Forging Silver into Stars

Forging Silver into Stars

Brigid Kemmerer

BLOOMSBURY

NEW YORK LONDON OXFORD NEW DELHI SYDNEY

BLOOMSBURY YA
Bloomsbury Publishing Inc., part of Bloomsbury Publishing Plc
1385 Broadway, New York, NY 10018

BLOOMSBURY and the Diana logo are trademarks of Bloomsbury Publishing Plc

First published in the United States of America in May 2022
by Bloomsbury YA

Text copyright © 2022 by Brigid Kemmerer
Map by Virginia Allyn

Bloomsbury books may be purchased for business or promotional use.
For information on bulk purchases please contact
Macmillan Corporate and Premium Sales Department at specialmarkets@macmillan.com

Library of Congress Cataloging-in-Publication Data is available
ISBN 978-1-5476-0912-3 (hardcover) • ISBN 978-1-5476-0913-0 (e-book) •
ISBN 978-1-5476-1124-9 (exclusive edition A) • ISBN 978-1-5476-1117-1 (exclusive edition B)
Book design by Jeanette Levy
Typeset by Westchester Publishing Services
Printed in Great Britain by CPI (UK) Ltd, Croydon CR0 4YY
2 4 6 8 10 9 7 5 3 1

To find out more about our authors and books visit
www.bloomsbury.com and sign up for our newsletters.

For Rhonda Barth,
whose light shined so brightly
and who so dearly loved these characters.

You are very missed.

THE ROYAL COURTS
OF THE ALLIED NATIONS
SYHL SHALLOW AND EMBERFALL

TITLE	NAME	RESIDING IN
Queen of Syhl Shallow	Lia Mara	Syhl Shallow
King of Emberfall	Grey	Syhl Shallow
Their Daughter	Princess Sinna Cataleha	Syhl Shallow
Queen's Chief Adviser and Sister	Nolla Verin	Syhl Shallow
Royal Physician	Noah of Disi*	Syhl Shallow
Counsel to the King	Jacob of Disi*	Syhl Shallow
Brother to the King	Prince Rhen, Acting Regent	Emberfall
Princess of Disi, Rhen's Beloved	Princess Harper of Disi*	Emberfall
King's Courier/Queen's Envoy	Lord Tycho of Rillisk	Both

*"Disi" is not a real country, though the people of Emberfall and Syhl Shallow both believe it to be the birthplace of Princess Harper. In truth, "Disi" refers to Washington, DC. When a curse tormented Prince Rhen years ago, Harper, Noah, and Jacob were magically trapped on the grounds of Ironrose Castle in Emberfall, with no way home aside from breaking the curse . . . but that's a different story.

FORGING SILVER INTO STARS

PROLOGUE

CALLYN

This was supposed to be a peaceful protest.

It's the only reason we came. Da kept insisting, "You owe it to your mother, Callyn. The queen should know the will of her people."

Maybe I do owe it to her. Maybe Mother would want me and Nora to be here. I reach up and rub the pendant that hangs over my heart the way I do anytime I think of her.

This was only supposed to be a gathering of like-minded people who opposed the king's magic. Safe. Small. Da wanted Nora and me to come because he said it was important to make a good showing so the queen would listen. He even tried to convince Master Ellis to come, along with his son Jax, my best friend. Their blacksmith forge was too busy to leave, though—and travel is difficult for Jax on his crutches. But now that we're all packed along the cobblestone roadway leading to the Crystal Palace, I don't know if any of us needed to come at all. There are hundreds of people here. Maybe thousands.

Most are armed.

All are shouting.

Nora squeezes my hand. "Those people have swords," she says, and her voice is nearly lost under the cacophony.

I follow her gaze. A *lot* of people have swords. And axes, and arrows, and hammers. I see bricks in a few hands. Anything you could reasonably consider a weapon. Guards stand in front of the gate, trying to talk people down, but there are only a dozen of them and a huge press of people straining at the steel bars. Behind the guards is a short stretch of shining cobblestones that end at the base of the steps leading up to the palace. The summer sun fills the air with heat, and the smell of so many sweating bodies pressed together is oppressive. It's doing nothing good for anyone's temper.

A shouting man tries to push through the crowd, and Nora stumbles into me, squealing when he stomps on her foot. He's got a dagger in his hand, and it comes dangerously close to my sister's eye. I jerk her out of the way.

"She's just a child!" I snap at him.

He gives me a rude gesture over his shoulder.

So peaceful. I scowl. Nora is only twelve. She shouldn't be here. I'm not entirely sure that *I* should be. I set my shoulders. "Da."

He's not even paying attention. He's chanting with the crowd. *Bring us the queen! Bring us the queen!*

"Da!" I shout over the noise. "Da, we need to get Nora out of here."

He doesn't look at me. "Queen Lia Mara will have to listen, Callyn. There are so many of us here. The queen must know: we're doing this for *her.*"

Nora clutches my arm. This is her first time seeing the Crystal Palace, and on any other day she'd be staring up at the massive glistening structure with her mouth hanging open. She'd be asking if I thought we had a chance to see the queen, or if the street vendors in the Crystal City make better meat pies than what we sell in the bakery.

Right now she's burrowing into my side, edging away from a man who has a hand on the trigger of a crossbow.

"*Da*," I say again. "Da, please—"

My voice is swallowed by sudden noise. A massive cheer goes up among the people, and at first, I'm not sure what's happened. I think perhaps the shouting really *has* made a difference, and I stare up at that gleaming staircase, wondering if the queen will appear at the top.

No. The crowd has broken through the gates. I see a guard lift a sword—and just as quickly, he disappears under the sudden crush of the crowd. Without warning, we're jostled forward, and Nora and I have no choice but to move or be trampled ourselves.

I keep hold of my sister's hand, and she clings to mine. I lose sight of Da almost immediately, and I cry out. "Da! Da!"

"Move, girl!" shouts a man to my left, and I take an elbow to the ribs. I stumble into Nora and we nearly fall. Luckily the crowd is so dense that we all but bounce off another woman. We're carried forward with the mob. Weapons glint in the sunlight. I hear a few screams in the crowd as others must be pulled under, but it's a quick burst of sound, and then it's gone.

My heart is pounding so hard that I can't breathe. My hand has gone slick, but I keep a tight grip on Nora's hand. I can't lose my sister. I *can't.*

I don't feel the steps, but we're moving upward. I can't see anything but the bright sunlight overhead, the mountains beyond the palace cutting a line through the sky. Glass shatters, and it seems to keep shattering. More screams ring out. The massive doors to the palace have been destroyed, leaving a gaping hole for everyone to stream through.

Bring us the queen! Bring us the queen!

The shouts are so loud, and they seem to come from every direction. My feet crunch on broken glass, and I realize we're about to be swept inside the palace.

No. My heart stutters and rebels. I don't want this. I'm not here to be a part of an attack on the royal family.

For an instant, I don't know what to do. Nora is crying now. Something must have hit her in the face, because blood is streaming from her nose.

There. To my right, a woman falls, leaving a gap in the surge of people. Bits of glass glint along the stone walkway leading to the doors. I give Nora's arm a firm tug, and we stumble out of the crush of people just as another cheer goes up inside the palace.

"They've found the king and queen!" a man yells. The cheering grows louder.

"What's happening?" Nora gasps between sobs. "What are they going to do?"

People are still surging past us. I've completely lost track of my father. "I don't know." I touch a hand to my pendant, pressing the warm steel into my skin. I wish Mother were here now. I consider the steps, the rapid stream of people, and I'm glad Jax didn't join us.

Soldiers are rushing up the stairs now, swords drawn, and I drag my sister farther away. Some of the protestors have turned to fight, and the clash of steel against steel makes my ears ring. Mother would have been right at home in the midst of a battle, but I'm only at home in the bakery. I've never wanted to be a soldier.

A man takes a sword right through his belly. He coughs blood onto the walkway.

I slap a hand over Nora's eyes, but she grabs at my hand and tries to see, her mouth wide with horror.

A man speaks from the shadows by the doorway. "She's a child! Get her out of here."

I can't tell if he's a soldier or a protestor. There's too much noise, too much fighting. But he's not in the melee, so he must not be a soldier.

"I'm trying!" I shout back.

"Go down the side stairs!" he yells, just as a soldier spots us.

I suck in a breath, but I have no time to react. A blade is swinging in our direction. Nora screams, and I shift to cover her with my body. I brace for the impact.

It never comes. Just a screech of steel as sword meets sword. I catch a glimpse of black armor, a flash of red hair.

"Go!" the man shouts.

I drag Nora. We run, half stumbling down the stone steps. The cheering in the castle has grown louder, carrying over the sounds of fighting. Screams sound from every direction. Suddenly, we're not the only ones running down the stairs.

"Magic!" a woman shouts. "The king's going to use his—"

Thunder cracks behind us, so loud that I nearly stumble again. I turn to see a blast of light flare through every window of the palace, brighter than the sun, like a million bolts of lightning all at once.

All sounds of fighting cease. There's a pulse of sudden, absolute silence—and then screaming. A man is on fire, stumbling out of the doorway of the palace. Then another. And a third. The soldiers at the top of the steps have stopped fighting, and they're staring in horror.

So am I.

Nora tugs at my hand. "Where's Da?" Her voice is high and panicked. "What happened to Da?"

I don't know. *I don't know.*

A woman shrieks from the top of the steps. "He killed them all," she cries. "The king's magic killed them all!"

More guards are beginning to arrive. Panic still fills my chest, but I'm aware enough to know that things won't go well for anyone left here.

"Come on," I say to Nora. I drag her toward the streets, and we slip into the city just as guards begin lining up to block the fallen gate.

I want to run, but guards might be looking for protestors now, so I hold tight to Nora's shaking hand and head toward a tavern, walking sedately. I keep my eyes locked ahead and focus on breathing. On moving forward. Everyone else is rushing toward the palace, so no one pays us any mind.

The sun is so bright and warm, and it seems like a cruel joke, as if the sun has no right to shine. My chest feels hollow.

Eventually, Nora stops crying, and she looks up at me. "Was that true?" she whispers, and the horror in her voice echoes what I feel in my heart. "Did the king's magic kill them all?"

"I don't know," I say.

But I press a hand over that pendant, because I do know. I saw that flash of light. I heard those screams. I saw the flames.

The king's magic once stole my mother.

And now it's stolen my father, too.

SIX MONTHS
LATER

CHAPTER 1

CALLYN

I've been staring out at the night for hours, daring the dawn to keep its distance, but the first hint of purple appears along the crest of the mountain anyway. When I was a little girl, my mother used to say that if you could throw a stone high enough, it would fly over the mountaintops and land in Emberfall.

She also used to say that if you were lucky, it would land on the head of one of their soldiers and crush their skull, but that was back when Emberfall was an enemy of Syhl Shallow.

I tried and tried when I was a child, but I never threw a rock over the mountain. Not even when rage over my mother's death propelled the rocks high into the sky.

I rub my hand over her pendant. I don't know why I'm thinking of my mother. She's been dead for years.

Any latent rage should be directed at my father, anyway. He's the one who left us with this mess. It's been six months, and there's no coming back from the dead. From what I hear, not even the king's awful magic can make *that* happen.

The moon hangs high over the trees, making the frozen branches glisten, turning the ground between the house and the barn into a wide swath of crystalline white. A few inches of snow fell at dusk last night, keeping away any customers Nora and I might have had for the bakery.

The weather didn't keep the tax collector away.

I glance at the half-crumpled paper with what we owe printed neatly at the bottom. I want to toss it into the hearth. The woman came by carriage, stepping fastidiously through the late-winter slush to enter the bakery—which is really just the main level of our *home*. Her lip curled when the door stuck, but I haven't been able to replace the hinges yet. She said we have a week to pay the first quarter of what we owe, or our holdings will be seized by the queen. As if Queen Lia Mara needs a run-down farm on the outskirts of Syhl Shallow. I'd be surprised if she knows the town of Briarlock *exists*.

A week to pay twenty-five silvers. Three months to pay the full amount due: one hundred silvers.

During the bakery's best weeks, my sister and I are lucky if we make ten.

If the tax collector sneered at the bakery door, I can only imagine her reaction to the rest of the property. It's likely a good turn of luck that she didn't want to see the barn. I can see the wood panel hanging crooked from here, snow swirling through the gap. The metalwork is rusted and bent. Jax said he'd try to fix it when he had time, but he's got paying customers, and he never likes to leave the forge for long.

Jax is a good friend, but he's got his own problems.

As usual, I wish Da had made a different choice. He could have kept on hating the king without risking everything we have. He could have participated in the protest without giving the rebels every coin we had. Now, the small barn and bakery are nearly impossible to handle on my own. Nora helps in any way she can, but at twelve, she's barely more than a girl. I can understand my father's desire for vengeance—but it sure didn't put food on the table.

But if Da were here, *would* he help? Or would he be like Jax's father, drowning his sorrows in ale every night?

Sometimes I don't know if I should envy Jax or if I should pity him. At least he and his father *have* coins.

I could sell the cow. She'd fetch at least ten silvers. The hens are good layers, and they would go for a silver apiece.

But if I lose my access to eggs and milk, I'll have to close the bakery.

Mother would tell me to sell the whole property and enlist. That's what she would have done. That's what she always envisioned for me. It was Da who wanted to keep the bakery, Da who taught me how to measure and knead and stir. Mother loved soldiering, but Da loved the art of feeding people. They fought about it before the battles with Emberfall. She was going off to war, demanding to know why he wasn't enlisting as well. Didn't he care about his *country*?

Da would counter that he didn't want to leave his children in an orphanage just so he could die on a battlefield.

Mother said he was being dramatic, but of course that's what she ended up doing.

And it's not like he did any better in the end.

Even still, I can imagine Mother staring down at this tax notice, looking around the bakery and the needed repairs to the house and the barn. "You should have enlisted six months ago," she'd be saying sternly.

And if I did, Nora would . . . go where exactly? She's too young to be a soldier. She'd hate it anyway. She blanches at the sight of blood, and she's afraid of the dark. She still climbs into bed with me half the time, after she's had another nightmare about the Uprising.

"Cally-cal," she'll whisper sleepily, my childhood nickname soft on her lips as she winds her fingers in my long hair. She's the only one who can make a name like Callyn sound whimsical.

She'd be put in an orphanage—if she were lucky.

She *will* be put in an orphanage if I can't pay these taxes. Or we'll be begging on the streets.

My eyes burn, and I blink the sensation away. I didn't cry when Mother died in the war with Emberfall. I didn't cry when Da died and we had to beg for passage back to Briarlock.

I won't cry now.

Out in the barn, the hens start to cluck, and Muddy May, the old cow, moos. The door rattles against the wood siding. That faint hint of purple over the mountains begins to streak with pink. In a few hours, the glistening snow will be slush and mud again, and Nora and I will be bundled up, thrusting a hand under the hens to find eggs, bickering over who has to sit in the cold to milk May.

But those hens keep clucking, and a faint orange glow suddenly pokes from below the creaking barn door.

I sit up straight, my heart pounding. It's been half a year, but the events at the Crystal Palace are still fresh in my memories. The clap of thunder, the flash of light.

But of course there's no magic here. Could it be a fire?

Underneath my flare of panic, I have the thought that I should just let it all burn to the ground.

But no. The animals don't deserve that. I grab for my boots, jerking them onto my feet without waiting to lace them. I sneak down the hallway past Nora's room, stepping lightly so I don't make the floor creak. If I didn't want her to see the note from the tax collector, I definitely don't need her to see the barn burning down.

I make it to the steps down into the bakery, but I trip over my loose laces and nearly go face-first into the brick floor at the bottom. I overturn the stool where I sit to take orders, and it clatters to the ground, rolling haphazardly into the shelves. A metal bowl rattles onto the bricks, followed by a porcelain dish I use for large loaves. That shatters, bits going everywhere.

Amazing.

I wait, frozen in place. My leg is at an awkward angle, but I hold my breath.

No sound comes from upstairs.

Good.

The cold hits me in the face when I slip out the door, but I hear the cow again, so I hurry through the frozen mud. I have a few weeks' worth of hay and straw in the loft, but I'm always good about stacking them away from the walls. Some must have gone moldy anyway, and moldy hay is always likely to start a fire. That stupid door needs fixing.

Like a working door will matter if the barn is a pile of ashes.

Halfway across the frigid yard, I realize the tiny glow hasn't spread.

And I don't smell smoke.

Muddy May moos again, and I hear the low murmur of a man's voice.

I freeze for an entirely new reason. My heart rate triples, the world snapping into focus.

Not a fire. A thief.

I grit my teeth and change course, striding across the yard to the small shed where we keep tools. Mother's old weapons are wrapped up under my bed, but I don't have much practice with a sword. The ax hangs ready, slipping into my hand like an old friend. I can split firewood without breaking a sweat, so I have no doubt I can make a thief regret his choices. I swing the ax in a figure eight, warming up my shoulder. When I get to the broken door, I grab hold and *yank*.

The door creaks and moans as it moves faster than the hinges are ready for. The shadow of a man shifts behind the cow. A blazing lantern sits not far off—the source of the orange glow.

I swing the ax around, letting the flat side slam into a wooden post. The hens go wild with clucking, and May spooks, jerking the rope where she's tied and overturning the bucket.

"Get out of my *barn*," I yell.

May spooks again, her hooves scrambling in the dirt as she shifts away from me, and she must slam into the man, because he grunts and then falls, tangling in the length of his cloak. Wood clatters to the ground beside him, and I hear a crack as it gives way.

"Clouds above, Cal!" he snaps, jerking the hood of his cloak back. "It's just me!"

Too late, I recognize the light hazel eyes glaring at me from under a spill of dark hair. "Oh." I lower the ax and frown. "It *is* you."

Jax swears under his breath and reaches for his crutches, dragging them through the straw. His breath clouds in the frosty air. "A good morning to you, too."

I'd offer to help him, but he doesn't like help unless he asks for it. He rarely needs it anyway. He rolls to his foot smoothly, if not agilely. He gets one crutch under his left arm, but the other snapped at the end, and it's too short now.

He looks at the jagged end, sighs, and tosses it to the side, then switches the good crutch to his right side to compensate for his missing right foot. "I thought you'd be asleep. I didn't realize I'd be taking my life into my hands by coming here."

I'm trying to figure out if I'm at fault here or if he is. "Do you want me to run back to the forge for some tools?" I offer. He used to make his crutches out of steel, but his father always said it was a waste of good iron. Now he's well practiced in making them out of wood.

"No." He tugs his cloak straight, then balances on one foot while he uses the good crutch to right the milking stool. "You can grab the bucket, though." He drops onto the stool, then blows on his fingertips to warm them. He puts a hand against the cow's flank. His voice gentles in a way that only happens when he talks to animals, never people. "Easy there, May."

The cow flippantly seizes a mouthful of hay and whips her tail, but she sighs.

I seize the frigid bucket and hand it to him. "You . . . you came over in the middle of the night to milk the cow?"

"It's not the middle of the night. It's almost dawn." He grabs hold of a teat with practiced ease, and a spray of milk rattles into the tin bucket. "I didn't want to wake you by firing up the forge." He hesitates, and the air is heavy with the weight of unspoken words.

Ultimately, he says nothing, and the breath eases out of him in a long stream of clouded air.

He studies the bucket. I study him.

Most of his hair is tied into a knot at the back of his head, but enough has spilled loose to frame his face, throwing his eyes in shadow. He's lean and a bit wiry, but years of forge work and using his arms to bear his weight have granted him a lot of strength. We've known each other forever, from the time when we were children, when everything in our lives seemed certain and sure, until now, when nothing does. He remembers my mother, and he sat with me and Nora when she didn't return from the war. He sat with me again when Da died.

He doesn't know his own mother, but that's because she died when he was born. When his father is drunk, I've heard him say that was the first mark of misfortune Jax brought on the family.

The second mark came five years ago, when Jax was thirteen. He was trying to help his father fix a wagon axle. It collapsed on his leg and crushed his foot.

I guess the third mark almost came courtesy of my ax. "I'm sorry I almost cut your head off," I say.

"I wouldn't have complained."

Jax is one for brooding, but he's not usually so sullen. "What does that mean?"

He lets go of a teat to thrust a hand under his cloak, then tosses a piece of parchment in my direction. I drop the ax in the straw to fetch it.

When I unfold the paper, I see the exact same writing that was on the parchment from the tax collector, the note that's still sitting in my bedroom.

The number on his is twice as large.

"Jax," I whisper.

"The tax collector came to the forge," he says. "She claimed we haven't paid in two years."

"But—but the forge has so many customers. I've seen them. You—you make a decent living . . ." I see his expression, and my voice trails off.

"Apparently when my father leaves to pay the taxes every quarter, he's not actually paying them." Jax is dodging my gaze now.

I wonder if that means his father gambled the money away—or if he drank it away.

Not like it matters. Both options are terrible.

May's milk keeps spraying into the bucket rhythmically. I grab the other milking stool from the corner and plop it down beside him. Jax doesn't look at me, but he ducks his face to toss the hair out of his eyes.

I watch his hands move with practiced efficiency. His fingers are red from the cold, scarred here and there from forge burns.

I wish I knew how to help him. I barely know how to help myself.

My midnight worries feel so selfish suddenly, when I have options. They're not options I want, but they're options I have. I *can* sell the farm. I *can* enlist. I'd probably never make it past the rank of cadet, not with Father's stain on our family, but I could do it. Nora *can* go to an orphanage—or I could possibly use part of a soldier's pension to pay for her to have a guardian somewhere.

Jax can't do any of those things. His father barely stays sober long enough to work *now*. Jax is the one keeping the forge in business. He can't be a soldier. With a missing foot, few people would take a chance on Jax as a laborer—or anything else.

If they lose the forge, they'd lose everything.

I put a hand on his wrist, and he goes still. "You don't have to milk the cow," I say quietly.

He turns to look at me. There's a shadow on his jaw, and I wonder if he got the bruise when May knocked him down—or if his father did it. They live all the way down the lane, but when they fight, I can often hear it from here.

He must notice me looking, because he turns away—which says enough.

I let go of his wrist.

He keeps milking.

"We owe a hundred," I whisper so softly that I don't think he'll hear it.

But he does, of course he does, because he turns to look at me again. Our breath clouds in the air between us. He always smells faintly of smoke from the forge, and the scent is sharp in the cold air.

When we were younger, after he lost his foot, I would bring him sugared twists of dough from the bakery every day, along with books from my mother's library. We loved tales of romance or history, but our favorite books were the stories of wind and sky and magic from the winged creatures in the ice forests to the west of Syhl Shallow.

I remember the day my mother stopped me. I'd been twirling around the kitchen, eager to go visit my friend.

He won't make a good husband, she said, and the feel of her disapproval was so thick in the air that I felt like she'd slapped me.

She didn't let me go. I didn't see him for weeks, until he found some crutches and hobbled his way down the lane to our bakery.

I never told him what she said.

It didn't matter, because he's never said or done anything to indicate he even saw me that way.

But there are moments like this, when it's cold and dark and the entire world feels like it's caving in, and I wonder, just for a heartbeat, what it would be like if Jax and I were more than friends. If we were in this together.

"Callyn?" Nora's worried voice calls from out in the courtyard, high and frightened. "Callyn?"

I jerk back and inhale sharply. "In the barn!" I call. "I'm here!" I look at Jax. "She doesn't know," I whisper fiercely.

He nods.

The door rattles and creaks as she tries to push it to the side. She's in a sleeping shift, her feet bare. Her hair is a wild mess of tangles that reaches to her waist, and she's shivering wildly. Tears seem almost frozen on her cheeks.

"Nora!" I exclaim. I pull my own cloak free. "You'll freeze to death. You need to get back in the house!"

"I—I was worried—"

"I know. Come on."

At the barn door, I pause and look back at Jax. To my surprise, he's watching me go.

I wish I knew what to say.

He must not either, because he gives me a nod, blows on his fingers one more time, and turns back to the bucket.

CHAPTER 2

JAX

My ears ring with the sound of iron against steel, but I don't mind. I was raised alongside the forge, so I can sleep through it if I have to.

Right now, the rhythmic clanging is all that's keeping me grounded. I haven't seen my father since midnight. When he disappears like this, frustration usually sets up camp in my gut, because without his help, I'll never catch up on the work we have due.

Today, I'm happy to leave him facedown in a puddle of spirits. Maybe he'll drown.

The forge is always busy this time of year. Farmers need new pitchforks and spades to prepare for the early planting season, and I can never make them fast enough. A man from the next town over requested new blades for his thresher, and I told him it'll take a week, but I should've told him two. Once the snows began to taper off, carpenters started buying so many nails that I've taken to forging them at night, just so I have a supply at daybreak. With the slush and mud, travelers are forever needing repairs to wagon wheels and axles. There's a blacksmith on the other side of Briarlock, too, but she's in her seventies, so she sends us anything big—and I try to return the favor by sending expensive detailed metalwork her way. She gets the fancy buckles and etched daggers, I get the sickles and horseshoes.

I think of that note from the tax collector and wonder if I should be taking any commissions I can get.

I swear under my breath and slam the hammer against the red-hot steel on my anvil. Two hundred silvers. All pissed away on ale or dice.

Wherever Da is, he's lucky. If he were here right now, I'd knock him into the forge.

The thought feels hollow. I can't knock him anywhere. That's why I've got a bruise on my jaw and an ache in my belly from where he kicked me. I might be a lot of things, but *fast* doesn't make the list. It's too easy to get me off my feet.

Off my *foot*.

The worst part is that I had put aside a little bit of silver for Callyn. She's too proud to ask for it, but I know how much she's struggled since she discovered her father was giving away their silver to help fund the attack on the king. I knew the tax collectors would be around eventually. It's only ten silvers that I stashed beneath my mattress, but it would have helped her a little. Cal would've taken it if it meant keeping Nora safe.

Now the tiny pouch of coins is going to have to help me save the forge—and it's nowhere near enough.

She always brings me bread and sweetcakes when the bakery has them left over—which is often. Surely I can spare five.

I don't know why I think that'll make a difference for either of us. We're both going to be on the streets in a matter of weeks.

My chest tightens, and then my throat. I'm used to my eyes burning from the heat of the forge, but this is different. I slam the hammer and shake off the emotion.

When I was a boy, Da used to talk about how I'd be able to turn around our misfortune when I became a soldier in the Queen's Army.

He was teaching me to hammer shields and swords as soon as I was old enough to pull steel from the fire. "An armory always needs a talented metalsmith," he'd say, beaming with pride at my evolving skill. "Mounted soldiers always need a farrier."

Then a wagon fell on my leg, crushing my ankle and foot. My entire future, burned out of existence. The village physician said I was lucky to survive.

Ah, yes. I feel so very *lucky*.

"Boy!" A woman clears her throat from behind me, her tone impatient. "I'm looking for Ellis the blacksmith."

My father. I grit my teeth and hope this isn't someone else we owe money to. "He's not here."

"And when will he return?"

The spade I'm fashioning has cooled, so I pull it off the anvil and thrust it back into the forge, then drag a sleeve across my forehead and turn. The middle-aged woman standing under the archway is unfamiliar, most notably because she's wearing belted silk robes in red and purple, and the hem is wet from the slush—meaning she's not from Briarlock. Anyone here would have the sense to wear trousers and boots, or to tie up their skirts.

But judging by the jeweled rings on her fingers and the wide chain of gold hanging from her neck, she's also clearly wealthy. I bite back the sour tone in my voice. "I don't know. But I can make you anything you need from the forge." I pause. "My lady."

She gives me a disdainful up-and-down glance, and I realize she has two different-colored eyes: one blue and one brown. I see the moment her gaze stops at the bottom of my leg. I have a small padded stool that I use to keep my balance when I need to stand, and it serves my purposes well—until people stare at it.

We need silver, so I can't let my temper get the best of me. I tightly add, "Does your carriage need mending? Or did your horse slip a—"

"I don't need any metalwork. I'm looking for Ellis. The blacksmith."

"Oh." I jerk the glowing steel back out of the fire with my tongs and hold it against the anvil. "Then you're welcome to wait." I swing my hammer hard, and I have the privilege of seeing her flinch.

"Boy. Boy!" She's shouting now.

I don't stop swinging. "What?" I yell over the clanging.

"I need to know when he will return!"

Hopefully never. "You can ask at the tavern." I glance past her without missing a swing. The morning sun shines through the trees, but I feel as though I've been awake for a week.

"I asked at the tavern," she says. "He hasn't been seen."

If anything would make my hammer go still, that does it. I turn and look at her. "Then I truly have no idea where he could be. You could try the gaming tables. Or the brothel."

"So you don't know when he's expected back?"

"No." I thrust the spade back into the forge. "I'm not my father's keeper." Her lips purse, so again I add, "My lady."

She studies me for a moment. "Do you know who I am?"

Something in the way she asks makes me hesitate. I look at her more carefully. She's not much older than Da, likely in her forties, with gray-threaded braids piled in an intricate pattern on top of her head. She's easily as tall as I am, and willowy, with intense eyes and a stern mouth that looks like it's never smiled.

But I've never seen her before. At least I don't think I have. "No."

"It's rare that I have an occasion to visit Briarlock. Your father has done some business for me in the past. I was hoping to hire him again, but time is of the essence."

My eyebrows go up. "I can do any forge work you need—"

"I already said I don't need metalwork." She glances down at my leg again. "But you do seem to have the advantage of staying right where I need you."

That makes me scowl. I jerk the steel back out of the forge and slam it against the anvil. "If you don't need metalwork, then I don't think I can help you."

She comes closer. "Are you as hungry for silver as your father?"

I snort and swing my hammer. "I don't think anyone is *that* hungry."

"Can you be trusted to hold a message?"

"Couriers run out of—"

She grabs my arm, stopping my swing. "I don't want a courier, boy."

She's a lot stronger than I gave her credit for. Her fingers dig into the muscles of my forearm, and I don't have the leverage to break her hold.

She doesn't let go. "You may call me Lady Karyl." The way she says it makes me think it's not her real name. With her free hand, she pulls a folded parchment from under her robes. A wide wax seal holds the paper closed. "A man will come to Briarlock this evening seeking the forge, because I intended to leave this with your father." She pauses, her eyes boring into mine. "He will expect it to still be *sealed*. Am I understood?"

I frown. "I—yes?"

She leans in, and her voice lowers, turning vicious. "If it is not, you'd best hide yourself well. The Truthbringers do not take kindly to deceit and fourberie."

Clouds above. My father is mixed up with the *Truthbringers*?

He couldn't be. He *can't*. He knows what happened to Callyn's father. I want to jerk my arm out of this woman's grasp.

When the queen of Syhl Shallow was first married to the magic-wielding king of Emberfall to bring peace to both countries, rumor said there were a few minor assassination attempts in the Crystal Palace. It was four years ago, so I was younger then, still trying to figure out how to manage on one foot. But I remember travelers would whisper about how the king had fooled the queen into marriage, how his magic was closely guarded, used only for his own gain. Our queen was new. Young. Untested. There were many people who wondered if the king was just biding his time until he saw fit to kill her, too.

Cal heard stories in the bakery, too. After what magic did to her mother, Cal's father was openly critical of the king, so Cal usually had better gossip than I did: like the night she told me about how the king wouldn't bother sending people to the stone prison because he could fracture all their bones at once—and then turn their skin inside out. Her little sister was only nine when Cal told me that story, and she later said Nora didn't sleep for a *week*.

Not long after the royal marriage, our queen had a baby, and the border between our countries was opened to all for travel and trade. It seemed like a tenuous peace had been achieved—but only on the surface. Whispers about the dangerous king continued, and Da and I would occasionally hear of calls for revolution. But Briarlock is a poor town that's a four-hour ride from the palace in the best weather, so most rumors were sparse with detail and lacking any real motivation. Da used to scoff and say most were just women and men filling the time while they needed a horse shod or a wagon repaired. They would arrive with whispers about soldiers who were burned to ash for speaking out of line, or tales of a magical creature who could be summoned at the king's whim to eviscerate his enemies. I'd heard enough to know *some* had to be true—but many seemed too grand. Too awful.

After that cursed beast tore apart her mother, Callyn's father believed every single one.

Late last summer, we heard of an opportunity to take a stand against the king, to protest against *magic* being present in Syhl Shallow. Those whispers about an uprising were suddenly backed by a plan. The Truthbringers had started as a close network of wealthy people who quietly opposed the king and his magic, but their thoughts had begun to spread among the people.

At the time, Da wanted no part in it. "We've got enough work for three men, boy," I remember him saying. "I've got to make do with one and a half. We'll leave *magic* well enough alone."

Cal's father, however, was one of the first to join up.

The protest turned into a revolt. Hundreds were killed, in a battle of swords and magic. That tenuous peace was rattled, and it's never calmed since. The Truthbringers see it as evidence of the dangers of magic, and they've been emboldened by what happened.

I may be desperate for silver, but I want no part of a plot against the royal family.

I swallow. "I need to put this back in the forge."

She lets go of my arm, and I take a deep breath. My head is spinning. This is worse than spending the coins meant for taxes. What has my father done? What has he involved us with? Didn't he learn anything from what happened with Cal's father?

I was worried about losing the forge. Now I'm worried about losing my *head*.

Callyn coming after me with the ax suddenly feels like a premonition.

But then Lady Karyl says, "He will give you ten silvers once the message is delivered."

I freeze. *Ten silvers! Ten!*

I hate that the promise of *silver* is making me consider this.

But if my father has already embroiled us in . . . *whatever* this is . . . the damage is already done. And if she's willing to pay *me* instead of *him*, there's a chance I can earn enough to pay off the tax collector. At least I can make sure the silver doesn't go right into the pocket of the local brewer.

My heart is pounding, but I take the folded parchment. "How often has my father done this for you?"

"Often enough."

"And you trust him?"

She laughs softly. "Of course not. I don't trust you either. But there is nothing in that message that can be traced back to me. And who would believe a crippled blacksmith over a well-respected governess from one of the Royal Houses?"

I bristle, but she's already turned away.

I think of Callyn and little Nora, who are probably thinking of splitting a boiled egg for their supper, just so they don't waste something they could use for the bakery. I consider the way Callyn stormed into the barn this morning, her ax swinging, her eyes full of torment and desperation.

She'd pass this message without hesitation if it meant a chance to save her farm. Cal wouldn't stoop to treason, but she has as much reason to hate magic as anybody.

The Crystal Palace is a long way off anyway. No one there cares about us, or about Briarlock—not any more than we care about their political intrigues. What's one little note?

I slide my fingers along the parchment, feeling the grooves in the wax seal.

Ten silvers. Whatever is inside this parchment must be *very* important. I look at the mud clinging to the hem of the lady's richly embroidered skirts, at the jeweled rings encircling her fingers. I consider the way she curled her lip at the state of my leg.

"Lady Karyl," I say. "I am not my father."

She turns back, and her eyes seem to darken. "So you will not do as I have asked?"

"Oh no, I will." I hold up the note between two fingers. "But my father is a lazy drunk. If you want this crippled blacksmith to help you out, it's going to cost you twice as much."

CHAPTER 3

TYCHO

No matter how many times I make the journey from Ironrose Castle in Emberfall to the Crystal Palace in Syhl Shallow, the sight of the guard station in the mountain pass always makes my heart skip. It means I'm only a few hours from home. The sun beats down, stealing some of the chill from the air, melting the snow that must have fallen overnight. It's turned the road to a slushy mess, but my mare has always been sure-footed, and today is no different.

I can—and do—make this ride in an easy four days, but this time it feels interminable. I've been at Ironrose Castle for six weeks, and I'm not usually gone so long. I miss home. My saddlebags are packed with gifts from Prince Rhen and Princess Harper, trinkets and toys and jewels intended for the royal family in Syhl Shallow, the public reason for my journey.

Tucked safely behind the breastplate of my armor is the real reason: a folded packet of reports from the Grand Marshals in Emberfall, detailing the movements of the Truthbringer faction and the warnings of violence.

They've spread more deeply into Emberfall than Grey suspected.

King Grey. Even now, it's hard to reconcile. When we first met four years ago, we worked side by side as stable hands. I was fifteen and he was twenty—and he was hiding from his birthright as the true heir to the throne. Instead of ruling a country, he was shoveling manure and teaching me to hold a sword.

Now he doesn't hide from anyone, but his position as king and the magic in his blood makes him a target. When rebels forced their way into the Crystal Palace, they killed guards and soldiers in their efforts to get to the royal family. It was too sudden, too overwhelming. The king was forced to unleash his magic, and it led to a lot of deaths on all sides.

Both countries are said to be united, but that doesn't mean the people feel that way.

A horn sounds through the valley, indicating I've been spotted by the guard station. At the upper level, one of the guards stands in the turret, looking down at me through a spyglass. There are longbow archers up there, too, but they're well hidden. I sit down in the saddle, drawing Mercy to a slow trot, then put two fingers between my teeth and whistle my pattern to them. The mare jerks at the reins, as eager as I am, prancing sideways as I wait for the guards to wave me through.

I rub a hand under her black mane and she settles, champing at the bit.

"Me too," I murmur to her.

"King's Courier!" the guard shouts in Syssalah, and they begin to roll the gates. It's not my first language, but like the guard station, hearing it is a reminder that I'm almost home.

Another man joins the first on the turret, and I recognize him. Captain Sen Domo. I lift a hand to wave.

"Tycho!" he calls. "We were starting to wonder if you were coming back."

"I missed you too, Captain," I call. Mercy paws at the ground.

He grins. "Do you need an escort?"

They're required to ask every time. I've only accepted once, about five months ago, not long after the Uprising. A man tracked me all the way to the border and tried to cut my hands off in the middle of the night. I'm not a magesmith like the king, but I wear rings of Iishellasan steel—metal that's infused with magical properties. They were gifts from Grey to afford me some protection when I carry messages between countries. I was able to fight the thief off and get away, but he got closer than anyone else ever had.

Today, I just want to get home. I shake my head. "I know the way."

He smiles and nods and waves me through. I slip the rein and cluck my tongue and Mercy takes off, flattening into a gallop.

"Not too fast," I murmur under the wind, and she flicks an ear in my direction. The mud is thicker here, still half frozen in spots, and I don't need Mercy to take a wrong step. I don't want to be careless when we're this close to home—but still hours away. This guard station is more remote, blocking one of the lesser-used passages into Syhl Shallow, because I like to stay off the beaten path.

I twitch the reins, but Mercy tugs right back and gallops on.

I smile. "All right. Another few minutes." Her stride eats up the miles, until the tree covering thickens, the road narrowing. The snow hasn't fully melted here, along the path where the leaves keep the ground in shadow. Branches begin to whip at my arms.

Now I really do draw back on the reins. Mercy is blowing hard, but she slows to a canter, then a reluctant trot. In hand, she's as docile as a children's pony, but when I'm on her back, she always seems to have a lot of *opinions*. Anyone else might find her exhausting, but it gives me something to focus on when I make the long journey between kingdom and queendom. I found Mercy at the bidders' market two years ago, and Nolla Verin, the queen's sister, burst out laughing when

I made a bid. The mare was razor thin, covered in welts, and lame in two hooves.

"You'll have to put that one out of its misery," Nolla Verin told me. "I thought Grey said you have a good eye for horses."

"I do," I said.

I've never regretted it for a second.

"Whoa," I say softly as Mercy stomps through the mud. "If you're not careful, you're going to throw—"

Steel *plinks* against a rock, Mercy stumbles, and I sigh.

Silver hell.

"A shoe," I finish.

I split an apple with Mercy while we walk. It's the last of the food I had in my pack, which wasn't a bother when I thought I'd be eating a hot dinner in the palace.

We've been walking for an hour though, with no sign of . . . anyone. There are a few small towns out this way, like Hightree and Briarlock, but I'm not familiar with them. Usually at this point in my journey, I'm galloping through, eager to get home.

Clouds have rolled in overhead, and snow flurries trickle down through the trees. Mercy blows a long breath out in a snort.

"This is your own fault," I say. "I have no idea where we're going to find a blacksmith." I bite a piece off the apple and feed her the rest.

Now that I'm not on her back, she plods along beside me like a loyal hound, the end of her reins looped around my wrist. The woods here are dense and thick with shadows, so I've unbound my quiver and bow from the saddle to string across my back. A sword and dagger hang from my belt, but I'd rather handle thieves from a distance if I have the option.

If I don't find a blacksmith soon, I'll need the bow to catch myself some dinner.

I sigh as loudly as Mercy. Despite the darkening cloud cover, I can tell the sun is still high overhead. It must be midafternoon by now. If I get desperate I'll pull the other shoe and try to ride lightly back to the palace. What I carry is too important to risk sleeping in the woods overnight.

I rub behind her ears, her brown fur soft under my fingers. "We'll give it one more hour. Deal?"

She leans into my hand. Answer enough, I suppose.

The snow begins to pick up, and I draw up the hood of my cloak. Maybe half an hour.

Somewhere off to my left, a branch snaps, and I whip my head around, a hand going automatically to my bow. The snow doesn't allow me to see too far into the woods, so I nock an arrow and wait for motion.

Nothing is there—but I feel *something*. I turn slowly, my eyes watching for a threat. I feel for the power in my rings. One allows for *seeking*, a kind of magic that's useful if I need to find food or water. Just now, I send power into the ground, seeking another person.

Before it gets far, Mercy jerks her head up and utters a low whicker. That means she hears another horse.

Then an arrow snaps into a tree to my left.

Another follows right behind it, so close that it brushes my arm.

Silver hell. I turn automatically and loose the arrow, following quickly with another. My magic snaps back to me.

Three people. Maybe four.

Two more arrows strike the tree behind me. I need to get off the ground.

I hook the bow over my shoulder, grab hold of her mane, and swing into the saddle. My hands find the reins without thought, and Mercy leaps into a gallop as soon as my heels brush her sides. I wince, hoping the ground is soft enough that it won't tear up her foot *too* much. We fly through the trees, the snow blurring the landscape as we run.

I wait for the sounds of pursuit, allowing her to gallop for a few minutes before slowing to a walk, and this time, she's perfectly obedient, as if she senses that the stakes are higher. I listen hard, studying the swiftly falling snow that surrounds us. I send magic into the ground again, stretching power as far as I can before it snaps back to me.

I sense nothing.

I give Mercy a looser rein and let her walk, but I stay on her back this time.

It has to be simple thieves. No one knows I'm here. I've been gone from Syhl Shallow for over a month.

I still can't shake the feel of danger in the pit of my stomach.

Mercy stretches out her neck, tossing snowflakes to the ground, and we come to a crossroads bearing a sign, which is brilliant news because it means we've finally neared a town. Food for me, a new shoe for Mercy, and hopefully a reprieve from the tension that seems to have leapt onto my back.

I let out a long breath and turn for Briarlock.

CHAPTER 4

CALLYN

Jax is sitting on the stool next to the table where I roll out pastry dough and knead my breads. He's back to two crutches again, and they rest against the wall. Nora sits on the other side of the room, near the roaring hearth, painting frosting onto the sweetcakes while a pot of stew boils over the fire behind her. I have to keep a close eye on her or else half the frosting will end up in her mouth.

"So what do you think?" Jax says, keeping his voice low so Nora doesn't overhear. He's told me about Lady Karyl and the Truthbringers and the promised silvers. His knee is bouncing, and I can't tell if it's nervous energy or excited energy.

I sprinkle flour across the smooth wood. I don't want to waste the stew, but I want to have a *few* meat pies ready on the off chance anyone comes ringing for supper. "I think you shouldn't have left the forge if you've agreed to do this."

"I left a note on the door telling this *lord* where to find me." He glances at the window, where snow swirls in the air, probably guaranteeing we won't see another customer today. "She said evening anyway, so I don't expect him until dark."

"Well, when I found you in the barn this morning, you said it was *dawn* when there were still stars in the sky, so—"

"Cal."

I throw a mound of dough in the middle of the circle of flour, then look at him. That bruise on his jaw is darker—or maybe I can just see it better now. "You know what happened to Da," I say. "I don't want to see you at the end of a rope, Jax."

He steals a bit of dough from the pile and twists it between his fingers. A shadow slides behind his eyes. "Your father didn't hang." He pauses. "You'd do this, too. I know you would."

Yes. I would. I still have nightmares about what happened in the palace, the way the protestors stormed through the gates, dragging me and Nora up the steps. I can still hear the clap of thunder in the cloudless sky, the flare of light blazing through the palace windows. There are dark rumors that say there were Truthbringers among the Queen's Army, allowing the insurrection to happen. I don't like to consider my father's role in the attack—but I don't like to think of my mother being slaughtered by a magical creature either.

I frown and thrust my hands into the pile, then blow impatiently at a lock of hair that falls into my eyes. "You could be sent to the stone prison."

"I'm not afraid. Rumor says they don't even keep a torture master anymore."

Those same rumors say there's no need for one because the king's magic can stop a man's heart. I sigh and glance across the room just in time to see Nora licking a long band of frosting from a blade. "Nora!" I snap. "You'll cut your tongue off."

She makes a face at me and licks the other side.

"You might slice it down the middle and look like a snake," says Jax. He makes a hissing noise, and she giggles, which makes him smile.

I wish he did that more. It brightens his whole face, stealing away some of his worries.

Nora gets a new knife, and I give her a warning look. She hisses at me, mimicking Jax.

I ignore her and tuck my loose hair behind my ear, then lower my voice again so she can't eavesdrop. "I'm serious," I say to him. "You need to be careful."

"I'm just holding a note. Not launching an attack on the palace." He takes another small twist of dough, but his knee is still bouncing.

Nervous energy *for sure.*

But for twenty silvers—I can see why he's taking the risk. We've never seen magic here in Briarlock. The closest we ever came was the book of stories we read as children, about the winged scravers in Iishellasa who could control the wind and ice, or the powerful magesmiths who fled Syhl Shallow only to be eviscerated in Emberfall. The stories said that scravers and magesmiths worked together, their magic combining to create something more powerful. Our magesmith king was said to have kept a scraver on a chain once, but the creature either died or escaped during the final battles with Emberfall. I don't know anyone who's ever seen a real one.

Nora still loves those stories, even after what she witnessed during the Uprising. Maybe the scravers seem too otherworldly, too inhuman. She'll trace the illustrations in our books with her finger. I remember doing the same as a child. They're beautiful and terrifying, with a body like a human, but with claws and fangs and twilight-gray skin—and wide wings that allow them to take to the sky. "They look like women and men," Nora will say, and I'll sigh and reply that men and women don't have claws and fangs—or *wings.*

Admittedly, I still find them rather fascinating myself. But it's not like I'll ever see one.

These thoughts feel a bit traitorous. A scraver didn't kill Mother, but it was still a creature of magic summoned to help win a battle. I rub at the old pendant under my shirt.

Either way, the Truthbringers themselves feel like a far-off threat. Most people in Briarlock are doing their best to get through each day, worried about staying warm in the winter or putting enough food on the table. We hear about scandals in the palace, but I can't summon any outrage about a noble lady losing a diamond during a carriage ride. Political intrigues just aren't intriguing when I'm trying to make sure Nora has boots that will last through the winter.

But I know what the Truthbringers want: an end to magic in Syhl Shallow. I don't disagree. And like Jax said, this is just a folded piece of parchment changing hands. It's not like he's an assassin.

I must be quiet too long, because Jax flicks a piece of dough at me. "Cal," he says softly. "Talk to me."

I flick it right back at him. "Did you get the coins up front?"

He nods. "Half. The person who shows up for the message will pay me the rest." He thrusts a hand into his pocket. He unfolds his fingers and ten silvers glisten.

I swallow. I'm happy he has a chance at saving the forge—and equally terrified for me and Nora.

Then he drops five onto the wood and nudges them toward me.

I startle and stare at him. "Wait—no. Those are yours."

"Ours, Cal." His voice is low and rough, and his eyes hold mine. "You're my best friend. I'm not going to save the forge and watch you lose your home."

For a breath of time, this feels like the moment in the barn this morning, when we sat beside each other, sharing our sorrows.

You're my best friend.

My chest tightens, and I thrust my hands into the dough again. "Thanks, Jax."

He reaches out and rubs a warm thumb across my cheek, and my breath catches—but he only says, "Clouds above, Cal. You're getting flour everywhere."

My cheeks warm, and I have to jerk my eyes away. Nora is licking this knife too. "Nora!"

She rolls her eyes and hisses at me again.

"Girl, you'd think you were five years old." I shove the pastry dough back into a pile, then stride across the room. I want to snap that we can't afford to waste ingredients now, but I also don't want to give her cause to worry. I'll probably give this batch to Jax anyway, along with some eggs from the barn. I've heard the forge clanging into the night lately, and I'm sure that won't change now that he needs every coin he can get. Guilt is chewing at my insides, and I want to slip the five silvers back into his pocket. Instead I jerk the knife out of Nora's hand and take away the platter of sweetcakes.

A boot thumps on the step outside, and then the door creaks and sticks before being forced open. The rusted bell above the threshold lets out a reluctant jingle.

A man steps through the opening, and everything about him is so startling that I nearly drop the platter. He's young, probably close in age to me and Jax, though the similarities end there. He's dusting snow out of his blond hair, which is short, though not as close-cropped as a soldier. He could be one, though, considering the sword and dagger at his waist and the knife-lined bracers buckled around his forearms. He moves like a soldier, too, as if he's very aware of the space he takes up in the world, and he's in control of every inch. But I remember what my mother's gear used to look like, and on this man, there's too much fine leather, too many gleaming buckles, too much detailed stitching on the cloak clasped over his shoulder. He has to be a lord, maybe even from one of the Royal Houses. Even the grommets on his laced boots seem to be fashioned from hammered silver.

"Forgive me," he says, and his voice is rich and cultured, with just the tiniest hint of an accent. He offers a slightly sheepish smile, and his eyes are a warm brown, though I see cunning intelligence in their depths. "I stopped at the tannery and they told me this was the way to the blacksmith, but I only seem to have found your bakery."

It takes me a moment for all the words to register in my brain.

He's a lord. Or something close.

Looking for the blacksmith.

Oh. OH.

I jerk my eyes over to Jax, who looks like he's swallowed his tongue. His eyes are narrowed, his expression completely closed off. His fingers grip the edge of my pastry table so tightly that I can see white around his knuckles.

I wish I could somehow transmit my thoughts to him. Is he reconsidering his actions? It's one thing to brazenly talk about helping the Truthbringers, but it's entirely different when you're looking treason right in the face.

"Jax is the blacksmith!" Nora pipes up cheerfully, and I watch said blacksmith's fingers tighten even more on my table. "He can take you there," she prattles on. "It's right down the end of the lane. You look like a lord. Are you from the Crystal City? We have sweetcakes, too, if you'd like some. I was frosting them before Cal took away—"

"Enough, Nora," I say. I have to clear my throat, and then I start rambling worse than she was. "I—yes. We do. He is. I mean—the blacksmith. Jax. The forge isn't far."

The man offers Nora a kind smile. "Perhaps I'll take some sweetcakes before I go." Definitely an accent. I wonder if he's from Emberfall, though it's rare for people over the border to be this fluent in Syssalah. When his eyes return to mine, they've gone from warm to a little more coolly assessing. Do I sound suspicious? I probably do. My heart is pounding. I suddenly hope Jax has the good sense to toss that note right into the fire and we can forget this whole thing.

"I'm the blacksmith." Jax's raspy voice speaks from behind me, and I hear his crutches clomp against the wooden floorboards. "You need something from the forge?"

The man hesitates, and I'm sure he's seeing what everyone else sees. I wait for him to frown at Jax's missing foot, or for his gaze to turn pitying, or, worst of all, for him to sneer, and I'm going to have to kick him in the shins.

But none of those things happen. "My horse threw a shoe a few miles outside town," he says. "I still have a ways to go before nightfall."

That . . . is not what I expected him to say. I wait for him to look pointedly at Jax, or ask for a letter, or . . . something.

Instead, we must look like we're up to something, because his gaze narrows another fraction. "Have I interrupted—"

The door is thrust open behind him, snow swirling through the opening. Another man comes through so forcefully that the bells above the door seem to chime angrily. This man is taller than the blond lord in front of us, but not much older, with fiery red hair and piercing blue eyes. He's dressed in fine clothing as well, with just as many weapons. Maybe more.

For an instant, something about him is familiar, but I can't imagine where I would've seen him before. Briarlock doesn't get a lot of travelers from the Crystal City, especially not nobles, not at this time of year. I've never had two lords in the bakery at the same time. I can't remember the last time I had two in the same *month*. Their weapons alone would probably fetch enough money to save the bakery and the forge combined.

The new man stops short when he sees the first. A look flickers across his face, almost too quick to catch it. Shock and alarm—followed quickly by disdain.

"Look at that," he says flatly, his voice full of contempt. "The king's pet has finally returned."

The first man looks equally stunned. "Lord Alek."

"*Lord Tycho.*" Lord Alek mocks the title—or his accent. Maybe both. "Some of us were beginning to lay bets on whether that foolish prince would keep you in Emberfall."

Lord Tycho has recovered from his surprise—and now has a hand on the hilt of his sword. "What are you doing here?"

Lord Alek's eyes narrow, and any mockery drains out of his expression. His hands aren't far from his weapons either. "I could ask you the same thing."

"Someone was shooting at me in the woods. Was that you?"

Lord Alek smiles, but there's nothing kind about it. He takes a step forward. "Scared you a bit, did it?"

Tension in the shop doubles. Lord Tycho's eyes flick to the door, to Jax, to the frosting knife that's still in my hand. Assessing escape routes and potential casualties. He might not be a soldier, but he definitely trained as one.

I move so Nora is behind me, and I change my grip on the frosting knife. "If the two of you start a sword fight in my bakery, you'll be scrubbing my pots for a month to make it up to me."

They both look at me in surprise—but at least those swords stay in their sheaths.

Lord Alek's eyes stay on my face for a moment too long, until I wonder if he's going to start trouble with *me* over that comment.

But then his gaze shifts back to the other man, and he lifts one shoulder in a careless shrug. "Why would I have cause to shoot at you? I have business dealings here in Briarlock. I can't help it if that forces my path to cross yours." He gives the other man another disdainful look. "But *you* don't have business here. Dallying in your duties?"

Lord Tycho glares at him, and his voice is low and even. "My horse threw a shoe on the way back to the Crystal City. I was looking for the forge." .

"What a happy coincidence! I'm looking for the forge myself. There was a note that I could find the blacksmith here at the bakery." He glances at Jax. "Would that be you?"

Jax is frozen in place. So am I. I feel like I've learned too much and not enough, all at once.

"Yes," Jax finally says. "My lord." He glances between the men as if unsure how to proceed.

"Is *no one* going to buy a sweetcake?" says Nora, peering around my shoulder.

I want to hush her, but it breaks some of the tension. Lord Alek reaches out a hand to clap Lord Tycho on the shoulder. "You were here first. I'm sure the king wants you back quickly. He has enough problems, so I won't delay you further. I'll settle up with the blacksmith later."

Jax swallows, but the man steps back out into the swirling snow.

Most of the tension goes with him, because Lord Tycho takes his hand off the hilt of his sword. "Forgive me," he says. "I didn't intend to cause trouble. He . . . took me by surprise." He looks at Nora. "Let me go see about my horse, and I'll return for sweetcakes. I promise." His gaze shifts to me. "And some stew if you can spare some."

"It's for the meat pies," Nora says. "Cally-cal makes the *best*."

"Or stew," I say hurriedly. "If you'd prefer."

"I'm not particular. Just hungry." His eyebrows go up. "Cally-cal?"

"Ah . . . Cal. Callyn. My lord." `

His eyes are intent on mine, and I'm either going to start blushing or I'm going to shove him out the door. He's just too intense, too mysterious, too . . . too many things I don't understand.

Now Jax is looking at me, and I can't tell if he looks more amused or more irritated, but somehow it's *both*.

"Come along, my lord," he says dryly. "Let's see to your horse."

CHAPTER 5

JAX

I can be quick on my crutches when the conditions are right. Generally that doesn't include mud, snow, and the weight of the realization that I almost handed this man a message that would've sent me to the gallows.

The snow swirls around us as we walk, and our progress feels painfully slow—emphasized by the fact that the young lord is all but *ambling* to keep pace with me, while I'm about to sweat through my clothes trying to go as fast as I can. Even his horse has tugged at the reins a few times, almost leading Lord Tycho instead of the other way around. I'm used to making this short trek alone, and I hardly think about the distance. Right now, the forge feels like it's ten miles away.

He hasn't said much since we left the bakery, and my heart is thrumming in my chest as the silence stretches on, punctuated by the *swish* and *clomp* of every step I take. I wish I could tell what he was thinking. That other man, Lord Alek, called him the king's *pet*, which definitely wasn't a compliment, but it implies Lord Tycho *knows* the king. He looks to be near my age, maybe a bit older, but he's clearly someone with money and status.

I'm worried this silence means he's suspicious. Callyn was about as subtle as she was in the barn this morning, when she was ready to swing an ax at my head. And then I almost handed him the message.

Here, my lord. Would you like to drag me back to the palace for sentencing, or should you draw your sword and save everyone a lot of time?

The tightness around my chest refuses to loosen. I don't have the mettle for this. I should have taken Lady Karyl's parchment and flung it into the forge the instant she left.

And then Cal and I would be five silvers poorer.

The thought is sobering. Surprise lit Cal's eyes when I slid the coins onto the table—surprise mixed with the smallest scrap of relief. Passing a message for the Truthbringers feels like the only option we have, especially since I'm walking beside a glaring reminder of everything that's wrong with my life. I'm willing to bet this man has never spent a single moment wondering where his next meal was coming from, or whether his father lost all their coins at the dice table.

My right crutch finds a hole or a branch or *something* under the slush, because it twists sideways and skids. I swear and try to catch myself, but I've got no leverage. It doesn't take much, not on that side, especially when I'm rushing. The ground is going to smack me square in the face, and I'll be doubly humiliated.

Instead, a strong hand catches my arm, holding me upright. Despite his grip, I have to hop once or twice to find my balance. The crutch topples into the snow, landing with a wet *squelch.*

My breath is a loud rush in my ears, my pulse pounding with a mix of adrenaline and embarrassment.

"Steady?" he says.

"I'm fine." I jerk free, and he lets me go so readily that I nearly fall down again.

He stoops to pick up my fallen crutch, then holds it out to me. Snow is collecting in his blond hair and along his shoulders. There's an emblem or a crest stamped into his breastplate, over his heart, but just the edge peeks out from under the cloak, so I can't make it out. He looks so bright and flawless, so fierce and worldly, that he could have said he was the king himself and I would've believed it.

Then he says, "Is it much farther?"

I grit my teeth and get my crutches under me again. "No, my lord," I say tightly. "Forgive me for the delay."

"That wasn't a complaint," he says easily. "I was worried Lord Alek might follow me. If it's a long way, I would offer you mercy. If you like."

I frown, turning that around in my head, and he adds, "My horse. Mercy."

The mare blows a snort against his shoulder.

It's a generous offer, and it takes me by surprise—but the last thing I need from him is pity. "No. I'm fine." I thrust my crutches into the snow to prove it.

"As you say."

He's being kind. I should be grateful. I don't know what's wrong with me. Anger and excitement are whirling in my gut, and I'm not quite sure where they'll land. I'm not even sure *why*. I keep my eyes on the snow ahead.

"Jax, was it?" he says, and I startle and almost lose my crutch again.

"Yeah. Yes. My lord."

"I'm Tycho." He pauses. "You don't have to be formal."

I'm not sure what to say to that, so I say nothing.

He continues as if we're in the midst of a conversation. "I'm being rude. Forgive me. I've been mostly on my own for days, with only Mercy for company. I sometimes forget how to have a conversation with another person."

"Forgiven," I say woodenly.

I'm not meaning to be funny, but the corner of his mouth turns up, just for a moment. "I didn't expect to find Alek here. He's from the north side of the Crystal City. His House mostly deals with fabrics and textiles. Does he visit Briarlock often?"

This, at least, I can answer honestly. "I've never seen him before."

I'm sure I'll see him later, though. The message feels like it's burning a hole through my pocket.

"I've been in Emberfall for well over a month," Lord Tycho says. "But his family has a history of . . . trouble. He doesn't like me much." He glances at me, and his voice takes on a heavier tone. "He's a dangerous man when he wants to be. Take care when you do business with him. You should warn your friend as well."

I find it interesting that a man armed to the teeth would call someone *else* dangerous, but I don't say that. I saw the way Lord Tycho's hand went to his sword when the other man came into the bakery. I'm desperately curious about who these men are, their relation to each other, and what's on this secret parchment in my pocket. The curiosity puts a sour taste in my mouth, but I can't shake it.

We come to the final bend in the lane, and I see my home up ahead, silent and dark. I added coal before I left so the forge would stay hot, and a thin trail of smoke floats into the sky.

I feel a momentary panic, thinking my father might have returned. I don't know why it would matter, but everything feels awkward and uncertain now, and my father would only make that worse. I can see Da being drunkenly vulgar, demanding too much silver or vomiting on the lord's polished boots. Lord Tycho is surely someone who wouldn't tolerate it.

But no, there's no motion, no sign of anyone. The vise grip on my chest loosens the tiniest bit.

"It's just up ahead," I say to him, nodding.

"Good."

I can't tell if that word means he's impatient, or if he's glad to have a reason to end this stilted conversation, but either way, I'm glad too.

I stoke the forge and light a lantern, because the sun is beginning to fall behind the trees. Now that I have a job to do, I can focus on the horse instead of the young lord who's peering into my workshop. In addition to a few low stools and several iron handles I've bolted to the wall or the tables, I have a dozen ropes suspended from the ceiling, positioned anywhere I need to move quickly without my crutches. When my father is being particularly wicked, he cuts them down. But under Lord Tycho's appraising gaze, I'm self-conscious, both about the workshop and my skills. I feel like I should grab a rag and wipe the place down. I teased Cal about the flour on her cheek, but there's probably soot on my face from this morning.

I have to clear my throat, and I point to a post anchored in the ground. "You can tether her there. Did you find the shoe or was it lost?"

"I have it." He ties the mare, then moves close to unbuckle a saddle bag. He pulls a bent shoe free and winces. "It's not in the best shape. We've covered a lot of ground over the past six weeks."

"I can make you a new one." I glance at the other forehoof and hesitate. The shoe on that one won't last long either. "For both fronts, if you like."

"Whatever you think is best."

I can't tell if he's being charitable or genuine, and it leaves me off balance. When Lady Karyl was looking for my father, it was easy to demand extra silver to carry her message. But with Lord Tycho, he's too calm, too easygoing. It feels as though it *must* be an act, like he's still suspicious. I drag one of my stools close to the horse and cast a glance his way, sure he's going to be watching me, but he's not.

Instead, he's moved away, peering at the tools and gadgets hung from the walls.

I have a ceramic jar of raisin biscuits that Callyn brought me last week, and I feed one to the horse. "Is your master always like this?" I murmur to the mare.

She presses her face to my chest and blows warm breaths against my hip. I grab hold of a rope to keep my balance in case she butts her head at me, but she's as gentle as a kitten.

I drop to sit on the stool and pull her foot into my lap—but then I see the scars.

She's a bay, with deep-brown fur, a black mane and tail, and a narrow white stripe down her face. But long stretches of white fur make streaks just behind the saddle girth, unnatural coloring that can only be caused by scarring.

In a location that can only be caused by spurs.

It makes me scowl. Maybe this is what I've misread. Maybe Lord Tycho is worse than cruel to this horse. Maybe that's why he seems so easygoing. Maybe he just doesn't *care.*

My gut clenches at the thought, and I'm surprised to realize I don't want him to be like that. So many people turn out to be a disappointment, and it's discouraging to think this fresh-faced young nobleman will be the same. I reach for my clamps and file and cast a dark look across the workshop to where he's meandered: the corner where we have a few forged weapons.

From here, I can't tell if he's wearing spurs.

He must sense my gaze, because he glances over, and I quickly look back at the horse.

If he noticed my staring, he doesn't say so. "May I?"

I have to look back, and he's gesturing to one of the swords.

"Yes." I scrape at the mare's hoof, creating a fresh surface for a new shoe. "They're nowhere near as nice as yours," I add roughly.

"I disagree." He cuts a pattern through the air, spinning an agile half-turn in the narrow space, making his cloak flare. "Incredible balance."

The praise makes me blush, and I'm not ready for it. The hoof is clean, so I grab hold of a rope to pull myself up so I can get to the forge, and I thrust a fresh shoe in. I'm glad this part takes my focus, so I don't have to say anything.

It doesn't stop him from talking, though. "Did you make this?"

I nod. "The swords are mine. My father made the daggers." I put the horseshoe against the anvil and swing my hammer to spare me saying anything else. Sparks fly and glowing steel splinters away.

Lord Tycho is more patient than Lady Karyl. He waits for me to finish banging, then says, "You do better work than your father."

I grunt and say nothing, returning to the horse. If my father heard that comment, he'd put his boot in my belly and it would hurt to sit up for a week. The hot shoe presses into the mare's hoof, and smoke rises. I murmur a soft word but she's steady as a rock.

Silence falls between us again, but I hear the moment he returns the sword to the rack along the wall. At first I'm tense, worried he's going to ask more questions, but he says nothing, waiting at a distance as I measure and bang and hammer. After a few minutes, this hoof is done, and I drag my stool to her other side to begin again.

"Forgive me," he says, and suddenly his voice is lower, quieter. "I know I interrupted you and your friend earlier."

I blink and look up.

He's leaning against the work table now. His eyes are intent, and he doesn't look away. "I sense that I've made you uncomfortable in some way. I didn't mean to."

I shrug, then duck my face into my shoulder to push hair out of my eyes. "You didn't."

He says nothing, so I glance over in the midst of my filing. His cloak is tossed back over his shoulder now, and I can clearly see the insignia over his heart.

I raise my eyebrows and look back at the mare's hoof. "You wear the crests of Syhl Shallow and Emberfall together."

He glances down. "Oh. Yes. I carry messages between the Crystal Palace and Ironrose Castle. Between the king and queen and the prince and princess."

My file goes still. "That makes you—"

"The King's Courier. Well, that's the official title in Emberfall. Here, I would be the Queen's Envoy, though no one calls me that. But either way, I try not to make a spectacle of it. There are many who'd make me a target if they knew."

Clouds above. And I nearly handed him a note from the Truthbringers. I may as well have handed it right to Queen Lia Mara herself.

At least that explains his accent, the tiny edge to his words. He must be from Emberfall originally, though his Syssalah is flawless. We're close enough to the border that I know a handful of words in Emberish, mostly words to ask travelers what they need from the forge. I would've learned more if I'd been able to enlist as a soldier. The last queen of Syhl Shallow was known to say it was the height of ignorance to not understand what your enemies are saying. I suppose I can add that to the list of things that makes me feel like a failure.

Once this hoof is smooth and clean, I head for the forge again. "You don't travel with . . ." I gesture around at the empty space. "Guards?"

"A lone man on a horse doesn't seem worthy of much attention." His mouth turns up in that slight smile. "A man trailed by Royal Guards generates a *lot*."

My eyes skip over his attire again. Now I understand the weapons and armor.

His gaze narrows just the tiniest bit. He sees me looking.

I flush, but I wonder if this is typical for him, judging everyone he meets, worrying that he's found himself in a risky position. It puts his silence on the walk in a new light. He's not sharing secrets, but somehow, this feels like an extension of trust. For a spare second, I want to explain why I've been so wary and anxious. I don't know if it's his easygoing manner or the fact that we're alone in the shop, but he doesn't talk to me like a lord speaking to a lowly tradesman. He doesn't speak to me like I'm *lesser*.

I'm such a fool. What even would I tell him?

I imagine confessing. *A woman named Lady Karyl paid me to carry a message for the Truthbringers. I don't know what it says, but I think Lord Alek is the intended recipient. She's paying me twenty silvers, so it's definitely something dangerous.*

I'd be signing my own death warrant. Especially if Lady Karyl was right that nothing in the note could be traced back to her.

But I consider the man leaning against the work table. *I would offer you mercy*, he said.

He was talking about the horse, but just now, it feels like he was saying something different.

"What?" says Lord Tycho.

I blink, and my eyes skip away. I was staring.

I swallow. My father is right. My world is nothing but misfortune.

"Nothing." I thrust a new shoe into the forge, then pull it out as quickly as possible so I won't have to talk over the pounding of steel against steel.

I don't have to worry. Lord Tycho says nothing more.

Minutes later, the mare is freshly shod, and I pull myself upright.

"You have my thanks," he says. "How much?"

"Oh. Ah—ten coppers."

He gives me a look and pulls two silvers from a pouch at his waist.

I don't want to take them. It feels dishonest.

Which is *laughable*.

I take the coins from his palm. "Thank you, my lord."

He takes the reins and draws them up over the mare's neck. "Tycho." He grabs a fistful of mane and swings into the saddle from the ground. "Be well, Jax."

His feet slip into the stirrups. *No spurs.*

He clucks to the horse, and she springs into a trot, splashing through the slush.

"Be well," I say, watching as the gently falling snow gradually turns them invisible. "Tycho."

I drop onto the stool beside the forge and breathe a sigh. I slip the two coins into my pocket and pull the note from Lady Karyl free. Just looking at it makes my chest tighten again.

The forge is right here. I can end this right now and toss it into the fire. Wash my hands of the whole thing.

Hoofbeats sound in the lane again, and I startle, grabbing a rope to stand. I thrust the note back into my pocket. Is he coming back?

But no. It's a tall chestnut gelding, coming from the opposite direction, being ridden too fast for the slippery conditions. The horse skids into the yard beside the forge, and the man dismounts before the horse has come to a full stop.

Lord Alek.

I grab my crutches. "My lord—"

He draws a sword and points it right at my throat. I backpedal too quickly, collide with my stool, and sit down hard in the dirt.

His sword follows me the whole way. I try to scramble backward, but I run into the work table.

That blade presses right into my neck, and it must break skin because I feel the sting. I'm afraid to swallow.

"Why were you talking to the King's Courier?" he demands.

I want to be flippant, but it's hard when I'm looking death in the face. "His—his horse—lost—lost a shoe."

He stares down at me, and his blue eyes are narrow and dark in the shadows. The light from the forge nearly makes his red hair glow. He presses on the blade, and I try to shrink back.

"I've never—I've never seen him before. I didn't know who he was."

He regards me silently.

"I'm just a blacksmith," I say. I shove a hand into my pocket and draw out the note. "Lady Karyl left this for you."

"Did you tell him about it?"

"No. No! Nothing. No one knows."

He takes the note. A moment later, he withdraws and sheathes his sword. "If you told him, we'll know."

I nod and press a hand to my neck. It comes away sticky with blood, and my breathing shakes.

Alek is a dangerous man.

Yes, Lord Tycho. I see that.

"I'll be back in three days," Alek says. "If you're telling the truth, I'll have another letter for you to hold. If you're not . . ."

I hold up my blood-slick fingers. "I got the message."

"Good." He strides away.

My thoughts are so scrambled up that I almost forgot the promised payment. I hate myself, but this isn't just about me. "Wait," I call. "If you want my silence, you're still going to need to pay for it."

"Sure." He swings onto the horse and throws a handful of silver into the slush. "Here are your coins."

Then he's off, leaving me on my hands and knees in the muddy snow, picking through for each one.

That's exactly where my father finds me, too, when he comes stumbling into the yard. He's bigger than Alek, and he might not be armed, but he has the capacity to be every bit as dangerous.

My breath catches. If he sees these coins, he'll take them, and there's nothing I can do about it.

"What are you doing?" he says, and while he's not fully slurring, it's close.

"I dropped the can of nails," I say. "I was just picking them up."

He grunts and turns for the house. "Typical misfortune," he says.

I look out into the darkness of the lane, where Lord Tycho first disappeared, and then Lord Alek. A bit of kindness chased by a bit of cruelty.

My father's right. Typical.

CHAPTER 6

TYCHO

I don't reach the Crystal City until very late, and the cobblestone streets are slick with fallen snow, forcing this last part of my journey to take longer than any other. Mercy picks her way along the darkened streets, and I listen for trouble, though all I've heard for hours are the rhythmic clops of her hooves and the whisper of snow settling across Syhl Shallow. I'm nearly home, but my thoughts are trapped back in Briarlock, and I can't settle on what's drawing my focus the most. The unexpected appearance of Lord Alek? I don't *think* so. He's hated me for years—and it's rather mutual. It's not like he caused an issue while I was there.

The tension in the bakery doubled when I arrived, too—a tension that followed the beguiling blacksmith all the way to his forge. I made Jax nervous, clearly, because I caught the many glances he threw across his workshop. I liked how gentle he was with Mercy, the way his voice went low when he spoke to the mare. *Is your master always like this?* I heard him say, and the memory makes me smile. I liked how he didn't try to overcharge me, even though he must have known I'd carry good silver.

Callyn didn't try to overcharge me either, and she blushed when I gave her two silvers, the same as Jax. The meat pies were incredible, though, the crust sweet and buttery, with the insides full of a savory mixture of chicken and vegetables. I feel like I should ride back to pay her more.

But I can't shake that overriding worry that I walked into ... *something*. Maybe it's just that I wear the crests of both countries, and lately that seems to be enough to cause tension.

When I reach the guard station at the palace gates, I don't recognize the guard there, which means she doesn't recognize *me*, and I have to wait for her commanding officer. I sigh inwardly and wait while Mercy paws at the slush.

"I know," I murmur and bite back a shiver. Those warm meat pies from Callyn's bakery feel like a distant memory. "We're almost there."

An army lieutenant named Ander reaches the station rather quickly, and I sigh with relief when I see him. We've never been friends, but I've known Ander since I was a recruit.

"Well met," I say.

He gives me a curt nod and looks to the guard. "Let him through."

It *is* the middle of the night, so I ignore his terse manner and cluck to my horse. Once we're past the gates, Mercy trots across the deserted training fields without any urging. The stables are dark and closed up for the night, but a sleepy stable hand comes down from the loft with an oil lantern when Mercy clops into the aisle.

"I'll take care of the horse," I say quietly. It's not his fault that I've arrived so late. "Go back to sleep." He leaves the lantern with me and shuffles back up the steps.

Mercy's tack is soaked and soiled from snow and sweat and days of hard riding, but that can wait till tomorrow. I tie her in the aisle and pile my equipment in the storage room, then grab some rags and a currycomb.

When I emerge, there's a cloaked man in the shadows feeding an apple to Mercy. I stop short in the doorway, but then he looks up. "Welcome home."

"Grey," I say in surprise. I smile, then put a hand over my heart and bow. "Ah, forgive me, Your Majesty—"

"Oh, stop it," he says lightly. "Give me a rag."

I hand one over. Mercy is only half finished with the apple he gave her, but she starts nosing at him for more anyway, slobbering a trail of apple bits along the front of his cloak. I catch her halter and pull her away. "Don't drool on the king."

Grey says nothing, he just takes the rag and begins to rub the sweat marks out of her fur. I hesitate, then do the same.

The people of Syhl Shallow—and Emberfall, really—have a lot of *thoughts* about the king: opinions about his once-banned magic, about his prowess on the battlefield, about whether he was earnest in his attempt to unite warring countries by marrying Queen Lia Mara. There are whispers that he was once working with an evil enchantress to destroy Emberfall, that his "alliance" is a farce to take advantage of the queen, that his magic will overwhelm Syhl Shallow and cause endless suffering to all who oppose him.

The *real* truth is that Grey is an honest man who was raised in poverty, only to later discover that he was secretly the heir to the throne of Emberfall. He's a *good* king, though: strong and fair, devoted to the countries he united. But I sometimes wonder if he craves quiet moments like this in the same way that I do. Moments where he doesn't have to be the fierce ruler and I don't have to be a well-armed messenger carrying word of threats against the throne, and instead we're just two people with a horse that needs tending.

I press the rag into Mercy's coat, rubbing hard. "You really did take me by surprise," I say to Grey, and mean it. "I thought the entire palace was asleep."

"I saw you cross the training fields," he says. "Lia Mara is sicker with this one than she was with little Sinna, so no one is sleeping these days."

My eyes flick up, and I study him over the crest of Mercy's neck. "The queen is pregnant again."

"Ah. Yes." He doesn't smile, but there's a warm light in his eye that only appears when he speaks of their daughter—but there's a hesitation in his voice, too. "You were gone before we knew."

I understand the hesitation. Another royal baby. Another potential magesmith.

Another target.

I think of the reports from Emberfall that are still wrapped up and tucked beneath my breastplate. Grey hasn't asked for them yet, but I know he will. I don't want to ruin the quiet by offering.

"Is Lia Mara well?" I ask instead.

He nods. "She misses you." He half smiles. "She says you're the only one allowed to teach Sinna to hold a sword, as it has been decreed by the princess herself—"

I snort. Princess Sinna is three. "Does she know *you* taught *me*?"

"Well, clearly I am no longer the favorite teacher." He fetches a currycomb from a rack, then rubs it into Mercy's fur, just below her mane. "How fares my brother?"

Prince Rhen. Grey asks me this every time I return, and the weight in his voice is always the same. Sometimes I wonder if it's about Rhen himself, because Grey and Rhen have a long, complicated, dark history that nearly broke them both—and nearly tore apart each country in the process. Grey seems to have moved past the curse that tormented them, but Rhen still wears the weight of his past like a cloak he can't shrug off.

But sometimes I wonder if this question is about *me*, as if the king worries that sending me to Ironrose Castle is asking more of me than he should.

Prince Rhen once tortured us both for a secret we kept.

Thinking about that moment always makes me feel weak, especially in front of Grey, so I lean into the currycomb and answer. "Prince Rhen is busy," I say. "When I first arrived, he'd received word that a small group from Valkins Valley had been shipping grain through the harbor at Silvermoon, but messages were found buried inside the sacks." It was a brilliant hiding place, because none of the messages would have been discovered if a sack hadn't been caught by a rusty nail and torn open. "At first the messages seemed ridiculous—nothing worth hiding."

Grey glances up. "What do you mean?"

"Like . . . *Mama fed the goats today. Papa didn't help her.*"

Grey frowns.

"Exactly," I say. "I don't think anyone would have paid any attention, but one of the dockworkers was in the marketplace talking about these mysterious letters in the grain sacks, and the Grand Marshal's guards overheard and demanded to see them. They hadn't kept all of them, but they had a new shipment waiting to go south on a ship, so they tore them all open—and found dozens of ridiculous messages."

I crouch to rub the mud from Mercy's fetlocks. "Marshal Blackcomb turned the messages over to Rhen, and you know how he loves a good puzzle. Well, one of the letters mentioned how 'Papa' couldn't see straight, which made Rhen wonder if it was a reference to *him*, what with his missing eye and all, so he went back through the messages and began to determine a code. 'Mama' was Harper, and 'feeding the goats' seemed to indicate a trip she'd taken to Hutchins Forge, because of the livestock market, and Rhen hadn't accompanied her—"

"So they were tracking Rhen and Harper's movements."

"Not just theirs," I say. "Yours and Lia Mara's, too. It took Rhen a while to figure it out, because you're *Father* and *Mother*, so for a while he thought it was interchangeable, but then they mentioned someone named *Nyssa*—"

"Sinna." His eyes flash to mine, and there's no questioning the sudden flare of fury and fear in his tone.

"Yes," I say. "We think so."

"Do you have these letters?"

"Yes. Some." I've already begun unbuckling the breastplate. "But there have been no threats to the princess. No threats to any of you, really. The vast majority of the letters are simply reports going back and forth between Syhl Shallow and Emberfall, tracking where you've been and what you've done."

I jerk free of the armor and unroll the leather that keeps their messages safe. "There's one line that appears several times, to *gather your best silver,* which we think could be an instruction to pool funds for another attack. But we're not sure. I was going to return at once, but Rhen felt it would be better to check shipments going through other towns, to see if we could find any true threats. But obviously, that's a lot of ground to cover."

Grey scans the first note in the pile, but looks back at me. "And did he find anything?"

"No. Nothing relating to the messages. Any true threats against the Crown seemed to be lone dissenters who were quickly captured and dealt with. But we did discover that there are small groups of Truthbringers that seem to be growing in number throughout most of the larger cities in Emberfall. He suspects that for now, these messages may be an attempt to set up some kind of . . . collaboration. Harper called it a 'whisper network.' They're seeing what messages get through, and what messages are stopped."

He's quiet for a moment, and when he speaks, there's a tone of resignation in his voice. "So they can plan something bigger."

He's thinking of the Uprising. I remember the rush of magic that swept through the palace, the way so many bodies dropped where they stood.

I also remember the way Sinna screamed when a dozen armed men burst into the nursery and killed her nanny in an attempt to capture the "magical princess."

My voice is equally resigned. "Possibly."

He flips to the next message in the pile, then frowns. Then the third. He sighs and folds them back up in the leather. "I shouldn't have troubled you with this now, Tycho."

"It's no trouble. I knew you'd be eager to hear. I would have been earlier, but Mercy threw a shoe just after we passed the border." I pause. "In that stack, you'll find that Rhen wrote you a letter detailing everything he thinks you should do."

"Of course he did." Grey pauses. "We'll have to search shipments here, too. I don't like the idea that messages could be passed right under our noses. Anything else?"

"No." I untie Mercy to lead her to a stall. "Maybe."

"Tell me."

I turn the mare loose in a stall and latch the gate. She immediately thrusts her face into a pile of hay. "I stopped in Briarlock to get a fresh shoe for Mercy. While I was there, I saw Lord Alek."

Grey frowns. "Did he say what he was doing there?"

"No—but you know how he feels about me. I'd have to put a sword through him to get an honest word out of his mouth."

"It's the same way he feels about me." Grey thinks for a moment. "But that's interesting. Was anyone with him?"

"No." I hesitate. I've been turning my time in Briarlock around in my head for hours. I keep thinking of the tension in the bakery, especially once Alek arrived. Was that because of my presence? Or was it something else?

"What is it?" says Grey.

I tell him about Callyn and Nora and the sweetcakes, then about Jax and his forge. "He said he'd never seen Alek before. But it's a small town near the border. Well off the main road. Alek would have no reason to be there. I can't imagine he would be overseeing fabric shipments himself."

I frown, turning it over in my head for the thousandth time. Alek has never been proven to be working against the throne, but his sister was caught working as a spy for Emberfall years ago. She died in the final battle. I was there. I might have shot the killing arrow. Alek doesn't let me forget it.

I was fifteen years old, and it was the first time I took a life. I don't let *myself* forget it.

So maybe all the tension and animosity was personal. Maybe I spent so many weeks in Emberfall looking for signs of treason that I found it in a remote bakery with a man I can't stand.

I look at Grey. "Alek knew I was looking for the forge. It was rather remote, and I was alone. If he were up to something, he could have ambushed me."

"He'd be a fool to ambush you." He pauses. He doesn't trust Alek either. "I know you've been gone for well over a month," he finally says, and his tone is grave, "but I'd like to know if Alek is still there. If I send soldiers, we'll spook him, but you can be explained away. How soon do you think you can return to Briarlock?"

I'm exhausted, and I've been thinking about my bed in the palace for longer than I'd admit out loud. But I pick up my armor and toss my cloak over my shoulder. "Your Majesty," I say grandly, partially teasing and partially not. "As soon as you need."

CHAPTER 7

TYCHO

I wake to weak sunlight against my eyelids and whispers from beside my bed.

"Are you going to sleep *all* day?" says the tiny voice. "The sun is up."

I blink and find myself eye-to-eye with Sinna, who's standing beside my bed. Her face breaks into a wide grin full of baby teeth. Her hair is a wild mess of red tangles, and she's still in a sleeping shift, one hand clutching the stuffed pony that Harper and Rhen sent to her. "You're awake!"

"I'm awake." My voice is rough, but I smile back. I could have done with another five hours of sleep. Salam, my cat, has no tolerance for toddlers or noise, so he springs off the bed to disappear somewhere. I glance past Sinna to see that my door is only open wide enough for her to slip through. I wonder which nanny she got away from this time. "Still being a bit of a sneak, hmm?"

Her grin widens and she puts a finger to her lips.

"Sinna!" a hushed voice whispers from the hallway. "Girl, it is *too early* for these games."

"You're going to scare your nanny to death," I warn softly.

Sinna scowls. "Mama said you would teach me how to hold a sword."

"I will." I run a hand down my face. I'm not awake enough for this. "If you let me go back to sleep, I'll let you ride Mercy, too."

She gasps, her eyes wide. "Mercy!" She squeezes the stuffed pony in her arms and bolts for the door, pulling it closed roughly behind her.

I pull the pillow over my head and fall back to sleep. The next time I wake, Salam's orange-striped body is curled around my feet, and my hearth has gone cold. By the time I make my way to the dining room, I've washed and shaved and put on cleaner clothes than I've worn in days. It looks as though everyone has already eaten, but I'm pleased that most of my friends are still present. The air is full of the scent of cooked meats, warm breads, and sweet honey, but it's the company in the room that's the most inviting. The king and queen sit at the far corner of the table, little Sinna between them. Noah, the palace physician, sits on the other side of the queen. The only people missing are Jacob, Grey's closest adviser and friend, and Nolla Verin, the queen's sister. I wonder if they're on the training fields already.

"Tycho!" Sinna cries, as if she didn't already wake me at dawn. She tries to tackle my legs, but I catch her and toss her into the air, and she shrieks with glee. But then she looks at me as sternly as a toddler can manage. "You're late for breakfast."

"You look like you needed the rest," says the queen. "Welcome home."

"Thank you," I say, but if anyone looks like they need some rest, it's the queen. She's one of the strongest women I know, but just now her eyes are heavy-lidded and her skin is a bit pale. I remember what Grey said about the pregnancy. Two slices of honeyed bread sit on her plate, but only one bite has been eaten. A steaming cup of tea sits in front of her.

Grey nudges the plate toward her. "You need to eat," he says softly.

"I will."

"I could try a bit of magic—"

"No," she says firmly, with the tone of a familiar argument. "You don't know what it would do to the baby."

There's a moment of tense silence in the air, but I say nothing.

Noah gives the plate a nudge, too. "He's right about eating, though."

"I have an idea," says Lia Mara. "The two of you can vomit all night and see how you feel about breakfast. Tycho, come eat so I can live vicariously through you."

I smile. "Gladly. Where's Jake—"

A strong arm grabs me around the neck from behind, but without dislodging the toddler on my one arm, I catch the hand, twist, and drive an elbow back.

I'm only doing it halfheartedly, because I'm used to his antics, but Jake grunts and falls back anyway. He coughs, then grins. "Damn, T." He rubs his stomach. "Welcome back. Who said something about vomiting?"

"Again, again!" says Sinna.

I laugh. "Let me eat first."

Grey stands. "We're due on the training fields anyway." He drops a kiss on Lia Mara's cheek, then stops beside me to do the same thing to his daughter.

Sinna lets go of me to grab him around the neck, looking into his eyes earnestly. "You be careful with your swords today, Da."

He smiles and flips her upside down before setting her on her feet. "I'll try my best."

I lose my smile and wish I'd woken earlier. "Should I join you?"

"You've earned a rest, Tycho. Take it."

Jake claps me on the shoulder, drops his own kiss on Noah's fore-head, then leaves with Grey. I pile a plate with food from the table, while Sinna spins in circles beside me, chattering endlessly. I'm almost as relieved as Lia Mara when a nanny appears in the doorway to take the princess for her morning lessons.

"Did you hear?" Sinna is saying to her as they head into the hallway. "Tycho is going to let me ride Mercy!"

"You're very patient with her," says Lia Mara when I sit at the table.

"I missed her," I say honestly. I glance between her and Noah. "I missed you all."

Lia Mara frowns. "Grey told me he's asked you to leave again."

I slather honey on my own slice of bread. "I know what I signed up for. When he's ready for me to go, I'll go."

Noah chuckles. "You'll be out on the training field with them in an hour."

I smile, abashed. "Maybe." That said, I like being *here*, too. I like their quiet thoughtfulness. Grey and Jake are at home with a sword in their hands, and I am too, but there's something calming about being with people who wield warmth and empathy instead of weapons.

"Grey has told us about the 'whisper network' you discovered with Rhen," Lia Mara says. She keeps her voice low so we're not overheard. Her eyes might be tired, but her mind is as sharp as ever. "My sister has already taken the letters to a few key advisers. I know shipments are being searched in Emberfall, but I do not want to spread word of our suspicions *here* yet."

I nod. "I think it took Rhen by surprise how widespread it was."

"Me too," she says. "Grey said you were concerned that Alek was so far northwest of the city."

I make a face. "Maybe it's just me."

"Briarlock is such a small village I had to ask one of my advisers to find it on a map. Alek deals in rich textiles and fabrics. His House should have no business there."

"I'll try to find out," I say. "I can leave today if you prefer."

"No," she says. "You need at least a day to rest. Two! I'll speak to Grey."

Her voice is strong and decisive, but when she reaches out to pat my hand, it feels like hers is trembling. She really should eat something. I wonder if she's truly worried about Grey's magic. Ever since so many died in the Uprising, there have been whispers about whether the king can adequately control it.

"I'll do whatever you need." I stab a piece of ham with my fork and smile. "I don't mind. Truly."

She's quiet for a moment. "We ask too much of you," she finally says. "This role leaves you no time for friendship, or courtship, or even—"

I almost choke on my food. "*You* are my friends," I say. "And *courtship*? Who would I court?"

"We certainly don't leave you with time to meet anyone. I could see if there are any eligible suitors within the Royal Houses."

"Like when I was sixteen and you encouraged me to pursue Nolla Verin? I tried to hold her hand and I thought she was going to cut my fingers off." I grin. "You do realize there are rumors that she sleeps with her blades in hand."

Lia Mara rolls her eyes. "My sister does no such thing."

I imagine Nolla Verin and her vicious practicality. "Tonight, you should check. I think you'd be surprised."

She doesn't smile. "In truth, I hoped that part of the reason you were in Emberfall so long was because you might have met someone who"—she exchanges a glance with Noah—"encouraged you to linger."

"Then I'm sorry to report it was just plots against the throne that took up all my time." I push food around on my plate. I'm not sure how we shifted from threats against the royal family to my romantic interests. A new tension has crawled across my shoulders. "When I wasn't traveling with Rhen, I trained with the Royal Guard. Once we'd discovered all we could, I came home."

"You spent a great deal of time with Rhen, did you?" A tightness enters her tone. She witnessed what Rhen did to me and Grey. It was years ago, and they've put aside their differences, but I don't think she'll ever forgive him for it.

"As much as was necessary." I shove another bite of bread into my mouth. I wish I could shake off this sudden new attention. I should have followed the others to the training fields. Grey would stumble into his own sword before it would occur to him to interrogate me about *courtship*.

Lia Mara and Noah are quiet for a moment, and I have no desire to fill *this* silence, so I keep my eyes on my food.

"Since we're talking about Emberfall," Lia Mara eventually says, "I did have an idea." Her tone has changed to lightly musing. Maybe she feels the need to change the subject. "It concerns me that the only people working together across the border are conspiring *against* us. There has been so much unrest, but our countries have been at peace for years now, and I would like to plan something bigger, something to show our people that they can be *united* in their love for both Emberfall and Syhl Shallow."

"What did you have in mind?" I say.

"My mother used to hold a competition every year, called the Queen's Challenge. It was quite a spectacle, and it would draw people from all over Syhl Shallow."

I've heard of the Queen's Challenge. Many of the soldiers have mentioned it with longing in their voices. "You want to bring it back?" I say. "I think that would be a popular decision."

"I'd like to host it in Emberfall," she says. "We could call it the Royal

Challenge." She pauses. "The lands surrounding Ironrose Castle are even more vast than the training fields here. This would require a great deal of resources from both countries, as well as an opportunity for the people to mingle in a time of revelry." She takes another tiny bite. "What do you think?"

She's right about the lands surrounding Ironrose Castle, and they'd be perfect to host all kinds of competitions, both mounted and unmounted, from swordplay to archery to foot races—any challenge they could fathom. The idea lights a spark of eagerness inside me as well. "When Grey and I worked in the tourney, the stands were full nearly every night. And there are tourneys all over Emberfall. I think such a challenge would be equally popular there."

"Do you think Prince Rhen would be agreeable?"

She says this more tentatively. Grey is the king, so his word is law, but Rhen grew up believing he was the crown prince. Despite their dark history, Grey is always careful not to force his will on his younger brother. Sometimes I'm not sure Rhen is aware of that.

"I think . . ." I begin thoughtfully, remembering the prince eagerly poring over the letters with coded messages of potential treason. "I think he'd be open to the idea. Prince Rhen loves a challenge."

She smiles and pushes her plate away. She's only eaten three bites, but I know better than to say anything. "Good. When you return, please tell him we hope to see him compete."

Once Lia Mara is gone, I expect Noah to leave to attend to his own duties, too, but he pours himself another cup of tea, adding so much milk and honey that my eyebrows go up.

He sees me looking and smiles. "One day we'll bring you back a caramel macchiato from the other side, and it will wreck you for tea forever."

He and Jake came from somewhere called Washington, DC, just like Princess Harper. Noah wears two magic-infused rings like my own: one to assist in his healing arts, but the other allows him to cross over into his own world.

I don't know how often they go, but I don't think it's often. I've heard Jake say that the longer they stay here, the more jarring it is to cross over. A few years ago, not long after Grey first forged the rings, Jake and Noah went to "Disi" for a visit. They returned two hours later, and Jake had a split lip and bloodied knuckles.

They didn't tell me what happened, but I overheard them talking to Grey.

"In some ways, it's harder here," Jake said. "But in a lot of ways, it's a hell of a lot easier."

My plate is empty, and I can see soldiers taking to the training field outside the window, but I fill my own teacup and add an equivalent amount of milk and honey.

When I take a sip, I nearly choke, and Noah laughs.

"Maybe it's an acquired taste," he says.

"Definitely."

He says nothing, but he sits back in his chair and takes a sip of his overly sweet tea, and we both stare at the window for a while. Snow has begun to drift down from the sky, but it's only flurries now. Bits of frost have collected along the edge of the windowpanes.

"When the weather is like this," Noah says, "it makes me think of Iisak."

He says this almost offhandedly, but Iisak's name always dredges a bit of sorrow from my chest. Iisak was a scraver from the ice forests of Iishellasa who initially helped Grey find his own magic. Iisak was my friend, too, but he died during the battles between Syhl Shallow and Emberfall. The scraver could be viciously callous when he had to be, but he was deeply kind and loyal, with strong opinions on the duties of a ruler.

Iisak loved the snow. Even in the dead heat of summer, his magic could pull frost from the air. I take another deep swallow of my too-sweet tea. "It makes me think of him, too."

Noah studies me for a long moment. His voice drops. "How are you doing *really*?"

I glance at him. "I'm well, Noah. Truly."

"You were with Rhen for a long time."

"He doesn't treat me poorly."

"I wouldn't expect him to." Noah hesitates. "But Rhen has suffered a lot—"

"So has Grey," I say.

"So have *you*."

I almost flinch. Noah knows me too well. Better than anyone, probably. When I was younger, I used to seek his company in the infirmary whenever the rest of the world felt too overwhelming—which was often. At first, it was because the space was quiet and secure, and Noah is one of the few people in my life who has never demanded anything from me. But as time went on, I discovered that Noah was a safe confidant: never harsh or critical, just a good listener. I know he was a healer in Washington, DC, a doctor in something called an emergency room. He once said that he used to see people on the worst day of their life, and it was his job to help get them through it.

I'm certain he was very good at it.

"Rhen is an expert at keeping people at arm's length," Noah says. "And so are you." He pauses. "Lia Mara hoped you might have found . . . ah, *companionship* at Ironrose, but I'm worried you found the opposite: a little too much isolation."

"I don't mind being on my own."

"I know," he says. "And I know Grey relies on you quite a bit." His voice quiets further. "What happened to Rhen and Grey was terrible, but they were young men, and they made some terrible choices. You were fifteen—and you had no part in their conflict. You didn't deserve what was done to you." He pauses. "I know about the soldiers when you were young, too, what they did to your family." Another pause, and this one is more weighted. "What they did to *you*. You didn't deserve that either."

This time I do flinch. "Stop." I hesitate. "Please."

"You spent so many years with the army, and I don't care what you said to Grey, I know you didn't want—"

"I was a good soldier, Noah. I'd do it again if he asked me to."

"Would you?"

The question hits me like a knife. It's a little too piercing, a little too precise.

"Yes," I say firmly. "I would."

He reaches out a hand as if to touch mine, but I draw mine away before he makes contact.

Noah watches this and goes still, then rests his hand on the edge of the table. "You were very tense when Lia Mara was asking about courtship. I'm worried that everything you've been through—"

I stand, wishing for armor and weapons and an end to this conversation. "I should join Grey and Jake."

"Wait. Please." His voice is very gentle. "I didn't mean to chase you off."

"You didn't." But maybe he did. I respect Noah, though, so I pause before moving away from the table.

"There's nothing wrong with enjoying being on your own," he says. "I don't want you to walk out of here questioning that."

I nod and move to leave.

"Tycho, look at me."

I turn, but my jaw is tight.

"I just want to make sure you *enjoy* it," he says, "and that you haven't taken this job because it's a convenient way to hide when you don't want to feel vulnerable."

"I don't feel vulnerable anymore," I say. "Grey made sure of it."

Then I turn on my heel to head for the training fields, to prove exactly that.

CHAPTER 8

JAX

Melting snow drips from the roof over my workshop, and early morning fog clings to the sodden ground. Mud will be everywhere today, which might make for decent business. I've been up since before dawn with butterflies in my gut, because today is the day that Lord Alek said he'd return, and I'm not sure what to expect.

After he left three days ago, I headed back down the lane to Callyn's bakery. Nora saw the blood at my neck and looked like she was going to pass out, but Cal is more steady.

She cleaned the wound while swearing under her breath. "This isn't worth it if you're going to end up dead, Jax."

I thrust a hand into my pocket and pulled out the silver. "Here's another five. Do you still feel the same?"

She bit her lip—and pocketed the coins.

I saw her yesterday, and between the coins I've given her and what the bakery has made this week, she has fifteen silvers stashed away. I know Lord Tycho paid her generously for meat pies and sweetcakes, just like he overpaid me for his mare's shoes. I keep feeling a twinge in my gut every time I think of accepting his silver, as if coins earned honestly and those earned from disloyalty don't all spend the same.

This morning, I've filled a jar with forged nails to replace the ones we've sold, so I move on to other projects. I have an order from a farmer on the north side of town who needs a new hammer and a spade, so I feed a fresh ingot of iron to the forge, then roll out my shoulders and wait for it to heat.

"You're at it early," my father grunts.

I look over to find him in the doorway that leads into our home. He's relatively clear-eyed this morning, but that probably has more to do with the fact that he's run out of coins than any avoidance of ale.

"No earlier than usual." I glance into the forge, but the iron hasn't reached the right shade of yellow yet. "I boiled some eggs if you're hungry."

He makes a noncommittal sound, but turns to go back in the house, which is answer enough. I haven't mentioned Lord Alek to him—just like he's never mentioned the Truthbringers to me. It's no secret what happened to Cal's father. There's a part of me that wonders why he'd ever be willing to take the same risks.

Then again, *I'm* taking them now, so I'm not in a position to judge.

I can hear him rattling around in the kitchen. I wonder if he's planning to take up some of the work, or if he'll fall back into bed. He's not always horrible, and when he's sober, he can actually be somewhat decent. He's very strong, and quick with a hammer, and we've worked alongside each other in the forge for so long that we can stay out of each other's way. When I was a boy, he worked long hours, but we always had enough to eat, with a little left over for the occasional diversion. He'd send me running down the lane to Callyn's bakery with a few coppers in my pocket, telling me to buy some sweets for us both.

Then I got hurt, and it seemed like the village physician carved out a piece of Da's heart when he took my foot.

I pull the iron out of the fire with my tongs, then set it against the anvil. I've gotten one end nearly flattened by the time my father reappears. He takes a leather apron from a hook on the wall. My eyebrows go up, but I know better than to say anything. I thrust the half-formed spade back into the forge and try to ignore the flicker of hope in my chest.

"I'll need a hammer to go with this," I say.

He nods, takes an ingot of his own, and sets it in the forge. A minute later, we're both clanging away.

Moments like this always fill me with longing—or maybe nostalgia. We don't say much to each other, but my father has never been a talker. The air is cold and peaceful, but we've both got a sheen of sweat on our forearms from the forge and the effort. We're starting so early that we can make some good headway, and that flicker of hope that ignited earlier grows into a burning ember. I finish the spade and move on to a set of door hinges. Hours pass, and my list grows shorter—then longer, as a woman shows up with two axles that needs repairing, and she commissions us for new ones instead. With Da's help I can probably finish the thresher for Farmer Latham, too, and that alone is worth ten silvers. We can pay the tax collector and begin to save silver for when we need to pay the balance next month.

Maybe I won't need to hold a message for the Truthbringers again.

Around midday, my stomach is empty, but I don't want to disturb this tentative peace between us. It feels like a truce. Maybe I should have kept all the coins away from him years ago.

"Jax," says my father.

I don't look up. Hopefully he's hungry too. "Yeah."

"Where've you been hoarding the rest of the coins?"

A sudden chill grips my spine, but his voice is casual, so I keep swinging my hammer. "What coins?"

"Don't be daft. You know what coins. I see how much business you've been doing." He gestures at the table, where I've got a scrawled list of projects to complete by week's end. "Where's the money?"

I turn a flat piece of metal against my anvil, creating a twist in the steel for an augur. "Those coins are for the tax collector."

"Then you'd best give them to me so I can pay her."

I make a derisive sound. "That went so well the last time."

He grabs hold of my arm, and the metal I've been working with slides off the anvil to hit the floor. "Tell me."

I glare at him, my tongs tight in my grip. "Let me go."

To my surprise, he does. "This is my forge," he snaps. "Those are *my* coins."

I seize the steel from the ground and roughly shove it back in the forge. "I already paid her what I had," I lie.

He studies me. I ignore him and wait for the metal to heat.

After a moment, he shifts like he's going to return to his own work, and a bit of tension falls away from my shoulders. I reach to pull the steel back out of the forge.

And while I'm unsteady, he grabs my arm again, so roughly that it throws me off balance and I drop the tongs. I lose track of the stool and I flail, hopping on one foot so I don't fall right into the forge.

He grabs my wrist and pulls me closer to the heat, and he's strong enough that it jerks me to my knees. "Don't play games with me, boy."

"I'm not playing," I snap. I fight his hold, but he's got more leverage. "We owe two hundred silvers! Do you want to lose the forge?"

"Tell me where they are."

I grit my teeth. My arm is slick with sweat, so he's having a hard time holding on—but it also feels like I'm going to pull my arm right out of its socket. "Go ask the tax collector for them back," I grind out.

He holds my hand so close to the fire that I can feel the promised burn, and my breathing shakes. My father's dark eyes hold mine, but I grit my teeth. I can't tell him. I can't. I know what he'd do with those coins. We'll lose everything. I've been working too hard.

He pulls me closer, and my free hand scrabbles for the tongs I dropped. "Let me go," I say, and my voice is full of rage and fear.

"Tell me."

"They're gone." My fingers close on the tongs, and I swing for his arm.

He's faster than I am, or maybe my life really is just cursed by misfortune. Either way, he catches the iron tool, and he wrenches it out of my grip. When he swings for *me*, I've got nowhere to go. The tongs are heavy, and they crack into my upper arm hard enough that I'm going to have a welt—or possibly a broken arm. But it throws me sideways, and my opposite hand automatically reaches to stop my fall.

I grab onto the hot steel edge of the forge.

The pain doesn't hit me at first—and then it's all at once. Blinding and searing and impossibly overwhelming. My head hits the dirt floor of our workshop, and I'm distantly aware of my father shoving me away. I can't hear what he's saying because my heartbeat is a roar in my ears, and the sound coming out of my throat is a terrible keening sound I wasn't aware I could make.

"You foolish boy," he growls, but there's a lick of fear under his words now, too. Then he's got his arms under my arms, and he's lifting me, half dragging me. For a wild, panicked moment I think he's going to throw me into the forge, but instead, he tows me to the edge of the house, where there's a small pile of melting snow. He lets me collapse beside it, then thrusts my hand right into the snow.

That's worse. I'm panting and crying and I think I want to cut my hand off. I might actually be begging my father to do it.

But time passes, and I'm not sure how much, but my heart begins to slow. My breathing is still shuddering, and mud and snow have soaked through my pants to chill the lower half of my body.

My father is standing over me, and the expression on his face is almost identical to the moment when that wagon fell on my leg.

"You'll be fine," he's saying, as if he's trying to convince himself. "It'll heal. Good as new."

Nothing is ever good as new. I know that better than anyone.

I swallow and swipe hair out of my eyes with my good hand. The strands are damp with tears.

I'm terrified to look at my injured hand.

"Tell me," he says.

I don't want to look at him either.

"Jax." His breathing is shuddering, and I can't tell if he's afraid of what's happened—or if he's thought of something worse to force the truth out of me. "Just tell me where they are."

There's too much pain. My thoughts are scattered and lined with agony.

"Under my bed," I say roughly, and my voice is thick.

He draws back. "Next time, you give them to me. You hear me, boy? You give them to *me*. Maybe this will teach you to be honest." He tugs at the leather ties to his apron, and he goes into the house. The door slams behind him.

All that silver, everything I risked, and he's going to take it.

That hurts almost more than my hand.

Well. Not quite.

I finally dredge the courage from somewhere and look at the damage. The skin across the center of my palm is a straight line of blistered skin, a red so dark it's almost brown. Three of my fingers as well. I can't fully close my hand. I can barely move it.

I'll never be able to grip a hammer or tongs until this heals.

Or a crutch.

I draw a whimpering breath. I need to get out of the mud. I need to figure out what to do.

There's nothing *to* do. Nothing. I brace my good hand against the snow and lever to my knees, then shuffle back into the workshop, where I ease onto one of the stools.

If any part of this could be called *lucky*, it's that my injured hand is my left—which means I can still use one crutch. I'll be slower, but I was never really fast.

My entire hand is throbbing, and I can't *think*. I pull it close against my body, as if cradling it will help the pain. For the first time in my life, I want to ask my father where I can get the best spirits, because I would quite literally do anything to stop this pulsing agony.

How long could this take to heal? It'll be weeks, most likely. Months? Ever?

I'll never catch up on what we owe now.

I think of that moment when Lord Tycho stood in the workshop. The way he said, *I would offer you mercy.*

I've heard that they believe in fate on the other side of the mountain in Emberfall, and right this moment, I want to beg fate to send him back.

Nothing happens. Because, of course, if fate *does* exist, it's laughing at me.

I duck my face to dry the last of my tears on the shoulder of my cloak.

Then—*then*—hoofbeats sound in the lane. My breath actually catches, which is ridiculous. My legs are half frozen from kneeling in the slush and mud, and my hand feels like it's still on fire, but for a wild, crazy second, I don't care. I'll confess my crimes and he'll drag me away from here, and at this point I don't even care if I end up in prison because at least it will be better than this horrific misfortune that follows me every day.

But then I see the horse, and it's not a dark bay with a crooked stripe down her face, it's a blazing red chestnut gelding.

It's Lord Alek.

Ah, yes. *Thank you, fate.*

At least he didn't find me crouching in the mud. I tuck my injured hand behind the leather strap of my apron, because after the way he tossed the coins into the slush, I don't want to give him an excuse to be *more* of an ass.

His gelding skids to a stop in the mud. "It seems you kept your word," he says.

"I'm good for it." My voice still sounds broken, and I try to breathe slowly. I don't know where my father went, but at this exact moment I can't decide if I'm hoping he's gone off to find someone who will buy him a tankard of ale, or if it would be better for him to come take this message from Lord Alek so I don't need to be a part of it anymore.

"I have another message for you to hold," he says. "Lady Karyl will come for it in three days."

I should demand more coins. I should ask questions about the content of these letters. I should do *something.*

All I can think about is the pain in my hand. I can hear my own breathing shaking.

"Fine," I say.

Lord Alek extends the folded parchment to me. He doesn't dismount from the horse—and he's at least ten feet away.

I was wrong. This is worse than fishing coins out of the snow.

I find one of my crutches on the ground by the work table, and I get it under my right arm, then lever to standing. I feel sick, and there's a good chance I might vomit in the snow. Everything about him disgusts me, from the way he glares down at me, to the casual marks of wealth and prosperity that seem like a mockery of everything I'm lacking.

When I make it to his side, I have to reach out with my injured hand, because the alternative is letting go of the crutch. I gingerly take hold of the parchment with the tips of my fingers, but it makes me wince anyway. I thrust it into my pocket.

He's peering at me, those piercing eyes searching my face. "You look unwell."

"I'm fine." I eye the sword at his waist and wonder if I'm about to risk my neck. I wonder if it matters. If I can't replace the silver that my father is taking, I might as well throw myself onto a blade.

I have to take a breath. "Holding a message for three days carries more danger than just one."

His eyes narrow.

I clench my fingers on the crutch. "You yourself saw the King's Courier in Briarlock," I add.

"What are you playing at?"

"Ten silvers per day," I say.

He looks like I just told him to swallow a lit coal. "Ten silvers!" he seethes. "You greedy little—"

"In addition to the twenty I require to pass the message."

"I should kill you right now. I doubt anyone would care."

"You could. And you're probably right."

He says nothing. I say nothing. I have nothing to lose.

Eventually, I endure the agony of pulling the parchment back out of my pocket. "Here. Find someone else to pass your treasonous notes."

"I should kill you for *that*." His hand flickers toward his sword. "The Truthbringers are not acting against the queen. We seek to protect her from the harm magic will bring to Syhl Shallow. You haven't seen the destruction wrought on Emberfall, the way this king used his powers to rise from nothing and claim the throne. You don't see the way he shares magic with his inner circle, for their benefit alone. You didn't see the monster he created, or the way our people were casually slaughtered during the Uprising."

I go still. I do know about that.

He must see the change in my expression, because he settles back in the saddle. "If you think you're bargaining silver for *treason*, then that says more about you than it does about me."

I don't like the way those words make me feel.

I do know I need silver.

"Fifty silvers," I finally say. There's a part of me that hopes he'll refuse. That we can be done with this. "Fifty, or you can have your message back."

He glares down at me, and similar to the day Lady Karyl brought me the first note, I realize that whatever is inside this message must be *very* important. I passed the first message and didn't say a word about it—surely that makes me less of a risk than finding someone new.

"Fine," he says. "Half now. Lady Karyl will pay you the rest when she returns."

I gingerly slide the message back into my pocket while he opens a purse at his waist and painstakingly counts out twenty-five silvers.

This time, it's no surprise at all when he throws them on the ground.

CHAPTER 9

CALLYN

When I was a little girl, I used to dream of magic. Jax and I would read Mother's books and imagine we could conjure fire or bury our enemies alive. We'd imagine the winged scravers of Iishellasa and debate whether they'd be beautiful or terrifying. They were rumored to control the wind, and one of our favorite stories was about a scraver that called enough ice from the Frozen River to wall off the forest for a hundred years—the way the ice forests of Iishellasa got their name. I used to stare at the stars and wonder at that kind of power, what it would be like to have it at my fingertips.

These memories always feel like a betrayal to my parents. That kind of power only seems to bring pain.

Mother was never directly opposed to magic herself. It just wasn't present in Syhl Shallow before the king arrived. Maybe in the past, years ago, but not in my lifetime. Our books talk about how the scravers were treaty bound to leave Syhl Shallow, and I've heard enough rumors about the one the king used to keep on a chain. Mother was all about serving the queen: being a good soldier, raising strong daughters. Da was all about serving his wife. He was a devoted husband and a doting father. But when Mother died, it seemed like all his devotion needed to find a new direction. He found it in the Truthbringers.

I keep peering at the door or out the window, hoping Jax will appear. It's been three days since he handed the message to Lord Alek, three days since he came back down the snowy lane with enough blood soaking into the collar of his shirt that Nora went a bit pale when she saw him. The sound of steel against steel has been clanging in his forge from dawn until dusk since then, while Nora and I have been baking and stewing and bickering without any hope of a reprieve.

Until today. Nora hasn't shut up since dawn, but the forge went mysteriously silent at midday.

Typically, the only time the forge is silent is when Jax is sitting here talking to me.

"Who do you keep looking for?" says Nora. We're kneading dough together at the table because breads and rolls always sell a bit better in this dreary weather. Most of the snow has melted away, but the sky is overcast, trapping Briarlock in the grip of a damp chill that won't leave for months. The courtyard looks like a muddy mess, and when I put May and the goats out into their little paddock, even the animals seemed a bit dubious about the weather.

I've started another pot of stew so I can have meat pies by dinnertime as well.

"Jax," I say. "I haven't heard the forge for hours."

Lord Alek was due back today. I can't shake the feeling that I've seen the man before. I can't imagine *where*, however. I keep thinking of Jax's wounds, and I wonder if the lord did worse this time.

I knew this was a mistake. I keep hearing Jax's quiet voice saying, *You're my best friend.*

Once I set these loaves to rise, I might need to head down the lane to check on him.

"He's right there," Nora chirps, and I snap my head up. She's right. Outside the window, Jax is working his way down the lane, using only one crutch, which is unlike him. I shove my pile of dough aside and rush for the door.

"Are you all right?" I call.

"Help me in," he says back, and *that* is more telling than anything else. Jax never asks for help.

I wipe my hands on my skirts and jog through the mud to his side. His arm goes across my shoulders. There's soot on his cheeks, but sweat has formed tracks through it. Or tears, but that's not like Jax at all.

"That feels a lot farther on one crutch," he says, and his voice sounds more rough and worn than usual.

"What happened to the other one?" I say.

He hesitates. "I hurt my hand."

I pause and try to peer at the hand hanging limply over my shoulder, but he gives me a tug. "Come on," he says. "I need to sit down."

When we get into the bakery, he drops onto a stool beside where Nora is kneading. Without ceremony, he sets his hand on the table and uncurls his fingers slowly.

"Augh!" Nora cries. "Give us some warning next time."

I smack her on the arm. "Jax," I breathe. He's earned dozens of tiny scars from the forge, but nothing like this. The palm of his hand is a deep red, with blisters that are blackened at the edges. A few of his fingers are burned as well. "What happened?"

"Da and I were fighting. I grabbed hold of the forge by accident." He looks a little pale. "You got that burn from the oven last year. I was hoping you'd have something to help."

My burn from the oven was barely more than a stripe along the side of my wrist, from where I'd come too close to the roasting racks. It seemed to disappear in a day. Nothing like this.

"I have some salve," I say decisively, because he's come here for solutions and I don't want to let him down. Otherwise, I'm going to go get my ax and go after his father. "I have some muslin, too. We should wrap it."

He nods.

I fetch some supplies, along with a fresh bowl of cool water. When I try to put his hand in it, he grimaces and pulls away.

"You have to clean it," I say. "Jax, you've got soot everywhere."

I keep my hand wrapped around his wrist, and after a moment, he allows me to immerse it in the bowl. He swears and his eyes water, and I reevaluate those tracks on his cheeks.

"Nora," I say. "We'll need some fresh eggs for the next loaves. While I help Jax, can you see if you can gather any more from the coop?"

"The hens hate me! They always peck my wrists!"

That's true, but they peck *my* wrists, too. I inhale to tell her so, but Jax looks at her.

"Please, Nora," he says.

Maybe it's because he's not a sibling, or maybe she can hear the whisper of pain in his voice, but either way, she shuts her mouth and nods.

Once she's gone, the bakery is so quiet that I can hear his breathing, just a little too fast, with a bit of a tremor to every exhale.

I tear a square of muslin and dip it in the water, then touch it to his face. His eyes lift to meet mine in surprise, but he doesn't pull away.

"You're a mess," I say.

"Lord Alek returned," he says softly.

I draw a sharp breath and glance at his hand. "Did *he* do this to you? I knew something must have—"

"No. I told you. I grabbed hold of the forge."

I still find that hard to believe—but Jax has never lied to me. "Have you seen him before?"

"The day he came here," he says, then winces.

"No—I mean before that."

"No." His eyes search mine. "Why?"

I hesitate. The answer feels like it's on the edge of my consciousness, but I can't place it. "I don't know. Something about him seems familiar."

"Not to me." He pauses. "He agreed to pay fifty silvers this time."

"Fifty!" There will be penalties for asking for that kind of money, and I know Jax is only asking for so much so he can help me as well. It makes me want to give him back the silver that he's already given me.

Jax nods, then swallows. "I need you to keep it here." His voice catches. "I had to ask for more. Da took the rest."

I stroke another line of dirt off his cheek, but I hold his gaze. This feels risky in all the wrong ways. "What's in these letters?"

"I don't know." Jax fishes the folded parchment out of his pocket and tosses it on the table between us. "Even if I could get it open, I'm not sure I could re-create the detail to seal it closed again."

I study the broad circle of wax, with swirls of the green and black of Syhl Shallow. It features a horse head, a sword, and several deeper stars all entwined, encircled by delicate loops in silver. It's so intricate that it must be a House sigil of some kind, but I have no idea which one. Or maybe it's something exclusive to the Truthbringers? I just don't know.

He sighs disgustedly. "If I had the use of this hand, I could try to forge something close, but now . . ." His voice trails off.

I dip the muslin in the water again. My eyes shy away from the damage to his hand, magnified by the water now.

"Do you want to know what it says?" I say softly.

"I want to know what's worth fifty silvers just to *hold* it." He pauses. "I accused him of treason, and he all but said he's trying to protect the queen from magic—"

"You accused that man of *treason*?" I swear, he's going to get his head cut off. My eyes skip to his throat, but there are only the marks from a few days ago.

"Yes. And Lord Alek told me that the king was involved with the monster that slaughtered the Syhl Shallow soldiers. That he stole his throne by magic. That the Truthbringers are trying to protect the queen."

I freeze, but only for a moment. My mother was a part of that slaughter.

I look back at the folded parchment.

Then back at his hand.

Then back at his face.

His hazel eyes are full of shadows. No path seems like the right one. I lift the muslin to his cheek again.

Jax ducks away. "Stop. Cal. I'm fine."

"Oh. Good. I thought maybe you were suffering." I pull his mangled hand out of the water. He hisses a breath through his teeth, but I ignore him, tighten my grip on his wrist, and blot the water away.

"You're a terrible friend," he mutters.

There's enough pain in his voice that I ease up. I open the jar of salve and study the wound. "How did this happen?"

"I grabbed hold—"

"I heard that part. What were you fighting about?"

He says nothing.

When I glance up, it's like the shadows in his eyes have multiplied. His jaw is set.

"It was my own fault," he says.

Sometimes I don't know whether I ought to hug him or if he needs a good shake. He probably wouldn't welcome either. I touch salve to the wound and his breathing hitches again. He's so tense that the muscled tendons in his forearm are standing out.

"Do you believe what Lord Alek said?" I say quietly. "That the Truthbringers are trying to protect the queen?"

"I don't know." He uses his good hand to reach into his pocket, and a moment later a handful of coins jangle onto the table. "I believe we need *that* to save our homes. It's not like the queen is going to show up and offer us a pardon."

Jax's eyes are intent on mine, and I nod.

The bakery door is thrust open, making the bells ring, and we both jump a *mile*. I nearly overturn the bowl of water. Half the coins rattle onto the floor.

"It's all right," Jax murmurs, but he's already jamming the parchment back into his pocket. "It's just Nora."

She's chattering away as she comes through the door with a basket over one arm. "The hens hate the cold, you know. They keep pecking my wrists. I could barely get *three*, if you can believe that."

Honestly. "Enough about the *hens*, Nora—"

I break off and choke on my breath. She's not talking to me. She's talking to the young man following her through the door.

Lord Tycho.

Jax swears under his breath and begins sweeping coins into a pile. He must knock his injured hand because he sucks in a breath and swears again. A bloom of sweat breaks out on his forehead.

I quickly step in front of him to block Lord Tycho's view. "My lord," I say, trying to sound nonchalant, but probably sounding like I'm about to commit a crime. "Welcome."

"Cally-cal was about to make some meat pies," Nora is chattering, heedless of the tension. "We made fresh pastry just this morning! She makes the best in Briarlock."

His brown eyes flick to the floor, scattered with silver, and then back up to meet mine. "Is that so?" he says.

"Yes." I nod like a fool—then shake my head when I realize what I'm agreeing to. "I mean—no. They're not the best. You startled us. We were just tallying the day's take."

"Clouds above!" crows Nora. "Look at all that silver! We made that much today? I thought we only sold a few loaves this morning."

"Some was left from yesterday." I drop to a knee to gather the coins. My cheeks feel like they're on fire. I need to calm down. "I'm not too sure how much."

Several coins have fallen near Lord Tycho's boots, and he stoops to pick them up. I hold my breath as he glances at the silver, as if he could possibly know where they came from. But he straightens, then extends a hand.

For an instant, I don't move, as if I could absolve us both of guilt by refusing to touch them.

"Here," he says. "They're yours."

I quickly swipe them from his palm. "Ah . . . thank you." I slip the coins into a pocket of my apron.

Then I'm not sure what to say.

I need to *do* something. Offer him something. Ask him something. My mouth is as dry as a sack of flour. Of all the people who could walk into the bakery just now, he's the most terrifying. Lord Alek might have threatened Jax, but Lord Tycho could send us straight to the gallows.

He glances between me and Jax, who's leaning heavily against my work table, his injured hand clutched against his belly. His eyes narrow slightly. "I feel as though I've interrupted again."

Jax tries to straighten. "No, my lord." His tone is low and uncertain, undercut by pain. "We're surprised to see you."

"I've been sent back to Emberfall," he says. "I stopped here in Briarlock to see if Lord Alek had remained."

At least this I can answer honestly. My heart keeps pounding. "I haven't seen him, my lord. Not since the day you both came looking for a blacksmith."

Jax is silent for a moment, but he adds, "We don't often see the nobility here."

Lord Tycho gives him a longer look. "What happened to your arm?"

Jax clutches his hand more tightly against his body, but it must hurt, because a tiny gasp escapes his lips. "A burn from the forge." He draws a breath through his teeth and glances at me. "Cal was about to tend it for me."

"Yes!" I say, picking up the thread that Jax has offered. "Perhaps Nora could wrap up anything from the bakery for you, my lord. I can take Jax into the storeroom—"

"A bad burn?" Lord Tycho takes a step closer. "May I see?"

"It's *disgusting*," says Nora, and I pinch her on the arm.

"It *is*!" she cries.

Lord Tycho glances at her. "I can handle disgusting." He looks back at Jax. "A burned hand won't be the worst thing I've ever seen."

Jax stares back at him, and there's a defiance in his gaze that usually means he's going to get himself in trouble. A lock of hair has come loose from the knot at the back of his neck to fall across his face, and his eyes seem to have darkened a shade. But he swallows, then extends his hand.

It's clean now, from the water, and it looks even worse. There's no soot, but the burn stretches across his palm, all the way down into the muscle. The skin smells sickly sweet, and his fingertips are blistered. Two of his fingers are faintly purple now.

I don't know how he's not sitting here sobbing over it. I want to sob and I'm only *looking* at it.

"Who did this to you?" Lord Tycho says, and his voice has gone very quiet.

"It was an accident." Jax hesitates. "I grabbed hold of the forge."

The lord's eyes flick up. "I've never known a blacksmith to grab hold of a forge."

There's something alarming in the way he says that. Like he knows there's more that we're not saying. My eyes flick to his weapons again, to the royal insignia over his heart.

I glance at Jax. I can't help it. I don't know if Alek really *is* behind this, or if his father was just as cruel as he always is, but I know Jax isn't going to say a word about either.

But then Nora whispers, "His father did it."

"Nora!" Jax and I snap at the same time.

Nora looks affronted. "It's true! He's horrible to Jax and everyone knows it. You yourself said—"

"Hush!" I reach out to pinch her again. "That's not your business."

"It was an accident," Jax says again, and his voice is tight. "An argument. I lost my footing. That's all." He draws a shuddering breath. "So have a good look, my lord."

He's being flippant, but Lord Tycho reaches out and takes hold of his wrist anyway. Jax jolts as if stung.

"Steady," Lord Tycho says, and his voice is low and quiet. "I won't hurt you." When Jax doesn't pull away, he reaches out his free hand to uncurl the blistered fingers. Jax's breath catches.

"It's fine," Jax says, but the tiniest tremor in his voice says it's *not* fine. "Cal will wrap it." A fresh bloom of sweat has broken out on his forehead.

"It will take weeks to heal," Lord Tycho says. "Can you afford to not work for weeks?"

Jax bristles. "I'll make do as I can," he says. "We're not all from a Royal House in the Crystal City, my lord."

I feel like I need to pinch *him*, but Lord Tycho doesn't look offended. The corner of his mouth turns up in half a smile. "Well, neither am I. Do you fear magic here?"

I automatically press a hand to the pendant hanging under my blouse. "Everyone fears magic," I whisper.

Lord Tycho glances between me and Jax. "Would you fear it if I said I could heal your hand?"

He says it offhandedly, but I freeze in place. I don't know if I should laugh in his face or drag Nora away from him.

Jax scoffs. "What difference does it make? There's no magic here."

I can't tell if it's bravado or belligerence in his tone, but a light sparks in Lord Tycho's eyes like he's been offered a dare. "Well," he says. "There's a little."

Then he presses his fingers right into the center of the burn.

Jax swears and throws himself back, but the lord holds fast. Jax isn't big, but working in the forge has clearly paid off in muscle. He nearly drags them both into the pastry table.

"Just wait," Lord Tycho says, and his voice is tight with strain. "Just—give it—a moment—"

"Stop!" I shout. I don't know if this is magic or assault, but I grab a knife from the block with one hand and a heavy steel pan with the other. "Let him go!"

Nora shrieks. "Cally-cal!"

Almost as suddenly, Jax stops fighting. "Stop, Cal. Stop." He's breathing hard, his eyes wide and panicked like a spooked horse, but Lord Tycho lets him go and steps back. Jax grips tight to the edge of my pastry table.

It leaves me standing there with a knife in one hand and a skillet in the other. I'm not ready to put them down. Not until I know what just happened. I look warily from Lord Tycho to Jax. "Are you all right?" I say roughly.

"Yes." His voice is rough and wary, too. "Maybe. I don't know."

Lord Tycho is wearing enough weapons to eviscerate all three of us, but his hands lift. "Callyn," he says evenly. "I didn't hurt him."

Nora darts forward to grab Jax's wrist, examining the skin across his palm. "It's gone!" she says, and there's wild awe in her tone. "Jax, it's gone."

I glance over. I can't help it. The injury *is* gone.

Magic. I feel like I can't catch my breath.

"What else can you do?" says Nora, and her eyes are so wide and her voice so hushed that I can't tell if she's fascinated—or terrified. Maybe both. She lets go of Jax's hand and takes a step forward. "Can you melt the skin off someone's bones? Can you start a fire with your eyes? Can you—"

"*Nora.*" I need to stop my sister before she can get closer. "You're a *magesmith*," I snap at him.

"No," he says. "The king is the only true magesmith. My rings are Iishellasan steel. They allow me to borrow his magic."

His hands are still lifted, and I can see the rings, dark steel that encircles three of his fingers.

I don't know what to do with this information. I remember our books carrying stories of magical artifacts from Iishellasa, but I never realized that meant anyone could wield magic. I had no idea such a thing was possible. "So you just do whatever you want with them?"

"Of course not." He pauses. "Put the knife down." Another pause. "Please."

The *please* startles me. It's a bare courtesy that seems to be at odds with the magic he just performed—a courtesy that makes my world seem to tilt on its axis a bit, because he sounds so calm and reasonable, while I'm standing here with a weapon and . . . and a skillet.

I swallow and slide the knife back into the block, but I can't seem to convince my hand to let go of the baking pan.

"He healed Jax," Nora protests, and there's a note of hope in her voice. "He healed him, Cally-cal. He's not like the king."

Lord Tycho's eyebrows flicker into a frown. "The king would have done the same."

"The king doesn't care about Briarlock," Jax growls. He keeps hold of the pastry table to lever himself a hopping step closer. "You should have warned us."

"I tried."

Jax lets go of the table and shoves him right in the chest.

Lord Tycho falls back a step in surprise. His gaze darkens. His hands aren't up now.

"Jax!" I drop the pan and grab my friend's arm before he can do anything worse. "He is the King's Courier," I hiss. "You're going to end up swinging from a *rope*." I think of those rings, of what happened to my father. My heart thumps. "Or *worse*."

But Lord Tycho surprises me. "Not by my order," he says evenly. "Say what you mean to say."

"I don't need your pity," Jax snaps. His arm is tense under my hand, almost straining against my hold.

"It's not *pity*. You wouldn't have been able to work for months. Maybe not *ever*."

Jax flexes his hand, which bears no mark from the burn that existed there a few minutes ago. Even I can't help the thread of wonder that winds through all my fear. I saw the blisters, the broken skin.

"Fine," Jax says darkly. "It wasn't pity. It was a rich lord riding through a small town, throwing some generosity to the poor folk of Briarlock. Maybe our taxes pay for a life of ease in the Crystal City, where you can borrow the king's magic to solve all your problems, but here, all you've done is remind us of what we've suffered. Of what we *lack*." His voice has grown sharp with disdain. "So forgive me, my lord. You have my *thanks*."

Lord Tycho looks like Jax has slapped him. Even Nora is silent.

After a moment, the lord takes a step back. He nods to me and to my sister. "Callyn. Nora. I will have to take you up on the meat pies another time. I need to cross the mountain pass before nightfall."

I'm frozen in place. Too much has happened. But after a moment of hesitation, Nora grabs hold of her skirt and glances at me before offering him a brief curtsy. "Goodbye, my lord."

Jax's arm is still tight under my grip, his eyes locked on Lord Tycho. His hands have curled into fists. He says nothing.

For one long, tense moment, I worry that he's going to break free of my hold. That he's going to pick a fight he won't win.

But finally, Lord Tycho gives him a nod as well. "You're welcome," he says. "Be well, Jax."

Then he turns on his heel and he's through the door.

CHAPTER 10

TYCHO

When it comes to political maneuvering, Prince Rhen always has a lot of ideas.

When I arrived this morning, he read the queen's letter about a Royal Challenge, and now he's got books and maps and papers spread across a table in his strategy room, and he's been making a list of suggestions for the king and queen to review. Ironrose Castle is large, with wood-paneled walls, marble floors, and elegant tapestries, but the rooms always seem much more stuffy than what I'm used to in the Crystal Palace. In the days I've been gone, more letters have been found among shipments in Silvermoon and Blind Hollow, but when I riffle through them, they're all the same: nothing more than tracked movements written in simple code. Mama and Papa. Mother and Father. Nyssa. No threats, no warnings—at least none that I can discern. There aren't enough to make a pattern anyway.

Rhen doesn't really *need* me right now, which isn't uncommon, especially when he's got a task to occupy his thoughts. Normally I'd bide my time with his Royal Guards, or I'd ride out to Silvermoon to stroll through the marketplace. Sometimes Princess Harper would join me, and I like her company, because she reminds me of her brother, Jacob.

Today, though, I'm still replaying Jax's comments before I left Briarlock. He carries himself like a beaten dog, but there was so much anger in his expression when he shoved me away.

All you've done is remind us of what we've suffered. Of what we lack.

But more than that, I'm thinking of the moment just before, when his eyes blazed into mine with a wild desperation. He was in pain. Afraid. Ashamed.

Steady, I said. *I won't hurt you.*

And then . . . in his eyes, I suppose I did.

I forget sometimes that my experience with magic is vastly different from everyone else's. What I know came directly from Grey himself. I was never tortured by magic, never affected by the monster Rhen was once cursed to become.

The monsters who tortured me have all been of the human variety.

I forget, too, that the people of Syhl Shallow see the Uprising as less of an attack on the royal family, and more of an incident that proves the danger of the king's magic. They weren't in the palace to hear the screams. They didn't see the splintering wood as protestors broke through doors and invaded private quarters, searching for the king and queen with weapons drawn.

They only heard about the flash of magic that lit up the sky for miles. The flames that swept through the palace hallways.

The women and men who died for trying to attack a king who never would have meant them any harm.

I think of the queen refusing Grey's magic to help with her sickness from the baby. She's never shied away from his powers. I wonder if even she is affected by the fears of her people.

Callyn was so afraid of the magic that she shoved her sister behind her in the bakery. I've worn these rings for years now, but I remember the first time I found the sparks and stars in my blood that allowed me to wield magic. It was wild and wondrous—but not frightening.

I healed her friend, but she still found it terrifying.

I hate that.

I glance at Prince Rhen where he's scrawling notes on a piece of parchment. He only has one eye, because the other was clawed out during a battle with an enchantress. He wears a small leather patch over the worst of his scars, but he's allowed his hair to grow long to cover that half of his face. At the right angle, you can't even tell.

I have as much reason to hate him as anyone, but I don't.

What I said to Noah was true: Rhen has suffered a lot.

We're the only people in the room right now, aside from two guards stationed outside the door. Maybe that's part of why the rooms here feel so quiet and stuffy. At the Crystal Palace, there's always someone around, ready to play a game of dice or share a meal or go for a ride. There's always little Sinna looking for entertainment. But here, beyond Harper, Rhen doesn't have a close circle of friends.

Lia Mara said I should tell Rhen that she hopes to see him compete in the Challenge, but I haven't passed on that part of the message. I know he used to spar with Grey, but I haven't seen him engage in swordplay since he lost his eye. I wonder if he misses it. He buries himself in work whenever there's an opportunity, like now, so I think he might.

Honestly, I'm not sure Rhen would notice if I left.

"If you need a task," Rhen says without looking up, "I am happy to provide more of a diversion than *staring*."

Or maybe he would.

"I'll take a task," I say.

He smiles, but it's more ironic than it is amused. "You're one of the few people who would hear that as an offer and not a rebuke."

I shrug, unfazed, and reach for an apple from the platter of fruit in the center of the table. "What do you need?"

"Truly, I need nothing." He finally looks up, and his one eye narrows. "You're not one to sit idle. What troubles you?"

"Nothing." I take a bite from the apple.

He looks back at his maps, then makes a mark. I keep eating the fruit. I expect him to dig, the way Lia Mara or Noah would. Even Grey would pry answers out of me. But Rhen doesn't. There's no expectant weight to this silence.

Maybe that's why I talk. "Last week, when I returned to Syhl Shallow, Mercy threw a shoe, so I stopped off in a little town to find a blacksmith. I did—but I also found Lord Alek, from one of the Royal Houses."

Rhen glances up. "I remember Alek. His older sister was my spy. She found the first magical artifacts in Syhl Shallow."

I nod. "His mother was killed in the first battle with Emberfall, too." I pause. "But Alek was young when all that happened."

"That means nothing. You were a boy when you stormed my castle with Grey."

I suppose that's true.

"*And?*" Rhen prompts. "What was Alek doing there?"

"I don't know." I frown. "He wasn't doing anything wrong."

"If his presence there feels significant to you, I believe there is a reason." He pauses. "He has bothered you in the past, has he not? Grey should have locked him up in that stone prison."

"I can handle it." Alek isn't the only member of the Royal Houses who takes issue with my position as King's Courier—but he's the only one who has no hesitation in being openly antagonistic about it.

Rhen scoffs. "I know Lia Mara wishes to rule with a gentle hand, but if she and my brother do not keep a tight leash on their nobles, they'll seek every weakness. Any attack on you is an attack on *them*, and they should have taken action to put it to rights."

I shift my weight, fighting the urge to squirm. I don't like questioning Grey's actions, or Lia Mara's either. "Politically, it's tricky," I say.
"Lia Mara believes Alek is loyal to Syhl Shallow—just not to Grey. He
hates the magic, and he's not the only one."

"That is not *tricky*. Loyalty to your country doesn't matter if you're
disloyal to whoever is ruling it."

I'm the last person who's going to tell Lia Mara how to rule, especially if she can't eat and she's vomiting all night. I take a bite of the
apple to avoid saying anything.

Rhen sighs and pulls one of his maps closer. "Fine. So you have no
idea what this *politically tricky* potential traitor was doing?"

"He said he was looking for the blacksmith. It's innocuous enough
that it might not even matter. I mean, I was doing the same thing. Grey
asked me to see if he was still there when I rode through, but he wasn't. I
spoke to many people, but no one seemed overly familiar with him."
I pause, thinking of Callyn and Jax, and the silver scattered along the
floor, or the way Jax's hand was burned so severely.

"You've thought of something," says Rhen.

"No. Maybe? The blacksmith is friends with the girl who runs the
bakery. I saw them the first time, too, when Lord Alek first appeared.
The blacksmith was badly injured this time. A burn from the forge—
but it didn't seem like a casual burn. I got a close look when I healed it."

Have a good look, my lord.

Callyn was frightened, but Jax was so brazen. I realize now that it
was a camouflage for his own fear. I learned early on with skittish horses
that sometimes they need a quiet moment to allow an element of trust
to form before you ask something of them. People aren't much different. I know that better than anyone.

I wish I'd given Jax that moment.

Rhen's voice calls me back. "The burn seemed intentional?"

I nod, then frown. "He said his father caused it. I don't get the sense that they're working with the Truthbringers—but I can't get past the fact that Alek was there. They had so much silver. More than I'd expect for a small bakery in a tiny town. You remember those first letters mentioned *gathering your best silver.* So . . . maybe."

"Is Briarlock a merchant city?" he says. "Could this be related to the messages hidden in the shipments?"

I think about it. "Not really. It's a small village surrounded by farmland. A blacksmith and a baker wouldn't be involved in shipping much of anything."

"They'd be receiving things, though," says Rhen. He sits back in his chair. "A blacksmith would receive bars of iron and steel—though admittedly those wouldn't do well for hiding slips of parchment. I presume they know who you are. Do they seem disloyal to the Crown?"

"They seem less like traitors and more like people wary of a distant nobility. You know how these villages are with rumors and gossip. What you hear in Emberfall is only half as bad as what they say in Syhl Shallow."

"How so?"

I shrug. "A month ago I heard a woman telling a tavern full of people that her cousin had seen the king's magic twist a man into knots while he screamed. For courtly entertainment." I roll my eyes. Grey would never do any such thing.

Rhen sighs. "I suppose stories of benevolence don't generate crowds."

"I spent so long chasing down messages with you that I think I'm looking at *everyone* with suspicion."

"Good. That's a healthy way to stay alive."

I wonder if he's being facetious. He doesn't look like it. I sigh and take another bite of the apple.

"What's a healthy way to stay alive?" says Princess Harper, as she comes through the doorway. She's in high laced boots and calfskin riding breeches, her long curly hair pinned at the back of her neck. She walks with a limp, and I know she struggles with strength and balance on her left side. Some malady from her world that's plagued her since birth. There's a scar across her cheek, too, though nothing as severe as Rhen's. Another reminder that none of us survived the past battles unscathed.

I rise when she enters, but Harper doesn't stand on ceremony, so she waves me back into my chair.

"Seeing everyone with suspicion," I say, in answer to her question.

She drops into the chair beside Rhen, then leans in to give him a kiss on the cheek. He murmurs to her, something too soft to hear, but he lets go of a paper to give her hand a gentle squeeze, then brushes a kiss across her knuckles.

It's interesting to see the way they treat each other, compared to how open Grey's affection is for Lia Mara. Rhen and Harper's love always seems very gentle, very quiet, trapped in little moments between the two of them. I glance away, because something about it is potent, as if I'm witnessing something intimate and private.

At the same time, I wonder what it would be like to trust someone that much, to allow myself to be that vulnerable. I remember my conversation with Noah, and memories of my childhood begin to surface. That old, familiar tension begins to crawl across my shoulders again.

"I didn't expect you to return so soon," says Harper, drawing my gaze back.

"I didn't either." I shrug. "I don't mind the ride. I like the queen's idea of a competition."

"I do too," says Rhen. "It's good to give the people an event to rally around." He pulls several sheets of paper together. "But one big competition here might favor Emberfall too strongly. She should have preliminary competitions to narrow the field of victors—"

"Like semifinals," says Harper.

"Indeed." He looks at the maps again. "I believe there should be one in Syhl Shallow and another in Emberfall. Competitors can enter both. That would encourage travelers to cross the border and spend coins in both countries, which I presume is her intent." He points at the map. "Here. This is farmland, yes?"

I peer at the map. The area he's indicating is an hour's ride north of Briarlock. "Yes."

"The Crown could rent the land during the summer months, and host a competition." He points to an area near the castle. "We can host one here, too. It would be widely accessible, especially with our proximity to the harbor. I'll include this in my return letter to Grey." He makes a note. "And the final competition could be held here in late autumn, well before the snows block the mountain pass."

I wonder if Lia Mara will want to travel in late autumn, but I nod. "I will let them know as soon as I return."

Maybe Rhen hears something in my tone, because he glances up. "Has Grey asked you to return quickly?"

I shake my head. "No. But I spent so much time here that Lia Mara began to assume I was having a clandestine romance. I'd like to avoid that if possible."

Harper snorts. "Really? With who? The Royal Guard?"

I smile. "Well, Noah is just the opposite. He thinks I—"

I break off as I remember *exactly* what Noah said, the way he compared me to the prince.

Rhen looks up, of course. "Noah thinks what?"

I lose the smile. "He thinks I use this role as a means to keep people at arm's length." I pause. "He implied you do the same."

"Noah thinks I keep people at arm's length?" Rhen straightens. "Harper, do you believe that to be true?"

"Well. You spent like a million years trapped by a curse, during which you stayed in this castle with no one but Grey for company. Gee, let me think—"

"That's quite enough."

"Hmm." Harper smiles and taps a finger to her lips. "Truly, it is a mystery."

He sighs—but he picks up her hand and kisses her knuckles again.

"I will finish my message this evening," Rhen says to me. "And you are free to return tomorrow, if you like." He pauses. "But here is what you should do." He pulls the map closer, indicating towns that lie near my path back to Syhl Shallow. "There are tourneys in Kalmery, Blind Hollow, Wildthorne Valley, and Gaulter. Stay an evening in each. Attend the tourney. Spend some silver. Spread word of what is being planned. See how this is received among the people so you can share what you find with Lia Mara and Grey."

I nod, eager to have a task. Eager to have a *plan*.

Maybe I'm more like Rhen than I think.

"Yes, Your Highness," I say. "As you wish."

CHAPTER 11

JAX

I've hardly seen Callyn in days. The forge, as usual, has been busy, and I've been glad to keep my head down and work. My father has been spending more time in the workshop with me, but I've got nothing to say to him. He clearly has nothing to say to me either, and I can't tell if he's feeling guilty about what happened, or if he's still mad about the silver I was "hiding." Either way, our conversation is limited to non-committal grunts and occasional requests to pass a tool. Any flares of hope have been fully extinguished after what he did. Not even an ember is left.

For the first few days, I kept my hand wrapped, because I didn't know what to say about Lord Tycho and what he did. I'm still not entirely sure how I *feel* about it, so I'm definitely not ready to introduce my father's opinions to the matter. But after the healing magic, the skin left behind was fresh and new, and working in the forge pulled open calluses across my palm anyway. Nowhere near as painful as a burn, but the blistered red skin must look pretty similar, because my father hasn't said anything about it. If he's surprised I'm able to work, it doesn't show.

Good as new. Hardly.

While my father's presence has improved the speed of what we're able to get done, it has the disadvantage of him collecting any coins when we're due payment. Coins I don't see again. I'd grown used to his frequent absences, but now I'm worried he'll be here when Lady Karyl returns for this note, and he'll be the one to collect those coins, too.

It's now the third day, and worry has begun to eat up my insides.

I'm finishing the final blade on the thresher when my father coughs and says, "That girl should have enlisted years ago." He spits at the ground. "What's she still doing here?"

I look up and see Callyn wandering down the lane, a basket over one arm. "Taking care of her sister," I say.

"Her father was a good man." Da pulls a piece of steel out of the forge and slaps it against his anvil.

Her father was part of an attack on the palace. But I don't say that. It reminds me again that my father was doing *something* for the Truthbringers. Something I've taken over. So I'm not one to criticize.

"He wouldn't like her staying here," he continues. "A military pension would do her sister a lot more good. I suppose you wouldn't know anything about that."

I'm so used to his digs that I don't waste emotion on irritation. "I suppose not."

Cal steps into the yard. All of the snow has melted, but there's still a chill in the air, and she's got a cloak drawn around her shoulders. Her hair is usually tied up in a braid that she twists at the back of her head, but today it's long and unbound, light brown curls tumbling down her back. I remember the way she seized a knife and a skillet to defend me.

She's strong and capable enough to be a soldier, but she always seems most at peace when she's in the bakery, wrist-deep in dough.

Or maybe that's just what I think because Cal is my only friend, and the thought of her leaving Briarlock is too much to bear.

She steps into the workshop, so I set my iron aside and grab hold of a rope to pull myself upright. "Hey, Cal."

She waves me back. "Don't stop working. I can't stay long. Nora 'accidentally' doubled this batch of sweetcakes, so I figured I would bring some down here." She casts a glance at my father and sets the basket on the table. Her voice cools. "Master Ellis."

If he notices, he ignores her tone. "Callyn." He finishes the piece he was working on, then tosses it onto the table. "Jax is working," he says.

As if I'm the one who spends half my waking hours at the alehouse and *he's* the one who's been keeping the forge running.

"I can see that," she says. "I just *told* him to keep—"

"Cal." The last thing I need is her picking a fight with Da. I give her a look and put a new piece of steel into the forge.

She sighs tightly.

I'm sorry, I mouth to her, and shrug.

My father unties his leather apron anyway. "I've got business in town."

"I'll bet you do," I mutter. I jerk the steel out of the forge and slap it against the anvil.

"What did you just say to me, boy?"

I slam my hammer against the metal and don't look up. "I said you'd better get to it," I call over the clanging.

He grunts and turns for the door.

I keep hammering. Cal keeps standing.

After a moment, I realize that she's not saying anything and *I'm* not saying anything, and I wonder if our few days of not seeing each other is less about being busy and more about . . . everything else.

I finally glance up from my work. "Thank you for the sweetcakes."

"I should have brought some stew. You've been busy."

I jerk my head toward the doorway where my father disappeared. "He's been here every day."

She frowns. "How's your hand?"

"It's fine." I think of the moment Lord Tycho let me go. The memory of the healing—of the sudden, shocking pain, followed by honey-sweet warmth and relief—should be bitter, but it's not. I should be afraid of the magic. I know Callyn was. I know a lot of people are. I *know* about all the damage magic has caused.

But I keep thinking of the light in his brown eyes. His voice, soothing and low. *Steady. I won't hurt you.* The way his fingers curled around my wrist, more gentle than I expected.

The way he didn't back down from my anger. The way he didn't retaliate, when he surely could have.

I need to *stop* thinking about it. I thrust the steel back into the forge.

Callyn is quiet for a moment. "Are you upset about the magic?"

I'm not. I probably should be, but I'm *not*. He was right. I wouldn't have been able to work for months. Just the memory of the pain is enough to make me break into a cold sweat. Despite everything I said to him, I'm grateful.

But admitting that feels like a betrayal to my best friend.

I keep my eyes on the iron of my anvil. "I don't want to talk about it."

I consider what Alek said about the queen, how the king's magic coerced her into marriage. I consider all the rumors I've heard. I consider what happened to Callyn's father.

Her father was a good man, Da said. Was he? Does Da regret not being a part of the Uprising?

For a flicker of time, I realign everything I know of my father: the drinking, the despondency. The irritation in his tone every time he addresses me. For the first time, I wonder if it's about more than just a disappointment for a son and a monotonous future forging tools. I wonder if he wishes he'd been a part of what happened.

I flex my hand. It's the first time I've ever seen magic with my own eyes. I've heard Callyn's descriptions of the fire that went blazing through the halls of the Crystal Palace to stop the attack. I know about what happened to her mother on the battlefields of Emberfall.

Those stories are hard to reconcile with a young man who'd see my injury and take it upon himself to heal it.

Callyn speaks into my silence. "Did you know anyone other than the king could do something like that?"

"Well—no."

"Why would we not know? Who else can do that?" She pauses. "Doesn't that worry you?"

In truth, I think it's pretty spectacular. It's part of the reason I feel so conflicted about what I said to him. Lord Tycho didn't have to help me at all.

Cal shifts closer. "I keep thinking about my mother. About Da. That kind of magic killed them both." She's absolutely silent for a moment. "Now . . . anyone could have it. Who else do you think the king has loaned his magic to?"

"I have no idea," I say.

"He could have *killed* you, Jax. He could have burned down the bakery. He could have—"

"He healed me." I finally look up at her. "That's all, Cal. He healed me." I hold up my hand. "I'm fine. You're fine. Nora is fine." I pause, then grit my teeth. "If you want to panic about anything, you should worry about all that silver. We're lucky he didn't demand answers."

She swallows. Her cheeks are flushed.

I sigh. "We should both have enough silver by tonight anyway," I say roughly. "Lady Karyl is due back. We can pay part of what we owe."

"Have you given any more thought to forging a new seal?" she says. "So we can see what's on these letters?"

I swallow and cast my eyes at the door. "I've thought about it."

I've sketched it out, too, in a small scrap of parchment I've kept folded into a tiny ball under my mattress. Forging the silver stars will be the hardest part. They're very tiny, very detailed. I can't work on something like that while my father is here. Such intricate work would likely take me a few tries.

And then there's the matter of reading these notes. It's one thing to pass them unknowingly. Entirely different to be *aware* that they're words of treason.

I don't know who I think I'm fooling, because it's certainly not myself.

The iron is beginning to glow yellow, so I seize my tongs and pull it out of the forge. "If we read these letters," I say, "there's no coming back from that, Cal."

She stares back at me. "I know."

I begin to hammer, and she waits.

"I thought you couldn't be gone long," I call over the noise.

She catches my arm, and I stop midswing.

"Don't you want to know what we're doing?" she says.

She's so fearless. I remember the moment she came flying into the barn, her ax swinging. The way she pulled a kitchen knife to defend me from Lord Tycho, who was carrying an armory's worth of weapons.

"And what will we do?" I say. "What will we do if they're letters of treason? What will we do if they call for revolution?" I jerk free and slam my hammer against the steel again. "Turn them all in, and then you can lose the bakery and I can lose the forge?" Every strike rings through the workshop. "Or maybe we'll all be hanging from a rope anyway."

"Jax."

She held me too long, and the metal cooled too quickly, so I have to shove it back into the forge. "What?"

"If we're committing treason, we should know."

I look down at my hand, the one Tycho healed. I was hurt, and he healed it . . . and he asked nothing in return. The magic was powerful and terrifying and wondrous all at once. I shoved him in the chest and yelled at him, and he could have taken my head off right there. He didn't.

I would offer you mercy.

And we're sitting here talking about treason.

I pull the metal free and look at Callyn. "You're right," I say finally. "We should know."

Lady Karyl doesn't appear until sundown. This time she has two people with her, a man and a woman, both heavily armed. I don't know if they're guards or soldiers, but they don't look friendly. They hover in the shadows by the edge of the workshop while she draws closer. Her hair is still coiled against her head, her robes damp at the hem as she steps across the mud-slick ground. Her blue eye is bright, even in the dim light of my workshop.

I grab my crutches and stand, casting a glance between her and the people in the shadows. I've been expecting her all day, so her "note" is in my pocket, but she's not alone. I'm not sure if I should just hand it to her or wait for her to ask for it. After the way Lord Alek treated me, her showing up with an armed entourage doesn't seem *better*.

"My lady," I say carefully.

"I saw Ellis in the tavern," she says, and I go still. If she gives this business back to my father, I have nothing. No recourse.

"He asked why he hasn't seen me," she says.

I'm not sure what response she's looking for, so I say nothing. I glance at the people in the shadows again. Light glints on their weapons.

"You haven't told him," she adds.

"No," I say.

Her eyebrows lift a hair. "Have you told anyone?"

Callyn. I barely hesitate, but her eyebrows lift farther. "I understand you're close with the girl down the lane. Shall I send my guards to ask the baker what she knows?"

Cal wouldn't breathe a word. I know she wouldn't. They could put a blade right to her throat and she wouldn't break.

But I think of little Nora. *Clouds above, look at all that silver!* She's still afraid of the dark, so I can just imagine how she'd act if someone pulled a sword on her sister.

I swallow. "Callyn won't say anything," I say roughly. "I swear it."

"And the King's Courier has been through Briarlock twice," Lady Karyl says. "I find that an interesting turn of events."

"He was looking for Lord Alek," I say. "We told him he hasn't been here."

She frowns. "Has he asked about anyone else?"

"No."

"And you've never mentioned me?"

"No," I say again. "My lady."

She's quiet. I'm quiet. I'm thrown by her mention of my father and the implied threats to Callyn. I cast another glance at the shadows.

Lady Karyl notices. "If you're being truthful, you have nothing to fear from my guards."

"I'm being truthful," I say.

"I find it interesting that you've said nothing of my visit to your father."

"Well, he never mentioned you to me. Do you find that interesting, too?"

She frowns. "Your mouth is going to get you in trouble."

She still hasn't brought up the message, and I'm not sure what to say to that, so I fall silent again.

"I like that you've kept my secret," she finally says. "And your girl from the bakery must be a loyal friend, too, because many days have passed, and neither Lord Alek nor I have been implicated in anything." She pauses. "The queen is planning some kind of competition, that she would like to resurrect the Queen's Challenge." Her lip curls. "She plans to invite competitors from Emberfall."

"That won't affect Briarlock," I say. "We're a long way from the Crystal City."

"Yes, you may be, but if these plans for a competition continue, it will mean more people crossing the border. More business for you, and more business for your baker friend." She pauses. "More opportunities to carry messages of great importance."

"More opportunities for you to spend a bit of silver," I say.

Her gaze darkens, but she smiles a bit. "I've learned you are easily motivated."

I bristle at that, as if I only crave silver to line my pockets and live in luxury. Maybe that's what *she* would do with it, but she has no clue what life is like for us here. "Yes," I say tightly. "I am."

She dips her hand into the purse tied at her waist and withdraws a handful of silver. She counts it fastidiously, then holds it out. "The payment you requested." She pauses. "I will take my letter now."

I withdraw it from my pocket. There are smudged fingerprints all over it from my time in the forge, but I take the offered silver and watch as she inspects the carefully placed seal.

"Good," she says. She drops the letter in her purse and withdraws another, the parchment perfectly clean, each fold crisp. Then she withdraws another twenty-five silvers.

She keeps them both close to her body. "I've told your father that I've found a new messenger," she says.

I nod, but my heart kicks to see that much more silver in her hand.

"You've proven yourself trustworthy," she says. "Lord Alek will return in a week. Don't disappoint me."

I take the parchment. The coins rattle into my hand. My heart is beating as hard as it did when I grabbed hold of the forge and wanted to die from the pain. I wish I could run to Callyn right this very moment.

It's enough, I want to shout. *It's enough to save the bakery right now.*

"I won't, my lady," I say, and my voice nearly trembles.

She turns away, but just before she reaches her guards, she stops. "Blacksmith?" she says.

"Yeah."

"I heard you worried this was treason," she says. "There's nothing treasonous about protecting Syhl Shallow. I'd think someone like you would be grateful for nothing more than the opportunity."

I might be used to ignoring my father's comments, but hearing it from *her* stings.

"I've heard stories," I say hollowly.

"Good." She nods. "We're counting on you to help us protect the queen."

Then she's gone, and I'm left alone with the flickering light from the forge.

I pull the parchment from my pocket and look at the seal, at the tight, crisp folds of the paper.

We're counting on you to help us protect the queen.

I scowl at the forge. At my missing foot. At the stools scattered all over my workshop. Maybe she's right. Maybe I should be grateful.

I brush my fingertips over the intricate seal. Then I pull out a fresh piece of parchment and a stick of kohl to try to sketch the design so I can later re-create it in steel.

Maybe this is treason, maybe it's not.

Like I said to Callyn, we should know for sure.

CHAPTER 12

TYCHO

I haven't been to a proper tourney in years, and now I've been to three in as many days. I'd forgotten the press of people, the smell of spilled ale and horse sweat, the way coins change hands as people bet on their favorite challengers. I'd forgotten the way fights would erupt at the end of the night, the way men would bicker and swear and draw blades when they'd drunk their way beyond any common sense. When I was a boy, I found the crowds intimidating—and the soldiers terrifying. It wasn't until Grey joined Worwick's tourney that I learned I had options other than hiding.

Now I'm grown, and I've spent enough time as a soldier that I still carry myself as one. If anyone has a mind for trouble, their eyes skip over my weapons and look away. At each tourney, I spend silver on ale that I don't drink, and I do as Prince Rhen suggested: I spread gossip that the king and queen long to host a competition on both sides of the border.

Some people are intrigued. Some are eager.

Some are wary.

Many murmur about how they can't wait for an opportunity to legally spill the blood of people from Syhl Shallow. It's been four years since a truce was formed between the countries, but bitterness lingers.

By the fourth night, I have one tourney left before I can return to the mountain pass that leads toward home. This one is two hours' west of my usual path, nestled into a valley at the base of the mountains, and I'm almost tempted to skip it. But no; I asked for a task, and I'll see it through.

We ride into the town of Gaulter at dusk, and the livery isn't crowded, so I pay extra for Mercy to have a stall instead of a tether. I don't get as lucky at the inn, which only has group rooms left, which means I'll have to sleep in my armor again. I inwardly sigh. At least my horse can get a good night's rest. I've grown so used to being on my own that night after night of crowds and conversation has exhausted me in a way I didn't expect. I'm eager to be done.

Most tourneys are situated similarly: a large arena surrounded by raised seating, further looped by a wide track where food and ale are sold, weapons are bought and traded, and horses are kept. I find this one to be a bit smaller than I'm used to, but Gaulter is more remote, and it's not dark yet: early enough that the track isn't full of people. There are more vendors here too, selling trinkets and cloth and jewels. I linger at each, trying to get a sense of the people here, because the atmosphere is slightly different: less drinking and gambling, more jovial and excited. Some children are in the crowd, which isn't exactly rare, but it's definitely less common.

Maybe this tourney won't be too bad.

One of the vendors is selling painted wooden figurines, and I pause to trace my fingers over a red horse that's been expertly carved. Then my eyes land on the figurine of a scraver, the wings fashioned with singed black silk, the claws made of steel.

Iisak. I frown.

But no. That's impossible. It must be a coincidence. He's been dead for years.

The girl working the stall sees my attention and turns my way with a wide smile. "Do you like the fantastic, my lord?" she says. "I have dragons and mermaids, too." She holds out a hand to indicate an array of brightly colored creatures, each more elaborate than the last.

I inhale to say no, but a shout from farther down draws my attention, followed by a startled cry and a rattle of metal against wood. Then the clear sound of a slap. The girl's smile turns a little strangled.

"Just one of the champions," she whispers. "They're always a bit tense before the fights."

I stride away from the vendor stalls, chasing the sound of trouble. We're close to the horses, and the scents of hay and soiled bedding are thick. I weave through the thickening crowd toward the stables, and I don't have to look far before I find a grown man in armor pinning a boy to the wall, the front of his shirt gripped in the man's fist. The boy can't be more than ten, and his cheek is flushed red. There's blood on his lip.

"I told you," the man says, seething, "to have *my* horse saddled first." He lifts his hand to strike again. "I shouldn't have to wait for your lazy—"

I catch his arm. The boy gasps, but the man swings his head around, and there's a murderous look in his eyes.

"Let him go," I say.

"This isn't your business," he growls.

"Surely not," I say. "I can saddle my own horse. I don't need a boy to do it." I keep a tight grip on his arm. "Let him go."

He lets go—but he also jerks free to turn and face me. He's older, with a thick graying beard and small, dark eyes. He's bigger than I am, too, but I'm used to that. When his hand reaches for his sword hilt, mine is already half drawn.

"Easy, gentlemen," another man drawls, his words slow and lazy from behind me. Something about the voice is familiar, but I can't place it. "Raolin, if you fight for free in the aisles, you'll be out of a job."

Raolin clenches his jaw, but he lets go of his sword. He spits at the ground at my feet. "Put some coins on the line and we can finish this in the arena."

"I try not to humiliate people in public," I say, and he glowers in response, but the man at my back speaks again.

"Go, Raolin," he says. "You're due in the arena in ten minutes anyway." He pauses, and his voice tightens. "And the lord is right. You can saddle your own mount if you're going to waste time abusing the help."

Raolin swears under his breath and turns away.

I look at the boy, who's watched this whole interaction with wide eyes. "Are you all right?" I say to him.

He nods quickly and swipes the blood off his lip. "Yes. Yes, my lord."

I want to offer to heal his lip, but I remember the way Jax and Callyn reacted, so I keep my hands to myself. It's a minor wound anyway.

The man at my back moves to my side. "Go ahead, Bailey," he says kindly. "Get to the other horses."

The boy nods and dashes off.

"Forgive my fighter, my lord," says the man as I turn to face him. "The odds are against him tonight, so he's got a bit of a temper—" He stops short as his eyes lock on my face, and then he does a double take. "Silver hell," he says. "Tycho?"

"Journ," I say, and I'm equally surprised. For a flash of time, I'm fifteen again, looking up at one of the tourney's champions.

He shakes off the shock, then claps me on the shoulder. "You've grown!" He looks me up and down, then offers me a warm smile. "And you've gone far."

"Well." I smile. "A long way from Worwick's." I always liked Journ. He was good in the arena, a fair fighter who'd put on a good show. He was also a kind man, someone who carried sweets in his pockets for the occasional children in the crowd.

"You're a long way from Worwick's, too," I say. Journ's hair has gone more gray, but he's still built like a fighter. No armor, though, so he must not be fighting tonight.

He shrugs, and something dark shifts in his eyes. "After the king was discovered, we had to leave Rillisk. There were many who thought I knew. The threats were . . . awful." He sighs and breaks off. "Abigale nearly lost the baby from the stress of it."

I lose the smile. "I'm sorry." I pause. "I didn't know."

"It's all right. It's been a long time." His voice is quieter now. "We're in a good place here."

Maybe he is, but I can't quite tell if he blames the king for what happened or if he sees it for a simple twist of fate. I wonder how he'll take the news of what Grey and Lia Mara are planning. "Still fighting?" I say.

"Nah, not so much." He hesitates and glances out into the aisle where the crowds are steadily growing. "Walk with me? Or do you have . . ." His eyes skip over the insignia on my chest. "Duties?"

"I'm glad to walk," I say.

The crowds yield to him readily, and kind greetings are common as we walk. He's well liked here, but that's no surprise, because he was well liked at Worwick's, too.

"I came to Gaulter as a fighter," he's saying, "and I still go in the arena on occasion. But a few months ago, Talan Borry, the old man who owns the tourney, fell into poor health. I've been looking after the place more and more."

"No wonder it seems so well tended," I say, and he smiles.

"It's not as big as Worwick's," he says, "but we do a good amount of business. We break even on the champions, but the scraver fights pull in a *lot* of silver."

I jerk my head around, sure I misheard him among the cacophony from the crowd. "The *what*?"

"You remember. Worwick had one, too. Maybe it's the same one, since Worwick's escaped during—"

I grab his arm. "You have *scravers* here?"

He looks at me like I've grown two heads. "Well—just the one. We get a lot of men who like to try their luck with it in the arena. It's good silver if you can last. But I told Talan they've got to be sober. We had a man nearly get torn apart last spring." He shudders. "We keep it on a chain now—"

"You keep him on a *chain*?" I feel like we must be talking about two different things . . . but then I remember how I first met Iisak. Worwick kept him in a cage. Iisak never spoke, never gave any indication he could understand a word that was said to him. He was vicious with his claws, too, if anyone got too close. It wasn't until later, once he escaped, that he befriended me and Grey and became somewhat trusting of humans. I remember the night we were all hiding in the woods, desperate and starving and exhausted, how Iisak brought us food and, later, how he taught the king to find his magic.

A cheer goes up in the crowd, and hooves thunder into the arena. The festivities must be starting. "I need to get into the stands," Journ says.

I follow him. "Can I see him?"

"Who?"

"The scraver."

Journ offers me a smile as we climb the steps. "Care to give it a try? Scratch up that pretty armor?"

He thinks I mean in the arena. I inhale to tell him *no*, that no scraver should be kept on a chain or in a cage, that they're magical and wise, not terrifying and ignorant.

But I'm thinking of Iisak, as if *he* is the scraver who could be at the end of that chain. As if I'd walk up to his cage, he'd say, "Ah! Well met, young Tycho," and I'd turn him free.

A man nearly got torn apart last spring.

This can't be Iisak. This can't be my friend.

But I remember the night Iisak died, and I know of one other scraver who was in Emberfall—one who definitely wasn't anyone's friend.

I fish in my purse for silver. "How much?"

Journ loses the smile. "Tycho—it's a monster. I've seen it slice through armor—"

"How *much*?"

"Five silvers," he says. "Odds are four to one if you can last five minutes." He pauses. "Twenty to one if you can last ten."

"How many people last ten?"

He laughs, but it's a little strained. "No one yet."

I nod. "Put me on the list."

CHAPTER 13

TYCHO

When I first learned to fight, my early lessons were always about making a decision instantly and carrying it out. No hesitation. Taking any opportunity available. I spent hours in Worwick's dusty arena learning footwork, memorizing all the different paths a blade could travel. Learning how to parry, how to dodge, how to attack. How to defend myself—and, ultimately, how to kill. I was young, and small for my age, but I was quick. Grey taught me how to use that. "When you're afraid, thinking takes longer," he said. "You have to teach your body to act without thought."

Now I'm waiting at the edge of this arena, glad for my years of training, because my thoughts are spinning. I've had to sit through hours of mounted games and sword fights, and nervous energy has my hand twitching toward my weapons.

Journ put me up first, which I suspect was done as a favor to me. But it also means I haven't yet seen the scraver, so I'm not sure what I'm up against. It's been four years since I last saw one, when Iisak's son had taken an arrow through his wing. When I tried to help Nakiis, his claws sliced right through the buckles on my bracer.

The crowd is impatient, feet stomping on the wooden floorboards. Metal bars are being erected and chained together to form a massive cage, the first part of this that's given me pause.

"Does the scraver try to escape?" I say to the steward at my back.

"Nah," he says, his voice bored. "That thing's on a chain. It's mostly the men who try to run." He coughs and hitches his pants up as he nods at the bars. "Those keep it out of the crowd."

My heart beats steady and hard as I process this information. "Oh."

"Don't grab the chain, though. It tore some poor sap's hand off." He swipes at his nose. "You ready?"

I nod, and he unchains a bar to let me in. Once I'm through, the metal clinks back into place and the crowd erupts with cheers. The first bit of fear pricks at my heart.

I turn to look at the steward. "Which way does the scraver—" I begin to say, but an earsplitting screech tears through the tourney, bringing an ice-cold blast of wind with it.

I cringe involuntarily, looking for the source. It's been years, but I forgot they can *sound* like that. I forgot their magic that brings a chill to the air.

I see nothing, though. The cheers from the crowd redouble, mixing with the shrieks, until the sound is deafening. I move to the center of the arena and turn in a circle, looking for an opening, but the crowd seems to press in around the cage, until I can't see a break in the faces.

Without warning, the shriek is closer. A chain rattles at my back. A dark shape rockets into the arena, and I register coal-black eyes, wings the color of night, and then nothing else because the scraver slams right into me.

I swear and hit the ground rolling. A claw slices through my upper arm, but I draw my sword as I roll to my feet. I sense more than see his second attack, so I spin a tight circle with my blade, barely nicking his forearms.

The scraver shrieks and retreats to the air, wings beating hard as it prepares to attack again. Blood is a bright-red streak against the darkness of his skin. The chain is attached to a manacle around his ankle, trailing all the way to the side of the arena.

I don't know if it's Nakiis. It's been too long.

"I don't want to fight you," I say in Syssalah. The crowd is so loud, but I keep my voice low. I know he can hear me. "I just want—"

He dives for me, heedless of my sword, his claws outstretched, fangs bared.

I don't want to hurt him. I swing my sword but duck under the movement, and he sails past. Claws drag against my armor anyway, tearing through the buckles at my shoulder. The crowd gasps as I stumble to a knee. Blood slips down my back, but stars flare in my vision as I call for the power in my ring. The injury closes just as the scraver tackles me again, and I crash into the dirt. My sword goes skittering away.

I roll quickly, before he can pin me. My sword is just out of reach.

But the chain is right there.

I grab hold as he takes to the air. The chain jerks taut, but he must be used to this tactic, because he changes course to round on me before I can blink. His shriek echoes through the arena, so loud it *hurts*. He's too fast, too hostile.

It tore some poor sap's hand off. Silver hell.

I don't duck this time. I let go of the chain and leap for him.

Those claws slice through the straps on the left side of my breastplate and drive into the skin below. But my arms close on his rib cage, and I can feel his shock. His wings beat hard, but he can't support my weight. We crash into the ground, but I don't let go.

"I don't want to hurt you," I gasp. "I just—"

His fangs sink right into my jaw. The pain steals my vision, my thoughts, my grip.

This was perhaps a bad idea.

"We've reached three minutes!" the announcer calls, and the crowd cheers. "Can he go for five?"

There's a good chance I'll be dead in five. I throw a punch, and it dislodges the scraver. Skin and muscle tear, robbing me of breath. But it gives me the tiniest bit of leverage, and I'm able to flip him onto his back. I'm panting, blood dripping from my jaw, soaking into my shirt beneath the armor, but I brace my arm across his neck. He's struggling, his claws digging for purchase, but now he's scrabbling at my bracers. My vision is still spotty from blood loss, but I can feel the magic in my ring working. I just need to stay conscious long enough for it to knit my skin back together.

The scraver's wings beat against the dirt floor as he struggles, but this close, I can see the scarring on the underside of one, where he was once taken down by an arrow.

"You *are* Nakiis," I say in surprise, and for a fraction of a second, he stops struggling. His eyes fix on my jaw, which has stopped bleeding.

"I can help you escape," I say in a rush. The crowd is roaring now. "I can—"

"No magesmith can help me," he growls, and then his claws sink into my upper arm, digging deep, severing muscle and tendon. I cry out and jerk back—and it's all he needs to wrench free.

I am quickly reconsidering my vow not to hurt him.

He's in the air before I can blink, those chain links rattling. I scramble to get my sword before he can pounce on my arm.

But he doesn't. He's ten feet above me, clinging to ice-coated bars, his chest rising and falling rapidly. Blood drips from the small slices along his forearms. I'm breathing hard, too, and my armor is holding on by nothing more than a few strips of leather and a prayer to fate. I can taste my own blood.

"We've reached five minutes!" the announcer cries. "Will this man be the first to make it to ten?"

The crowd screams, but I don't take my eyes off Nakiis.

"I used to spar with your father," I say, and my voice is still low. "I'm not going to let you hit me again."

A light sparks in his eyes, and he launches himself off the bars. He's fast, but so am I. He dodges my blades, but he can't get close enough to make another critical hit. Still, I earn a few slices across my arms—and so does he. The air has turned so cold that my breath fogs, and frost has formed along the ground. I leap the chain so many times it begins to feel like a second adversary. We begin a dance of advance and retreat, and my entire focus narrows to this moment, this battle.

Nakiis soars low, darting under my dagger arm. He takes a swipe at my legs, but I block him and spring out of his way.

The chain catches my ankle. I go down hard on my back.

He's on me instantly, all but crouched on my chest. One foot pins my sword arm. Those clawed fingers close around my throat. Each individual point digs into the muscle. I hold my breath, but he doesn't break the skin.

The magic in my ring won't help if I'm dead before I can use it.

He leans close, until I can feel the chill of his breath against my face.

"I remember you now," he says.

"Oh good." I draw a ragged breath, then wince as his claws tighten. "I trust you've been well?"

"Foolish magesmith," he says. "Enjoy your silver."

I frown. "What?"

A bell rings, the crowd cheers, and chains rattle. His fingers scrape free of my throat as he's dragged off me by the chain. Suddenly I'm lying in the dirt, and he's being forced backward through a gap in the bars, toward a waiting cage.

My heart is pounding. "Stop!" I find my feet and sheathe my sword. "Stop!" But my voice is drowned out by the cheering crowd.

Journ appears beside me. He claps me hard on my shoulder, and I wince again. "That was incredible. I thought it was going to rip your head off."

I rub at my throat, and my fingers come away with blood. "Me too."

Journ claps me on the shoulder again. "Let's go."

"Go?" I still feel a bit stunned.

"To get your silver, boy! You've set a standard for the rest of them, I'll say." He gives me a firm shove in the opposite direction, but I can't help glancing over my shoulder. I've lost sight of the scraver altogether.

There's a man waiting at the gap in the gates, and the steward looks equally bored.

"What's happening next?" I say to Journ. My thoughts are spinning.

"You didn't think you were the only one, did you?" The bars clang closed behind us, and they're chained shut.

The crowd roars, and Nakiis shrieks. Journ propels me forward, into the crowd, but at my back, the scraver's second match begins.

I watch Nakiis fight nine more men. I should be buying ale and spreading gossip about what the queen intends, but instead, I sit on a wooden bench and lock my eyes on each match. The scraver is swift and brutal, and while some men last five minutes and call for the match to end, many others try for ten—and suffer for the effort. By the end of the night, Nakiis has a dozen bleeding stripes on his limbs, but the men have more. The dust underfoot has turned to mud in some spots where blood—and worse—has spilled.

When it's all done, they lock him back in a cage and drag it out of sight.

I've been entertaining the thought of asking Journ to release Nakiis. But he doesn't own the tourney, and I'm not even sure he'd do it.

What did Journ say? *The scraver fights pull in a lot of silver.* I heard the way the attendants talked about Nakiis, the way they dragged the cage out of the arena. He's an asset, not an individual.

Journ wouldn't turn him loose.

If this tourney is anything like Worwick's, the next hour will be spent cleaning up spilled ale, washing tankards, oiling tack, and locking up the weapons. There's no sense in me lingering now.

But if I'm going to free Nakiis, I'm going to have to come back prepared.

I return to the inn, but not to sleep. I need food, and while I'm eating, I buy scraps of leather off some of the men there, then use it to lace my armor closed in spots. Several buckles are completely missing, and there are gouges everywhere, many that go down into the steel. I'm close to the Syhl Shallow border, probably a full day's ride from the Crystal Palace, but that's still a lot of ground to cover.

Guilt pricks at me. Rhen's return letter to Grey and Lia Mara is still wrapped in leather and strapped to my chest, untouched. It's not the most secret letter I've ever carried, but it's a document that would've been uncovered if I'd been killed. I wonder if Grey would have faced Nakiis in the arena too, or if he would have considered it an unnecessary risk.

It's hours past midnight now, and the common room in the inn has emptied, leaving no one but me and the barkeep and a dwindling fire.

"Will you be needing anything else, my lord?" the barkeep calls, his voice low.

"No. Thank you." I pause. "I don't think I'll be needing the room after all." I leave a coin on the bar and go to fetch Mercy.

By the time I return to the tourney, it's dark and silent, nighttime cold pressing down around us. The moon hangs high overhead, a narrow crescent that doesn't provide much light. Mercy's hooves clop on the frozen ground rhythmically, her breath streaming in two long clouds. I don't expect guards, so I'm not surprised when I find none. Outside of the weapons, which are kept locked in the armory, there's generally not much worth stealing from a tourney, especially not one this small. I tether Mercy out of sight and find a rear door. Even that is unlocked. I slip inside and creep through the darkness.

I've come through on the side where the stables are kept, and one of the horses offers a soft whicker. I stroke a hand across its muzzle and ease down the aisle, my feet silent on the straw-littered ground. I'm not sure where they'd keep the scraver here, so I let stars flare in my blood and my vision as I send seeking magic into the ground. The power tugs at me, drawing me down the aisle, easing past horse after horse.

The space is small, and the scraver isn't far, tucked away at the opposite end of the stables under a low overhang. I don't make a sound, but his eyes flick open as if he sensed the magic. He's in a cage, which I expected, nowhere near big enough. His wings are tucked tight against his back, but they still spill between the bars. He uncurls slowly from the ground to sit up and face me. In the dark, he moves like a shadow.

"You're more foolish than I thought," he says, and a cold wind slithers through the stable to make me shiver.

"Probably." I step closer to the cage, but his hands flex against the bars. Something in his focus tightens, shifts.

I stop and lift my hands. "I can break the lock."

"You can keep your distance." I see the edge of his fangs.

I frown. "You don't want to be freed?"

"*Freed.*" He scoffs, those fangs fully bared now. "I've had many offers of *freedom*, boy. None were true."

"The king freed you once. He healed your wing and let you go."

"I remember the magesmiths and their dealings," Nakiis says. "He will collect one day. I have no doubt."

I shake my head. "He won't." I pause. "I would offer you freedom, too."

"You will not *trick* me," he growls.

"It's not a trick." I take a step closer. "I have no chain. No ropes. I'm not a magesmith. I'll break the lock and you'll be—"

He shrieks at me, and a cold blast of wind tears through the stables. I cringe. The horses pace nervously in their stalls.

"The king kept my father bound," Nakiis snaps. "I saw it."

"He wasn't bound! Iisak was a *friend*—"

He shrieks at me again, and I shiver. His magic makes frost form along the knives in my bracers and the hilt of my sword. Ice crawls up the walls of the stables.

I glare at him. "You'd rather stay in a cage?"

"Their demands are few," he growls. "I'm treated well. I cannot say the same of you or your magesmith king."

"Your father once said that nothing in a cage is ever truly *well*."

Nakiis says nothing to that.

I sigh. It's the middle of the night, and I've got a long day of riding ahead of me.

"Fine," I say to him. "Stay here if you want. But I'm going to break the lock, and then it can be your choice."

I expect him to shriek at me again, but he goes very still.

I draw my dagger. His eyes widen.

I lift my hand to slam it against the steel—but then I hesitate. "My name is Tycho," I tell him. "If you choose to leave, you are welcome to accompany me to the Crystal Palace in Syhl Shallow."

He hisses like he's caught me in a lie. "Scravers are unwelcome in Syhl Shallow."

"Not anymore," I say. "Lia Mara is queen. She would welcome Iisak's son, as would King Grey."

"Liar."

"Fine. Suit yourself." I slam the dagger against the lock with all my strength. Then a second time. The steel twists but doesn't quite give. Once more will do it. I raise the dagger for a third strike, just when I hear a small voice behind me.

"What are you doing?"

Nakiis growls, and I whirl.

Bailey, the boy I saved from a beating earlier, stands by the edge of the stables. He's shirtless and barefoot, with mussed-up hair and a cloak thrown haphazardly over his shoulders. His eyes are wide, and he's frozen as if he's unsure if he should run or scream.

At my back, the scraver shrieks again, and the bars of the cage make a loud *clang* as they give way. The door swings wide enough to slam into me, and then he's free, tearing past me as if I'm going to make a move to stop him.

Bailey gasps and shivers as Nakiis soars through—and then the scraver is gone.

I'm breathless. So is the boy. He's wide-eyed and staring at me. I watch as his gaze snaps from my face to the dagger in my hand, and he swallows.

"I—I didn't see anything, m-my lord—"

"Good," I say. The sack of coins I won earlier is heavy in the purse at my belt, and I tug it free, then sheathe the dagger. "Here."

His eyes widen farther, but he takes the coins and clutches them to his chest, then hesitates. "He used to talk to me," he whispers, his voice so low that I almost can't make out the words. "No one believed me." He pauses. "But you talked to him."

"I did."

He frowns. "I would've let him go. I couldn't break the lock."

"You can let him go now." I offer half a smile. "Me as well."

He nods quickly. "Yes, my lord."

"Go back to sleep," I say.

He scurries off, his bare feet silent as he slips into the stables. I don't know if he'll keep this secret, but it won't matter. I'll be gone in minutes, and it would be hard to prove that the King's Courier had been liberating mythical creatures in the middle of the night.

I find my way through the stables back to Mercy. I listen for the scraver's shrieks in the night sky, but I hear nothing. There's no sign of him.

I sigh. "Come on, girl," I say quietly, clucking to her with my tongue. "Let's go home."

CHAPTER 14

CALLYN

Snow falls again overnight, making the morning trudge to the barn a true delight. Nora is snoring away, so I leave her to it, wrapping myself up in a cloak to go milk Muddy May. The chickens are excited when I scatter grain, and May is lowing for her own breakfast. I scoop grain into a bucket for her, too, then grab the milking stool. The morning air is quiet, but I don't mind. Sunlight breaks through the cracks of the barn door, a wide stripe of light shining through the area where it hangs crooked.

This morning, I'm glad for the quiet, for the task. It gives me time to think.

I've heard a dozen stories about the monster that killed my mother. The soldiers that returned from Emberfall were broken and battered, soaked in blood, some with dried viscera caked to their armor. Their eyes were dark and haunted, and they all had stories about a large white creature that sailed out of the sky, bringing terror and death. Some talked about the glistening scales and fangs like a dragon, some said it was more like a winged horse, others talked about the talons that plucked soldiers off horses to tear them in two.

I don't know if that's what happened to my mother. Maybe she survived the monster to fall to the army in Emberfall. Maybe it was both.

I know it terrified my father. He was such a kind, thoughtful man before she died. That didn't quite change after she was gone—but maybe that thoughtfulness went awry. Maybe he couldn't stop thinking about the magic and what it had done to Mother. That's why he got tangled up with the Truthbringers—and why he's dead now. I know he didn't expect the protest to swell into the palace the way it did.

I know he didn't expect the king to turn his magic on our people. I rub at Mother's pendant under my shirt.

I keep thinking about these messages. I've begun to wonder how my mother would feel about our activities.

I wish we knew what was in these notes.

Jax has gotten pretty close to the design, but he's not there yet. What's more concerning is the wax. It's a complicated swirl of green and black, with flecks of silver. I walked to town last week, but there's nothing available at the stationers with so much detail. When we melt green and black wax together, we don't get pretty swirls—we get a darker green. It might be nothing anyone would notice—or it might be the most important thing of all. We might get a dozen opportunities to read these letters if we get the mixture right, but I'm pretty sure we'd only have one shot if we get it wrong. Then our blood would be swirling in the dirt.

I finish milking May and set the bucket by the door, then turn her loose in the small paddock so I can muck out the barn. Nora should be awake by now, but she likely saw me doing the barn chores and decided to start the dough for bread. Hopefully.

When I go to dump the wheelbarrow on the muck heap, something in the woods draws my notice. I'm not sure if it was a bit of sound or a bit of movement, but I hesitate, looking out through the ice-laden trees. A bitter wind tears through the barnyard, and somewhere out in the woods, an animal shrieks. I shiver.

I want to ignore it, but I can't shake the feeling that I'm suddenly not alone.

I finish dumping the wheelbarrow, then turn back for the barn. That feeling won't shake loose. I wish for the ax.

"Jax?" I call.

No response. I can hear the forge distantly clanging anyway.

"Nora?" I say. "Nora, if you're fixing to trick me, I'll make you fetch the eggs for a *month*."

Nothing. Some of the hens wander through the open door out into the yard. Muddy May looks over from her pile of hay.

I put my tools away, fighting the urge to hurry out of sight. When I go to slide the crooked door closed, it protests with a loud creak—then stops altogether. The gap is a foot wide now. I sigh.

I jerk at the door, but it's frozen in place. Now it won't open or close in either direction. No amount of swearing or pulling or kicking will get the door to move. Sweat begins to gather under my cloak.

"May I help?"

I startle and whirl. Lord Tycho stands there in the snow.

I stumble back a few feet before I stop myself. "Oh. Hello. Ah . . . my lord." I feel flushed and uncertain. I can't stop thinking of the magic he bears.

Magic that helped Jax.

The same magic that's caused so much harm.

His eyes are shadowed, and a day's worth of beard growth covers his jaw this morning. Even his armor seems scratched up. There's definitely a slice through the emblems of Syhl Shallow and Emberfall.

"Forgive me." He pauses. "I didn't mean to startle you."

His voice is kind, and it sounds as if he's apologizing for more than just this moment. My heart is still pounding, and I wish it would stop. I wish I could reconcile the kindness of his actions with the terrible power he bears.

Has he been here awhile? I wonder if he was waiting on the other side of the bakery, where the door is locked. Maybe it was his horse that I heard.

Then I remember what he said when he came through town before. "I don't—the meat pies aren't ready yet—"

"I didn't expect them to be. I'm earlier to Briarlock than I expected." He nods at the barn. "I heard you battling with the door. May I help?"

I frown. Knowing he's at my side makes me even more aware of the peeling paint, the weathered wood, the bent hinges and crooked track.

He's stepped up to my side, and I shiver, but he only points. "Your door has slipped off the track a bit."

He's right. Jax warned me about it a month ago, saying he could fix it, but I didn't have the coins to pay for a new track, and I wasn't going to beg him for steel. He already does enough for me.

"I've been hoping it would hold through the winter," I admit—then worry he's going to offer magic to fix it somehow, and I won't know what to do.

"Almost," he says encouragingly. "Do you have a ladder? I can lift it back into place."

I stare at him.

"Or you can," he says. "If you'd rather."

His eyes are bright and guileless. I don't know if I should be afraid of him or grateful to him or something else entirely.

But Lord Tycho is looking at me expectantly, and I have no idea how to chase him out of here when he's being so . . . so *harmless.* My heart keeps pounding against my ribs, but I drag the ladder out of the barn, set it against the wall, and—despite his offer—I begin to climb.

I see what he means about the track: it's weathered and worn and the wheel has come a bit loose. But when he lifts from the bottom, I try to maneuver it back into place.

While I'm huffing and puffing and trying to shift the wood, I hear the back door of the bakery creak open. "Cally-cal!" Nora calls. "I think Lord Tycho is nearby. I know we're supposed to hate magic, but he *did* heal Jax. Don't you think he's handsome? I think I might fancy him. If he didn't have magic, I think *you* would fancy—"

"Nora!" I shout. My cheeks are on fire, and I don't dare look down at Lord Tycho. If anyone could turn my fear of magic into exasperated mortification, it would be my little sister. "I'm fixing the barn door."

"I saw his horse tethered out front! I fed her one of the apples for the tarts." She must be crossing the barnyard. In an instant, she'll see him. That's a good thing because if she keeps going, I'll fall off this ladder. "I think he's very kind. For a lord. Don't you think he's very— Oh, hello, Lord Tycho!"

"Hello, Nora," he says genially. "I'm certain Mercy offers her thanks for the apple." He's a little bit breathless, straining with the weight of the door. It's probably better that he's down there and I'm up here. I fight to get it fully on the track.

"Your horse's name is Mercy?" I hear her chirp. "She's very gentle."

"She can be," he says.

"Clouds above, Nora," I snap. "Leave the poor man al—*ouch*!" The door slings back onto the track, but my fingers pinch under the metal before I can get them out of the way. Blood appears on my fingertips, and I shake my hand as if that'll get rid of the sting.

"Cally-cal!" shouts Nora.

"I'm fine," I say. "Just foolish." I give the door a shove, and it slides perfectly now. My fingers leave bloody spots on the wood.

When I climb back down, Nora sees the spots of blood on my

fingers and blinks wide eyes up at Lord Tycho. "Will you do the magic again, my lord?" Her smile is bright. "Please?"

That brisk wind tears through the barnyard again. "Nora," I hiss. "You can't ask—"

"I don't mind." Lord Tycho puts out a hand.

I jerk back without meaning to, and he frowns.

I swipe the blood on my skirts and take a step back. "It's . . . it's not bad enough for all that."

He studies me for a long moment, then nods and lowers his hand. "As you say."

I can't read his expression, and I'm worried I've offended him. My heart keeps up its brisk pace, but he *did* just help me fix the barn door. He did heal Jax's hand. I'm the one who drew a knife. Jax is the one who hit him.

It feels wrong to invite magic into my home, but Lord Tycho isn't a monster. He's not a winged creature out of a storybook.

He's not even the man who set the palace ablaze and killed my father.

I swallow. "I know it's early for meat pies, but I have the dough ready for apple tarts." I hesitate. "If you have time today, my lord."

"I do," he says, but now there's an odd silence between us.

I have to turn away. "Well," I say. "Come along."

The bakery is warm from the fire, and probably for the first time in my *life*, I'm glad for Nora's chattering, because it spares me the need to say anything at all. I trim dough and lay apples and ignore my stinging fingers—all while she rambles about nothing for twenty straight minutes and the bakery swells with the scent of cinnamon and sugar.

"A woman was through two days ago," says Nora, "and she said the queen is expecting another baby. Is that true?"

"It is," he says. Lord Tycho has taken a seat on the bench by the window, leaning back against the wall. The sunlight gleams in his hair. Nora was right—he is very handsome. There's a hint of weariness to his frame, though, and now I can see that one side of his armor is barely held together by crudely tied strips of leather. I wonder who he fought with, and why.

"Do you think she'll have another girl?" says Nora. "Two daughters are supposed to be very lucky."

He smiles. "So I've heard."

"I'm so excited," she squeals. "I love babies."

I roll my eyes. As if she'll be meeting this one personally.

"Maybe she'll be a *magical* princess." She sighs. "I'm sure people will have a lot to say about that."

Lord Tycho's eyes meet mine, and I think of that moment in the barnyard when I refused his magic. "What do you think they'll say?" he asks her, but his eyes are still on me.

"Everyone is worried that Princess Sinna might be a magesmith like the king. Do you think so, Lord Tycho?"

"I think Princess Sinna is fairly determined to be whatever she wants to be." He pauses. "They needn't worry. The king and queen are fair and just, and they're raising their daughter to be the same."

I'm not sure my parents would agree, but I don't know what to say. I certainly can't tell him that my father was part of the attack on the castle six months ago. My cheeks are warm, so I thrust my hands into a fresh ball of dough and say nothing.

Nora, however, has no hesitation. "But even if she doesn't, she could get rings like yours, right?" she's asking with awe in her voice. "Do many people have them?"

He's been very patient with her prattling, and I'm curious about this one myself, so I keep my eyes on the tarts while I wait for his answer.

"Very few," he says. "They're made of special steel from the ice forests in Iishellasa." He flexes his hand, and they catch the light. "It takes the king quite a bit of time and effort to make them."

That must mean that the king chooses who gets to wear them. Something about the idea twists up inside of me. Why should one person get to choose?

"Can you heal anything with them?" Nora is asking.

"Not anything," he says. "I'm nowhere near as fast as the king would be. It's borrowed magic. Like . . . like a pair of boots that don't fit quite right. I can't summon it as quickly as he can, so if an injury is bad enough, I can't stop it. It's . . . it's very draining, too."

I glance over when he says that. I wonder if he was harmed in battle, if that's why he looks so worn and tired. If he were badly injured and then healed the wounds, it would match the damage to his armor.

"Magic won't undo healing," Tycho is saying. "So once it sets in, I can't reverse whatever damage has been left behind. The king can't either. But he saved a pregnant woman once, who'd taken a dagger to the belly." He pauses, gesturing to his face. "He even saved a man's eye after it had been gouged out. It simply started re-forming in his head—"

"Ugh!" cries Nora.

"Ah . . . forgive me." Lord Tycho looks abashed. "Sometimes I forget my audience. Too many days with no one but Mercy for company."

"She deserves it for being so nosy." I cast a wicked glance at my sister, but in my head I'm thinking of everything he said. Surely if magic can heal a wound, it could cause one just as easily.

Nora makes a face at me. "What do your other rings do?" she asks him.

"Nora!" I snap. "Quit badgering the man."

"It's all right," he says. "I have a friend who always says that a little knowledge can make the mysterious less frightening. I've heard many of the rumors about magic. Most of them are untrue." He hesitates.

"I can seek things, like water or food. Or a person, if they're not too far off. I can start a fire if I need to."

Nora loses the smile. "The king's magic started a fire."

I go still. "Nora," I say quietly. "That's enough about magic." I glance at the apple tarts. They've browned nicely around the edges, so I use thick woolen mitts to pull the pan out of the oven. The entire bakery smells like apples and crisp pastry. Tycho joins me by the table as I slide the tarts off the pan.

"Don't steal one," Nora warns. "She'll break your knuckles."

That startles a smile out of him. "I've been warned."

I glance up. When my eyes meet his, the expression fades away.

"Forgive me," he says. "I frightened you with the magic. That wasn't my intent."

"I'm not afraid." I pause, and I can feel my heart pounding again. Maybe it's the mention of the king's magic, but I *am* afraid. For a heartbeat of time, I want to pull away, because I'm sure Tycho is going to force me, to show me how harmless it is. I hold my breath, waiting.

But he doesn't.

I touch a hand to Mother's pendant and let the breath ease out. "I'm the one who should apologize. I shouldn't have pulled a knife on you."

"You were defending your friend. It's admirable. You shouldn't apologize for that."

"You're welcome to take one," I say without looking up. "I'm sure we've delayed you long enough, my lord."

"I'm not delayed," he says. "And please. Call me Tycho."

I shake my head. "It wouldn't be right."

"I wasn't born to the nobility," he says quietly. "It wouldn't be wrong."

That makes me stop and look up at him. His eyes are warm and intent on mine. There's no smile on his lips now.

"What were you born?" says Nora.

It jolts me out of my staring. "Nora!" My sister, I swear.

But Tycho doesn't hesitate. "My mother was a seamstress. My father was a . . . well." He shrugs, but there's a weight to his voice now. "He wasn't much of anything, as it turns out." He casts a glance at Nora. "But I remember what it was like to have a little sister. Two, in fact."

"You were so lucky," I tease, trying to take some of the sudden weight out of the moment.

He smiles, but there's a shadow in *his* gaze all of a sudden. An uncertainty that reminds me a lot of how I felt a moment ago.

I'm not sure what this conversation has triggered in him, whether it's sadness or nostalgia or something else entirely, but I do know my sister doesn't need to keep butting her nose into his business. I fetch two small bags of muslin and begin to lay the apple tarts in each of them. "Nora, I want you to run up the lane and take a pouch of these to Jax."

"Jax," Tycho says, and a spark of dark intrigue slides into his voice. "How is *Jax*?"

I bite at the edge of my lip, chagrined. "Well, it's been several days since he *last* yelled at the King's Courier, so . . ."

"So perhaps I'm due?"

"No!" My eyes flare wide. "That's not what I meant at all."

"I know." He smiles, then gestures for the pouch. "Allow me."

Dumbfounded, I hand it to him. "I just—he won't—I didn't—"

"I insist." Tycho bows to my sister, teasing with great flourish, and she giggles. "My lady Nora," he says, "I will save you the trip."

CHAPTER 15

JAX

I hate how often my father is in the forge now.

It's a bit ironic, because I spent months hating how much time he was spending facedown in a puddle of spirits. I was telling Callyn that it's like he realized I was getting silver from somewhere, and now he doesn't want to miss out. Our first payments are due to the tax collector tomorrow, but all that silver is safely stowed away in the bakery. If we do this for a few more weeks, we'll be able to pay it *all* off.

It snowed overnight, so the ground outside the workshop is coated in a layer of white, though it's turned to slush near the forge. Business is always a bit slower when it snows, and today is no different. My father seems irritated by that, but I can't control the weather. When he vanished this morning. I was hopeful that he'd be gone until nightfall, but he reappeared a few hours later, reeking of ale and smoke. I've seen him nearly strike his hand three times.

Maybe he'll grab onto the forge himself.

Good as new, right, Da?

I scowl and keep my head down. This would be the worst time to get into it with him, and I'm still a bit wary after everything that happened.

"This one coming has got money," Da calls. "You be on your best behavior, boy."

"Yes, Da." In the midst of my hammering, I glance up at the lane, then do a double take. A bay mare with a stripe down her face.

Lord Tycho.

I miss the anvil entirely, and my hammer goes sailing into the dirt. The hinge I was working on isn't long behind it. It lands with a loud clink.

My father swears, then heaves himself off his stool. "Do you have to make us look incompetent?"

I can't breathe. I can't move. I remember every word I said last week, the way I chased Lord Tycho out of Callyn's bakery.

I don't want him to see my father. I don't want him to see *me*. My hand, the one he healed, clenches closed. I have half a mind to dash into the house, and my father's warnings be damned. But he's already in the courtyard, his mare blowing steam and kicking up slush.

I'm angry. I'm humiliated. I'm afraid. I don't know what I am.

And he hasn't even dismounted his horse yet.

My father clocks me on the back of the head. "Are you addled, boy?" he hisses. "Take his horse."

I duck my head and grab my crutches. For the first time, I look at Lord Tycho the way I'd look at Lord Alek. Rich and powerful and someone who wouldn't glance at me twice if he didn't need something from me.

I take hold of the mare's rein, but I keep my eyes on her shoulder, on his oddly scuffed boots, on anything but his face. "What can we offer?" I say woodenly.

He swings down from the saddle, and for a moment, he says absolutely nothing. The silence swells between us. I wait for him to cuff me on the ear or make a demand or worse—to tell my father what I said.

But Lord Tycho doesn't do any of those things. "My mare's hind shoes are loose." His voice is cool and dispassionate. "I still have a few hours' ride ahead of me. I wondered if you could replace them."

My heart seems to pull free of the vise grip to start pounding. I nod. "Yes, my lord." I tether Mercy to the post, and she presses her head to my chest, breathing warmth against my thighs. I want to hold tight, to press my forehead to her mane and let her strength hold me up, but I'm being ridiculous, and my father would knock me in the mud if I tried.

So I give her a gentle pat along the crest of her neck, then grab my tools.

Lord Tycho says nothing. I wait for him to say that I've shod his horse before, or that we know each other, but he stands there silently. I still haven't fully looked at him. I tuck a lock of hair behind my ear and drop onto my stool.

"Work quick," my father snaps, as if I'm one to dawdle.

The first shoe pulls loose and drops to the ground with a clink. Behind me, my father mutters instructions I don't need, as if I haven't been shoeing horses independently for the last few years. He's trying to earn an extra coin or two, I can tell. The master blacksmith keeping a close eye on his "apprentice." The whole time, Lord Tycho is silent while my father grows louder and harsher with his criticism, so I work fast and hard so this moment can end.

Eventually, it does. Mercy has two fresh shoes, and my father is charging him two silvers. I want to wince, because I know Lord Tycho is aware it's not what we usually charge. But the lord hands over the coins, the metal sparking in the light, and my father eagerly pockets it.

I untether the mare, stroking a hand down the stripe on her face, wishing I had a cookie to feed her when she noses at my fingers. "Be good, sweet Mercy," I murmur under my breath.

Then I hand the reins to Lord Tycho. When his fingers brush mine, a jolt goes through me, just like the day he fixed my hand. I wonder if it's his magic. I hold my breath and let go.

I haven't met his eyes since he arrived—and now he's about to leave.

"Master Blacksmith," Lord Tycho says to my father. "I left a carriage down the road toward town, and the springs have gone rusty. Can I borrow your"—he hesitates—"*apprentice* to assess whether it's something you could repair before I'm due to leave tomorrow?"

My father inhales, and it sounds like he's going to protest. I'm not sure if he's going to say that Lord Tycho should bring the carriage *here*, or if he's going to insist that he should go, as I'll obviously take too much time. But the lord tosses him another silver, and says, "I'd be much obliged for the service."

My father sounds like he's choked on a rock. "Yes—yes, of course, my lord."

Wonderful. Maybe I can trip over my crutch again.

Or . . . maybe Lord Tycho is getting me away from my father so he can beat the piss out of me for what I said in the bakery.

That's a new thought that hasn't occurred to me, and now that it's entered my brain, it refuses to shake loose. It would explain his cool demeanor, the way he interacted with my father, the way he stood silently while I shod his horse. My fists are tight on my crutches as we make our way down the lane, away from the forge, and I brace myself. He'll likely wait for the stretch of woods between my place and Callyn's, where nothing will be seen. If I fight back, it'll probably make it worse. It's not like I can run. Could I play dead to get it over with more quickly? I feel like I could be rather convincing.

When his hand reaches out, I flinch, jerking left. Mercy throws her head up and snorts.

"Steady," Lord Tycho says, and I'm not sure if he's talking to the horse or to me. He's quiet for a moment, and my heart gallops along in my chest. I chance a glance over, and he's holding out a small cloth pouch. "Cal sent some apple tarts. Would you like one?"

It's so far from what I was expecting that it's like he's speaking another language. This is the first time I've really looked at him since he arrived, and now I see that his pristine armor bears deep gouges, and he's missing a few buckles. But Mercy is unharmed, and he's still got all his weapons, so whoever he fought with, he didn't lose.

His eyebrows go up, and I realize I didn't answer his question. I have to clear my throat. "No. My lord."

We walk on. He eats one of the apple tarts, and the smell is heavenly. I shouldn't have refused. My emotions refuse to settle anywhere. We keep walking down the lane, past the turn to Cal's house, heading south toward the miles of woods that lead out of Briarlock.

I stop short, and that lick of fear I felt a moment ago returns. "You said your carriage was on the way to town."

His lip quirks. "I don't have a carriage."

"But—"

"You know who I am. You know what I do. What courier would take a carriage?"

His voice is easy, but I still don't understand. I draw a long breath, letting the steam out through my teeth.

"I wasn't tricking *you*," he says carefully. "I was tricking your father."

"I wasn't worried about you *tricking* me," I say darkly. "I thought you were dragging me out here to fill my back with arrows."

"If I were going to shoot you, Jax, it wouldn't be in the back."

I still can't tell if he's angry with me or if I'm angry with him—or if we're both just so different that we practically *are* speaking different languages. I stab my crutches into the snow again, and we keep walking.

"So where are we going?" I finally say.

"Anywhere you like," he says. "I had no destination in mind."

Now I round on him. *This* emotion is unmistakably anger. "If you don't have a carriage and you aren't dragging me out here to leave me for dead, then just let me go back to the forge."

"Do you really want to go back?" he says, and the way he's looking at me is piercing, like he knows every emotion I'm not voicing.

I inhale like I'm ready to breathe fire. I'm tempted to hit him with a crutch. I'm ready to snap at him that I'm *busy*, that I don't need his pity, that I don't need some stupid spoiled lord from the Crystal City to interfere with my life when I'm in the middle of trying to save the forge through unscrupulous means.

But then he says, "I wanted to apologize." His voice is low, and quiet, and earnest, and it stamps out some of my fire. "I would have done it at your workshop, but . . ." He takes a breath. "Well. If I had to stand there and listen to him much longer, I would have held *his* hand in the forge."

Warmth heats my cheeks, but I don't look away. "You don't owe me an apology," I say. I swing my crutches forward and start walking again.

Lord Tycho falls into step beside me without missing a beat. "I do, actually." He pauses. "I should have warned you about the magic. I shouldn't have assumed. But you were so cavalier, so bold." He cuts a glance my way. "It wasn't until you began lecturing me on *kindness* and *suffering* that I realized I made a misstep."

I was tripping over the words *cavalier* and *bold*, but this makes me flush. I'm the one who should be apologizing, truly, but I'm not sure what will come out of my mouth if I open it.

We walk in silence for a while, until we've traveled so far that I know I'm going to hate the walk back. I don't often go farther than Callyn and Nora's. But maybe that's why I keep going.

"Did you really think I was dragging you out here to shoot you?" he finally says.

I keep my eyes on the snowy trail, but I nod. "Either that, or you'd beat me senseless."

"Really!" He actually sounds shocked.

I glance at his scarred armor, at the weapons strapped to his body. "Yes, my lord," I say dryly. "I realize such a thing could hardly be foreseen."

"Hmm," he says, and for such a simple word, the tone is interesting, weighted in a way I don't expect.

Wind whistles through the trees, blowing snow from the branches overhead, and I shiver.

He holds out the little cloth bag of apple tarts again. "They're still warm."

I hesitate, then nod. When I take one from the pouch, I worry that I'm going to be forced to use crutches and eat at the same time, which is never a dignified experience. But Lord Tycho stops, and he feeds the horse one of the tarts, too.

"Callyn would have a fit," I say.

He smiles. "Our secret." He rubs the horse under her mane, then leans back against her shoulder. "Mercy won't tell."

Somewhere deep in the woods, a branch cracks, and I'm both surprised and not at how quickly he whirls, pulling a bow and arrow from behind the saddle. He doesn't aim, but he's alert, staring out between the trees. I look, too, but I don't see anything. Snow whispers down through the trees to settle in his hair and along the shoulders of his cloak.

I wonder if I would have been like this, if I'd followed the path my father assumed lay ahead of me. If I hadn't lost my foot, if I'd grown up to enlist and become a soldier. If I'd be wary of loud noises in the woods instead of ignoring them in favor of finishing an apple tart.

After a moment, I say, "Probably just a branch. From the weight of the snow."

He nods. "Probably." But he hangs the bow over his shoulder and leaves it there, then shoves the arrow under his sword belt.

"Are you worried about whoever you fought with?"

His eyes snap to mine. "What?"

I glance at his gouged armor. "Whoever did that."

"Oh. No." He doesn't say anything else, which feels deliberate.

When he starts walking again, he's quiet, and I wonder if he's still worried about the noise in the woods. My crutches are loud, while he moves so silently that he could be a ghost, and I wonder if he's regretting . . . whatever this is. Our random walk through the woods.

He finally says, "I have a history with Lord Alek. He resents the king, and he resents the presence of magic in Syhl Shallow. He's made no secret of that. His House is one of the most influential, and he has many allies at court. He can't openly attack the king or the queen . . . and truly, he shouldn't attack me, either, but . . . well." He hesitates, and I can tell there's more he's not saying. "Alek is very clever. He's very good at claiming innocence." He looks out at the snowy woods again. "Since I saw him in Briarlock, I've been wary."

Absently, I rub at my neck. The wounds Lord Alek left have healed, but they'll scar. I remember what Lord Tycho said about Alek being a dangerous man, and I don't disagree—but I also know what Lady Karyl said about the king and his magic and the harm it brought. I know how Callyn's mother died, and she wasn't the only soldier from Briarlock to fall to the monster. Knowledge of the sealed letter in my pocket burns in my thoughts. I don't know what to believe about anyone.

Either way, it's another reminder that these men matter, and I . . . do not.

"You must spend a lot of time fighting," I say.

"Less than you'd think." He looks over. "Or maybe not. I'm not sure. Are you a fighter, Jax?"

The question wraps a dark band around my thoughts. I keep my eyes on the icy path and say, "No. I would have enlisted once I came of age, but . . ." I shrug and nod down at my leg. "So now I just make weapons. I don't really know how to use them."

He's quiet for a while, and it's a weird kind of silence that I'm not sure how to read. I remember that moment in Cal's shop when he healed my hand, how he had something that we didn't. Offering magic was a kindness, yes, but something about it still smarted. I don't want pandering now either. I've heard all the comments. *At least you're a good blacksmith. You're lucky you've still got the forge. As misfortune goes, yours isn't too bad.*

But Lord Tycho doesn't say any of that.

Instead, he says, "Want to learn?"

CHAPTER 16

JAX

Lord Tycho is mocking me. Surely.

But he doesn't look like it. He looks like he's waiting for an answer. My eyes flick to the sword at his waist, to the knives at his wrists, and finally to the bow on his shoulder. I can't use a sword—even I know the very basis is *footwork*—and I doubt I could hold my balance to shoot an arrow. My heart is beating at a rapid clip, but I narrow my eyes, ready to refuse.

Before I can, he jerks the bow off his shoulder and holds it out. "Here. Hold this."

"I—yes, my lord." My hand closes on the cold wood.

He cuts me a wry glance. "Tycho." He tethers Mercy to a tree and feeds her another apple tart. Before he turns back, he unbuckles the quiver of arrows from behind the saddle and loops it over his shoulder.

I watch him dubiously. This would be a lot of effort for ridicule.

He pulls the arrow out of his sword belt and holds out a hand for the bow. "When Grey first taught me to fight," he says, "one of the first things he did was ask what I was afraid of. It's the worst question in the world, and he wouldn't let me get away from it. I'll never forget it." He lowers his voice to imitate someone more stoic and unyielding. "'No, Tycho, speak your fears. You cannot *challenge* them if you cannot even *voice* them.'" He rolls his eyes. "But he was right. He usually is."

I'm staring at him. "Are you talking about the *king*?"

"Yes," he says, like it's nothing. "Here. Watch." He lifts the bow, nocks an arrow, and draws back the string. "Keep your arm level. Draw back and release." The arrow flies off the string and cracks into a tree thirty yards away.

Then he looks at me. "What are you afraid of, Jax?"

I'm afraid I'm about to make a fool of myself. My cheeks are already warm. "That *is* the worst question in the world."

"Right?" He doesn't make me answer, he just holds out the bow. My fingers tighten on my crutches uncertainly, but he shrugs and glances behind me. "Brace against a tree."

This feels awkward, but I lever myself backward a few steps until I'm against a narrow trunk, snow trickling down my neck when my cloak tugs a bit loose. But I drop the crutches and take the bow. I've tried archery before, when I was a boy, my father explaining the movements. But it was years ago, long before I got hurt, and everything feels foreign. I try to mimic the movements, slipping an arrow onto the string and drawing it back, letting the shaft rest along the shelf.

"More," he says. "Don't be afraid to put some strength into it."

I draw it back another inch. It'll be a miracle if the arrow doesn't fall off the string. "I'll never be able to shoot as far as you did."

"Why? I've seen you swing a hammer. You're likely stronger than I am."

I almost drop everything right there. "I doubt that." But I draw the bow back another inch, and before I have a chance to hesitate—or even think about something like *aim*—I let go. The arrow shoots off the string with more power than I expect, and I'm glad for the tree at my back. But he was right: it soars past the tree he struck, going so far down the path that I have no idea where it lands.

Lord Tycho throws his hands up and whistles. "See? I told you." He pulls another arrow from the quiver.

"I didn't hit anything." But there's joy in his voice, so it lights a spark of joy in my chest, too.

"Who cares? Here."

I take another arrow and nock it on the string again. I blow a lock of hair out of my eyes and try to aim this time, focusing on the same tree he hit. It's a broad target, with a wide trunk. I take a breath and let it fly.

This arrow shears off some of the bark but sails past the tree.

"Even better." He pulls another arrow out of the quiver. "Soon I'll have to worry about you putting an arrow in *my* back."

The praise stokes the warmth in my chest—but it's a reminder of who he is and why he's here. He's this beautiful, strong, skilled noble- man, and I'm . . . well, I'm *me*. I frown. "My lord—I shouldn't—"

"Silver hell, Jax." He whacks me on the arm with the arrow. "Shut up. Shoot."

"Ow. Fine." This somehow feels like bickering with Cal.

But also not *at all* like bickering with Cal.

This time, the arrow cracks into the trunk six inches below the one he shot, just barely sticking. But it's there. I'm a little breathless, staring.

Lord Tycho—*no, just Tycho*—grins. "Do it again."

I should refuse. This isn't right. I have duties—and so does he, I'm sure.

But this is also the first time I've felt a flare of . . . of *challenge* from someone, especially another young man. The first time in a long while that I've felt a glimmer of pride, too. Is this some kind of militaristic camaraderie? Is this what I've missed by not becoming a soldier?

Or is this more?

I shoot another—and then another, until the quiver is nearly empty. Many of my arrows flew past the tree, but some did not. At least half a dozen are buried in the trunk near the first one Tycho shot.

"Hold on," Tycho says. "I'll fetch them. At least the ones I can find." Without waiting for an answer, he swings aboard Mercy and she lopes down the path.

I stare after him, bemused. And possibly a bit fascinated. I can't tell if it's *him* or if it's . . . all of this. My fingers have gone a bit numb from the cold, and my leg is stiff from bracing against the tree for so long, but I'd stand here all night if it meant this feeling in my chest wouldn't dissipate.

But I can't, and it will. Ultimately, this won't be a fond memory. It'll serve as a reminder of everything I lack. The thought makes me frown. I get my crutches underneath me again and straighten.

Tycho is already loping back, the quiver mostly full again. When he sees that I've moved away from the tree, he looks startled. "I know you're not bored of shooting."

"No—but Da will grow suspicious if I don't return soon." I hesitate. "It'll take me a while to make the walk back."

His expression darkens, but he nods. "As you say." He leaps down from the horse. "Here. You ride."

I inhale to refuse, but there's a note in his voice like the moment he smacked me in the arm with the arrow and challenged me to shoot.

What are you afraid of, Jax?

My heart is pounding. "Fine."

"Grab the saddle. Bend your leg. I'll boost you up there."

I do what he says, but when I'm facing the horse, I say, "You do know I can't ride."

"Well, you couldn't shoot an hour ago." Then his hands are on my leg, and suddenly I'm in the air. By some miracle I grab hold of her mane and keep myself from sliding out of the saddle. I take a deep breath and hold it. I feel very high off the ground, and there's nothing to keep me up here.

"Steady," he says, and like before, I don't know if that's for me or for the mare. But he picks up my crutches, ties them behind the saddle where the quiver was, and takes up the reins. "Just let your legs hang. She won't take a step wrong."

I nod. I don't trust my voice.

And then Mercy starts walking.

My breath catches and Tycho glances up, but I fix my eyes on the trail. I can't decide if I'm afraid or exhilarated. Probably both. Like shooting the arrows, I'm dreading the moment this ends, because the memory will only be painful, when the experience itself is bringing joy.

It's a pretty sedate pace, but judging by Tycho's stride, we're going twice as fast as I would on foot. As I relax into the rhythmic motion, I realize this is the closest I'm ever going to get to feeling this type of freedom. The thought makes my chest tighten, and I try to breathe around it. We've covered half the distance before I'm even aware that Tycho hasn't said a word; he's just striding beside the horse easily.

I thought healing the burn was a gift. Or showing me how to shoot arrows. Or the extra coins he paid for Mercy's shoes.

But this is the gift. *This.*

I'm going to get emotional in a moment and then I'll have to throw myself in the forge, so I force myself to talk.

"Were you a soldier?" I ask him. My voice is breathy, and I tell myself to knock it off. "Before you were the King's Courier?"

"I was," he says. "For a few years. I started as a recruit, and then a cadet, and then a cadet sergeant."

He seems young to reach rank, but he doesn't say this with pride. Just a statement of fact. "Did you like it?" I ask.

He shrugs. "I love the drills, the weapons. I'd match blades and spar from sunup to sundown if I could." He really would; I can hear it in his voice. He probably would have shot arrows till it was too dark to see.

Then he adds, "The actual soldiering . . ." Something in his voice darkens. "Not so much. After the Uprising, I was . . ." He hesitates. "I was glad to have an opportunity to do something else."

I wonder what that means. Surely he wasn't afraid. But then I think of Callyn's father and what they saw, and I'm not sure what to say.

He glances up. "Do you like blacksmithing?"

The question is startling, which is ridiculous. I'm not sure if anyone has ever asked me that. I've never known anything else. "I love watching iron take shape. But some of it gets tedious." I sigh. "I'm *forever* making nails."

He smiles. "I never really thought about that."

"I had a carpenter leave an entire jar of nails out in the rain and they all rusted. Of course he needed more *immediately*, so he stood over me the whole time, wanting to know why I couldn't make them faster." I roll my eyes and swear. "He's lucky I didn't nail his hand to the table."

Tycho bursts out laughing. It feels like I've won a prize. I smile and look away—and my eyes find the forge in the distance.

The sight of it steals the joy from my chest. I'm home. This is over. At least there's no rhythmic clanging, which must mean my father has given up on work and he's taking the silvers he got from Tycho to the alehouse. I've been spared any further humiliation.

"Is it hard?" says Tycho, and I blink. I've completely lost the track of our conversation.

"What?" I say.

"Making nails?"

"Oh. No. Rather quick, actually." I cut him a narrow glance, then offer half a smile as I mimic his faint accent. "Want to learn?"

My father must have been gone for a while, because the flames in the forge have cooled to nothing. I strike a match to light it, very aware of the way the shadows skip along the walls of the workshop, turning Tycho's hair to gold and making his weapons gleam. I was mostly teasing with my offer, but now he's leaning against the table, waiting, while I'm sitting on a stool, fidgeting with my tools.

Well—I was *partly* teasing.

I inwardly sigh. If I'm being honest with myself, I wasn't teasing at all.

I glance over. "I'm sure you have duties you should be attending to."

He winces a little. "I'll return to the Crystal City by tonight. I carry nothing of urgency this time." He pauses. "I'm sure news hasn't made it to Briarlock, but the queen intends to host a competition with Emberfall."

I nod without thinking. "I've heard a bit about that."

His eyebrows go up. "Really. Then word *has* spread quickly."

I almost freeze. I forgot that I heard about the Royal Challenge from Lady Karyl.

Tycho and I spent an hour in the woods shooting arrows, and somehow I forgot that he's an attendant to the king and queen, and I'm a poor blacksmith holding a note of treason in his pocket.

I'm such a *fool*.

I swallow, then shrug and poke at the forge. "We see a lot of lost horseshoes and broken carriages this time of year. Travelers always want to talk."

"I'm sure." He says this lightly, without a hint of suspicion. I feel guilty anyway.

The forge has begun to glow, but it's nowhere near red enough to heat iron, so I keep my eyes focused ahead and wish I had something to say. He's quiet, too, but I can feel the weight of his gaze, and I'm suddenly self-conscious.

"I sense I've made you uncomfortable again," he says.

"Oh, *now*?" I say. "Not when you were whacking me with an arrow?"

"Yes," he says. "Now."

I'm not sure what to say.

He's studying me. "Is it the magic?"

I look up in surprise. "What? No."

"Because it clearly unsettled your friend."

I frown. "Callyn's family has a bad history with magic."

"And you?"

I shake my head. Maybe I'm being disloyal to Callyn, but it's not the magic.

He frowns. "Do I make you nervous, Jax?"

Yes. For a thousand different reasons. But I don't say that.

He kicks at a stool near me, beside the forge, and says, "May I sit?"

My heart will never settle. "Sure."

He drops to sit beside me. "I spoke true earlier. When I came up the lane with Callyn's apple tarts, I really was just going to apologize and leave the food." He shrugs a little. "But . . . but then I saw your father."

I go very still.

"No!" Tycho says sharply. "I'm not sitting here saying I pity you. Silver hell, Jax." He makes a disgusted noise. "I should likely leave you in peace."

"You *were* going to leave me in peace. I offered a lesson."

That makes him smile, but only for a moment. His eyes are on the forge, and his expression is serious, firelight bouncing off his cheeks. "I wasn't born to privilege," he says slowly. "My father was a drunk who lost everything over a game of cards. My family suffered. Grey—Grey has been like a brother to me. A mentor. A friend. He taught me how to defend myself when . . ." He hesitates. "When I needed to know how.

And I love Lia Mara like a sister. My friends in the palace are the only family I know, but—" He swears and breaks off. "Forget it. I'm not even sure what I'm hoping to say."

I take my tongs and shove at the coals in the forge, then hold them his way. "Here," I say quietly. "Take one of those ingots of iron and bury it in the fire."

He does as I say, but I grab his wrist before he pulls the tongs out, leaving the bar there. "Don't let it go. We need to watch the color."

His wrist goes tense under my hand, which takes me by surprise. But he keeps hold of the tongs, and after a moment, he relaxes. I should probably let go of him.

But I don't. I chance a glance up.

Instead of looking at the forge, he's looking at me. This isn't just militaristic camaraderie.

Ah, this memory is *definitely* going to hurt.

"I do have duties," he says. "Responsibilities. Reasons for being here. But I've spent so much time as a soldier, so much time at court. I've done . . . so many things." He hesitates, flexing his hand, making the firelight glint dully on his rings. "I have a bit of magic, and people fear it. I have a bit of silver, and people think I'm a spoiled noble. That day I healed your hand . . . I thought you and Callyn were up to something. I didn't . . . I didn't realize that I'd grown so far from who I once was. That I would be seen as the type of person who'd drag a blacksmith into the woods to beat him senseless over a few honestly spoken words." He looks at me. "I didn't realize that I almost forgot what it was like to just be . . . Tycho."

My breath catches. I'm not sure what to say. I'm not sure what I *want* to say.

Either way, I don't get the chance, because Lord Alek chooses that exact moment to ride up the lane.

CHAPTER 17

TYCHO

I'm on my feet so quickly that I distantly register Jax's tongs rattling to the floor. My hand finds my sword, but I don't draw. Not yet.

Knowing Alek, it'll come to that, especially since he's not alone. Two guards ride behind, every bit as armed as I am.

I *knew* I sensed someone in the woods. I knew it, and I ignored it. All I carry is a letter from Rhen to Grey about the Royal Challenge, but for Alek, that would be enough. He'll steal what I have, just for a chance to prove that I shouldn't have this role. Just for a chance to take an easy shot at the royal family.

My eyes skip to Mercy. I could be on her back and galloping away in seconds, but they'd give chase. She's fast, but we've been riding hard for *weeks*, and they look fresh and alert. They'd probably take her down.

If I stand and fight, they'll probably take *me* down. I finished yesterday in a bloody battle with a scraver, and I never slept last night. My armor is damaged, held together by a few scraps of leather. And Alek has many allies among the Royal Houses, while I have few. If I hurt him, the political ramifications could be immense.

I remember Grey's voice in the barn. *He'd be a fool to ambush you.*
I guess we'll see in a moment.

"Tycho!" Alek says brightly, though his blue eyes spark with hostility. "You've found a role better suited for one of your station. What luck."

"What are you doing here?" I demand.

"We've already done this once." He dismounts from his horse. "I do not answer to you." Alek steps closer to me, and his eyes flick across my form, identifying every weakness, I'm sure. I just sat here telling Jax that I long to remember what it was like to just be Tycho, but now I need every ounce of authority my role can carry. I don't have the respect of every Royal House, but Alek is the only one to treat me as lesser so *openly*. It's jarring, and somehow it steals a shred of my confidence every single time.

Maybe Alek can sense that, because he steps even closer. "Why is the King's Courier lingering in a mud pit near the border?"

I set my jaw. "Why are *you*?"

"My business takes me all over Syhl Shallow. Yours, however, does not." He reaches out a hand as if to touch the breastplate of my armor. "Does the king know about your little diversions from duty?"

I smack his hand away. "You have no business here, Alek."

"Run along, Tycho, before you get hurt. Curl up in the palace with your master." His voice lowers, and he takes a step closer. "I'm sure he's missing his whipping boy."

My blood turns to ice. There's not much he could say that would stop me in my tracks, but that does it.

Alek glances at the forge at my back, his gaze settling on Jax. "Haven't you heard there are plots against the throne? I think the queen would be interested in hearing that her trusted messenger is having secret meetings with a roughshod laborer in the middle of nowhere."

"I am doing no such thing," I say.

"You've been speaking privately for *hours*. I'm sure the queen would feel rather betrayed." Alek doesn't draw a weapon, but his eyes skip over my form again. "Maybe we should see how much use that armor has left."

"My lord," says Jax quickly, his voice a rough rasp, and Alek's blue eyes shift left. "My lords—please—"

"Go in the house," I say to him.

"No," says Alek. "I have business with this blacksmith. Business *you* are interrupting."

"Find another," I snap.

"I've already hired this one." Alek looks at Jax. "It seems your hand is no longer injured."

Jax's breathing is tight and shallow. He looks from Alek to me and back, then swallows tightly.

I step in front of him. "Leave him alone, Alek."

He stops, glaring at me. "This is your last warning, Tycho. You have no right to interfere with my business dealings. You are not the king. You are not of the Queen's Guard. You are not even a soldier in the army any longer. You are a *messenger*."

I don't want to fight him. I don't. There are three of them and one of me.

Regardless of what I want, Alek tries to step past me, toward Jax, and I grab hold of his arm.

It's all the excuse he needs—and it's not like he needed one at all. Alek draws a blade, and almost without thought, I'm drawing my own, swinging. Deflecting. Fighting.

He's always been a good swordsman. He blocks every swing, matches every parry. A strain builds in my forearms, and I try to call magic to reinforce my strength, but it's sluggish. *I'm* sluggish.

I swing my blade viciously, knocking his sword out of his hand. One of his guards steps forward, but Alek ducks, using his dagger to deflect my second attack, and before I'm ready, he's stepped inside my guard.

His hand shoots out, catching me by the throat. He's quick, his fingers digging into the tendons there with vicious accuracy. One of his guards has a blade against my sword arm. The other has an arrow pointed at my throat. I collide with the work table, and Alek has me pinned.

"You can't kill me," I grit out.

"I can hurt you."

Yes. He can. He already is. The pressure of his hand on my throat is like a burn every time I inhale. It's reminding me of another time a man pinned me with a hand against my throat, and I have to force my thoughts to stay present, to stay *smart*. "The king will take your head off for this."

"For what? For preventing his messenger from committing treason? Don't think I haven't figured out how his hand was healed."

"I'm—not—committing—"

"Well, I certainly know what it *looks* like. Perhaps I should have my guards add a few more stripes to your back. Help you remember your place."

I surge against his hold and he laughs, shoving me back down. The edge of the work table is pressing into my spine.

"You're awfully brave with those magical rings," Alek says, his voice low. His blade glints in my peripheral vision. "Maybe I should cut your hands off and see how you fare."

My hands are wrapped around his wrist. I don't think. I let the magic flare. Flame erupts on his sleeves.

Alek shouts and jerks back, smacking out the flames. I'm suddenly free, choking on air, and my sword is gone, but one of my knives finds my hand.

I've never been so grateful for training. I step forward to throw—

Alek ducks my blade, deflecting with his bracer. His dagger stabs into my waist, just where the armor hangs a bit loose.

The pain is sharp and immediate, and it steals my breath. My knees hit the icy ground. I scrabble for the blade, but he's stabbed it deep. I try to breathe around the pain, to call for the magic in my ring, but I swear the blade reaches all the way to my spine. I'm wheezing, and I think I've got a hand on the ground now. There's too much blood, and I can't get a grip.

He's staring down at me. "You said I couldn't kill you. Let's see how true that is."

Jax is shouting, but I've lost track of where he is. I've lost track of what's happening. My forehead hits the ground. Blood is in my mouth. That can't be good.

"Now give me my message," Alek is saying.

I don't understand. My thoughts are full of pain and anguish. "What—what—"

But he's not talking to me. He's talking to Jax, who's nodding, his eyes wide and full of fear. "Yes, my lord." He holds out a folded, sealed piece of parchment. I watch it change hands.

Alek tucks it beneath his cloak. His breathing is a bit ragged, and I smell singed fabric. "As you see, Tycho, this has nothing to do with you."

"I'll find you," I growl, then cough on my own blood. "The king will—"

"The king will do nothing. You attacked me with magic. I defended myself. My guards witnessed it. This blacksmith witnessed it." He leans close, his hand catching my throat again, fingers digging in. "I *should* cut your hands off and watch you bleed to death."

My vision is blurring. I can't tell if it's lack of air or if it's all my horrific memories assaulting me at once. I want to curl into a ball, but I need to find my weapons. I need to—I need to—

"No!" Jax shouts, and glowing steel swings in front of me. Alek flinches back in surprise. The guards rush forward. Firelight glints on their weapons, and I hear a body hit the dirt.

But Alek laughs humorlessly. "No. Leave him. He's done his duty." Alek flings silver into the snow. "You have my thanks, boy."

I take a breath and cough on blood again. *"You're* committing treason."

"If I were committing treason, I'd kill you both right now."

My head is spinning with confusion and betrayal and uncertainty. Nothing makes sense. I'm not sure what to make of this. But they're turning away. I blink, and hooves pound the earth.

"My lord." Hands are pulling at my clothes, rolling me over. "My lord. *Tycho.*"

I blink again and I'm looking up at Jax. His hair has spilled loose from its knot, and it falls across his face. His hazel-green eyes look gold in the firelight. He's exquisite and terrifying. I can't tell if he's a friend or an enemy.

"Tell me what to do," he says in a rush. "Tell me—should I pull the blade?"

My hand is still struggling to get a grip on the hilt. I can't breathe. I can't speak. I can feel the magic, but there's so much damage, so much pain, and I'm having trouble focusing. I do know I can't heal with a blade in the way. I nod. At least I hope I'm nodding.

He takes hold. The dagger is wrenched free.

It drags a shout from my throat, then a sob. The blade hurts just as much coming out.

Jax is on his knees at my side, pressing his hands to the wound. He's swearing, looking from the wound to my face. There's a streak of blood on his cheek. "Can you heal it? Tell me you can heal it."

I don't know. *I don't know.* The pain is so intense I might vomit in the dirt. But stars flare in my vision as the magic begins to work, sparks of power swirling in my blood. It only takes a minute for the wound to close, but it's the longest minute in the history of time. My insides will take longer. Blood is still in my mouth, hot and metallic. I feel wrung out. Magic has a price, and I've paid it many times today.

But Jax is still kneeling above me, his eyes golden pools. That dagger is somewhere.

I have business with this blacksmith.

I roll away from him, staggering to my feet, landing in a crouch. I'm panting from the effort, but I've got weapons in hand.

His eyes widen, and he draws away. I watch his gaze go from my blades to my face and back.

"Was this a trap?" I growl, and my voice sounds like I've swallowed gravel.

"No!"

"Were you to delay me? Were you working with him?"

"You came *here!*" he snaps. "You dragged *me* into the woods!"

That's true. I have to breathe. I have to think.

"You should sit down," Jax says. He shifts toward me.

"*Stay where you are.*" I tighten my grip on my weapons.

He goes still. "You've lost a lot of blood."

"He said he hired you," I say.

"I was asked to hold a message for him," he says. "That's *all.*"

"What kind of message?"

"I don't know. I didn't read it."

I take a slow breath through my teeth. My head is beginning to clear. I study him. The feeling of betrayal is still thick in the air, sour and potent. But now that I'm looking at him, I can't tell if it's on my side, or if it's on his.

I just sat here and told him I long for the days when I was just Tycho—and now I'm facing him with weapons in hand.

But I told him about Lord Alek. I told him that he was a dangerous man—and he said *nothing.*

"What was that?" I grind out. "How did you stop him from—from cutting my hands off?"

Jax hesitates. "Most people won't mess with hot iron. I pulled the ingot out of the forge." He points.

The block of steel is lying in the dirt. I stare at it for a moment too long.

He's very lucky Alek and the guards didn't kill him. His blood could be spilling into the dirt right here beside me, and he wouldn't have Grey's rings to protect him.

Jax is right about today, too. It *was* my idea to come here. It was my idea to shoot arrows, to ride Mercy, to linger.

It was my idea to provoke Alek.

All my idea. All my fault.

I think the queen would be interested in hearing that her trusted messenger is having secret meetings with a roughshod laborer.

Politically tricky indeed. I slide the weapons back into their sheaths and run a hand across my face. I need to get to my feet. I need to get back to the Crystal City.

But I look at Jax. That wariness is back in his eyes. It had almost completely vanished when we were sitting by the forge. My blood is a rich red streak on his cheek. His hair is much longer than I'd thought, shining black tangles spilling down across his shoulder.

His cheeks redden as if he sees me staring, and he gathers most of his hair back into a knot at the back of his head, then shoves a thin bit of steel through to hold it in place.

I straighten, rising to my feet, but I feel a bit off balance. I jerk my armor into place—or as close as I can get. My trousers are tacky with blood along my hip, and an alarming amount has soaked into the dust at my feet. That dagger did a lot more damage than the scraver did. I'm nowhere near rested enough for this much healing magic. "I need to return to the palace."

"Maybe you should wait for a bit," he says.

I shake my head, and the world goes a bit fuzzy around the edges. I don't know where Alek went, but I can't decide which would be worse: him spreading rumors that I'm disloyal, or coming back to finish the job. I'm definitely not in any shape to defend myself now. I stumble as I approach the horse, and I have to grab hold of the strap for her breast-plate to keep myself on my feet.

"Are you sure you can ride?" Jax says.

"Better by the minute," I lie. I take a long breath before pulling Mercy's tether loose.

Jax stops in front of me. "My lord," he says softly. "I worry—"

I reach out a thumb to brush my blood off his cheek.

He freezes. My fingers graze the tangles of his hair. "Thank you," I say. "For . . . for what you did."

"I didn't do anything."

"You risked your life."

His breath catches, and he ducks away. "My lord—*Tycho*. You're not thinking clearly. You're in no condition to ride. Lord Alek could return—"

"Right. *Yes*. Lord Alek." I grab the saddle and *leap*. Somehow I end up on her back, but I know I'm going to rely on Mercy's steadiness to get me most of the way to the palace. I want to press my face into her withers, but I force myself upright. I inhale deeply, and it helps.

"Please," Jax says softly. "Wait."

"I can't."

Then I touch my heels to Mercy's sides, and we're off.

CHAPTER 18

CALLYN

By the time dusk falls, I've spent my afternoon slicing and measuring and pouring and kneading. I've been expecting Jax to show up to tell me what happened with Lord Tycho, but he hasn't appeared. Worry has started twisting in my gut. Did Jax tell him off again? Maybe he offended the young lord so badly that Tycho rode out of Briarlock for good. Part of me wants to scowl at the thought—but another part wonders if maybe that would be better.

I rub at the pendant under my shirt. I keep thinking of my mother and what *she'd* think of all this.

Nora edges up beside me, taking a damp rag to the wood to wipe it down. "You're waiting on Lord Tycho?"

"Definitely not."

She smiles. "I still think he's very handsome."

"Yes, you were very subtle."

She's quiet for a while, and when she finally speaks, her voice is small. "I know he has magic, but what if he fancies you?"

"Oh, Nora. Why would he fancy *me*?"

"Well, he *has* been here several times."

I suppose that's true. And she's right that he's rather striking. But I consider the magic in his rings, his loyalty to the king, and I shiver.

Nora is missing all the spots where flour has caked to the table, so I take the rag out of her hand to rub harder at the wood. "You know what Da did. And Lord Tycho is far above our station."

"He said he was born—"

"It doesn't matter where or how he was born," I say firmly. "He's clearly someone of consequence *now.*"

But I remember the intensity in his eyes when I said, *It wouldn't be right.* And he so evenly responded, *It wouldn't be wrong.*

I glance at the window, which only reveals the lightly falling snow beyond. An animal shrieks somewhere in the forest, and I shiver again.

"Maybe he fancies *me,*" she says. "He *did* call me Lady Nora."

I laugh. "You keep right on believing that."

She steps away from the table and twirls, but her patched hand-me-down skirts are too heavy to flare very much. Then she drops into a ridiculous curtsy. "Why, *yes,* Lord Tycho," she intones, "I would gladly take your hand in marriage. We shall have twenty-five children—"

I burst out laughing. "Twenty-five!"

"He seems *quite* virile—"

"Clouds above, Nora," I snap, as if he could possibly hear us. "Do you even know what that means?"

"Of course I do," she says pompously. She curtsies again. "For I am a *lady.*"

"I'm not sure I know many *ladies* who'd be commenting on . . . well, *that.*" I glance at the darkening window again. "I don't think he's coming back anyway, so you can save your marriage acceptance for someone else."

"Do you want to get married, Cal?"

For a second, I think she's being playful, so I almost give her a glib answer. But when I look over, her expression is serious, her eyes searching mine.

"I don't know," I say.

She grabs the broom from the corner. "Mama always used to say you were wasting your time pining after Jax. I never understood why. I think he'd make a good husband, too."

She says this so simply, but the words hit me like a rock. Nora was barely eight when our mother died, and it's rare that she mentions her. "Mama . . . what?"

Nora begins sweeping. "When you'd go up the lane to bring him sweetcakes, she'd always say it to Da." She glances over. "Don't you think Jax would make a good husband?"

"No. I mean—yes. He's very—" I stumble over my words. Jax is a lot of things. I spent way too much time thinking of the way he brushed flour off my cheek. Or the way he fled here after he burned his hand. "Jax is my friend. Our friend."

"I suppose he'll never have a soldier's pension," she prattles on, musing while she sweeps. "But you'd never want for new baking pans. And we could make *him* fetch the eggs every day!"

"So generous." I snort. "So now I'm marrying Jax?" I say, amused. "I thought I was marrying Lord Tycho."

"Marry them both." She winks at me. "I've read of such things."

I stare at her, torn between laughter and shock. "What on earth are you reading?"

"Mama's old books," she says. "She has so *many*."

Yes, she does. Stacks and stacks, high enough to line the back wall of my bedroom. When she wasn't on duty as a soldier, she'd be curled up in the bakery window with an old romance while Da was doing the mixing and measuring and baking. He used to tease her that we'd have plenty of kindling for the ovens, but he never dared. I had no idea Nora had started reading the love stories on her own. I want to chastise her, but I'm hit hard with a memory of reading with Jax after he hurt his leg. We weren't much older than Nora, and I remember giggling with him over the racy bits in some of Mother's books.

"Is that really what it's like?" I remember asking him.

He'd blushed *so* fiercely. "How should I know?"

It makes me smile now to remember it.

The door is thrust open roughly, making the bells jangle. I suck in a breath, wondering if it's Lord Tycho.

Instead, I get Lord Alek. My heart stumbles in my chest. "Nora," I hiss. "Go upstairs."

"*You* go ups—"

"Go!" I snap. I keep hold of my rag and move closer to the end of the table, where I keep my knives. Lord Alek is through the door, followed by two guards, and he glances after my sister, who's scurrying up the steps.

"Is your sister running from me?" he says.

"No, my lord," I lie. "I sent her to fetch some more rags. We were just about to close for the night."

"Then I'm just in time." He moves closer to the table, and I swallow. My left hand is flat against the wood by the knives, my right hand slowly moving the damp rag.

I remember thinking Tycho moved like a soldier, but this man moves like a predator. There's no easy smile, no light in his eyes. Just sharp features and tight movement. Even his red hair is thick and dark, making me think of the color of dried blood, his eyes blue and piercing like someone took the essence of ice and locked it in his gaze. When he draws close, I want to edge away.

"What would you like?" I say evenly. "I have fresh meat pies. One raisin loaf from this morning. Maybe even—"

"That's not why I'm here." He steps up to the side of the table.

My hand slips left, reaching for a knife.

He's quick, though, and he reaches out to smack my hand down against the wood, pinning it there.

I'm quick too. I snatch a knife with my opposite hand.

He grabs my wrist, his fingers pressing into the bones and tendons there. I try to jerk away, but he holds fast. It turns into a struggle, and I swear, aiming a kick for his shins.

Then my back hits the stone wall beside the oven, hard enough to make me cry out. He slams my wrists into the stone over my head, pinning them there. Only sheer luck keeps the knife in my hand instead of dropping it on my head.

"Cally-cal!" Nora is yelling. I hear the guards' boots shift against the floorboards.

"No!" I shout. "Nora, stay upstairs."

"Stay upstairs," Lord Alek calls more casually. "Your sister and I are only exchanging words." He glances at the knife in my fingers. "Right?"

My breathing is too quick, rough and furious. I strain against his hold, but he's too strong. He tightens his grip, and I have to bite back a whimper.

"Answer me," he says.

"Yes, my lord," I seethe.

"Now, tell your sister."

"We're just—we're exchanging words," I call. I draw a breath and try to keep my voice even. "Nora, it's all right. Go pick a book for us to read together."

I don't know if she listens, but I don't hear feet on the steps, and the guards haven't moved farther.

"I drew no weapon on you," Lord Alek says. "What stories has the blacksmith been telling you?" He pauses, his eyes narrowing. "Or have you been hearing lies from the king's fawning lackey?"

"No one needs to tell me any stories," I grit out. "I saw what you did to Jax."

His eyebrows go up. "What I did to *Jax*? Jax, who accused me of treason? Who demanded a fortune in silver to hold a slip of paper?" He leans closer. "If he doesn't like such dangerous games, he shouldn't play."

Damn, Jax. I knew he was asking too much. Risking too much.

"What were you going to do with the knife?" Lord Alek says.

I glare at him. "Let me go and I'll show you."

He laughs lightly. "I like you better than that greedy blacksmith." He pauses. "This is quite a welcome for a man who once saved your life. Was I wasting my time?"

My breath catches, because for a moment, I don't know what he's talking about.

And then, in a snap of realization, I *do*. I remember the flash of red hair, the loud clash of his sword stopping another.

She's a child! Get her out of here.

"The Uprising," I say. "That was *you*?"

Alek nods. "I find it fascinating that your friend accuses *me* of treason when you were right there on the palace steps yourself."

I try not to struggle, because I don't want to give him the satisfaction. "So were *you*."

"I had my own reasons for being there," he says. His blue eyes search mine. "You were there, but you didn't breach the castle. Where does your loyalty lie?"

"I wanted to protect my sister."

"That's not an answer." He pauses. "Jax made the choice to carry our messages, but why are you keeping his secrets?"

I swallow, and my breathing shakes. "He's my friend."

"So you're willing to hang alongside him? Is that it?"

I think of Jax sliding silver across the table to me. I think of finding him in the barn, milking Muddy May. I think of him blushing over stories or forging iron or letting me cry on his shoulder after my mother died.

Where does your loyalty lie?

With Nora. With Jax. With the people close to me.

"Yes," I whisper. "I am willing to hang next to him. Just like I was willing to take that blade meant for Nora."

Alek blinks, then withdraws a bit. His hands slide off my wrists.

"Maybe I *wasn't* wasting my time," he says. "Put down the knife."

I hesitate, glancing at his guards, then set it on the table. "Fine."

"Lady Karyl suggested that you were trustworthy," he says. "But she had not met you."

I resist the urge to rub at my wrists. "So you came to find out?"

"I did, in fact. I wasn't sure I recognized you on the first night I came here. I needed to return to be sure." He pauses. "But I don't like when people work for nothing more than silver. It makes it far too easy for them to be swayed by the highest bidder." He pauses, and his voice takes on a note of anger. "And I watched Jax spend the day with the King's Courier. It makes me wonder which side he's playing here."

Now it's my turn to stare. "He . . . he did?"

"He did indeed. I was going to wait and seek my message privately, but I determined it would be better to claim it before it could fall into the wrong hands."

Oh, Jax. *What are you doing?*

"Jax is trustworthy," I say. "I'd stake my life on it."

"Would you?" he says brightly. "I'm glad to hear it." He pauses. "Tell me why."

I fumble for words. "Because he's been my friend forever." That's all I want to say, but Lord Alek is still watching me intently. Waiting.

"Since . . . since before he lost his foot," I add. "Since we thought he'd be a soldier." I hesitate. "Since before my parents died."

"How did your parents die?"

The words pull at my heart, and I don't want to answer him—but surely he can find out. "My father—he was part of the Uprising." I swallow. "That's why we were there."

"Killed by the king's magic, then." He pauses. "And your mother? Was she involved as well?"

"No. She died in the war." My voice is so soft. "The war against Emberfall. She was slaughtered by the monster."

Lord Alek goes very still. "Our king was involved with that *monster*."

I swallow. "That's rumor."

"That's *fact*."

"I don't—I don't know—"

"He's a magesmith. His daughter is a magesmith." His lip curls. "That monster was created by magic. His bond with our queen was forged with magic." His voice drops. "Our country has been *stolen* by magic. Your blacksmith accuses me of treason. But our *king* commits the greatest treason of all." His eyes hold mine. He's so close, his voice so low. For the first time, I notice a light smattering of freckles across his nose, and it's the first sign of anything that makes him look less severe.

Then he adds, "That monster killed *my* mother as well."

My breath catches.

He nods. "And then the king and Tycho killed my sister. For daring to be the first to take a stand against magic."

I'm frozen in place. "Your sister was the queen's adviser," I whisper. Father used to tell us stories of the woman who found artifacts that could bind magic. *Iishellasan steel*, like Tycho's rings. There was supposedly a dagger that could kill the king.

"Yes," says Lord Alek. "She was. And my mother was a general in the Queen's Army. When that creature attacked, it tore through the officers first."

"That's what I heard as well." My voice is a broken rasp.

He hesitates, and his voice is very quiet. I don't know if we've simply surprised each other, but the air between us has somehow changed. "What was your mother's rank?"

I have to clear my throat. It's weird, and startling, to learn this about him. He must think so, too, because the way he's looking at me is different. It's no longer so calculating. Maybe that's what makes me answer. "My mother—she was a captain."

He frowns, his eyes tight. "So many good people were lost. Too many." His jaw is tight. "The old queen would have retaliated. *Was* going to retaliate. But after she died, Queen Lia Mara allied us with them—with *him*—less than six months later." He shakes his head and looks away. "My sister was a true loyalist—and she was slaughtered for it. When people air a grievance, they're accused of sedition. When we speak out against the king, we're accused of treason. Meanwhile, his power grows by the day. We're *lucky* that he was not raised among the magesmiths, that much of his power still remains a mystery. And the people of Syhl Shallow are simply supposed to yield to this? We're supposed to forget those who were lost?" He runs a hand across the back of his neck, and for the first time, I realize there are burn marks along the leather of his bracer, stretching up along his sleeve. "I come here to talk, and you pick up a knife because you think *I* am a threat. Yet you allow Tycho to sit in your window as if you've known him your entire life."

I don't know what to say. *Tycho frightened me too.*

"What happened to your arm?" I say quietly.

He blinks as if startled, then drops his hand to his side. "I demanded answers from the King's Courier, and he attacked me with magic."

He says this so evenly, but it makes my heart pound again, for an entirely different reason. Too much has happened. I've seen too many sides to this. Tycho may have saved Jax's hand—but now he's used his magic to attack Alek. Alek may have threatened Jax—but he once saved me and Nora.

I hesitate, then reach for his arm. "Are you burned? I have some salve."

"First you were going to kill me, and now you're going to mend my wounds?"

"I probably owe you for saving my life." Those words sound too heavy, and I dodge his gaze as I add, "But don't worry. I might still kill you."

He smiles, then offers his arm. The bracer looks like it took most of the damage, but at the bend of his elbow, his shirt has burned away to reveal a three-inch stretch of reddened, blistered skin that reminds me too much of the injury Jax received from the forge.

I fetch my jar of salve from under the work table, then smooth it onto the damaged skin.

He hisses a breath, and I fix him with a look. "Oh, don't be a baby."

"Don't be so cruel."

"If you don't like such dangerous games," I say, imitating his tone, "you shouldn't play."

He doesn't smile, but his eyes don't leave mine. The air is heavy and quiet between us. I grow very aware of the weight of his forearm in my hand, the curve of the muscle under the burn I'm treating.

I swallow and let go, then swipe my hands on the rag. "There. Now we're even."

"Indeed." After a moment, he takes a step back. "You say Jax is trustworthy. I think your friend is hungry for silver."

"No! He's just—we're—"

"It doesn't matter." Lord Alek pulls a folded piece of parchment out of his pocket and tosses it on the table. There's a smear of blood across the cream vellum, just a drop on the black-and-green seal I've seen before.

My breath catches. I don't touch it.

"Open it," he says.

My heart is pounding. We've been desperate to know what's inside these messages. Jax has been trying to re-create the seal for *days*. And now Alek just . . . wants me to open it?

"Go ahead," he urges.

I hesitate, then reach out for the folded paper. I slip my finger under the seal, and the paper tears slowly, then gives all the way.

2 *Full bolts of damask - purple*
3 *Full bolts of silk - white*
7 *Full bolts of muslin*
1 *Half bolt of cotton*

I don't read the entire list. My eyes flick back up to meet his. "It's—it's not a letter."

"Surely not. A fabric order. Some of my customers pay dearly for confidentiality."

"So—so these aren't letters of treason at all." I don't know whether to be disappointed or relieved.

"Not this one. I'm quite literally doing my job." He pauses. "I'll return in a fortnight, and you can tell me your decision then."

Two weeks. I make a quick calculation on whether we have enough silver to pay the tax collector now—and whether that will allow us enough time to gather more to pay what we owe.

But then I realize what he said, and I frown. "My decision on what?"

"I'm not sure I can trust Jax. But you and I are a bit alike, I think." He leans in, and his voice is very low. "A decision on whether to help me."

There's danger in his tone. *This* might just be a fabric order—or it might not. Or maybe only some of his messages are treasonous, mixed with regular ones to lessen the risk.

There's no way to know.

Before I can say anything, he straightens. "You have my thanks for the salve," he says. "How much for the meat pies?"

"Ah . . ." I scramble to make my thoughts make sense. "Five coppers apiece."

"Done." He glances at his guards. "Wrap them all. We can eat while we ride."

They do, and he pulls coins from his purse and slips them into my hand. "Think on my offer. It's not treason to question whether someone is loyal." He folds my fingers around the coins.

I nod. "Yes, my lord."

He keeps a grip on my hand, holding my fingers closed. "Don't tell the blacksmith."

I swallow hard. "But—"

He shrugs. "Your decision. Choose wisely. I make a very dangerous enemy, Callyn."

Oh, Jax. I think of him telling off Tycho. I have no *idea* what he might have done to the man in front of me. But I knew he was playing with fire—and I might be, too.

I don't know what to say.

So I nod. "I'm truly sorry about your mother. And your sister."

Some of the arrogant stillness seeps out of his expression again, and for an instant, he's not a terrifying lord, he's a young man who understands grief and loss as potently as I do. "I'm truly sorry about yours," he says softly.

Then he lifts my hand with the coins and brushes a kiss across my knuckles. Before I can react, he's through the door, and cold wind swirls into the bakery, making the fire flicker. Somewhere in the distant forest, an animal shrieks again, and I latch the door. My heart is pounding so hard I'm sure my sister can hear it upstairs.

Nora. I fly to the base of the stairs, but she's sitting there on the top step, just out of sight. Her eyes are wide.

"Don't marry that one," she whispers.

"Don't worry, I won't." But then I think to open my palm, and my breath catches.

No coppers at all.

Twenty silvers.

Don't tell the blacksmith.

Oh, Jax. I drop the coins into my skirt pocket and ease up the stairs to my sister.

CHAPTER 19

JAX

I don't sleep at all. I stare at the ceiling for hours. Part of me wants to run down the lane to tell Callyn everything that happened.

Another part wants to keep all of it bottled up inside my chest, to turn each moment around from every angle. Not just the fight with Alek. Everything that happened before.

And everything that happened after.

I keep thinking of the space of time when Tycho's thumb brushed the blood off my cheek. *You risked your life.*

But he was dazed and disoriented. Maybe it means nothing. I should've tried to keep him here. I'm not entirely sure how I would've done that, but there was so much blood. When he climbed aboard his horse, it wasn't graceful and sure. I have no way of knowing if he made it safely back to the Crystal City. Would Lord Alek have gone after him?

But he was gone, and I can't chase after a horse. I settled for kicking dirt over the blood in the workshop, then wiped Alek's dagger clean and hid it under my mattress. I imagine I can feel it through the layers of linen, straw, and feathers. Maybe that's what's keeping me awake. This traitorous dagger poking at me with reminders of everything I've done wrong.

When my father lumbers into the house after midnight, I let my eyes fall closed. He must stop in my doorway, because I can hear his heavy breath. The scent of ale is thick in the air. I lie in tense silence, wondering if he's going to wake me.

But no, his footsteps thump through the house, and eventually his door creaks closed.

I stare at the ceiling again and replay every moment.

I wasn't tricking you. I was tricking your father.

You're likely stronger than I am.

Silver hell, Jax. Shut up. Shoot. I can close my eyes and hear that one over and over again. I can see the challenge in his eyes.

After Alek stabbed him, I thought I was going to watch Tycho die in the dirt. But he used that magical ring, and then he rolled to his feet so quickly. He faced me with weapons in hand. That easy smile was gone, replaced by a vicious intensity. In an instant, he was a thousand times more terrifying than Lord Alek ever was.

You're working for him.

I'm not. Not really.

Am I?

I don't like this feeling. I want to reverse time. I want to gather every piece of silver I've "earned," just so I can give it back.

But for as generous as Tycho was, he's gone. He showed me how to shoot arrows. He let me ride his horse for a quarter hour. He can't save the forge. He probably won't return.

By the time the first spark of light glows at the horizon, I haven't slept. Another long day of hammering steel beside the forge awaits me. I think of yesterday, shooting arrows in the woods, the air so cold that it made my fingers ache. I remember the first arrow I shot, how Tycho put his hands in the air and whistled like it was some kind of victory. I remember grabbing his wrist to hold the iron in the fire, or the way he touched my cheek, his fingers grazing my hair.

I press my hands into my eyes, then reach for my crutches. I was right. The memory is only going to bring pain.

The steel rim of the forge is ice cold this morning, and I blow on my fingers while I wait for the coals to burn. I head for the far side of the work table and pull my sketch of the seal out from under the pile of random scrap metal and mismatched planks of wood that we keep for minor repairs.

I scowl and crumple the paper. I'm going to throw it into the forge.

But then I notice a curved stretch of wood at the bottom of the pile, thick with years of dust, and I remember my father's old bow, long since abandoned with the scraps. I move bars of iron and broken spades to get to the bottom, coughing when half of it crashes to the floor and sends a plume of dirt into my face.

It's surely useless by now, after so long, but I dig through the mess until I can pull it free. The wood is tacky with dirt and grime, and the string is coiled around the shaft. I expect it to be brittle or chewed by mice, but it seems fairly solid.

I rub a thumb against the bow, and beneath the filth, I discover a deep-red stain on the wood. The leather on the grip is dry-rotted, but I have more leather. I glance at the warming forge, waiting for all the iron I'll feed it today, then back down at the weapon in my hand.

I'm not even sure I remember how to string a bow. Or where the arrows are.

I shift a few more things below the workbench.

The arrows are there, though only four are usable. The others are snapped from the weight of everything we've piled on top of them over the years.

Four is better than nothing. Well—the arrowheads are rusted. At least that's something I can replace, and easily.

I hardly want to think about what I'm doing. I cast a glance at the door that leads into the house, as if my father might appear at any moment. I don't know what he'd say if he found me out here trying to string a bow. I don't want to find out.

I fetch a rag and some oil, along with some scraps of leather.

In less than an hour, I have a questionably strung bow, four arrows, and a pounding heart.

It's still early. Surely the forge can wait another half an hour.

I sling the bow over my shoulder, tuck the arrows under my belt, and take up my crutches.

I don't go anywhere near as far as we went yesterday, just halfway down the lane toward the bakery. Out of sight from both. The woods have brightened with early sunlight, and my breath eases out of my mouth in a long stream. I try to remember every instruction Tycho offered, from nocking the arrow to drawing my arm back to finding my aim.

I have no idea if this will work. The string might snap, or the arrows might go sideways, or my father might catch me, break the bow in half, and demand that I get back to the forge.

But maybe I don't want to settle for a pitiful memory.

What are you afraid of, Jax?

Less than I was yesterday.

I brace myself against a frozen tree, draw back the string, and shoot.

CHAPTER 20

TYCHO

I wake in a dim, unfamiliar room, lying on a narrow bed. A fire crackles somewhere nearby. I remember Alek and my hand flies to my waist, but my weapons are gone. My armor is gone. With a gasp, I shove myself upright.

"Slow down," Noah's voice calls from behind me, and then I realize where I am.

The infirmary. The Crystal Palace.

I . . . have no idea how I got here. Weak sunlight filters down from the windows, but I don't know if that means it's dawn or dusk. I remember arguing with Alek. Jax. The dagger. The pain.

I remember Jax saving my life. My blood was on his cheek. His eyes were shining in the light of the forge.

I remember climbing onto Mercy. I don't remember much after that.

But I remember *before*. Walking in the woods with Jax, watching the bitterness in his eyes soften into something like eagerness when the first arrow shot off the string. Sitting beside the forge when I should have been riding home. Feeling his hand close on my wrist. Sharing thoughts I haven't revealed to . . . anyone.

I almost forgot what it was like to just be . . . Tycho.

My cat is sleeping at my feet, but Noah appears in front of me with two steaming mugs, so Salam slithers off the cot to sneak beneath it.

Noah ignores the cat. "Here," he says, holding out a mug as he drops to sit on the cot beside me. I inhale the scent of oranges and cinnamon. "How's your head?"

I frown and lift a hand to my head, but nothing hurts. I'm in a simple linen tunic and loose trousers that I don't remember wearing. My frown deepens. "I don't remember getting here."

"Well." He takes a sip of the tea. "When you rode up to the guard station last night, you were unconscious."

I stare at him. "Really."

He nods. "Collapsed over your horse's neck," he says. "Covered in snow. Blood everywhere. They thought you might be dead."

I fight for memories, but after cantering out of Briarlock, none come. Oh, sweet Mercy. She brought me home. I'll need to bring her an entire bushel of apples.

I rub a hand over my face and take a sip of tea.

"Grey has been here every few hours," he says. "He's been waiting for you to wake up. But he said you'd healed anything critical on your own." He pauses. "He fixed the rest of it."

I remember crawling in the dirt in front of Jax's forge, wondering if I'd stay awake long enough to keep the magic working. Grey's magic will flare and protect him even if he's not consciously aware of it, but I don't have that luxury.

"I saw your armor," Noah says more slowly. "Who came after you?"

I look up—and hesitate.

"Should the answer to that wait for royal ears?" he says dryly. He rises from the cot. "Grey asked me to send word when you woke. I'll call for breakfast, too. You've got to be starving."

Breakfast. So it must be morning.

The king arrives before the food does, which takes me by surprise. His expression is tight and severe, and he's fully armed, which means they called him in from the training fields. Just as I'm about to tell him that I'm fine, that he didn't need to rush away from his soldiers, I realize that he's trailed by others. Jake, whose expression is unusually fierce instead of jovial. General Solt, one of the most formidable commanding officers when I was a recruit, who's no less intimidating now. Nolla Verin, sister and adviser to the queen, and also one of the most brutally powerful women I've ever met.

They're so imposing that I shove myself to my feet and stand at attention before remembering that I'm not a soldier anymore.

Did Alek make accusations against me? Do I need to explain myself? A ribbon of fear tugs at my spine. Training and protocol are so drilled into me that I nearly salute. "Your Majesty," I say to Grey.

"Who did this?" he demands. "You were still carrying silver, so it wasn't common thieves. I only found the one letter from Rhen. Were there more?"

"What?" I don't understand all the intensity, and it takes my thoughts a moment to catch up. "No. I wasn't attacked for what I carry. I wasn't—"

"Just tell us how many there were," says Nolla Verin. She cracks her knuckles.

"And which direction we have to go to find them," Jake adds darkly.

"It wasn't one fight." I stifle a grimace, because I'm responsible for both confrontations. "It was two, and the latter—"

"*Two,*" growls General Solt. "Tycho, where?"

They're completely getting the wrong idea here. They look like they're ready to call up the whole army, and I just want to lie down and pretend nothing happened. "The latter was Lord Alek," I say evenly. "So—"

"Alek!" Grey snaps.

"You don't need to go after him," I say.

"Oh, I don't?" he says sharply. "Nolla Verin. Go. Deliver a summons. Bring him back."

"Gladly." She's out of the doorway so quickly that I half expect her to drag Lord Alek back here in less than an hour—and that will lead nowhere good.

I stare at Grey. "Please do not rattle the Royal Houses on my behalf. I'm fine."

"You're lucky you made it to the gates. I saw you when they brought you in."

"It was a misunderstanding," I say. "We had—we had an altercation—"

"You found him in Briarlock again? Why did he attack you?"

"No—Grey, he didn't—it wasn't an *attack*." I grit my teeth, remembering. As usual, Alek pushed, but I responded. "Not *really*."

"You were soaked in blood," says Jake. He leans against the doorjamb. "Seems super friendly."

"And your armor," says Solt. "I haven't seen damage to armor like that since we left that scraver in Emberfall."

I scowl and inhale to protest, but there's just too much. I'm not sure how to explain things like this, with all of them in my face. I know their intentions are good, but I wasn't prepared to wake up and admit my failings to the most powerful people in the city.

"He just woke up," Noah calls gently from where he's sitting near his work bench. "Maybe you all could take it easy with the interrogation. He should probably sit down."

That doesn't help. "I'm *fine*," I say.

Grey studies me for the longest moment. After a while, he turns to Jake, and his voice is lower. "Go with Nolla Verin."

Jake nods and turns away from the doorway. "I've got your back, T," he yells over his shoulder to me.

"I'm counting on you to curb her temper," Grey calls. "Not to provoke it."

But Jake is already gone. Grey glances at Solt. "Return to the fields. I'll join you shortly."

The general departs—followed almost immediately by Noah, who says he needs to fetch some fresh turmeric from the kitchens. It leaves me facing the king alone. That should be better. In a way, it is.

In a way, it's not.

Grey puts out a hand, indicating the cot. "Sit."

I don't need to sit. I don't *want* to sit. But I feel like I've earned a reprimand, and there's no give in his tone, so I obey.

Once I'm seated, Grey unbuckles his cloak at his shoulder and drops it unceremoniously on the cot across from me. Then he drops himself right next to it and runs a hand across his jaw.

"When the guard station sent their first report," he says, his voice low, "they told me your horse brought back a body."

I go still.

"You were covered in snow," he continues. "Barely breathing. Blood everywhere, Tycho."

"I'm fine!" I hold up a hand. "Truly, Grey. I'm fine. The ring worked. I was exhausted, but Mercy got me—"

"You were half frozen to death," he says. "Your lips were blue. Another hour and you might have lost your fingers to frostbite."

I flex my hands. "Noah didn't mention the frostbite."

Grey gives me a look. "So you'll forgive me for sending Nolla Verin to fetch Lord Alek."

What did Alek say? *I think the queen would be interested in hearing that her trusted messenger is having secret meetings.* Lia Mara wouldn't believe him—but he wouldn't tell her in a private conversation. He'd say it in whatever way cast the greatest doubt on the royal family.

But if they haven't heard from Alek, then that means he hasn't been here to spread rumors about *me.*

"Tycho," says Grey. "Talk."

"I got to Briarlock earlier than I expected." I twist the mug in my hands, but I don't take a sip. "I've become friendly with a few people in town since Mercy threw a shoe, and I wanted to see if Alek had returned. He took me by surprise," I say. "But . . . I misread the moment. I thought he was there to hassle me. He was merely asking for a message that had been left for him."

Grey waits, studying me. When I say nothing more, he says, *"And?"*

"He provoked me," I admit. "And I . . . may have provoked him back."

"It must have been one hell of a provocation."

I wince, thinking of all the things Alek said. Since the moment I first met him, he's always known the right words to say. Every verbal taunt feels like it's a breath away from drawing blood. I can defend myself with blades and arrows, but when Alek whispers things like *whipping boy,* it always seems to crawl under my skin and turn me into a sniveling child again.

I don't want to share any of that with Grey. "We fought," I say. "He had guards with him."

He had his hands around my throat.

Grey knows my history, what happened to me when I was a child, but I don't want to share this detail either. I have to shake off the memory. "I threatened him with magic," I say. "I used it against him. He retaliated."

Grey thinks about that for a moment, studying me.

"Please," I say. "There is already enough tension over magic here. Don't go to war with the Royal Houses because of one incident."

I wish I could read his expression, but much like his brother, he's very good at schooling his face to hide everything that matters. "I will speak with Lia Mara. But I still expect Alek to explain his actions."

I nod. "As you say."

He's quiet, so I'm quiet, and I stare into my tea. The mug is warm against my fingers, but I can't shake the feeling that I've disappointed him, and I don't like it.

I'm sure you have duties, Jax said.

I shouldn't have strayed from them.

"You said two," Grey says eventually.

"What?"

"You said there were two battles. That Alek wasn't responsible for the state of your armor."

"Oh. Yes." I hesitate, wondering how this is going to go over. "I found Nakiis at a tourney in Gaulter. Kept in a cage, the way Iisak was." I pause. "They forced him to fight. Do you remember Journ?"

His eyebrows go up. "Of course."

I nod. "He was running the tourney there." I frown. "He told me they've kept Nakiis there for years."

"I will send soldiers. Have him liberated. I'm surprised you didn't send word immediately—"

"You don't need to. I broke in and freed him."

Grey goes still. "*Tycho.*"

I can't tell if he's shocked or outraged, so I rush on. "He was earning them too much silver! They weren't going to let him go. You remember how Worwick was with Iisak. So I paid the entry fee and faced him in the arena. At first, I don't think he knew who I was. But he did by the end. He had his claws over my throat, and he could've killed me, but he didn't. So I snuck back into the tourney that night, and I broke the lock. I offered to bring him back here, but he's—he's—" Grey's expression has darkened, so I falter for words. "He's *afraid*. Afraid of being trapped by another magesmith. He's worried you'll demand a debt for healing him years ago. I told him he would find friends here, but as soon as I broke the lock, he slammed through the door and disappeared."

He draws a long breath. "So the King's Courier entered a *tourney*," he says, "risking his *life*—"

"Again, I'm *fine*."

He gives me a narrow look, and I clamp my mouth shut and scowl.

"And you broke in!" Grey says. "What if you'd been caught? Can you imagine the scandal? We already have enough pressure from the Royal Houses."

"You would've done the same."

"No," he says fiercely. "I wouldn't."

"Because you're the king," I say, "and you wouldn't *need* to. Would you rather I had left him there?"

"For the two days it would've taken you to get *here*? Yes. I would have."

"It doesn't matter," I say tightly. "I freed him, and he's gone."

"You freed a *scraver* who bears resentment for *magesmiths*."

I'm not sure what to say to that.

Grey's voice is very careful. "He was not Iisak, Tycho. He was not your friend."

I have to look away.

He sits there, regarding me, and again, I feel as though I've earned a reprimand. Maybe I deserve one—or maybe I owe him an apology. But I don't feel remorse. Not about freeing Nakiis, and not about what happened with Alek.

Not about the time I spent with Jax.

Maybe Grey can sense my reticence, because he draws back a bit. "Did anyone see you?"

I inhale to say no, but then I stop. *Bailey.*

"A stable boy," I admit. "But he won't tell."

"You'd better hope he doesn't tell."

I scowl. "Who would believe him?"

"It takes little effort for a bit of rumor to cause a lot of grief," Grey says. "Especially after what happened with Alek. I don't need anyone thinking you're using magic for malicious reasons. And I don't need anyone casting doubt on your loyalty."

That makes me flush, and I glance away.

"Look at me," he says, and because his voice leaves no room for disobedience, I look at him.

"Your loyalty is not in question with *me.* But there are threats throughout both kingdoms." His voice is so low that there's no danger of him being overheard. "Like in Emberfall, we've discovered secret messages among shipments here in the Crystal City. We are trying to determine the source, but it's too widespread, too unfocused. There are no threats, simply declarations of movements and thoughts. There have been references to a game of chess, which we now think stands for the Royal Challenge that Lia Mara wishes to host." He pauses. "There have been mentions of pawns taking the king."

I stare at him. "I didn't know."

"There are few who do." He frowns, and for the first time, a flicker of worry crosses his face. "The queen is far sicker with this baby than she was with Sinna, but we cannot reveal any sign of weakness while unrest grows in the streets. It is important that now, more than ever, Syhl Shallow remains aligned with Emberfall. *You alone* carry missives between royals. Alek and others like him may imply you are unsuitable because of your birth, or because of your association with me, but that is because they do not want to call it what it is: a position of power and access."

I nod, but his eyes are intent on mine, his voice very serious. "Do not *ever* think your role is insignificant, or that the choices you make do not have far-reaching ramifications."

"Yes, Your Majesty," I say.

My voice is as serious as his, but it's rare that I call him that, and now I've done it twice in five minutes. He studies me, and I wonder if he thinks I'm being flippant. "Lia Mara suggested that perhaps you should travel with guards."

I scowl. She doesn't mean that as a punishment—but it would feel like one.

The corner of Grey's mouth turns up, *almost* a smile. "I thought that would be your reaction. I want you to stay here until we speak with Alek. But I told her I didn't think assigning guards was necessary yet."

"*Yet.*"

He loses the smile, but he reaches out to ruffle my hair, ending it with a friendly shove. It makes me feel like a child, which is never reassuring. I bristle.

He notices this look, too. "If you don't like people worrying about you, don't show up at the gates half-dead." He stands, tossing his cloak over one arm. "I need to return to the fields. I'll let you know once the others return with Alek."

I can't wait.

He's nearly through the door when I call him back. "Grey. Would you really have left Nakiis there?"

He turns. "Yes."

"Even before you were the king?" I press.

He hesitates. "I was a guardsman before I was the king," he says. "I would've followed orders, Tycho. Whatever that meant."

He's said that to me before. It feels more pointed now. I nod.

Once he's gone, Salam crawls out from under the cot and leaps up to sprawl beside me, erupting in purrs when I rub behind his ears. I don't understand how I felt so free yesterday, and now I'm one misstep away from being under guard when I leave the castle. I never mentioned Jax to Grey—or even the reason I lingered in Briarlock at all. I wasn't deliberately keeping any of that a secret, but it feels like one all the same.

Right this moment, I don't think I mind.

CHAPTER 21

CALLYN

I don't see Jax for three days.

The banging from the forge has been nonstop, though, so I know he's busy.

The first morning after Alek visited the bakery, I was relieved when Jax didn't wander down the lane, because I didn't want to feel like I was keeping a secret from my best friend. Alek's warnings kept pounding against the inside of my head. I don't know what to think about any of it. The message he showed me wasn't anything concerning—but I know they wouldn't be paying this much silver if they were all this innocuous. Was this a trick? A test? Did Jax fail? Will I?

And . . . *do I* want to carry these messages? Alek saved my life. Do I owe it to him? Jax was willing to do it for *me*. Does that mean I owe it to *him*?

But what was he doing with Lord Tycho? The last time we discussed this, Jax was going to try to fashion a new seal so we could discover the contents of these messages . . . but then he spent hours with the King's Courier?

I don't know what to make of any of it, and I don't like the way my stomach has begun to twist with feelings of distrust and betrayal—on both sides.

By the *third* morning, I'm beginning to wonder who's keeping more secrets: me or Jax.

He comes down the lane at midday, easing his way into the bakery with soot on his knuckles and an unconcerned expression on his face. "Hey, Cal," he says, like we just saw each other hours ago.

"Jax," I say in surprise.

Nora tackles him with a hug, and Jax smiles, letting go of a crutch long enough to give her braid a tug. "It's good to see you, too," he says.

Then his eyes meet mine, and I find a spark of wariness there. The distance between us feels like a hundred miles, and I'm not sure if it's on my side, or if it's on his.

My tongue feels tied up in knots.

He frowns and straightens. "I . . . wanted to talk to you," he says to me.

I swallow. "Sure."

Nora sighs dramatically. "I'm not going to collect eggs again, Jax. So don't even think about it. I'm tired of being left out of your gossip."

He rolls his eyes, but I shrug and say, "Fine, Nora. We'll go get the eggs. You watch the bakery."

She stares at me as I stride across the floor. "But Cally-cal—"

I hold the door for Jax, and then I let it slam in her face.

"She won't follow?" he says.

"She knows I'd cut her braids off in her sleep if she left the bakery unattended."

A bitter wind tugs at my skirts when we cross the barnyard, and I grab one of the milking buckets when we slip through the door. The hens do peck at my wrists, but I'm quick, easing the eggs into the steel bucket.

After a minute, I realize Jax hasn't said anything.

Neither have I.

"What did you want to talk about?" I ask him.

"I think I owe you an apology."

Of anything he could have said, that surprises me the most. I stop and turn to look at him. His hazel-green eyes are shadowed in the dim light of the barn.

"An apology?" I say. "Why?"

"Because I think I've lost the trust of the Truthbringers." He pauses. "I don't think they'll be having me carry any messages anymore."

I'm such an idiot that I almost say, *Oh! I knew that.* But Alek warned me to keep his visit a secret. Would I be putting Jax in danger if I revealed this? Would I be putting *myself* in danger? And where would all that leave Nora?

I don't know how this all got so complicated so fast.

I stop my thoughts and clear my throat. "Why not?"

"Lord Tycho came to the forge," he says. "A few days ago." He tells me how Tycho told Master Ellis a story about a broken carriage, how they spent the afternoon talking.

I remember what Alek said, about how Jax wasn't trustworthy. My heart sinks. "And you told him?" I say quietly.

"What?"

"You told Lord Tycho about the messages you've been carrying?"

"No!" Jax says in surprise. He shoves a loose lock of hair behind his ear. "You think I'd be standing here if I'd admitted *that*?"

I frown. "Then what happened?"

"Lord Alek showed up and demanded the letter." Jax looks away. "I hadn't had time to try to re-create the seal. I have no idea what it said. But Lord Tycho tried to get him to leave, and he wouldn't, so then they fought. And it—it was awful." Jax runs a hand across his jaw. "There was so much blood. I thought Lord Alek killed him."

My heart is pounding. I remember the smear of blood on the envelope. This had to be the same night Lord Alek came to the bakery.

But Lord Tycho attacked him with magic. I saw the injury myself.

And they fought over a message about fabrics? I just don't understand.

"Alek attacked him?" I say.

He twists up his face. "It seemed pretty mutual. Alek provoked him, but Tycho threatened him with magic. And when Alek put hands on him, Tycho set him on fire."

I remember Nora's voice when she talked about the way Tycho healed Jax. She wondered if he could melt the flesh from someone's bones.

"I don't like any of this," I say to him, and my voice is rough.

"I don't either." He pauses, taking a long breath that he blows out through his teeth. "I should've told you earlier, but Da has been spending so much time in the forge. And . . . I've felt so guilty about losing the silver, Cal."

"Never mind about the silver." I set the bucket of eggs in the straw beside my feet. "I'm glad you weren't hurt."

"I thought he was going to kill me."

"Tycho?"

Jax frowns. "No. Lord Alek." He pauses, and a new note enters his voice. "Tycho was . . ." He runs a hand over the back of his neck. "It doesn't matter. I'll likely never see him again."

I study him. "Lord Tycho was what?"

Jax shrugs. "It's nothing."

But it's not nothing. He's blushing. Just the tiniest bit. I'd attribute it to the cold if I didn't know him better.

I've been feeling guilty about keeping secrets, but suddenly I don't feel like I'm the only one.

"You *fancy* him," I whisper.

"No." But his blush deepens. "He's the King's Courier, Cal."

"Trust me. I know."

He blinks and studies me. "You're angry?"

I don't know what I am. I'm afraid. I'm desperate. I'm tired.

Underneath all of that, I feel like I've taken a fist to the gut. And it's stupid. I *know* it's stupid. I've known Jax forever, so it's silly to wonder why he wouldn't fancy *me*, when we've grown up alongside each other.

For my mother, the war was more important. For my father, avenging my mother was more important. For Jax . . .

Mama always used to say you were wasting your time pining after Jax. I never understood why.

I'm such an idiot. He's not rejecting me, and I know that, but my chest is tight and hot anyway.

He's choosing someone else. He's choosing someone else with *magic*.

"I need to go," I say, and suddenly I sound like I'm a breath away from crying. "If I don't get back in the bakery, Nora is going to come looking for me."

"You *are* angry." He's frowning now, his eyes locked on my face.

I pick up the bucket of eggs and turn for the barn door. "I'm glad you weren't hurt," I say.

"Cal!"

I toss him a look over my shoulder. "You're such a fool, Jax. You're lucky you weren't killed."

"Because of the silver? The Truthbringers? Cal, would you stop?"

I don't stop.

I'm halfway across the barnyard when he calls out to me. "Cal, I said I'm sorry."

"You didn't do anything wrong," I call back, and then I'm through the door into the bakery.

I stand there, breathing heavily, and I wait for him to come after me. He doesn't.

I called him a fool, but he's not.

I am.

"What's wrong?" Nora whispers. "What happened to Jax?"

"Nothing," I say, and to my surprise, I have to swipe tears out of my eyes.

I hear her boots rushing across the floor, and I expect her to burst through the door and go after Jax. Instead, I'm startled when her arms wrap around my waist.

"It's all right," she says softly. "Whatever it is, it's all right. I still love you, Cally-cal."

I hug her back. "For as annoying as you are," I say, "you have your moments."

"I'm only hugging you because you fetched the eggs."

It makes me laugh through my tears, but I quickly sober. It wasn't Jax's responsibility to save the bakery. He's always been my best friend, and nothing more. He can fancy whoever he likes.

My responsibility is to Nora. To the bakery. To myself.

Lord Alek asked if I'd be willing to hang right alongside my best friend, and I said yes. I meant it when I said it.

But honestly, I'd rather not hang at all.

I wonder what Mother would think of Lord Alek and the Truth-bringers. I remember how she used to tell me to throw a stone over the mountain to crush the skull of soldiers in Emberfall.

Emberfall, the birthplace of our king. The king, whose magic supposedly summoned that monster that killed her.

The king, whose magic is in those rings on Tycho's fingers.

I don't have to wonder. I know what side she'd be on.

Mama always used to say you were wasting your time pining after Jax.

She was right. Maybe she was right about a lot of things.

No matter what happened with Jax and Lord Tycho, he was putting himself at risk to help save us both. My parents put themselves at risk for the same reason.

For the first time in my life, I have a chance to do the same thing.

When Lord Alek returns, I take his note, I take his silver, and I keep my mouth shut.

CHAPTER 22

TYCHO

Despite the king's summons, Lord Alek does not appear.

He's traveling, we're told by the servants of his House, reviewing shipments and deliveries of wool and silk, but the order will be obeyed the *instant* he arrives. A message is received detailing Alek's accounting of what happened, and just as I expected, he paints me as the assailant, that he feared for his life when confronted with my "limitless magical power." He says he was merely accepting a confidential message about a fabric delivery—and sends "proof" by way of an opened blood-stained letter that bears his House seal. He calls for me to have the rings stripped away if I can't be trusted to use them responsibly.

I spend a lot of nights not sleeping. I worry about Nakiis, the scraver who might bear animosity toward Grey. I think about Alek, and whether he's up to no good—or if he simply hates me and anything to do with magic. I consider Prince Rhen, and his comments about *politically tricky* rivals, and whether this Royal Challenge will make any impact on the people of Syhl Shallow and Emberfall—or if a competition will just be an excuse for more rivalry to breed.

And when it's very late, and very dark, and the palace is quiet, I think about Jax: his watchful eyes, his cautious smile, his fierce determination that revealed itself in the most surprising ways. Like how he seemed almost afraid to succeed at something like archery—followed by clear eagerness to learn once he didn't fail. I think about his hand on my wrist when we sat by the forge, how I wanted to pull away at first. I think about how his voice was low and soothing, how his fingers were so gentle against my skin that it held me in place.

I think about Jax more often than I'd like to admit.

I keep waiting for an assignment to return to Emberfall, just so I can ride through Briarlock again. But I'm not given any messages to carry aside from brief, unimportant missives to local nobles. At first, this seems typical, but as days—and then weeks—go by, boredom begins to set in, and I seek out further duties.

"Remain here," Grey says every time I ask. "I have nothing yet to send to Rhen." He's tense and distracted, his eyes hard when I see him on the training fields. Lia Mara has been staying out of the public eye—the only visible hint that she's unwell, but I know she hasn't been sleeping. And neither, it seems, has Grey.

"It's been many weeks," I eventually say. "I could see if he's discovered any further troubling messages—"

"Tycho," he says firmly. "*Stay here.*"

Excitement for the Royal Challenge has built among the palace staff and the soldiers. Preparations for the first competition in Emberfall have continued, which means *someone* is carrying messages across the border, just not me. I know it's not personal—the Royal Challenge is no longer a secret—but I can't shake the feeling that I've let the king down, that this is a punishment. My role always felt like freedom, but now I feel as chained as Nakiis.

I try to keep busy, spending time on the training fields every morning, running the courses or sparring with any recruits looking for extra hours with a blade in their hands. But when Grey appears, his shadowed expression becomes a daily reminder of what I've done wrong. I always seek my horse and ride into the woods surrounding the soldier barracks, or I disappear into the palace. I begin to dine with the soldiers in the mess hall, or with Noah in the infirmary, skipping morning meals altogether.

I'm probably not being subtle. But after a *month* passes and I've been given no duties at all, I no longer care about subtlety.

By the sixth week, the wind and snow from the mountains have lessened, the air softening as winter begins to yield to spring. Mercy sheds her winter coat, and the servants pack heavy cloaks away. Buds form in the palace gardens, the promise of color to come. When I spar on the training fields, we're sweating under our armor instead of shivering. My mood turns lighter than it's been in weeks.

One morning, Jake surprises me by arriving on the fields early, when the air is still fresh and cold. I'm in the middle of a match with first-year recruits who've barely graduated from wooden training swords.

"Come on, T," he says, drawing his weapon. "Let's give them a real demonstration."

There's no bitterness between me and Jake, and I'm not one to turn down a challenge. I grin and whirl to face him almost before he's ready. He's athletic and blocks quickly, though. He's strong and relentless with a blade, but there's not a lot of finesse to Jake's fighting: he'll throw a punch or swing a dagger or drive your face right into the dirt if he gets the chance.

But this is my element: swordplay in the sunlight, facing someone who won't easily yield. When he tries to get me off my feet, I counterattack and get him off his. But throwing knives unexpectedly spin free of his hands, forcing me to keep my distance, allowing him to get his feet underneath him again. A small crowd has gathered, mostly the early soldiers, but I keep my eyes on the battle before me.

Jake swings hard, forcing me to yield ground, and I swear. A light of victory glints in his eyes, and he bears down, single-minded and ruthless. "You're going down, T."

I smile and block, then attack just as hard. "We'll see."

A voice speaks from behind me. "Tycho won't go down."

Grey. Silver hell. I grit my teeth and try to focus. What was supposed to be fun now feels like *pressure.* Especially when Jake takes advantage of my moment of distraction. He spins and tries to hook my blade. It puts him close, and he's nearly strong enough to wrench the sword out of my hand.

This reminds me of the battle with Nakiis. Or the fight with Alek. All the mistakes I made when I let my guard down. Grey is here, judging every movement, every step.

I can't break Jake's hold, so I draw my dagger and aim for his throat. He jerks back in surprise, but it's all I need. I bring my sword down, and he's off balance, so he can't block effectively. Now it's his turn to swear. He's going for his own dagger, but I slam my shoulder into him hard. He grabs hold of my armor, and we go down together. We roll, grappling for leverage. I feel his fist connect with the side of my rib cage, right at the base of my armor.

It's no harder than I'm used to, but it steals my breath. It's right where Alek stabbed me.

I blink and in my mind, it's night. There's snow on the ground and the forge is glowing.

Perhaps I should have my guards add a few more stripes to your back. Help you remember your place.

I swing a fist without thinking. His head snaps to the side. I can feel his surprise, but now I've got the advantage. I pin his arm before he can swing a dagger this time, and I draw back my fist again.

"Tycho." A hand catches my arm. "Hold."

It's Grey. I'm panting, my arm straining against his grip. The sky is blue and the air is warm. Below me, Jake has blood on his lip, and his jaw is already reddening. "What the hell, T. I said I *yield*."

I stare at him for a moment. It looks like I've hit him more than once. "Jake. I—I'm—"

"It's fine. Let me up."

Grey lets me go, and I get to my feet. I put out a hand to Jake.

He spits blood at the turf—but he takes my hand. "What got into you?"

"I don't know." My side aches where he punched me, and my hand is tight and sore. I flex my fingers. It *feels* like I hit him more than once. I don't know what made me so angry. "I'm sorry."

"Don't be sorry." He studies me, then claps me on the shoulder. "Gave them a good lesson on being cocky. I thought I had you."

He nearly did, but I don't say that.

"Find your units," Grey says to the gathered recruits. "We'll run drills in ten minutes."

My insides are a jangled mess. My emotions won't settle anywhere. I don't know how I went from lighthearted sparring to slamming my fist into a friend's face.

Grey is studying me.

Oh wait. Now I know.

I slide my weapons into their sheaths. I haven't met his eyes yet.

"I have messages for you to take to Rhen," he says. "They're bound and ready."

That gets my attention. I look up, my irritation forgotten. "Of course," I say readily. Relief floods my veins. I haven't failed. "I can leave this morning."

"Good. Jake will go with you."

The breath I'm inhaling turns to ice. I'm not sure what expression takes over my face, but it must not be good, because Grey holds my gaze.

I don't know if I take a step or make a sound or just look like fire, but

Jake hooks an arm around my neck and begins to pull me away. "Come on, T. We're going to have a great time."

I let him drag me.

The alternative is getting into it with the king of Emberfall in the middle of the training fields, and I don't want to do that.

But he's watching Jake drag me, and I'm sure he can read every thought I'm not voicing.

"Let me go," I say to Jake.

To my surprise, he does—but he throws an arm across my shoulders instead. "I know that look. Keep walking."

I grit my teeth and do it. "You knew," I say. "You knew when you came out here and asked if I wanted to spar."

"I did," he says. "But Grey wanted to tell you."

I say nothing and stomp alongside him. Now I want to punch him *again*.

"I told him I wanted to see my sister," Jake says. "It's not a punishment."

I grunt and set my jaw. I don't believe that at *all*. "I'll be ready to leave in an hour. Try to keep up."

We ride hard and fast toward the border. The air is brisk and the footing is sure, so Mercy makes the miles vanish. When we near the road that leads to Briarlock, every instinct is begging me to call Jake to turn, to wait.

As if she can read my thoughts, Mercy slows as we near the signpost.

I hesitate, considering—but Jax has probably forgotten I exist. We shot arrows and shared apple tarts. It was fleeting. A diversion. His father will drink himself to death and Jax will end up marrying Callyn and they'll have a dozen beautiful children.

I scowl, cluck to Mercy with my tongue, and she puts her head down to flatten into a gallop.

I could talk to Jacob for a distraction, but I'm worried he's going to dig at me about Grey, and that's not better. I set a hard pace instead. It pays off, because when we stop at night, we've covered more ground than I usually do, and we're both too tired to do anything more than pitch forward into sleep.

By the third afternoon, however, heavy clouds roll over Emberfall, bringing cold rains, with enough wind and lightning to force us into an inn earlier than I'd like. I see to the horses while Jake arranges for lodging. There are men in the stables, speaking low while they rub down their own horses, but I'm so tangled up with my own thoughts that I'm barely paying them any attention.

But then one of them says, "I haven't seen that much damage to an animal since that monster was ravaging the towns."

"When I was in Gaulter," the other man says, "I heard the mountain lions would sometimes get their livestock."

"This wasn't anywhere near the mountains," says the first. "Three of my best ewes, clawed from neck to flank."

I turn Mercy loose in her stall, then latch the door slowly, listening.

"I heard this king once conjured a monster just like the old one," the first man continues roughly. "Were you at the town meeting when those Truthbringers were talking about the things he's done in Syhl Shallow?"

"I don't care what he does over there. After the way they marched on us, they deserve whatever they get. The king wouldn't turn a monster on his own people."

"*Are* we his people?" the first man scoffs. "How long has that bastard been in Syhl Shallow?"

I'm frozen in place. I shake out my saddle blanket again, just for an excuse to be in the barn. It reminds me of the way Callyn was terrified of my magic, or the way Nora made whimsical comments about little Sinna having powers of her own. It's so odd to be on both sides of this: to *know* that the king and queen truly do care about their people, but to hear the way gossip and rumor fly through towns so quickly that Grey and Lia Mara could never hope to stop it. Just like the conversation I'm hearing right now: anecdotes are accepted as fact, while true announcements from the Crown are viewed with skepticism—if not outright suspicion.

"Marlon," the second man is saying. "Don't be spinning stories about magic just because you don't have enough dogs watching your sheep. I suspect Bethany might have a few words about the ale you've been drinking."

"Dogs wouldn't have stopped whatever did this! It's not normal, I tell you. I think those Truthbringers might be right. Whatever magic they have on the other side of the border is coming here . . ."

His voice trails off as they walk out of the barn.

I try to decide whether any of this is significant. We've known that Truthbringers were becoming more prevalent on this side of the border. It's not like wariness about magic is exclusive to Syhl Shallow. Emberfall has its own share of trauma.

It's just a few dead ewes, though. Why would anyone do *that* with magic? We're too far southeast for mountain lions, but wolves aren't uncommon here. But then I realize what he said.

Three of my best ewes, clawed from neck to flank.

My heart thumps hard in my chest. I know a creature with claws that could do damage like that. A creature I broke out of a cage weeks ago.

Maybe the king was right.

I scowl, finish with the horses, then head for the inn.

I plan to lock myself in a room, but Jake has found a table near the hearth, and there's enough food to feed an army.

"Quit hiding from conversation," he calls to me mercilessly. "Sit and eat."

I sigh and drop into a chair. "I'm not hiding."

"Oh really?" He grins and grabs a roasted chicken leg. "Has someone been chasing us?"

Maybe being away from the Crystal City has taken some of my edge off, because that makes me smile. "We're not going *that* fast."

"Wait—are you *smiling*?" He reaches out to grab my chin. "Hold on—is this a disguise?"

I knock his hand away, but my smile widens. "Stop it."

"Grey should have told me to drag you away from the palace weeks ago."

That's a reminder I didn't need. The genial expression slips off my face. I've been irritated since I made the decision to skip the turn to Briarlock, and I can't seem to shake it.

Jax may have forgotten about me, but I haven't forgotten about him.

"Oops," Jake says. "I broke it."

"I don't need a guardian, Jake. I'm not a child."

He pushes a platter of food toward me. "Who said you did?"

I give him a look. "You're here."

"I really did want to see my sister."

I finally pick up a chicken leg of my own. "You can see Harper anytime you want."

"Maybe I wanted the pleasant company."

I grunt and eat my food.

"Just like that," he agrees.

I say nothing. We eat. The inn is packed with people trying to escape the rain, making the space too warm when combined with the heat from the hearth. No one draws near our table, though. Jake is a good four or five inches taller than I am, and broader across the shoulders. He's not imposing—at least, *I* don't think so—but he's got a solid build, and eyes that promise a willingness to brawl at any given moment. Strangers usually give him a wide berth.

I've always liked him. As a couple, he and Noah couldn't be more different. Noah is coolly practical and has no taste for violence. Jacob would step into a tavern fight just to stave off boredom. That bellicose spirit is part of why he's so good with the recruits—and why he and the king are such close friends.

I have no doubt there's a reason Grey chose him to accompany me instead of one of the palace guards. It's the same reason I've been pushing the pace and keeping my mouth shut: Jake will tell Grey everything I say and do.

At this point, I would have preferred a reprimand.

"He doesn't think you need a guardian," Jake eventually says.

I take a second slab of meat. "Good. Go home."

"Wow!" His eyebrows go up. "First you beat the crap out of me, and now—"

"I didn't beat the crap out of you."

He doesn't respond to that. I keep my eyes on my food.

Eventually, his voice drops, and he says, "Why would you break into a tourney?"

I swear. "Is that why he wasn't sending me anywhere? Does he think there are chained-up scravers all over the countryside?" As I say the word *countryside*, I think of those three ewes the men were talking about in the stable, and I have to shake it off. "Iisak was your friend, too, Jake."

"Iisak was. Nakiis wasn't *anyone's* friend."

"I just let him out of a cage. He's scared of being bound by a magesmith. He wants nothing to do with Grey."

"You hope."

He's right. I do hope.

I still don't regret what I did.

Jake is studying me. "Grey is also worried that Alek is going to spread rumors that you can't be trusted with magic."

That's a little too close to what Alek himself said right to my face, and I scowl. "I shouldn't have threatened him."

"He shouldn't have laid a hand on you." Jake frowns. "We searched his fabric shipments. Lia Mara thought we'd find messages like those from Emberfall."

I snap my head around. "Really."

He nods. "Grey might have told you if you weren't working so hard to avoid him."

That has the sound of a trap waiting to be sprung, and I'm no fool. "Did you find anything?"

"No," he admits. "Not among Alek's shipments. Not among anything that can be traced to the Royal Houses. But Grey suspects threats about the Royal Challenge."

"Threats to him, or to Lia Mara?"

"To him." He pauses, and his voice drops further. "The people are always vocal in their love for her. They're afraid of him."

I think about that evening with Jax, when Alek stopped to pick up a message. Would he be so bold as to pick up some kind of treasonous message right in front of me?

Maybe I *should* have stopped in Briarlock. Maybe I should have tried to find out.

Maybe I'm just looking for a reason to stop.

"What are you thinking?" says Jake.

I look up. "Rhen thought perhaps the different shipments weren't about passing messages of worth. That they're trying to establish a method that's *not* caught."

"So when we find it in a sack of grain, they stop sending them that way."

"Yes." I hesitate. "Alek was picking up a message from the black-smith in Briarlock."

Jake studies me. "You think maybe all these messages in shipments are a decoy? That they're using trade workers in the towns for the *real* ones?"

I think of Jax, his hazel-green eyes boring into mine as I bled all over the floor of his workshop—just after Alek had thrown a handful of coins at him for holding a sealed message.

It's not enough. That message could've been from anything.

I consider the first day I walked into the bakery, the first time I saw Alek in Briarlock. The tension was thick enough that I worried I'd walked right into a battle.

And then the next time I was there, Callyn was scrambling to pick up all those coins from the floor.

Look at all that silver! little Nora said. *We made that much today?*

My heart clenches. Her voice was so bright. I remember what it was like to be desperate.

"Maybe," I say to Jake, my mood darkening. "Or maybe I just hate Alek enough to want a reason for someone to lock him up."

He doesn't say anything to that, and I pick at my food.

"Something else is up with you," he says.

"Nothing," I say, tearing a biscuit into pieces that I gracelessly shove into my mouth. "Truly."

But as I say the words, again I'm reminded of what Noah said, how I keep people at arm's length. I almost wish someone *would* start a brawl while we're sitting here, just so I could escape Jake's careful scrutiny.

I should have stopped. I should have asked.

I should have done a lot of things.

"What's his name?" Jake says, and I choke on a mouthful of biscuit.

"Who?" I say, when I can breathe.

He looks at me quizzically. "The tradesman. The blacksmith with the message."

Oh. That one. "Jax."

"Do you remember how to find his forge?" he asks.

I school my face to remain neutral, and it takes a lot more effort than it should. "Probably," I say.

"We should stop. On the way back. Check it out."

My heart skips in my chest, and it takes everything—*everything*—I have not to ask if he'd like to turn back right this very second.

But I know my duties, and if I've learned anything from Grey, it's how to swallow emotion and stick to the matter at hand.

So I nod, then shrug, then reach for another biscuit. "As you say."

CHAPTER 23

CALLYN

The world shifts into spring like it's revealing a poorly kept secret: bitter winds and icy mornings yield to sunlit afternoons and bursts of greenery that appear overnight. I'm always glad when milder weather sneaks into Briarlock. My fingers don't freeze to the bone while I'm trying to milk May, and Nora doesn't give me as much trouble when I tell her to fetch the eggs. I've held two more messages for Lord Alek and Lady Karyl now, with forty more silvers to show for it. The coins are in a wooden box I keep hidden beneath my mattress, and I feel guilty about every single one.

I haven't told Jax. I know where the coins are, and as soon as this is all done, I plan to give him his half. But every time I see him, which hasn't been often, I think of our last meeting. He didn't betray me, but disappointment and loss lurk in my thoughts anyway.

It doesn't help that Jax has been keeping his distance, too.

Maybe it's better this way. I can't shake the memory of Lord Alek's threats, and I worry that the nobleman is going to swoop down from the trees and wrap a rope around Jax's neck if I dare to speak to my friend.

Or . . . maybe not. Alek's visits have been brief, but not unkind. He always buys whatever the bakery hasn't sold for the day, and while he's arrogant, he's never condescending. On his second visit, when Nora scurried up the steps upon seeing him again, Lord Alek called up the stairs after her. "Surely you have a bit of your sister's bravery. You clearly share her beauty."

"She shares my common sense, too," I said to him, loudly enough for her to hear. "Which means she won't fall for pretty words from bold men."

He looked at me without a hint of humor. "Those aren't pretty words."

Nora poked her head down the steps. "I think they are," she whispered loudly, and he smiled.

She didn't run from him the next time.

Lady Karyl is more aloof, but she also buys a few sweetcakes when she comes for her messages, and on her second visit, she buys twice as many. She also comments sternly on Nora's posture. "You are speaking to a lady from one of the Royal Houses, girl, and I understand your mother was an officer in the Queen's Army. You should stand tall." Then she took my sister's shoulders in hand and made her stand up straight.

I expected Nora to mouth off—or to wither from embarrassment, like I was doing. But my sister nodded solemnly and said, "Yes, my lady."

Later, when Lady Karyl was gone, Nora said, "She reminds me of Mother. I like her two-colored eyes, don't you?" My sister has been standing more properly ever since.

I don't want to like either of them, especially because I know how they treated Jax. It's hard to reconcile the way they treat *me* with the stories of how they treated *him*. But just when I start to think I should wash my hands of all of it, business for the bakery begins to flourish. I've never seen so many customers, ranging from the lowest common-ers to wealthy nobles who flip silver onto my counter without think-ing. Some are travelers, boasting about their intentions for the Royal Challenge, whispering about the queen's new pregnancy. A new baby is always cause for celebration, but there are worries about the birth of another magesmith, and I hear them all. The bakery is a bit off the beaten path, so random travelers and gossip can't account for *all* this new business.

Then one morning I hear one well-coiffed woman mention to her companion, "Alek was right. These pastries are *divine*. Well worth the journey."

Her companion murmured back, "Did you hear him say her father was a part of the Uprising? I *told* my husband that the Truthbringers would find more allies in these remote towns. I simply feel safer know-ing we're far from the king's magic."

I looked up in surprise when she said *that*, and the woman caught my eye and gave me a knowing smile, and then a nod.

For a frozen moment, I wasn't sure what to do. But I knew what my *mother* would do.

I nodded back. "Yes, my lady," I said quietly. "I do too."

If I hate anything, it's that I feel like I can't trust my instincts about anyone lately. Tycho was so kind, and he clearly has the favor of the king. But he used his magic to heal Jax's hand! Like it had never hap-pened! Just because of a few rings? Who else has them? What else can they do? It's terrifying to think that the king isn't the only one who can wield such power. It's not as if Tycho has only ever used it for benevolent reasons. I saw the burn to Lord Alek's arm.

And while no one would ever label Lord Alek as *kind*, he hasn't been cruel to me or to Nora. He saved our lives! He could've abandoned

Briarlock altogether, instead of bringing his business to me when Jax's actions upset him.

The warmer weather doesn't stop the rain from falling, and it doesn't stop the chores in the barn. I've been so busy in the bakery that much of what I could accomplish in the daytime has now been shifted to the evening. Mucking stalls is miserable in any weather, but particularly so when I have to push a wheelbarrow through the mud. The barn is only half done, and I'm all the way soaked, my hair a sodden rope hanging down over my shoulder. Once the sun goes down, the nights are a reminder that winter isn't a distant memory yet, and I'm shivering while I push the wheelbarrow back inside to clean out the cow's area. A persistent dripping is somewhere in the corner behind the henhouse, and I don't want to investigate to find out how bad it is. It's a miracle that the barn hasn't fallen down entirely.

A scratch at the wood overhead makes me freeze and look up. Somewhere out in the night, I hear an animal screech, and I jump. We had foxes get into the henhouse last year, and I always worry about wolves in the woods. A gust of wind blasts the barn, and it seems like every wooden panel rattles around me. Another leak starts in an opposite corner, a persistent *drip-drip-drip*.

I scowl. Maybe the barn will crash down on me right *now* and spare me a lot of trouble.

A nagging thought in the back of my head screams that I could pay for repairs from the money I'd set aside for Jax.

I tell that nagging voice to go away.

Another gust of wind, and that animal shrieks to the night again, the sound faintly echoing against the mountains, followed by a loud roar of thunder. Muddy May stomps nervously.

"It's all right," I murmur to her.

The barn door creaks, and I'm sure Nora is bolting out here because she's scared of the thunder, though she'd never admit it. But when I turn to look, a man in a hooded oilcloth cloak is coming through the door. I only have one lantern with me, so I can't see his face, but the shadows and the thunder and the darkness serve to make him a thousand times more terrifying.

I suck in a breath and grip the pitchfork, lifting it menacingly.

He steps closer and shoves back the hood. Lord Alek's red hair looks black in the lantern light, raindrops gleaming on his cloak. The corner of his mouth turns up in a bemused smile. "I've never been attacked with a *pitchfork*."

I lower the pointed end and swallow. "I didn't expect you to come to the barn."

"Nora told me where to find you."

I wince at the thought of the muddy courtyard, the door that barely slides. "You could have waited in the bakery, my lord."

"I know." He steps closer. "The rain has never bothered me."

Spoken like someone who can afford an oilcloth cloak. I shiver and turn to shovel another pitchfork full of straw. "Do you have another message for me to carry?"

"Not today." He pauses, looking around. "Your barn has fallen into disrepair, Callyn."

He says this disapprovingly, so I shove the pitchfork at another soiled pile. That persistent dripping sounds like it's mocking me now. "Well, I'm a baker, not a carpenter."

"And the world is luckier for it." He looks around again. "I'll send a worker to do the repairs."

He says this so casually, but I stop and stare at him like he's addled. "What? Why?"

He stares at me like I am. "Because I can?"

I turn back to the mucking. If he doesn't have a message, I'm not sure what he's doing here. Not knowing leaves me off balance and uncertain. "I'll get to it eventually. Don't trouble yourself, my lord."

"It's no trouble. I can't tell people about a wondrous little bakery in Briarlock if they arrive and it looks as though the farmhouse will collapse at any given moment."

I flush. "Ah, so it's to keep up your reputation. Perhaps you could simply stop telling them."

"Are you displeased with your newfound popularity?"

"I don't need charity."

"It's not charity."

His voice sounds closer, and I look up to find him right beside me. My heart beats a steady thrum in my chest to find him so close. He's taller than Tycho, taller than Jax even. And while Lord Alek isn't strikingly handsome, there's something about him that makes you look twice. Maybe it's the dark look in his eye or the strong set of his shoulders—or maybe it's the casual arrogance that seems to say that he might not be dangerous right *now*, but he just needs a second.

I shiver again, and this time I'm not sure if it's the cold or if it's him.

"You're not dressed for this weather," he says.

"I'm fine. I just need to finish the barn chores." I suck back another shiver. "If you don't have a message for me to hold, then why are you here?"

"I have deliveries in the neighboring villages, and I thought to stop."

"Nora could have wrapped some meat pies for you."

"I wasn't stopping for the food, Callyn."

I can't read his tone, so I frown. "Are you stopping to make sure I'm keeping your secrets? I haven't told anyone anything." I set my jaw. "Not even Jax."

"Oh, I know."

I glare at him. "Are you spying on me?"

A wicked light sparks in his eye. "Not me personally."

Ugh. I make a disgusted noise and turn away from him.

"I'm still trying to figure out why you're doing this," he says. "You're not greedy for silver like your friend. Yet you're not opposed to the king. At least . . . I don't think you are."

"My thoughts on the king don't matter. It's not as though I'll ever meet him."

Lord Alek scoffs. "Trust me, he's not worth your time."

I blow a strand of hair out of my eyes, and it sticks to my rain-damp forehead. "Well, *your* thoughts aren't much of a mystery."

"With all your recent business, have you heard the gossip about the queen?"

"That she's pregnant again? It's all anyone wants to talk about. That and the competition."

He shakes his head. "More than just her pregnancy. She's hardly been seen. I have friends in the palace who say she's very sick." He pauses. "That she hasn't been eating. That she grows weaker by the day."

"I've heard that can happen."

"Wouldn't you think her magesmith husband could put his magic to good use?"

I freeze. I don't know the answer to that question. I think of Tycho and his magic rings, how he mentioned that the king would be quicker at healing, more thorough. He said something about how King Grey saved a pregnant woman once, or regenerated a man's missing eye.

Why would he leave his wife—our *queen*—to suffer?

I don't like all the answers that rush to my thoughts. I stab the pitchfork into the straw again. "I don't know how his magic works."

"No one does," he snaps, "and that's the problem."

"Well, you're not going to find the answer here in my barn."

"Maybe not answers about magic." He pauses. "But you see a lot of customers. I think the people should know."

"Oh, so you want me to spread the word?" I say, then frown. "I'm not a gossip mill."

He swears, his composure breaking for the first time. "This is not idle gossip. I am not telling you that our queen prefers red jewels over green ones. Our queen is *unwell*. The king is attempting to distract the people with a competition that will span both borders, while Queen Lia Mara suffers behind closed doors." His gaze darkens, and standing turns to looming. "I wish to bring the truth to the people, and you act like I'm trying to sow discord."

Lord Alek takes a step closer, and I tighten my grip on the pitchfork.

He glances down at my "weapon," before his blue eyes lift to blaze into mine. "You're afraid of *me*, when I've been nothing but kind to you."

Honestly, I don't know what I am. My heart is slamming against my rib cage. Talking to him is so different from anyone else I know. I lift my chin and steel my spine. "I'm not stupid. You said you make a dangerous enemy. I know what you've done to Jax."

"Your greedy friend who was demanding twice as much silver to hold my messages?" Lord Alek takes another step closer to me. "Jax is lucky I didn't take off his hand to match his leg."

I swallow. My hands have gone slick around the handle. "You're right, my lord. How could I *possibly* be afraid of you?"

"You're as mouthy as he is, but it suits you better." He steps even closer, and I lift the pitchfork. He smiles.

Before I'm ready, he grips the handle and tries to jerk it out of my grasp, but I don't let go. His eyes flare in surprise, but I use his momentum to slam it into his chest, and he falls back a few steps. I redouble my grip and shove *hard*.

He recovers quickly, wrenching the pitchfork to the side, and for a long moment, we grapple for it. I'm stronger than I look, and I think

I take him by surprise. Eventually, though, I'm no match for his size, and he twists it out of my grip one-handed. I'm gasping, trying to recoil, but he catches the neckline of my blouson and pulls me forward, his fist tight on the wool.

"Here's what I think," he says, as if I'm not scrabbling at his wrists to get him to release me. "I think you want to honor your mother's memory, but you're afraid." He pauses. "I think you know she'd agree with me. I think she'd be doing more than just holding messages."

"I think I'm going to stab you when I get the chance," I grind out.

He laughs. "I rather doubt it, Callyn. I'm going to let you go, and you're going to tell people about the queen and her sickness, because it's the truth." He leans in. "And because I think you're more like me than you want to admit."

"I'm *nothing* like you."

"You've attacked me twice, and I've never even drawn a weapon."

I swallow. My fingers slow against his bracer.

"You're keeping secrets from your friend," he continues. "A friend you said you were willing to hang beside. So clearly you're having doubts about *something* in your life."

Alek isn't wrong.

Oh, I'm a horrible friend. My hands fall away. "Please let me go."

He does, and it's so sudden and so unexpected that I stumble back.

"I'll return soon," he says. "Think on what I said." He unbuckles the cloak at his shoulder, then holds it out. When I don't move, he says, "Take it. As I said, you're not dressed for this weather."

"You don't need to concern yourself with my attire."

"Attire is quite literally my business." He smiles. "Besides, it would be inconvenient if you were to catch a chill, fall ill, and die."

"Inconvenient," I echo.

"Of course! Who else would try to stab me with a pitchfork?"

"I'm sure *someone* would be eager to oblige."

His smile widens, but then it slips away altogether. He gestures with the cloak again, but I don't take it.

He sighs, shakes it out, and sweeps it around my shoulders. It's heavier than I expect, and warm from his body. It smells good despite the rain, like leather and cinnamon. I hate that anything about it is reassuring and inviting.

While I stand there thinking, he's working the buckles at my shoulder.

I can't remember the last time anyone buckled a piece of clothing onto me, and I stand there, trapped in a moment that feels unexpectedly . . . caring.

"I didn't send people your way out of charity," he says equably. "I sent people your way because your apple tarts and meat pies are some of the best I've ever eaten, and my business puts me in contact with many who'd patronize your little bakery. And I'm not repairing your barn out of charity either, but because you've proven yourself to be trustworthy and loyal. I've told you before, and I will tell you now: I'm not a traitor. I care about our queen, and I care about the threat of magic to all of Syhl Shallow. There's a reason the magesmiths were not allowed to settle here, and a reason they were nearly all killed off by the king of Emberfall decades ago."

Once he's done, he steps back. "And finally, I did not stop here today to *use* you. Tell people of the queen or not. I simply thought you should know."

I nod.

He brushes a finger under my chin, so light that I might have imagined it. "I stopped here today to see you. No more, no less." He smiles. "The attack with the pitchfork was simply a bonus."

I'm not sure what to say.

He glances at the corner of the barn, where the dripping has gotten worse. "Expect someone to repair the roof in the next few days."

I have to clear my throat. "Yes, my lord." I hesitate, wondering if I can bring myself to *thank* him.

He doesn't wait for gratitude. While I stand there deliberating, he's already through the door, lost to the windswept darkness.

CHAPTER 24

TYCHO

When we reach Ironrose Castle the following evening, I deliver my messages to Rhen, offer my greetings to Harper, and then disappear into the room I always use, claiming exhaustion from the ride.

It's hardly even a lie. I close myself into the room, grateful for the chance to finally lose my armor, soak in a hot bath, and collapse into bed.

This isn't supposed to be a long visit, and I'm glad. Despite what Jake said, I feel like I'm being watched. Like I've lost a bit of Grey's trust.

In the morning, I train with the Royal Guard. They're more skilled than the army soldiers in Syhl Shallow, and I always enjoy the challenge, especially since they admit me into their ranks without question. The Queen's Guard in Syhl Shallow is more cloistered, and I've never been allowed to train with them, so it's one of my favorite parts of coming here. Jake is with Harper, Rhen is doing whatever he should be doing with Grey's missives, and I'm . . . adrift. At least I can lose myself in swordplay and forget about everything happening at home, especially since many of the guards are eager to hone their skills for the Royal Challenge. They're full of questions, too, which I didn't expect.

Teach us how they fight on the other side of the mountain, they say to me.

Is it true that the king's magic has been welded into their blades?

Are their weapons lighter? I've heard they're lighter.

"Faster," I say. "But not empowered by magic."

This lasts for exactly one hour. Rhen appears at the side of their training arena. "Commander," he calls to Zo, his senior officer, who's overseeing the training exercises. "I need Tycho."

"Yes, my lord," she says with a nod, and she gestures for me to exit the arena.

Prince Rhen might be the only member of the royal family that I don't currently have any friction with, so I sheathe my weapons and duck through the fence around the arena to face him.

Without preamble, he says, "Jacob has indicated you and my brother are engaged in a bit of discord. Explain."

I make a mental note to beat the crap out of Jake again later. "There is no *discord*."

"So Jacob is lying to me."

Silver hell. "No—he's not. It's just—" I sigh tightly. "There's no discord."

"You've said that." He turns. "Walk with me."

I hesitate, but he's not waiting, and I don't want there to be discord with him, too, so I jog to catch up. When we approach the doors leading out into the courtyard, guards swing them open, and we step into the sunlight. Two guards trail us, but I'm no danger to Rhen, so they stand along the back wall of the castle.

I wish I knew what Jake had told him. I'm bracing myself, waiting for another lecture on duty and obligation.

But Rhen only says, "I do not like to linger in the arena."

"You don't want to distract the guards?"

"No. I shouldn't be a distraction." His voice takes on a dark note, and he frowns. "Too many . . . memories."

He and Grey were once trapped here. I've only heard bits and pieces of what they endured, but it was enough to know they were tortured by the magesmith who held them captive with magic, and most of the time, Rhen took the damage to spare Grey. I don't know what *specifically* happened in the arena, but I can imagine it was a lot, because Rhen seems to involuntarily shudder. He takes a long breath, glancing at the sky, then up at the castle. After a moment, he seems to shake off the emotion.

Maybe someone else would comment on it, but I don't. I often have to do the same thing when I think of my childhood. Rhen endured something terrible. So did I.

For the first time, I feel a spark of kinship with him, and it takes me by surprise. I'm not sure what to do with it.

"If we're speaking *those* kinds of truths," I offer slowly, "I do not like to linger in the courtyard."

It's where I was chained to the wall and flogged, once upon a time.

Rhen glances over but says nothing. Wordlessly, he changes course, heading along the cobblestone walkway toward the stables.

"Forgive me," he says after a while. "I did not consider it. I should have."

I'm off balance now, because I wasn't anticipating this kind of conversation. Maybe he wasn't either.

"It was a long time ago," I say.

And it was—for both of us. But I can't look at the walls of the courtyard without remembering the flickering torchlight, the shackles clamped around my wrists, the bite of the whip as it tore through my flesh over and over again. Until that moment, I'd thought nothing could be worse than what those soldiers did to my sisters and me when I was a child.

Now it's my turn to involuntarily shudder—to look at the sky, the trees, to inhale the spring air and center myself. To feel the armor on my back and the weapons that are never far from my hands.

I'm here. I'm safe.

Once I'm steady, Rhen glances over. "You're far more generous than I would be."

He yielded a kingdom to his brother, so I'm fairly sure that's not true. But I shrug and keep walking.

We've never talked about this. I'm not sure what to say.

"The courtyard isn't *all* bad memories," I offer. "Sometimes I have to remind myself that it's just a place."

"The arena isn't all bad memories either," he agrees, and it almost sounds as if he's trying to convince himself. "Grey and I would match swords every day to try to stave off the boredom. He was very good. He'd never yield."

"Do you miss it?"

"The curse?" His shoulders are tense. "Never."

"No." I glance over. He never wears weapons or armor, but he must have been a great swordsman, especially if he sparred with the king. "Do you miss the swordplay?"

He gestures to his face, his missing eye. "It wouldn't be the same."

"Have you tried?"

He doesn't answer. We've reached the stables, and the guards there step forward to roll the doors open. Two dozen equine heads poke their heads out to see who's coming in, hopeful for an extra ration of grain. Mercy rattles her hoof against the door and whickers when she sees me, her ears pricked.

I smile. "I'll have to bring you an apple later," I call to her.

"Here," says Rhen, and I turn to see him offering me a handful of hard caramels.

I'm doubly surprised. But maybe this was always his destination, because he keeps some for himself, then feeds them to his own horse.

Mercy laps hers from my palm, then blows warm breaths against my neck while she mouths the candies, leaving a trail of drool to find its way inside my armor.

"Lovely," I say to her.

Rhen joins me by her stall, rubbing under her mane. She noses at him for candies, too, and he feeds her one.

"I haven't tried," he admits, and it hasn't been so long that I've lost the track of our conversation. "After I lost my eye, the simplest things caused me difficulty. Pouring a glass of water. Walking down steps. When we travel to unfamiliar cities, Harper has to walk on my blind side. Swordplay would just be one more way to fail."

"You'd learn to accommodate," I say. I think of Jax, how he was so reluctant to put his hand on the bow, and then his first shot flew fifty yards. "I think you'd surprise yourself."

"Maybe." He feeds Mercy another caramel. "I didn't bring you out here to talk about me. Tell me what my brother has done wrong."

I sigh. "The fault is mine. Grey's done nothing wrong."

He scoffs. "I highly doubt *that*."

I whip my head around, and Rhen smiles, a little shrewdly, a little sadly. "You are more ardently loyal than even he was, Tycho. If you and Grey have found a point of conflict, I would bet good silver that the fault is on his side."

I shake my head and stroke a hand down Mercy's muzzle. "No. It's mine." I explain about Nakiis and the tourney—and then, when his expression doesn't change, I tell him about Jax and Lord Alek and what happened in Briarlock.

"I don't really know what draws me there," I say, and my voice is quiet. I'm not sure why I'd admit this to *him*, of all people, but perhaps admitting our fears to each other has opened a door I never realized was closed. "Maybe it's the reminder of what my life used to be like—but that's hardly a comfort. I don't know. But I shouldn't have lingered when I was due to return. Too much is at risk."

Rhen listens attentively and feeds my horse another candy. He makes for a good audience, and he waits, saying nothing until I'm done.

"So you see," I say. "The fault is mine."

"I disagree." He turns from the horse, heading toward the opposite end of the barn, which leads to another path that eventually meanders through the woods.

Intrigued, I follow.

"You've mentioned this blacksmith before," Rhen says. "If this Jax is as innocent as you hope, then Alek will consider his messenger to be too risky, and he'll move on to someone else, likely some*where* else. If these people are no threat to the Crown, then I see no harm in chasing whatever you seek, whether it's friendship or romance or even just a few hours of simplicity." He pauses. "Grey himself made many missteps along the way, and he should not be too critical of moments of levity and amusement. Maybe you should remind him that instead of claiming his throne, he spent months hiding at some tourney in Rillisk."

I laugh. "You will forgive me if I am not the one delivering that reminder to the *king*."

"Fine," he says without laughing. "Then I will."

He's so serious that it chases the amusement off my face. "Yes, Your Highness."

"I mentioned before that Grey does not yield," he says. "That sounds like a strength, and in many ways, it is. He stayed by my side through the eternity of that curse." Rhen glances over. "But when I needed answers from him, he refused to give them. Even when you ended up chained on the wall beside him. Even when the guards uncoiled their whips."

He's never spoken about this so directly, and I feel as though Rhen has driven a sword right into my side. My steps almost falter.

"Again," Rhen continues, "in a way that is a strength. He held a secret so dearly that nothing could force the words from his lips. I know my role in that moment, and how much harm I caused. You would be right to hate me for what I did, Tycho. But *I* was trying to protect my people. You were trying to protect *him*." He pauses. "Grey was trying to protect *himself*. So when I hear that you and my brother are in a moment of discord, I wonder if he is once again unwilling to yield in a moment when he very well should."

No one has ever said anything like this to me. I don't know if I can speak. I don't know if I can *breathe*.

"On the day that Grey returned to Ironrose," Rhen says, "I asked him what I had done to lose his trust. And Tycho, I had done nothing. The fear was inside his head—and we all paid the price. So if our king has made you feel as though you are not worthy of his trust, then he has made a grave misstep indeed. True loyalty is a gift."

We're approaching the woods, and I'm glad for the shadows, for the cool air, for the fact that we're alone, because I think I'm about to choke on my breath.

"Pull yourself together," he says pragmatically, "for it's one thing for *me* to know this, and entirely another for Grey to be aware of it."

"I'm together." But I'm not. Not yet.

"I didn't realize that would shock you."

"No one ever speaks of him that way." I give him a rueful look. "This entire conversation feels treasonous."

He stares at me in surprise. "Treason! He should *hope* any treason comes from the likes of someone like you. He has held on to his throne for years, when there was a time I worried it would only be a matter of months." He glances over at me. "But there have been attacks on the palace, and now these letters are changing hands. The insurrection has crossed the border. I'm worried his first true test as a ruler has come."

"Me too," I admit.

"Don't doubt yourself, Tycho," he says. "Grey is lucky to have you."

I wish it were that easy. But I nod. "Thank you."

We walk in silence for a while, until we take the loop that leads back to the castle.

"I do miss it," Rhen admits, and my eyebrows go up. "Swordplay," he adds.

"The guards have followed," I say. "Borrow a blade. We could spar right now."

He hesitates. "Not yet."

"As you say."

He's quiet again, and I think that's it. But then he says, "Next time, perhaps."

I smile. "Your Highness. Whenever you're ready, I stand willing."

Rhen smiles in return. "My brother is a fool indeed."

CHAPTER 25

JAX

The forge is busier than ever now that the winter snows are well behind us and more travelers take to the road. Word has spread widely about the Royal Challenge, and travelers needing a blacksmith are full of gossip: what cities are already boasting champions, what prizes the Crown will offer, what competitions will be held. Callyn's bakery is busy, too, and I see horses and carriages out in front of her shop more often than not. I heard hammers pounding a few days ago and went to look, and there were roofers replacing worn and rotted shingles on the roof of her barn. Business must be going *very* well. Cal used to bring me her leftover pastries every afternoon, but now days will pass before I'll see her—and when I do, she's always rushing back.

Like the change in the weather, something has shifted between her and me.

Lord Alek hasn't returned. Lady Karyl hasn't returned. Any silver I had is gone, paid to the tax collector or lost to ale, courtesy of my father. At first, I was glad for their absence. After watching Lord Alek put a blade into Tycho, I haven't been eager to see him again.

But as the weeks have drawn on, I've begun to worry about how we're going to pay the rest of what we owe.

I wonder if Cal is still mad at me. Our last argument haunts my waking thoughts.

I'd ask her if I could find a chance to *see* her.

My days have found a new routine anyway. I wake early every morning, pull the bow and arrows from beneath my bed, and venture into the woods for a few hours before I attack the forge. I've never been weak on my crutches, but trekking out to retrieve my arrows every morning has given me a greater endurance I didn't realize I was lacking. I have the balance and strength to stand and shoot without bracing against a tree now. Two dozen arrows have joined my first four, and I've acquired a heavy quiver, too, thanks to an early spring hunting party. They needed a wagon axle fixed and asked if I was willing to barter. A few weeks later, a fur trader noticed bruising along the inside of my wrist from where the bowstring snaps, and she offered a well-worn bracer. It covers my palm and stretches the length of my forearm, with brass buckles and a small sheath for a knife.

While I was shoeing her horse, the trader leaned against the work table and said, "Are you trying to qualify for the Royal Challenge?"

I laughed without any humor and didn't look up from my work. "Sure," I said caustically. "I think I've got a real shot."

"My sister is hopeful, too," she said. "You might see her there. Her name is Hanna. She has a green kit, with black stars on her quiver."

I glanced up, confused, but then I realized she wasn't teasing—and she heard my answer as truth instead of sarcasm.

It was the first time anyone looked at me as capable of anything other than swinging a hammer, and I think about that moment a lot— a lot more than I'd like to admit. After that, the idea of the Royal Challenge became wedged in my thoughts, and I can't seem to shake it loose.

It's a ridiculous idea anyway. It costs five silvers to enter. If I had five silvers, I'd hide them away for the tax collector.

I shoot every morning, I work the forge all day, and I collapse into bed at night. I try not to think about how we'll pay the rest of what we owe.

But when it's very dark, and very late, and very quiet, I allow myself to think of Lord Tycho, and how that fur trader wasn't the *first* person to see me as capable. I'll remember his encouraging voice or the snow in his hair or the way he let me ride his horse. The way he sat with me beside the forge and spoke quietly about his life.

You fancy him, Cal said.

Maybe I did. Does it matter? I may as well fancy a star in the sky.

I don't know if he ever made it back to the palace, but surely gossip about harm to the King's Courier would've made it to Briarlock by now. It's been almost two months since his blood was soaking into the dirt beside the forge. I've given up hope of ever seeing him again, which is fine. Better, actually, because the memory no longer stings like I once worried it would. Befriending a member of the nobility is an impossibility. He's very likely forgotten all about Briarlock, about the blacksmith he once taught to shoot a bow.

Which is why I nearly put a hammer right through my hand when I see him riding up the lane.

He's not alone today. Another man rides alongside, mounted on a large black gelding with four white socks. The man is older than Tycho, though not by too much, and seems taller too. He's got curly dark hair that's a bit windblown, along with a thin beard. He's trimmed in armor that's every bit as fine as Tycho's, all rich leather and gleaming buckles, though the insignia over his heart is different: the crest of Syhl Shallow backed by a shield of gold.

Clouds above. I don't know what it means, but this man is clearly someone important. I seize my crutches and stand before they reach the courtyard.

Tycho leaps down from his horse first. He looks every bit as wind-blown as his companion, with a few days of beard growth coating his jaw, but his eyes are bright and alert, no hint of the tense exhaustion that clung to him the last time he was here.

"Jax!" he says so brightly that it forces a smile onto my face. "Well met."

"Well met," I say, and I can feel warmth in my cheeks. "Lord Tycho." I glance at the man swinging down from his horse more sedately. "My lord."

"This is Jacob of Disi," Tycho says. "Counsel to the King, Man-at-Arms to the Queen's Army of Syhl—"

"Jake is fine," the other man says. He's got more of an accent, so he must originally be from Emberfall as well. He gives me an appraising glance that would make me bristle if it didn't seem so unprejudiced. This is a man who sizes up everyone he meets, I can tell. He glances at Tycho and then back at me, and a light sparks in his eyes as if he's solved a puzzle. "Well met." He smiles. "Jax."

I'm so surprised that they're here. The last time I saw Lord Tycho, his blood was spilling into the dirt and I was worried he wouldn't make it home. Now he's here, and he's well, and I almost can't stop staring at him to reassure myself that this moment is real. I'm not quite sure what to say, but I have to say *something*. "What can I offer?"

Lord Jacob turns to look at his companion, and his smile broadens. "Yes, Lord Tycho," he says. "What can he offer?"

Tycho gives him a shove. "We're on our way back to the Crystal City. We were going to stop at Callyn's bakery first," he says to me, "but she has a line out the door, so we decided to come here."

They're friends. Or . . . something close. A militaristic camaraderie that reminds me of that moment when Tycho hit me in the arm with the arrow. I'm off balance, uncertain how to respond. "Do you need something from the forge?" I glance at Lord Jacob again. "My lords?"

Tycho loses the smile. "Oh. No." He hesitates, and his eyes flick past me to the glowing forge. "Forgive me. I should have realized we would be interrupting your work—"

"No!" I say. "It's not an interruption."

But then I'm not sure what else to say. Maybe he's not either, because he stands there until an awkward silence builds between us.

"Silver hell," Lord Jacob mutters. "Tycho mentioned that the last time he was here ended in bloodshed, so he wanted to make sure that Alek hadn't caused any further . . . issues."

"No." I was more worried about Tycho, but I'm unsure how to voice that. "I haven't seen Lord Alek since that day. He may have business in town," I offer, "but I rarely have cause to leave the forge."

Lord Jacob nods. "That's what Tycho said, too." He pauses. "Do you know what his messages might have contained?"

I shake my head quickly. "They were sealed." I hesitate and try not to squirm under his scrutinizing gaze. There's a part of me that wishes I *had* broken the seal, just so I'd have something to offer now. But of course that's ridiculous, because if I read treasonous messages and passed them on, I'd be headed for the gallows myself. "I never read them," I say hollowly.

Tycho says something to him in Emberish, his voice low. I don't catch the words, but the tone sounds a lot like *I told you so.*

Lord Jacob nods. "The merchants in town might know something," he says in Syssalah. He gives me a nod and turns back for his horse.

They're leaving. I swallow. This . . . this can't be it.

But of course it is. I'm not sure what I was expecting.

"Find me later, T," Lord Jacob says as he swings aboard the gelding. "I'm going to seek out some food and talk to the shopkeepers."

Tycho hesitates. "You don't need me to come with you?"

"Nah. We've been setting a hard pace. I could use a break. I'll go lose a few coins at the dice tables, too." He grins. "Stay here for a while.

Get some sweetcakes if the line dies down." He gives me a nod. "It was nice to meet you, Jax."

He clucks to his horse, the gelding whirls, and he's gone.

A cool breeze swirls through the courtyard, pulling smoke from the forge and scattering a few dried leaves along the turf. Tycho stands beside his horse. All the quiet openness from our last meeting is long gone, much like the radiant smile from when he arrived and leaped off his mare.

I don't understand how I can fearlessly demand coins from a cruel man like Lord Alek, but when Tycho is in front of me, I can barely get it together to say my own name.

"I truly did not mean to be an interruption," he finally says.

"You're truly not."

He smiles, and something about it is a bit bashful. "Want to shoot arrows again?"

His voice is lightly teasing, and I think he really is joking, but now it's my turn to smile. "I'll get my bow."

I enjoy Tycho's surprise at my bow and my bracer, but that's nothing compared to when we get into the woods and he sees my targets.

"Whoa," he breathes. "You've been busy."

"It's not much," I say, but I'm pleased. "Just what I can carry." I have a dozen steel rings suspended from tree branches, set at various locations and distances, as well as scraps of leather that I've nailed to numerous tree trunks.

He turns in a circle to see them all. "This is great." His eyebrows go up when he sees some of the far targets. "That's quite a distance."

"I haven't been able to hit them *all* yet."

"Show me."

I pull an arrow from my quiver. The woods are cooler. Darker. I'm keenly aware of his presence. It's one thing to shoot by myself, with no one to witness my many misses—entirely different to know he could probably hit every single one of my targets blindfolded.

But I nock the arrow on the string, aim for something midrange, and take a slow breath. The arrow sails through one of the steel rings to embed itself in a leather square fifty feet away. I draw another and hit a tree farther down. But when I go for a third target, the arrow drifts to the ground well before reaching it.

I wince. "As you see."

He shrugs. "That's not you, that's the bow. You're trying to hit a seventy-five-yard target with a thirty-pound draw. Here." He holds out his own.

I've shot his bow before, but now, after weeks of using my own, I realize how much heavier the wood is, how much more tension in the string. I nock an arrow and aim. The bow snaps *hard*, and I'm doubly grateful for the bracer. I have to hop once to keep my balance.

Thwick. The arrow snaps right into the leather square.

Tycho whistles. "I know soldiers who can't hit a target at that distance."

"That can't be true."

"My word that it is. You should be entering the Royal Challenge."

He's the second person to suggest that, but it means a lot more to hear it from him. I hold out his bow and try not to blush. "Can you?"

I mean for it to be a genuine question, but it comes out like a dare. Tycho draws *four* arrows from his quiver, and before I can blink, he's flipping them across his knuckles and firing them off the string in rapid succession. Each arrow drives into a separate tree beside the one I shot. *Thwick. Thwick. Thwick. Thwick.*

I blink and stare. There's a part of me that doesn't want to shoot in front of him again—but a bigger part that wants to know how he *did* that.

He smiles at my reaction. "That's just army training."

"Do it again," I say.

He does, but this time, he shows me how he pins the extra arrows in his palm, hooking them with his middle finger as he needs to flip them into place. After he shoots, he takes two more arrows. "Give me your hand."

He folds my fingers around the wooden shafts, just above the fletching. His hands are warm against mine, and it puts us very close. I'm aware of his breathing, of the way the sunlight brings out the gold in his hair, of the bare edge of corded muscle just above his bracer. I find myself wanting to wind my fingers through his, to step just a bit closer, to hear his voice deepen. *Show me. Teach me. Tell me. Anything. Everything.* Every time I see him, my thoughts don't want to process that he's here, that this moment is happening, that he's invited me to shoot arrows or share apple tarts or ride his horse.

And the instant I have the thought, I realize that this moment will end, just like the last one, and it'll be weeks or months or years before it happens again. *If* it happens again.

"Jax."

I glance up, and I realize that he's said something I've missed completely. His eyes are such a dark brown, searching mine.

My chest is tight, and I can't get a handle on my emotions. I don't know what I'm doing here. I don't know what *he's* doing here. Just like last time, I can't tell if this is charity or pity or if he still thinks I'm involved with whatever Alek is doing, but none of it matters. The last time he left, it was agonizing. That's not his fault—but it's not mine either.

I don't want to do it again.

I grip the arrows and shove them into his chest. "I—I should really get back to the forge." I seize my crutches and start walking.

"Jax!"

I ignore him. An icy breeze comes down from the mountain to whip through the trees, defying the spring sunlight. I'm not sure where my anger came from, but now I have nowhere to put it. An hour ago, I was flailing because they were leaving, and now I wish they'd never come. My crutches stab into the ground with each step. "Surely Lord Jacob is waiting for you," I call.

"What just happened?"

Nothing. Everything. I don't know. But much like the moment he healed my hand, this might feel like a kindness from his side, and it *is*, but from my end, it'll just serve to show me everything I lack.

CHAPTER 26

JAX

The cool breeze wraps around me as I walk. I think I've left Tycho with a half dozen of my arrows, but I don't care. I've reached the edge of the woods, and I cast a look down the lane. Callyn's bakery has a dozen carriages and horses out front. I've never seen her place so busy, and this has been going on for weeks. At this rate, she'll have her tax debt paid in no time.

It's a new level of bitterness for my thoughts, and I wish I could shove it away, but I can't.

Hoofbeats and booted feet are jogging up behind me, and I swing my crutches forward again. "Don't follow me."

He does anyway. "Why are you angry?"

"I'm not angry." But I am, and I *sound* like I am.

"Jax?" He sounds nonplussed.

I round on him so quickly that Mercy throws her head up and tugs at the reins. Tycho murmurs, "Steady," but his eyes are on me.

"Don't *follow* me," I say again.

He frowns. "I don't—"

"Maybe you seek a reminder of what it felt like to be just Tycho, but I will *never* be anything more than just Jax. So if you need nothing from the forge, my lord, then please, just go away."

He looks like I've slapped him.

For just an instant, it makes me regret every word. Not all of this anger is about him. Not even a quarter of it. But I turn away before emotion can tighten my chest and wring out my voice.

He doesn't follow this time. My crutches stab into the ground with every step, my breath hot in my lungs. When I get back to the workshop, I recklessly shove the bow and arrows under the table. Wood cracks, but I don't care. I don't know what I was thinking.

I shove a lock of hair out of my face and stoke the fire in the forge, then drop onto one of the stools. When I look up, Tycho is still in the lane. Mercy is tugging at the reins again, pawing at the ground.

"Go *away*," I shout.

After a moment, he nods. His expression closes down, turning as cold as Lord Alek's. "As you say." He turns for his horse, drawing up the reins. He swings aboard, but I look away. I've seen him leave often enough. I don't need to watch it again.

The door to the house slams behind me, indicating my father is home.

Excellent.

I don't turn and look at him, but I can smell the ale from here.

He speaks from behind me. "What are you doing, boy?"

"I'm working." I shove an ingot into the stove, even though it's nowhere close to hot enough.

My father grabs my arm from behind, dragging me upright so roughly that I have to hop to keep my balance.

"Did you just yell at that lord?" he hisses in my face, and his breath is nearly enough to get *me* drunk.

I try to jerk free. "Just go back to the tavern," I growl.

He cuffs me across the cheek. It's not hard enough to knock me down, not with the way he's gripping my arm, but it snaps my head to the side and I taste blood.

Today is not the day. I hit him back.

This time he hits me so hard that I crash into the work table, and papers and bits of iron and equipment go everywhere. I grip the edge and scrabble for the tongs, but he's quicker. He swings me around and cracks me in the jaw again, and I land in the dirt. Before I can decide which way is up, he kicks me right in the stomach, not once, but twice, and my body starts to reflexively curl into a ball. He grabs hold of my shirt and drags me upright again, and my vision spins. I see his fist coming, and I know this time is going to put me out for good. There's a part of me that's glad.

But the hit never comes. My father is jerked away so roughly that I go sprawling again. I put a hand against the ground and cough. Blood speckles the dirt. My breathing is ragged.

My father makes a sound that's half-rage, half-roar, and I force my head to lift just in time to see him take a swing at Tycho. The young lord ducks the strike, then returns two of his own. Before I can blink, my father drops to the ground and moans. He tries to put a hand against the dirt, but it looks like *he's* having trouble figuring which way is up.

"Jax." Tycho is looking at me, extending a hand. "Jax, can you stand?"

I don't know. I swallow and it hurts. Blood is bitter on my tongue, and my vision is blurry. There's a chance I might empty my stomach right here in the dirt.

But my father is trying to shove himself upright.

"Watch out." I stumble over words. My jaw doesn't want to work. "He's—he's going to get up again."

Tycho's eyes are like fire. "Then I'll put him back down. Here. Take my hand."

I have to put an arm against my belly, and it takes me a while to get to my knees.

My father is groaning in the dirt. "You lazy boy. I'm going to—"

"You're never going to touch him again," Tycho snaps, his voice so cold that it sends a lick of ice through my body—but also a bolt of warmth, too.

"Please," I say, and it comes out like a whisper. I'm not sure what I'm begging for. For help? For Tycho to not kill my father? For something I can't even fathom?

His hand is right there, and I grab hold. I'm not sure how I manage to get myself upright, but Tycho gets my arm across his shoulders. He's all but carrying me, and I don't even know *where* until I practically faceplant into Mercy's shoulder.

"I need you to help me," he says, and his voice is lower, rougher than I'm used to. "Grab hold of the saddle."

Everything hurts and I can't focus. "Where—where—"

"Jax, if I don't get you out of here, I'm going to do something I'll regret, and I'm already in enough trouble. Grab hold."

I blindly grab hold. I'm in the air, and then I'm in the saddle. I curl over and clutch sweet Mercy's mane. It's horrible. Agonizing. Embarrassing sounds are coming out of my mouth. My eyes feel damp, but he's so fierce and fearless that I don't want to cry in front of him.

"Just hold on," Tycho says. "Tuck your hands under the breastplate if you need to."

I slide my hands against her fur, and it's all I remember doing until Tycho's voice is soft and low. "Jax? Jax. We're almost there. I'm going to help you down."

My foot hits the ground, and it sounds like I've landed on a plank of wood. Tycho has my arm over his shoulder again. We're surrounded by noise: the clamor of voices, the rhythmic clopping of hooves on dirt and cobblestone. Someone somewhere has a hammer, and I hear a woman calling for a child. We're in town, but I'm not sure where.

I blink, and Tycho pushes through a door, and the noise quiets. I know I'm hopping, but there's a good chance Tycho is fully supporting my weight. A man stands behind a counter, and I see him look from me to Tycho and back. I must look even worse than I feel—or maybe exactly the same as I feel, because his eyes are wide and alarmed.

"We do not want any trouble here," he says in a rush. "This is a peaceful boarding house."

"No trouble," says Tycho. "You have my word. I simply need a room."

The man inhales sharply, but Tycho slides half a dozen silver coins across the wood.

That changes the man's tone *immediately*. "Yes, my lord. Of course."

Tycho flips another coin onto the counter. "And I need a message sent to the tavern. Or maybe the gambling house. Tell Lord Jacob of Disi that he's needed here."

"Certainly. Right away."

My heartbeat is a roar in my ears, and I don't hear what else they say. I have to press an arm to my stomach again. I feel as though my ribs are caving in. Or maybe I'm inhaling shards of glass. My breathing seems thin and reedy. Suddenly, Tycho is walking again, all but dragging me. But soon we're in a room with a low fire and a locked door, and he eases me into a lavishly plush chair that might be nicer than anything I've ever sat in.

Too bad I can barely appreciate it. The room spins again, and I choke on my breath.

"Don't vomit," he says, and I wince, because it's exactly what my body feels like doing.

"Forgive me," I say, and my voice sounds garbled. I can't tell if the problem is my ears or my mouth. I draw a slow breath and try to make the room stop swirling.

"No, I don't care if you do. But it'll hurt like hell with broken ribs."

Oh. His voice is so practical that I'm nodding before he's even finished speaking—and that's all it takes for my body to start dry heaving.

He's right about the pain. I'm doubled over, and that's almost worse, but my body won't stop curling in on itself. Tears are on my cheeks and I can't speak. I can't *think*. I taste blood again.

Tycho kneels beside me and lifts my shirt, and then his hand is against my chest. Like the day he healed my hand, at first it hurts so badly that I involuntarily jerk away, my teeth clenched. But the pain softens into something warmer, something easier. My body was so tense, tighter than a bowstring, but I can suddenly breathe without feeling like my bones are coming through my skin. I sag in the chair and try to force my thoughts into order.

"Forgive me," Tycho says, and I can't possibly imagine what he's apologizing for, but he adds, "I should have done this before I made you get on Mercy. I didn't realize how bad it was—and I was worried your father was going to come after you again." He grimaces. "When you carry a lot of weapons, they start to look like the only solution. Ribs all right now?"

Does that mean he would've killed my father? Or something else? I stare at him, dumbfounded, and I have to force myself to nod.

He sits back on his heels, and only then do I realize that Lord Tycho was touching my bare chest, and all I could think about was not emptying my stomach onto the floorboards. My thoughts scatter wildly again. He might have fixed my ribs, but my head won't stop spinning.

Tycho lifts a hand as if he's going to touch my face—but he hesitates. "I know you hate the magic," he says carefully. "Or . . . or *me*, maybe. But your face doesn't look very good either."

I have to stare at him again. "I don't hate you." I swallow, and all I taste is blood. "You don't like my face?"

"That's not what I meant." He smiles, and it's half amused, half sad.

"He got you good. Noah would likely say you have a *concussion*." Tycho lifts that hand again. "May I?"

He could be offering to set me on fire and my thoughts wouldn't be able to process it. "Yeah," I breathe.

Despite what he said, and despite what *I* said, I'm still startled when his fingertips settle on my cheek. My whole body gives a jolt, but his other hand catches the good side of my face, forcing me still.

"Shh," he says gently. "It just hurts for a moment. You remember."

And he's right. I do. A quick flare of white-hot pain sears through my cheek and my jaw, followed by that honey-sweet warmth. But then I'm healed, my head is clear, and I'm staring at Lord Tycho from inches away. His eyes are so dark in the dim firelight, his hair flickering with gold. When his thumb brushes against my lip, my breath catches.

"Better?" he says quietly.

Yes. No. Both. Much like every other memory I create, this one is only going to bring pain. For a lot of reasons. But seeing as I'm only good for misfortune anyway, I close my eyes and lift a hand to hold his palm to my face.

I expect him to jerk away, but he doesn't. He goes still, then lets out a long breath. After a moment, he shifts his hand, his thumb tracing the arch of my cheekbone.

Too late, I realize he's brushing away tears. I frown and duck away.

He lets me go and sits back on his heels again.

"Forgive me," I say again, and I swipe at my face. I'm not crying over pain anymore, and I'm not sure how to reconcile it.

"It's not the first time I've seen a man cry," he says. "There's no shame in it." There's a kindness to the way he says that—but also something sharp and dark. It reminds me of the moment I asked if he liked being a soldier, how he said, *The actual soldiering, not so much.*

I shift in the chair until I'm more upright, and then I rub at my face, swiping the last of the tears away. Surely whatever tears he's seen have been for bigger reasons than this. My shoulders feel tight suddenly, as if he's seen too many things I keep hidden from everyone but Cal.

"You should take me back," I say softly.

That breaks whatever spell kept him quietly at my side. Tycho uncurls from the floor, and he runs a hand along the back of his neck. "Your father should be dragged in front of the magistrate, Jax."

"It was a misunderstanding. He didn't know why I was yelling at you."

"I didn't know why you were yelling at me either, and I didn't break your ribs over it."

That makes me flush, and I look away, into the fire. "Thank you," I say. "For what you did."

"You're welcome. Maybe next time we should work on how to block a punch instead of shooting arrows."

Next time. I don't know how to unravel any of this. I'm trapped in this horrible middle ground of never wanting to go back to the forge— and worrying that the longer I'm gone, the worse it will be when I get back.

"I need to wait for Jake," Tycho says, and there's a note in his voice that's a bit rueful. "He'll have some thoughts, I'm sure." He's moved across the room, and I hear something land on the bed with a soft *thump.* I glance over to discover that he's unbuckled his sword belt to toss the weapon on the quilt, followed quickly by his knife-lined bracers. His hand goes to his side next, flipping the buckles loose that hold his breastplate, and he only undoes half before dragging it over his head. He's wearing a linen tunic beneath, and it's pulled to his neck with the armor, revealing a long stretch of muscled waist before he catches the fabric to drag it back down.

What I see makes all the breath leave my lungs in a rush. Long ropes of scars cross his lower back.

He must hear me, because he looks over. I jerk my eyes away.

He says nothing. I say nothing. The silence swells between us. Eventually, he breaks it, heading for the washbasin in the corner, where he splashes water on his face.

Your father should be dragged in front of the magistrate.

And then what? He can come home and do worse? He won't be imprisoned for long. I know from experience.

I don't want to think of my father. But the alternative is thinking about Tycho and his hand on my cheek or those scars on his back or his easy smile or—

The latch at the door clicks. We both jump.

It's Lord Jacob, and his watchful eyes search the room when he enters. They settle first on Tycho, and I can see the spark of relief when he sees that his friend is unharmed. But then his gaze lands on me.

I'm not sure what to read in his expression, and despite the healing, I'm aware of what I must look like: filthy and blood spattered, with the distinct possibility of humiliating tearstains on my cheeks. I tense, but Lord Jacob only sighs.

"Silver hell, T." He runs a hand back through his hair. "I knew this one was going to be trouble."

CHAPTER 27

CALLYN

After what happened in the barn, I shouldn't be surprised when I find Lord Alek blocking the doorway out of my pantry, but somehow I am. As it is, I've got my arms full with a sack of sugar and a platter full of butter, and I nearly walk straight into him.

He catches the bag of sugar before it can spill out on his boots, and I somehow manage to avoid getting a face full of butter. We're down the hallway from the main part of the bakery, and I can hear the bustle of the people waiting in line. I scowl up at him. "Have you ever considered announcing yourself like a *gentleman*?" I demand.

"What do you know of gentlemen?" he says.

"Not much from you."

He smiles, but there's something tense about it. "Do you have any letters from Lady Karyl?"

I frown. I was ready for him to banter back, and the fact that he doesn't is . . . disappointing. But of course that's ridiculous. He's never here for *me*, he's here for business.

I square my shoulders and shove these thoughts out of my head.

"No. I haven't seen anyone since I tried to stab you with the pitchfork." I peer past him. "My lord, Nora is alone with the customers—"

"This is important."

"So is my sister."

He sighs, then moves to set the sack of sugar on the floor.

"Just give it to me," I say, gesturing. "I need to get back into the bakery."

"Callyn—"

"If you didn't want me to be busy, you shouldn't have sent all these customers my way!"

Alek moves closer and drops his voice. "Tycho has returned to Briarlock. Lord Jacob is with him this time." He says this with the gravity of someone delivering news of a death in the family, and his blue eyes are burning into mine. "They were seen approaching your friend's forge."

I feign a gasp. "Not Lord Jacob."

He nods, but I stare back at him and respond with equal gravity, though mine is a little mocking. "I don't know who that is."

He swears and looks away, running a hand through his hair. "He is the king's closest friend and adviser."

Oh, is *that* all. "Well, you're from one of the Royal Houses. Surely he can't be *too* intimidating."

"He's not *intimidating*, he's—" He breaks off and swears again. The sack of sugar hits the floor, and he grips my arms. "Do you not understand? If he's here, I need to know why. I need to know what he's doing. We chose Briarlock because it's not a popular town. Lady Karyl chose Jax because his father had been loyal in the past. But the King's Courier has been seen here many times—and now he's joined by Lord Jacob. How do you not see—"

"I see!" I try to wrench free. My heart won't stop pounding, and I can't believe that a moment ago there was any part of me that was hoping he'd come here for any other reason than to save his own neck. "Would you *let me go*?"

He doesn't. "Have they been here?"

"I haven't seen Lord Tycho." Alek's eyes are dangerously intent on mine, and I swallow. "I *haven't*. And I haven't talked to Jax."

After a long moment, his hands gentle on my arms, and he sighs. "Forgive me."

"I need to get back to the front." I hesitate. "My lord."

"I need you to find out what they want. Why they're here."

I want to punch him in the face. "I've hardly talked to Jax in weeks, because of *you*, and now you want me to suddenly ask why two lords were visiting his forge? Maybe they needed iron work."

"Maybe they'll visit the bakery next, and when I see you again, you'll be swinging from a rope." His voice is cold, but surprisingly . . . that doesn't sound like a threat. It sounds like a worry. I can't tell if it's for himself or for me, and I hate that there's something about him that's even raised the question in my thoughts. "Callyn. Truly. I need to know why they're here. *You* need to know why they're here. Think of your home. Think of your *sister*."

I swallow. "I'm always thinking of my sister. It's the only reason I'm helping you at all."

His expression doesn't flicker. "Is it really?"

Yes. No.

Maybe it *was*. But it's not anymore. I wet my lips and shake my head. "What—" My voice is breathy, and I tell myself to knock it off. "What do I do if they come here?"

He pulls coins from a pocket and presses them into my palm. "You're going to tell the truth. I came here, gave you a few coins, and took a few pastries. You don't know my plans."

"What *are* your plans?" I say.

He smiles. "If I tell you that, your answer will be a lie."

"Cally-cal!" Nora calls from the main room. "Cally-cal, I need you!"

I glance past him. "I need to get back."

"Of course you do." He picks up the sack of sugar and hands it to me. "Until later, Callyn."

"Until later," I say flippantly. I turn away, but then think better of it, and turn back to ask what will happen if this Lord Jacob brings more than just questions.

But Lord Alek is already gone.

CHAPTER 28

TYCHO

This isn't where I expected my day to end up. I thought I'd spend a few hours shooting with Jax, I'd find Jacob at the dice tables, and then we'd ride back to the Crystal City.

Instead, I've all but kidnapped Jax and left a man half-conscious in the dirt.

Jake closes the door and leans back against it, then rubs his hands over his face. "Tell me everything."

I do.

Well, mostly everything. I leave out the moment when Jax was yelling at me to go away. I'm not sure what happened there, and he still hasn't said. I keep thinking about the way his hand lifted to press over mine. Was that fear? A moment of vulnerability? Or something else?

Jake listens to every word, and after all that's happened with Grey, I expect him to give me a censorious glare and insist that we leave this mess behind us while we return to the Crystal City.

But he doesn't. "I *am* going to the magistrate," he says.

"It won't matter," Jax says bitterly. "You should take me back."

"You're not the only one with a shitty father," Jake says, and Jax looks surprised that his tone is equally bitter. "Trust me. I'll make it matter." He looks at me. "Stay here. I'll be back. Are you hungry? I'll have some food sent."

He doesn't wait for an answer to any of this; he just goes through the door.

The air between us still feels prickly and uncertain, and I'm not sure how much of that is on my side, and how much is on his.

"You said he's . . . Counsel to the King?" says Jax.

"His closest friend, in fact." I grimace a little, wondering how word of this excursion is going to sound when it hits Grey's ears. Rhen told me there was nothing wrong with seeking moments of levity, but right now, I think the king would disagree. Strongly.

But then I think about the way Jax smiled when he said, *I'll get my bow.* Or the way tears made tracks through the blood and dirt on his face.

Much like freeing Nakiis from the tourney, I wouldn't undo it.

Jax uncurls from the chair, and I look up. His eyes scan the floor, likely searching for crutches that aren't there.

I wince. "I should have thought to grab them," I say. "I was more worried about getting you away from your father."

"It's all right."

"I can help you."

He shakes his head. "I'm used to it."

This isn't said with scorn, but I frown anyway. He hops across the room to the washbasin, where he splashes water on his face—and seems surprised at the amount of blood that washes away. Somewhere along the line, he lost the nail that pinned his hair in a knot, and it hangs down over his shoulders again, a wild mass of shining black waves. He's pushed back his sleeves, revealing the cords of muscle in his forearms, honed from what must be years of work as a blacksmith.

If you need nothing from the forge, my lord, then go away.

I jerk my eyes away. I shouldn't be staring at him. I suddenly realize why the awkward silence exists at all. "I can leave," I offer. "Surely they have other rooms. Or I can wait for Jake in the tavern."

He dries his face and hands on the towel there, but his eyes are on the window. "I don't understand."

"As usual, I sense I have made you uncomfortable, Jax."

He laughs without any humor, but he doesn't look at me. "*Uncomfortable* is not the right word, my lord."

Ah. We're back to *my lord* again.

I give him a nod and reach for my weapons. "As you say."

He looks over in surprise. "No! I didn't mean . . . you don't have to leave."

I hesitate with my hand on my sword and bracers. I wish we were in the woods again, where we could shoot things, where our conversation could revolve around arrows and fletching and aim.

Jax is studying me now, his hazel-green eyes a bit narrower. Every time I'm with him, I feel as though we wordlessly dance around our real thoughts and true intentions. Some of it is due to our relative positions, I'm sure.

But some of it is not.

"Back at the forge," I finally say, "why did you tell me to go away?"

Jax leans back against the table with the washbasin and folds his arms. Sometimes, when his eyes dodge mine or heat crawls up his jaw, his emotions seem as easy to read as text printed on a page. But other times, like now, like the moment he told me so emphatically to *go away*, his expression will level out, locking everything away. It's a very measured look, revealing nothing, and it reminds me of Grey.

I don't expect him to answer, but he does, his voice very quiet. "Because I didn't want to spend hours in your company again, only for you to disappear for weeks or months or . . . forever."

Ouch. I frown and take a step forward. "Jax—"

"You owe me nothing," he says earnestly. "Truly. I know my life is . . ." His voice trails off a bit, and he shrugs. "Marked by misfortune. I am grateful for what you've taught me. For what you did today." He flexes his hand, the one he burned that I healed. "For what you did before. But you will return to your duties in the Crystal Palace, and I will return to the forge. It doesn't matter if Lord Jacob drags my father before the magistrate. You will be gone and my father will eventually come home, and my life will continue as it has."

There's something so bleak about the way he says that, because there's no tone of resignation. This is a fact that Jax believes to the core of his being.

The worst part is that . . . he's not wrong. Not entirely.

I draw a long breath and take another step. "Jax, please, allow me—"

"To explain? You don't need to explain. I know who you are. I know who I am. I know what my life is." His eyes are piercing now. "Do you, my lord?"

Maybe I shouldn't have taught him how to use weapons, because he's clearly capable of eviscerating a man with nothing more than words. I wish he would stop calling me that—but maybe that's exactly the point he's making.

A knock sounds at the door, and we both jump.

"Jake said he'd send food," I say evenly, and I open the door to a serving girl, grateful for the interruption.

CHAPTER 29

CALLYN

I haven't started calling the daily crowds *typical* yet, but there's usually a lull before the dinner hour, and I'm often glad for the break.

Today, I'm not. I've been glancing at the doorway all afternoon, waiting for armed guards to storm into the bakery and drag me off to the gallows, while Nora wrings her hands and wails after me.

I should give my sister more credit. She'd probably attack a cadre of guards with a pastry knife. Or, more likely, she'd try to sell them a platter of sweetcakes.

These worries are surely foolish. No one has accused me of anything. No one has accused *Jax* of anything. I've had nobles through the bakery for weeks, and the most drama I've seen was when two women argued over which was finer, my meringue-topped peach tarts, or the savory egg pies I laced with cinnamon and cloves.

I wish Alek hadn't appeared. He could have told me *nothing* and my answers to anyone from the palace would have been the same: *I haven't seen him. I don't know what he's doing.*

Ugh. He's insufferable.

But also . . . not. The barn has been repaired. The door leading into the bakery. Even the manger in the barn was replaced one day, and two new pairs of boots were left by the door, along with an oilcloth cloak for my sister.

His voice was full of worry when he told me about Lord Jacob. Worry . . . for me? It's a new angle to all his visits, and I can't quite make it match up. But it lights a flicker of intrigue in my chest, one I can't quite douse.

I keep trying to balance all his acts of generosity and kindness with the way Alek treated Jax, and I never end up in the same place. Was Jax too greedy? Am I too gullible? Did Tycho really threaten Alek with magic, or was Alek the aggressor?

I don't know, and I can't ask Jax without making Alek think I'm revealing his secrets.

Nora is sweeping the floor while I fold meat and vegetables into pastries for travelers seeking dinner.

Outside, hoofbeats thunder in the lane, and my heart jolts. I wipe my hands on my apron and head for the window just in time to see three horses gallop past the bakery.

But the only thing down the end of this lane is the forge.

Jax.

Nora is at my side. "Clouds above. Was that the magistrate?"

Yes. It was. The horses were going too fast for me to identify the others. Just dark horses, two men and one woman.

My heart won't stop pounding. I know he doesn't have any more messages from the Truthbringers. Would Jax have taken to doing something else to get silver? Or could this be related to the first messages he carried?

Guilt drops in my stomach like a red-hot stone.

"Do you think Jax is all right?" Nora says. "Should we go see?"

I don't know. I don't *know.*

I do know Alek won't like it. But I don't care. Jax is—*was?*—my best friend.

I return to the table and finish folding the pastries together, crimping the edges as quickly as I can.

"I'm going to go see about Jax," I say to Nora. "I'm going to put these in the oven, and I want you to watch them. No drifting off into your stories just because I'm not here, you hear me? If we have a dinner rush and we don't have meat pies, I'm going to make you tell all the nobles you got lost in a saucy romance. If you need something to do, you can make a few more cheese biscuits."

I expect her to roll her eyes at me, but she glances worriedly at the window. "We haven't seen him much, Cally-cal. Do you think he did something very bad?"

I swallow, and it feels like there's a rock in my throat.

"No," I say roughly. *I'm worried that I did.* "I'll be back as soon as I can."

I don't run, because I don't want to give the impression that there's cause for concern. I'm just walking up the lane to see my friend. But nerves keep prodding me, and my feet nearly sprint anyway.

I'm halfway there when the magistrate rounds the bend, walking on horseback, a rope tied to her saddle. She rarely comes out this way, and I don't think I've ever seen her quite this close, but she's a striking woman, stately and stern, with deep brown skin and close-shorn hair.

The other end of her rope is attached to the bound hands of Ellis the blacksmith. Jax's father.

Ellis has a black eye and a split lip, and he's stumbling along like he's still drunk. His eyes alight on me, and he says, "Callyn knows me! Tell the magistrate, girl." He hiccups and stumbles, then makes a retching sound and spits at the ground. "Tell her," he croaks. "Tell her I'm a good father to Jax."

He must be joking.

The magistrate does nothing more than give me a nod before giving the rope a sharp jerk. "I've already heard enough about your son from Lord Jacob," she says. "The only person who can speak for you now is the queen herself. Now *walk*."

Lord Jacob. Oh Jax, what happened?

I stare from Ellis to the magistrate to the lane leading to the forge, which suddenly feels twenty miles long. I don't know if I should run the rest of the way—or turn around and run back to the bakery and get Nora out of here. An unusually cold wind whistles through the trees, making me shiver despite the warmth in the air.

I force my mouth to work. "Is Jax all right?" I call after Ellis.

"He won't be!" he snarls back. "Not after what he's done!"

Oh. Oh no. Does this mean— Should I go back for Nora—

But the magistrate hardly glanced at me. Those horses didn't stop at the bakery—and I'm sure they wouldn't have gone galloping past if they suspected me of being a part of something. I grab hold of my skirts and hurry the rest of the way down the lane. I don't know what I expect to find, but everything my thoughts conjure is terrible. Jax on his knees, in chains, begging for his life. Jax being mouthy and irreverent with the magistrate's people, earning himself a trip to the stone prison.

Or worse, Jax broken or bleeding or dead. Or all three.

When I come skidding into the courtyard, there are two men in the workshop, but no Jax. One man is middle-aged, a bit more round and portly, with ruddy cheeks and thick brown hair peppered with gray. The town crest for Briarlock is on his sleeve, so he must have come with the magistrate. He says, "I'll check the inside, my lord."

"Sure," says the other man casually. He's younger, in finer armor, with what must be a dozen weapons strapped to his body. He's tall and broad-shouldered and looks like a fighter. He's frowning down at his palm, at something he must have picked up from the work table, something too small for me to identify from here.

I don't know if I make a sound or if he senses my presence, but his eyes snap up in surprise. He slides whatever he was looking at into a pouch on his belt, then gives me a clear up-and-down glance. "Hello," he says.

"Hello." I offer a quick curtsy and wonder if this is the Lord Jacob that Alek mentioned. "My lord."

"If you need something from the forge," he says, "it seems that both blacksmiths are unavailable for the time being."

His accent is unusual, slightly different from people who come from Emberfall, his words not quite as hard edged. It throws me for a moment. "I . . . ah . . ." My eyes sweep the area. No sign of Jax.

The man steps out from under the overhang. "Who are you looking for?"

My eyes snap back to his. He's savvy, this one. "No one," I say, and his eyes narrow just the slightest bit. I take a breath. "I mean—I'm looking for my friend." I frown. "I saw his father. Is—is there trouble?"

"I'm not entirely sure yet." He pauses. "Who's your friend?"

"Jax."

"Would that make you Callyn? You own the bakery?"

"Yes." I hesitate. "Is Jax all right?"

"He will be." His voice is grave. "His father roughed him up. The magistrate will hold him for a couple weeks."

Those words take a moment to register and rearrange all my thoughts. My pounding heart begins to slow. This has nothing to do with the Truthbringers—and everything to do with Jax's horrible father.

"You're sure he's all right?" I say.

"I think so. Tycho will bring him back once we're done here." He pulls a few coins from a pocket and holds them out. "I get the sense he might have a hard time getting around. Can you make sure he has enough to eat?"

"Of course!" I shake my head. "You don't need to *pay* me."

"Food isn't free." He takes my wrist and drops the coins into my hand.

Tycho will bring him back. I'm frozen in place for a moment, because I can't wrap my head around all of this. Has Jax befriended Lord Tycho? Is Lord Alek right?

I close my fingers around the coins just as hoofbeats pound in the lane again. I'm expecting the return of the magistrate, but instead, a chestnut gelding slows to a stop beside me, and Alek himself swings down from the saddle to stand at my side. "Callyn," he says. "Is Lord Jacob troubling you?"

"No," I say. "I heard the horses—and I was worried about Jax, so—"

"Alek." Lord Jacob looks absolutely gobsmacked—but it takes him less than a second to recover. His gaze darkens. "You've been ignoring a royal summons," he says, with unveiled anger. "I know what you did to Tycho. I should drag you back to the palace right now."

"A royal summons?" Alek says. The air flickers with danger. "I feel certain I sent word regarding *my* side of the events."

"Fine. I'm going to give you *my* side." Lord Jacob draws a blade.

So does Lord Alek.

Clouds above. Like a fool, I jump right between them. "Stop!"

"Move," Jacob snaps. "You don't know who he is. What he's done."

"I can tell you what *he* has done," says Alek. "Jacob was involved in the first assault on Syhl Shallow's army."

My heart freezes in my chest.

Alek isn't finished. "He was commanding the soldiers who killed your mother. The same soldiers who killed *my* mother." His voice is ice cold. "He was with the soldiers who slaughtered my sister."

"Your sister was a *spy*."

"My sister was loyal to Syhl Shallow," Alek snaps. "While *you* were involved in the insurrection that allowed this magical king to take the throne."

"If you want to talk about *insurrection*," Lord Jacob growls, "maybe we can talk about what *you* are doing *here*."

The words fall like a guillotine. I'm not sure how or why, but the tension seems to triple.

The flat side of Alek's sword touches my elbow. "Step aside, lovely. I'm not sure words are going to solve this."

Maybe my mother would think I'm a coward, but I'm not going to watch them hack each other to bits right in front of me.

"He's here for *me*," I say to Lord Jacob. I wish I'd thought to bring that ax I keep near the barn. I focus on what Alek just said about my mother. About his family. That same fire from his voice lights a spark in mine. "I don't know anything about a royal summons, but Lord Alek has been coming to Briarlock to see *me*." I take a step forward, toward his blade, and Jacob falls back a step. "He's here *now* because he saw you talking to me, and he doesn't trust you. If what he said is true, then *I* don't trust you." Those coins are still clenched in my fist, and I fling them at him. "I'll take care of Jax. I don't need your money."

The coins scatter in the underbrush. Lord Jacob is staring at me in disbelief. His eyes go from me to Alek and back. "Look," he says to me. "I don't think you understand who he *is*. What he's *done*."

"I haven't treated Callyn with anything but kindness," Alek says from behind me.

"And you drew your sword first," I say sharply.

Lord Jacob swears in a language that's not Syssalah. His jaw is tight, his eyes full of anger. "Fine. *Fine*." He sheathes his weapon. "I will gladly return to the Crystal Palace to inform the royal family that I found you here, and you feel your presence at court is not warranted."

"Oh, I'll return to court," says Alek. He hasn't put his sword away at all, and there's enough vicious promise in his voice that I worry he might finish the fight that Jacob almost started. "When I decide I have the time. My business keeps me rather occupied."

"I'm sure."

Alek inhales, and I realize he really *is* going to continue this fight, so I turn and put a hand against his chest. "I've left Nora alone too long. Would you walk me back?"

He falters, which is more surprising than the almost-violence.

"For certain," he says. He gives Lord Jacob a contemptuous nod, takes up the reins of his horse, and turns to walk by my side.

We're both silent, our footsteps crunching on the lane, underscored by his horse's hoofbeats. Lord Alek says nothing as we walk, leaving me with my own swirling thoughts. Jax and I only wanted to save our homes. Now we've somehow ended up on opposite sides of a brewing rebellion.

But of course, instead of wholly focusing on *that*, a tiny part of my brain is replaying the moment when Alek called me *lovely*.

When we get to the bakery, I expect Alek to leave me at the walkway, but he tethers his horse and walks me right up to the door instead—and looks like he's going to follow me in.

I stop on the doorstep. "You don't have to come inside," I say to him. "You really didn't need to walk me home. I just wanted to make sure you two didn't slice each other in half."

"You were very brave," he says.

My heart skips, but I roll my eyes. "I jumped in front of his sword. I was very stupid."

"They often look the same. But I know the difference."

That makes me flush. I'm not used to anyone calling me *brave*. I spend so much time thinking I should have followed in my mother's footsteps, that remaining here in the bakery was dishonoring her memory. But Alek's words light me with a glow that refuses to dim.

"Did you really ignore a royal summons?" I ask him.

He lifts one shoulder in half a shrug. His blue eyes haven't left mine. "I sent a letter."

"Why didn't he . . . I don't know . . . arrest you?"

"Do I give the impression I would've gone willingly, Callyn?"

The chill in his voice makes me shiver. My eyes skip over the weapons he wears, which are every bit as plentiful as the other man's. "No," I say truthfully.

"I have many allies among the Royal Houses. Not many of them are content with the queen's alliance and marriage to a magesmith. With the queen being so ill and out of the public eye, rumors have continued to spread. The Truthbringers don't have to sow discord when it's obvious that something is amiss with the royal family. The king's magic can kill hundreds of citizens crying out against magic, but he can't protect the queen? If Jacob wants to forcibly drag me back to the Crystal Palace, he wouldn't be doing it unscathed—and it wouldn't be seen well politically." His eyes narrow. "I'd make sure of that."

I have to fight not to shiver again. "Do you feel better about him being here?"

"Yes. In truth, it no longer matters why I come to Briarlock now."

"Wait. Why?"

"Because *you* declared quite passionately my reasons for being here."

Well, *that* makes me flush. "I didn't—it wasn't—" I hiss a breath of air through my teeth. "It was true. You do come here to see me."

"Indeed. Who else would attack me with a pitchfork?"

This entire conversation is wildly terrifying and breathlessly exhilarating, like being spun through the air as a child.

"Follow me out to the barn and I'll do it again," I say.

A light sparks in his eye. "If I follow you out to the barn, we won't be sparring with pitchforks."

"Oh no?" I tease. "What will we be doing?"

Alek takes hold of my waist and presses his mouth to mine.

Whoa. I was being coy. Alek was *not.*

Based on the strength in his hands and the intensity in his mouth and the sudden fire in my belly, Alek is probably *never* coy. I keep waiting for my thoughts to catch up, but instead, I'm leaning into the warmth of his body, feeling his hand slide up my waist to graze my breast, stroke my neck, and bury his fingers in my hair. My throat keeps making helpless little sounds. He tastes like the cinnamon and sugar of my apple tarts, but *better,* like I need to add him to my recipe. I'll never be able to eat apples again without thinking of this moment. Without *longing* for this moment. This can't be simple kissing. This is—this is—

The door clicks. "Cally-cal?"

I break free of him, and it feels like I've been tossed into a snowbank. "Clouds above, Nora!" I cry.

She starts prattling like she didn't just interrupt the most captivating moment of my life. "I think I did the meat pies right, but the edges are a *little* more brown than—"

"I'm sure it's fine," I gasp.

"Well, I need you to come look, because the tops are a bit soft, and yours are always—"

"Give us a moment, please, would you, Nora?" Alek's eyes are shining.

"Of course." She gives him a flourishing curtsy—but then she doesn't close the door.

"GO INSIDE!" I snap.

"*Well,*" she huffs. "If you—"

I yank the door shut so hard that the glass panes rattle. Then I put a hand over my eyes.

"Just leave me, my lord," I say. "Allow me to die, right here, on this step—"

"Alek," he says, his voice rough and soft and right against the shell of my ear.

I inhale sharply, but he's right there.

"Alek," I whisper, and he smiles.

"The meat pie situation seems rather urgent," he says. "I should leave you to it." He casts a glance up the lane. "I do not want to face Lord Jacob again."

I nod, then swallow. My thoughts are still disorganized, and I want to pick everything up right where we left off.

"I'll be back soon," he says. "You have my word."

"No messages?" I whisper.

"Not this time." His hand finds my face, his palm gentle against my cheek. When he kisses me this time, it's slower. Warmer. Lazy sunlight instead of a bonfire. Forget the barn and the pitchforks. I want to hook my fingers in his sword belt and drag him up the stairs.

Then he's gone, and I'm all but falling through the door. It clicks closed, and I lean against the door frame and sigh.

Nora clears her throat emphatically.

"I know, I know," I say. "Don't marry that one."

She giggles. "That was better than Mother's old books. I think I might have changed my mind."

CHAPTER 30

TYCHO

Jax returns to the chair by the fire while I divvy up the food. Jacob arranged for sliced beef and cheese to be delivered, along with a loaf of bread, a pitcher of raspberry wine, and a variety of fruits. Jax hasn't said anything, so I haven't either, and I'm glad to have something to occupy my hands. I take the other chair, and we eat in silence for the longest time. But maybe the food or the fire or the closeness eases a bit of the tension between us, because after a while the quiet becomes more amiable.

Uncomfortable is not the right word, he said.

I want to know what the right word is.

Jax ate hesitantly at first, as if he wasn't sure he should dare. But I piled as much food onto his plate as I did my own, and it doesn't take long before he's eaten it all. I think of how far his forge is from town, and I remember Callyn sending him the apple tarts. I'm sure Jax is mostly reliant on his father for food, and I wonder how often he has to go hungry in addition to dealing with that awful man.

I don't ask if he wants more. I just take his platter and load it with more food when I take my own.

"You shouldn't be serving me," Jax says, and it's the first thing he's said since the food arrived.

"If you can hop on one foot while balancing a full plate of food and a glass of wine, I will be truly impressed."

"The glass might be a challenge."

I ease the food onto the table between us and drop into the other chair. I'm not really hungry anymore, but I'm tired of making him uncomfortable, so I pick at the bread and cheese.

"I did not mean to disappear for months," I say quietly.

He doesn't look at me. "As I said, you owe me no—"

"Shut up, Jax. Eat." I wish I could smack him with an arrow again.

He dutifully stabs a fork into a piece of meat. "Yes of course, Lord Tycho."

His voice is both wry and a bit sad, and now it's my turn for warmth to crawl up my neck. I take a long swallow of wine while I fight to remember what I was going to say.

"I made a misstep with the king," I eventually admit. "After what happened with Lord Alek, I wanted to return to Briarlock, but Grey all but ordered me to stay at the Crystal Palace. For *weeks*, I begged for the chance. But then . . . well, he sent me to Ironrose Castle with a chaperone. It felt like a punishment." I breathe a long sigh. "I would have stopped here on our way to Emberfall, but I was worried Jake would see it as a deviation from my duties, which . . . in a way, it is."

Jax stabs another piece of meat, but his eyes are on me now. "What was your misstep with the king?"

You.

But I can't say that. And it wasn't just him, anyway. I have no idea how to explain everything that's gone wrong since I first rode into Briarlock.

I inhale to answer, but he's set down his fork to pick up his wine, and I find myself watching the movement of his arm, the way his fingers curl around the stem, the way the glass touches his mouth. I keep thinking of that brief moment when his hand lifted to press my fingers to his face, when tears were making tracks through the blood and dirt. As he sets the glass down, a solitary pink droplet clings to his lips. A lock of dark hair falls across his face, and he absently shoves it behind his ear.

Without thinking, I reach out to tug it loose again, my fingers lingering on the strands before I let go.

He instantly goes still. His eyes lock on mine.

I have to shake myself. "Forgive me." I drain my entire glass.

"You apologize a lot."

That makes me smile, and I feel heat on my cheeks again. "Well."

But then I'm not sure what else to say.

Jax drains *his* entire glass.

I raise my eyebrows. "More?"

He hesitates. I fetch the bottle and pour for us both.

He doesn't take another sip. His voice is rough. "I . . . don't want to turn into my father."

"I've seen the man. You could never."

Jax traces a finger around the base of the glass, but he still doesn't pick it up. He doesn't nod—but he doesn't deny it either. "I've heard wine will make me too honest."

"That doesn't sound like a problem."

His lip quirks up, but the smile doesn't reach his eyes. If anything, there's a spark of sadness in their depths. "You do realize this is quite possibly the finest meal I've ever had."

"I can send for more."

"No." His voice is the tiniest bit husky. The wine must be hitting him. "Thank you. My lord."

"Please stop calling me that."

"Please stop leaving me with memories that will only hurt later."

I freeze.

Jax swears, then sighs. He pushes the glass away by a few inches.

I want to apologize again. I want to take away all the reasons these memories will hurt, because I know what he means—maybe too well. I want to shoot arrows and feel the heat of the forge and learn how he pulls a useful shape out of a block of iron.

But not just that. For the first time, I want *more*.

I want to teach him to fight so his father never dares to lay a hand on him. I want him to press my hand to his cheek again. I want—I want to feel—

My thoughts stumble to a stop. Like the day I told Rhen I don't like to linger in the courtyard, my emotions are such a tangled mess. I keep thinking of what Noah said, how I keep people at a distance. I can't even argue the point. I spent weeks avoiding Grey in the Crystal Palace—and then I rode right past the turn for Briarlock when Jake and I were heading for Emberfall. Even now, my chest is tight, and there's a part of me that wants to draw back. I don't know what's wrong with me that fighting and swordplay feel *safe*, but sharing a quiet moment feels terrifying.

Please stop leaving me with memories that will only hurt later.

I turn the words around in my head and examine them from all angles, until I see them from the clearest one: the first three words. *Please stop leaving.*

I reach out and touch his hair again. My fingers barely graze his jaw, and I wonder if he's going to pull away, but he doesn't move. His eyes are intent on mine.

I follow that strand to the end, then do it again. He's so still, his breathing slow and even. Outside of training and sparring, I never touch anyone else. I rarely allow anyone else to touch *me*. This is hardly *touching* anyway. This is . . . I'm not sure what this is.

I know I don't want to stop.

When I do it a third time, a strand winds around my finger and nearly tangles, tugging gently before going loose, and Jax lets out a breath.

He gives me a rueful look. "You're going to make this memory hurt more than the others."

I draw back, but he catches my hand, his thumb gentle against my palm. "I don't think I'll mind the pain of this one."

That makes me blush and smile, and I duck my head. "I've never— well." I shrug a little, then chance a glance up. "I don't know much about . . ." His eyes are so intent, and now it's my turn to look away and stumble over my words. "Ah, that is to say, I have very little experience in . . . in *courtship*, if that's what this *is*—"

"With a commoner?"

"With anyone."

His eyebrows go up. *"Really."*

"You don't have to look *so* shocked."

He grins, and it's truly amazing how transformative it is for his face. He wears his worries so plainly, but when he smiles, his eyes practically gleam.

I need to stop drinking wine. Or maybe I need to drink *more* wine.

Especially when he says, "You're the most beautiful person I've ever seen, so forgive me for finding that hard to believe."

"I think you've had too much to drink."

"Well." His smile broadens. "Admittedly, I rarely leave the forge."

I laugh outright. He turns his hand so our fingers are loosely intertwined, but just for a moment before he lets go.

"I have little experience with *courtship* either," he says, lightly mocking my so-serious tone.

"Not . . . Callyn?"

He shrugs. "We grew up together. Cal is like a sister."

"She is very fond of you," I say, and mean it.

His smile fades, and a dark look slides through his gaze. Something has happened between him and Callyn. I wonder if he'll tell me—or if I can ask. We're still dancing around truths, but we seem to have tightened the dance floor.

I take a sip of wine that nearly turns into a gulp when I realize Jax is watching the movement.

I have to close my eyes and take another sip. I can't stop hearing him say, *Please stop leaving.* But I'm going to leave. Probably by nightfall. And once again, I'll be stuck at the Crystal Palace, awaiting my next orders.

And Jax will be . . . here.

"Why?" he says.

My eyes flick open. He seems closer somehow.

"Why what?"

"Why no courtship?"

"Ah." I hesitate. "Not *none*," I say. "But very little. When I came to Syhl Shallow with Grey, we were seen as outsiders. There are many who would hate the king, but they cannot do so openly. They can hate *me* without provocation."

He's studying me. "Like Lord Alek."

"Exactly." I pause, riffling through my memories. "There was a girl who sought my favor a few years ago," I say, musing, "when I was a young soldier. But that quickly ended when I learned she was trying to anger her family. Lia Mara tried nudging me toward her sister at one point, and we've enjoyed a few moments together—but I don't think Nolla Verin will be happy unless she finds someone as bloodthirsty as she is, and that is *definitely* not me. I grew close with a soldier named Eason when we were recruits . . . and perhaps that might have been more, but romance among the ranks was not allowed." I shrug, remembering Eason's gentle smile, the way we'd stay up well past curfew because he'd beg me to teach him another card game from Emberfall. He didn't like being a soldier any more than I did, but it's tradition here for someone in every generation to serve in the army. The instant his two-year commission was up, he took his leave.

But looking at the memory now, I wonder if it was truly my commitment to duty that kept me in line, or if it was something more. The scars on my back aren't the only ones I bear.

I don't want to examine that thought too closely, so I look at Jax. "Why no courtship for you?"

"Not *none*, but . . ." He gives me a look. "Haven't you heard the saying that men are best suited for hard labor and dying in battle?"

"Yes. For what it's worth, the queen hates that expression. I haven't heard it spoken at court in *years*."

"Just because people can't say it openly doesn't mean they don't still think it. I can't take a commission as a soldier. I'm lucky that I can make a living as a blacksmith—but there are still people who see my missing foot and demand that my father do the work, even though he's drunk half the time." He pauses. "I've had . . . *romantic* offers from travelers. Once or twice I've been intrigued, but no one ever stays for long. They're usually bored traders who think I'm an easy mark or a quick lay. I don't need anyone's pity." A vicious glint shines in his eyes. "Sometimes they're not *asking*, if you get my meaning, but that's rare—and no one can get close enough to pin me down when I've got a white-hot iron in my hands."

I've gone still, and I have no idea what expression is on my face, because Jax frowns. "What?"

I have to shake off a memory before it can grab hold, but his words— *no one can pin me down*—have dragged it to the forefront of my thoughts. It was so long ago, but I can still hear my sisters screaming. I can still smell the fresh cut hay of my parents' barn. Tiny claws were digging at my chest. I'd shoved one of the barn kittens down the front of my shirt because a soldier was killing them.

I like when they squeak, he said. His fingers closed on my throat, pulling me forward. *I bet you'll squeak, too.*

Jax's fingers brush over mine, and I nearly jump.

"Something I said upset you," he says quietly.

"No." But I drain the rest of my wine.

"Clearly yes."

"I said *no*," I snap, and he jerks back.

His eyes flick from my face to the wineglass and back. There's a new tension in his eyes that wasn't there a moment ago, and his voice turns very careful. "Forgive me, my—"

"Stop," I say softly. I lift a hand, and I mean for it to be calming, placating. But he flinches, just a little, and I remember how he jumped a mile when I tried to offer him Callyn's apple tarts.

I remember his father, the reason why we're here at *all*.

This is what we've been skirting around. Not the spying or the messages. Not even the agony of courtship.

We're dancing with the trauma of my past . . . and his present.

"What you said—" I hesitate. "You caught me in a memory. It wasn't a good one. I shouldn't have snapped." I want to touch his hair again, to put my palm against his cheek and brush my thumb against the curve of his lip. But now there's a wary set to his gaze, and I don't know how to undo it other than offering my own truth.

"When I was a boy," I say slowly, "my father was . . . well, he wasn't like yours. He never beat me. He never hurt my mother. But he was a horrible gambler." I frown. "He nearly lost our home a dozen times. We never had enough food because every time we'd earn a coin, he'd lose it. One time he bet more than he had, and he made the mistake of playing with soldiers in the King's Army—in Emberfall. When he couldn't pay, they followed him home. There were three of them. My younger brother tried to hide with my mother—and he saw everything they did to her. I took my sisters into the barn, and we thought we were safe there. But—"

My voice chokes off. I don't think I'm breathing. The words won't come.

I glance at Jax's hazel-green eyes, and just like that moment with Rhen in the courtyard, I have to remind myself that I'm here, I'm safe, it's over, it's done. His gaze is steady, unflinching now, his expression patient.

He doesn't move. He waits, and he doesn't look away.

Maybe that's what gives me the courage to continue. I take a long breath. "I was twelve," I say. "I kept begging them not to hurt my sisters, and they said that *I* would have to do. I didn't even know what they meant. But I . . ." I have to grimace. "I learned rather quickly. And then, after it was done, my mother begged my father to figure out a way to make it right. So he went into town and tried to find someone to help with his debts. A man named Worwick owned a tourney, and he was known to offer good money for trade. I don't know what Worwick asked for, or if my father simply *offered* me, but I was sold into his service for five years." I rub at the back of my neck. "Worwick wasn't a bad man. I worked in the stables and I cleaned the tourney. I had food to eat, and I could scrape together a few coins of my own every now and again. But after what happened . . . the soldiers always frightened me. I used to hide . . ." My voice trails off. My body wants to shudder again, but I force myself still.

"Yet you became a soldier," Jax says softly.

"I did."

"Why?"

"Because . . ." I take a long breath and let it out. "Because Grey expected it of me. And I never want to disappoint him."

He's studying me so intently. "So when you said you made a misstep . . ."

"I spoke true. He ordered me to remain at the Crystal Palace after what happened with Lord Alek. But I don't regret the time I spent here with you. I don't feel remorse, and I think Grey can sense that. For the first time, it's put us at odds."

"You're at odds . . . with the *king*."

His tone makes me smile. "Well. Yes. But you must understand, our relationship has always been deeper than simple friendship, different from that of a ruler and his servant. When we met, Grey didn't just save my life, Jax. He put a sword in my hand and taught me how to save *myself*. He is *good* and he is *just* and he will do everything in his power to protect Syhl Shallow *and* Emberfall. I was the first person to swear fealty to him, and I would do it again right this very instant if he asked it of me."

Jax is staring at me, and I wish I could read his expression. The wariness is gone, though, and that heavy lock of dark hair has fallen across his forehead again. I reach out to twist it through my fingers.

"You didn't have to share that with me," he says.

"I wanted you to know." I let my thumb graze his mouth, and his lips part, just a fraction.

I shouldn't do this. All the talk of the king should be a reminder of my duties and obligations. Instead, I feel like the Crystal Palace is a million miles away, and here in this room, I'm just Tycho, and he's just Jax. His hair is like silk and his eyes are like jewels and now he knows my darkest secrets, just like I've learned his. I shouldn't be thinking about his lips or his hands or imagining the taste of his breath.

But I *am*, and once I have the thought, there's no room for anything else. I tangle my hand in his hair, then slip out of my chair to press my mouth to his.

CHAPTER 31

JAX

Maybe my father really did knock me out and none of this is happening. Because I can't imagine any version of reality where Lord Tycho, the King's Courier, would have his hands buried in my hair and his breath on my tongue.

Or maybe I'm dead. But if this is death, I'm not complaining.

I'm afraid to open my eyes, like I'll wake up and discover I'm dreaming. My other senses are overwhelmed, from the sweet taste of the wine on his lips to the heady scent of his skin, something earthy and raw like the forest in early morning. He touched my hair so delicately, and his hands are so gentle, but there's no restraint in the way he kisses me. My fingers find his chest, clenching in the fabric of his shirt, and my heart kicks against my ribs to find him so *close*. When one of his hands leaves my face to stroke up the length of my side, I gasp and suck in a breath.

He pulls back just enough to whisper against my lips. "Stop?"

It's enough to force my eyes open, though I wouldn't even stop if I were drowning. But then I realize how he's so close: Tycho has gone to his knees in front of my chair. His hair is gold in the firelight, his eyes shadowed.

I have to swallow. He truly is the most beautiful person I've ever seen. I'm afraid to touch him now, as if he'll vanish. But he's so close that I can't *not* touch him. I put my palm against his face, finding his jaw a little rough. When my thumb strokes across his mouth, his lips part, and I feel the edge of his teeth, the bare brush of his tongue. His hands settle on my knees, fingers pressing into the muscle there, and he leans in to kiss me again. Gentler this time. Agonizingly slow.

This is like the moment when he healed me, but a thousand times better, my entire body filling with honey and heat. My hands find his hands, sliding up his forearms until I reach the curved muscle of his biceps. There's a part of me that wants to tackle him to the floor, to feel the strength and power that I know hides behind his gentle touch. But when my hands slide up the column of his neck, his kisses stop, his mouth hesitating against mine.

I don't know if this is about what he just revealed about his childhood, or if it's related to the scars on his back, but I wait, letting him breathe against me. There's an element of trust to this, and I don't want to violate that. He's the one with the status and the magic and the weapons, but in this moment, none of that matters. He's offered me a vulnerable bit of *himself.* Possibly the *most* vulnerable bit of himself.

Maybe that's what gives me the courage to shift a little closer so I can whisper along his jaw. "Stop?"

He shakes his head, but it's a tiny movement, an uncertain movement, so I wait, our faces almost pressed together, my fingers still against his neck. His breathing seems too quick, and his pulse is a strong beat under my fingertips. I can sense his tension now, but he winds a finger through a strand of my hair again, almost as tentative as when he did it the first time.

He kisses me lightly, then withdraws to sit back on his heels. His cheeks are a bit flushed, his hair a bit wild. "As I said, far too little practice with courtship."

It's so unexpected and he's so serious that I almost burst out laughing. I have to rub my hands over my face. My brain seems incapable of forming a coherent thought, and I'm worried if I try to speak the only thing that will come out of my mouth is going to sound like *guh*.

"Jax," he says softly, earnestly, as if he's worried.

"Tycho." I pull my hands down and stare at him in wonder. "You saved my life and served me dinner and kissed me senseless—and now you're kneeling on the ground at my feet. Somehow you believe you have *too little practice with courtship*?"

He smiles, and something about it is bashful, but something about it is a little wicked, too. "Next time, I'll attempt a bit more proficiency."

"I'm not sure I'll survive it." But then I realize what he's said, and the smile falls off my face.

Next time.

Because he's leaving. Likely tonight, I'm sure. He and Lord Jacob have no reason to linger in Briarlock. He'd be gone now if not for my father.

Tycho notices immediately, because he rises up, taking my hands, pressing them between his. "It will not be weeks or months or never, Jax. I swear to you. I have to return to the Crystal Palace with Jacob, but now that plans have been set for the first competition of the Royal Challenge, I will be sent back to Emberfall. Soon."

I swear to you. I don't think anyone has ever sworn anything to me. My chest is tight all the same. I know his role, how his schedule is at the mercy of the king.

He lifts a hand to brush a thumb across my cheek. "A week," he whispers. "At most."

I nod.

I knew this part would hurt. And he's not even leaving yet.

His hand winds in my hair, tugging gently at the strands. My insides are turning to warm honey again, but I don't want to make this hurt more, so I force myself to speak into the silence.

"Are you going to compete?" I say. "Is that why you're going to Emberfall?"

"Not this one," he says. "The king and queen will travel to watch the first competition. I will ride ahead to ensure Prince Rhen is prepared for whatever they may need. There are always threats against the Crown." He pauses. "But I will not make you wait so long, Jax."

There are always threats against the Crown. Again, I've forgotten who I am and what I've been a small part of. I've wanted to confess to him before, but right now, I almost can't keep the words in my mouth. I want to tell him everything about Lord Alek and Lady Karyl. He's given me so much, *told* me so much. I feel as though I'm keeping a tremendous secret in the face of all his openness.

But I don't have any proof—and I don't want to admit how desperately we need silver to save the forge. I told him earlier that I don't want pity, and I meant it. Tycho's confession to me was about something real, something potent, a terrible moment in his life that he's grown past and found the strength to face.

Conning the Truthbringers out of silver seems to pale in comparison. Shame curls in my belly, and I bite my tongue.

I look into Tycho's brown eyes, so much darker than eyes native to Syhl Shallow. *I will not make you wait so long.*

"Yes, my lord," I whisper.

His eyes fall closed. "Jax."

A knock raps at the door. "T. It's me."

Tycho sighs. "Silver hell." He sits back on his heels again, then agilely rises to his feet. "Come in, Jake." Any hint of vulnerability is gone from his frame. Gone is the boy who carefully stroked his fingers through my hair, leaving only the former soldier.

I straighten in the chair as Lord Jacob enters. His eyes fall on me. "The magistrate jailed your father for a fortnight. I couldn't get more than that. But maybe that will sober him up and he'll realize what he did."

A *fortnight*. He's never been locked up that long, but I know it won't change much. I mentally calculate how much food we might have in the pantry. Callyn's bakery has been so busy, but maybe she can spare some meals. I think of my bow and wonder if I could hit a moving target to hunt.

He's waiting for an answer, so I force myself to nod. "Thank you, Lord Jacob."

He looks to Tycho. "Take my horse. Get him home. I'll settle up here. We should ride out before we lose the light entirely."

Tycho nods and reaches for his armor.

And just like that, it's over. Before I'm ready, Tycho is helping me onto Mercy, while he swings onto Jake's large black gelding. Dusk has begun to fall, throwing long shadows in our path. I grip tight to the pommel of the saddle, but Tycho leads at a walk.

He's quiet, so I am too.

Already, the memory is bringing me pain.

When we get back to the forge, the fire has gone cold. The workshop is a bit of a mess. I can see my bow has been snapped, shards of wood sticking out from under the table. I wonder if my father did that, or if I did it myself when I was so angry with Tycho. At the time, I didn't care, but now I do.

I shouldn't. I have bigger worries than archery. My heartbeat is a roar in my ears. Everything that happened in the boarding house feels like a cruel dream.

I find my crutches on the floor, and they slide under my arms. I can't look at him. "Be well, Lord Tycho."

He catches my arm, the first hint of true strength from him. When

I turn with vitriol on my tongue, he steps close, his hand catching my face. He leans in, almost an embrace, but his voice speaks right to my ear.

"I swore to you," he says softly. "Yes?"

I nod. "Yes."

"I keep my word." He pauses, drawing back to look at me. "In truth," he says, "you're the most beautiful man *I've* ever seen. And I'm not confined to the forge."

My heart skips. I can't speak.

I want to tell him everything. But now it's too late. He's leaving. Again. He ties up the black gelding's reins, then springs onto Mercy.

"One week," he says. "Maybe less."

I swallow and nod.

He takes a long breath, then closes his eyes. "Silver hell," he says under his breath. "I'm in trouble already."

"Then go," I say.

"Not yet." He climbs back down from the horse, strides up to me, and before I'm ready, he presses his mouth to mine.

I'm breathless and dizzy and I'm about to make nonsensical sounds again.

Tycho hits me in the chest with something, and I grab hold automatically. "Work on your long range," he's saying. "Remember what I said about your hands."

My thoughts are still tangled up in the feel of his mouth. "What?"

He swings aboard his horse and laughs lightly. "Be well, Jax."

And then he's gone.

It takes me a solid minute before I can look down at whatever he shoved into my chest.

His bow.

CHAPTER 32

TYCHO

I expect Jake to question me while we ride, or to tell me what happened with Jax's father, but he does neither. He's oddly quiet, but I don't really mind, because I can let Mercy canter along the darkening path while my thoughts remain firmly planted in Briarlock. My heart feels so light that my pulse seems to beat in time with her hooves. I feel like I've been smiling for hours, remembering the feel of his skin or the taste of his lips or the silken softness of his hair.

A week will be too long. There's no way to predict what Grey and Lia Mara will need when I return, but it's rather doubtful they'll need me for *much*. It's only a four-hour ride. I could be out and back within a day.

I don't want it to be a day.

"Tycho," says Jake. "Let's give the horses a breather."

I sit down in the saddle and Mercy slows reluctantly, tugging at the reins until she realizes that Jake's horse has dropped to a walk, too. *I* don't want to walk, though. My entire body feels jittery, full of an eagerness that I can't quite reason out. If Jake suggested sprinting on foot the rest of the way, I think I could do it.

Then he says, "So tell me about Jax."

I sigh, inhaling the cool air that's arrived with the twilight.

"Oh dear god," says Jake.

I cut him a glance. "Stop it."

"Look, as much as I love that you've grown up in a place where you've got absolutely no hang-ups about crushing on a guy, I'm going to have to shoot the stars out of your eyes for a second, T."

I turn that around in my head for a moment and come up with nothing. I've known him and Noah and Harper for long enough that they don't often find a phrase that I can't parse out. "Is that Disi talk?"

"No—well, sort of. I'm glad you've finally found someone to pine over, but—"

"I am not *pining.*"

He gives me a look. "There's a reason I knocked when I came back the second time."

"There was no reason to knock." But heat crawls up my neck anyway, and I keep my eyes on the path.

"Uh-huh. And where's your bow?" he says.

"I gave it to Jax. His bow was snapped in the fight with his father."

I expect that to launch a new round of teasing, but instead, he says nothing, and we walk in silence for a while. It's not an uncomfortable silence, but it's *weighted,* like he's thinking.

"What did you mean about 'shooting the stars out of my eyes'?" I say.

"I mean it's obvious you have a thing for this kid, and I get it. He's not breaking any mirrors." He pauses, and his voice drops a bit, gentling. "And I saw his father. I know why you got him out of there."

At the mention of Jax's father, I don't feel gentle at all. "I wish the magistrate had been willing to hold him for longer than two weeks."

Jake is quiet for a long moment. "You said Jax was holding a message for Alek, right? That's the night you were hurt?"

"Yes. He wasn't doing anything but holding the message. He hadn't read it. And today, he told me he hasn't seen Alek since that day. I don't think he was lying."

"If he's not, I know why." He pauses. "Alek has been seeing that baker—Callyn, right?—instead."

I go still. "What?"

"He was there when we were going through the forge. She said he's been coming to Briarlock to see *her*." He pauses. "He walked her back down the lane to the bakery. I didn't follow them too closely, but I rode far enough to see him kiss her at the door—and it sure didn't seem like a first kiss."

Alek and *Callyn*? I try to realign every moment I've spent with Callyn, and I can't draw any conclusions.

While I'm deliberating, Jake reaches a hand into the pouch on his belt and withdraws two small objects that appear to be a combination of wood and steel. When he holds them out, I take them from his palm. They look like wax seals, crudely formed. There are bits of black-and-green wax caked to the metal, along with a few spots of rust, and I study them, trying to determine whether I recognize the design.

Before I've figured it out, Jake holds out a folded scrap of parchment. I loop my free arm through Mercy's reins to take it. The paper is well worn, dusty and stained in spots, as though various items have been shoved on top of it. When I unfold it, I see a dozen sketches of a seal that I *do* recognize.

"The Truthbringers," I whisper. Something in my gut clenches. I look at Jake. "Where did you get this?"

But I know. I know before he even says, "At the forge when we went to arrest his father."

"Then it must be his father's," I say. "I asked Jax—"

"I asked his father. He swore he's never seen that before. I also asked if he was working with the Truthbringers, and he said he only provides what's needed from the forge. He says it was *Callyn's* father who got mixed up with the Uprising. Not him."

My mind won't stop spinning. I have so many questions. Does Jax know? Was he keeping that a secret? His voice was tense when he mentioned Callyn. Could this be why?

"The magistrate said the forge is a full two years behind on their taxes," Jake adds. "The bakery isn't much better. Did you know that?"

The clench on my gut tightens. I remember little Nora's voice. *Look at all that silver!* "No."

"Did you ask Jax about anyone else, or just Alek?"

"Just Alek." I frown.

Jax may have been telling the truth that he hasn't seen him in months, but that doesn't mean he hasn't seen anyone else. That doesn't mean he's not carrying messages for other Truthbringers.

I hand Jake the parchment and study the wax seals again. I don't want to think Jax could be involved.

But he could. I know he could. I remember the whispering with Callyn, the silver they'd spilled all over the floor.

I remember the way he lectured me about privilege and magic. The way Callyn flinched from my touch.

All the joy in my heart has iced over.

"I'm surprised you left them there," I say hollowly. Jake's eyebrows go up, so I add, "Instead of interrogating them. Or dragging them both back to the Crystal City with us." I hold out the seals. I don't want them in my hand.

Jake slips them back into his pouch. "Alek was ready to draw blades when he saw me talking to Callyn. I'm not starting a war over a few scraps of paper. We'll see what Grey wants to do."

I swallow at the implication in his words. "But it doesn't look good."

"No." He sighs. "It doesn't."

The horses plod along. I'm tempted to whirl Mercy around on the path and gallop back to Briarlock, to demand answers I'm not sure I want.

"You're the King's Courier," Jake says.

"I know."

"You have access to the entire royal family—more than just about anyone else—"

"I *know.*"

"I'm not trying to lecture you, T."

"On the day Alek stabbed me, Jax could have finished me off. I had information from Rhen tucked beneath my armor. But I was also with Jax for hours, shooting arrows in the woods." I search my memories of that afternoon. The air was sharp and cold, full of snow flurries. There was a sound in the woods—but we never saw anyone. "If Jax were plotting against the throne, he's had several opportunities to cause trouble. The first time I went to Briarlock was by accident, when Mercy threw a shoe. Alek—or Jax—could have ambushed me then, and he didn't."

"Are you trying to convince me, or yourself?"

I sigh. "Both."

"I'm not saying he's guilty. I saw his father, and that kid probably has a hellish home life. But . . . I know what people are capable of when they're desperate."

I whip my head around and glare at him. "*So do I.*"

He doesn't flinch from my gaze. "I know."

I flush, and now it's some combination of anger and humiliation and a whirlwind of emotions I can barely identify. I draw up Mercy's reins.

Jake reaches out to grab one, and she prances, fighting his grip.

"I didn't tell you this to upset you," he says quietly.

I say nothing. I'm not even angry with him. I'm not angry with Jax either, or even Lord Alek.

I'm angry at myself. I should have been paying attention.

I grit my teeth. "It's fine. I'm fine. Let's go."

"One more thing."

"What." I all but spit the word at him. Mercy tugs at the rein again, prancing sideways. "Let her go," I say.

He does, but I keep a tight grip, waiting to hear what he has to say.

"Grey needs to know," Jake says, and my eyes flash to his. "So," he continues, "do you want to tell him, or should I?"

I'm on edge when I walk through the palace. It's not so late that everyone is asleep, but the hallways feel tense and quiet, with few servants out and about. The tension must all be in my head. I left Jake with the horses, but there's a part of me that wants to change my mind, to hide in the barn with Mercy while Jake handles this conversation.

But that feels cowardly. I didn't want a chaperone—but that means I have to prove I didn't *need* one.

The hallway leading to the royal suites is flanked by guards, but they nod and allow me to pass. When I reach their private chambers, I ask the guards on duty if the king and queen have gone to sleep yet.

Please say yes.

Maybe I did need a chaperone.

"The king is meeting with advisers," says Tika, one of the guards. "But the queen is within. Shall I announce you?"

I hesitate. Lia Mara has been so sick and tired. I don't want to disturb her, especially if she's resting.

The Royal Guards aren't usually friendly with me—or anyone outside their ranks—but Tika hesitates, then leans close and drops her voice. "Her Majesty's spirits are rather low after what happened to the princess. I believe she could do with a bit of kind companionship."

I inhale sharply. "Something happened to Sinna? Is she all right?"

Tika nods. "The princess was found in the forest. She is unharmed."

That only leaves me with more questions, but Tika straightens and reaches for the door handle.

When I'm admitted, I expect the space to be brightly lit, every wall sconce flickering, but instead, the room is dim, the only light coming from the hearth. The queen reclines on a low sofa by the fire, Sinna curled against her, tucked under a light blanket. They're both asleep, a book open under Lia Mara's hand.

The moment feels peaceful and intimate, and I pause just past the threshold. But as my eyes adjust to the light, I can see the red rim of Lia Mara's eyes, the dried tear streak down one cheek. I don't think I've ever seen her cry. The queen has always been full of gentle strength. I've seen her hold the hand of dying soldiers, and she's never wavered.

There are stories all over Syhl Shallow about the king's brutal magic during the Uprising, how fire swept through many of the palace hallways to stop an assault on the royal family. I've heard the tavern tales of how the king's magic fractured limbs and stopped hearts—which are never quite as graphic as what I witnessed with my own eyes. As I told Jax, there was a reason I was glad for a chance to stop being a soldier.

But the stories of the queen's kindness and empathy aren't shared as widely. I walked at her back as she moved from body to body, checking for survivors, using the magic in her own ring to heal anyone she could.

"They're dissenters," I remember the queen's sister saying. Nolla Verin didn't check a single body. "You should leave them to rot."

"They're still my people," said the queen.

The young princess is curled so tightly against her mother. Something has happened. Something bad. I wonder if I should leave, or if I should wait.

While I'm deliberating, the door clicks open, and I turn carefully, putting a finger to my lips before the guards can announce someone new.

But it's not one of the guards. It's the king.

Grey doesn't look surprised to see me, though I'm sure one of the guards told him I was here. It's too dark to read his expression, but his eyes flick to Lia Mara.

When he speaks, his voice is a low rasp. "Is she asleep?"

I nod, then hesitate. "Tika said something happened to Sinna."

Grey draws closer, and I realize that same tension clings to the lines of his face. He looks as tired as Lia Mara does, but he nods. "Let me get them to bed. I'll tell you."

He reaches for the tiny princess, gently disentangling the girl from her mother. The toddler easily snuggles into Grey's shoulder, tucking her face into his neck without waking, but Lia Mara stirs.

"No," she says, and her voice breaks. "No, I want her with me."

"I know," Grey says gently, and there's a note in his voice I don't think I've ever heard before. He rests a hand against her cheek. "Come lie in the bed."

Her eyes are a little wild, not quite awake, and she blinks at him, and then at me. "Oh," she says. "Oh, Tycho. Forgive me."

"You have nothing to apologize for." I take a step back, to quietly leave them to privately deal with . . . whatever this is. But Grey meets my eyes and gives a small shake of his head.

Wait, he mouths.

I give him a small nod. When Lia Mara rises, she tucks herself against his side. There are dark stains at the edge of her chemise. But the family disappears into the bedroom, leaving me with the fire. The room feels heavy and melancholy, but I can't reconcile that with the rest of the palace, which seems tense, but not overwhelmingly so. Something has happened *here*. Between them.

It's not long before Grey reappears, closing the door gently behind him. When he comes to face me before the hearth, I say, "I feel as though I am intruding."

"You're not. I asked you to wait." He pauses, his eyes searching mine. I'm not sure what he finds there, but he says nothing.

There's so much tension in his frame that for a quick moment, I wonder if Jake got to him first, if Grey is going to confront me about Jax and Briarlock right this instant.

But . . . that doesn't match the heady emotion of whatever is going on in this room. Something fractures in his gaze, and Grey has to rub at his eyes. He's frozen in place, not even breathing.

I'm frozen, too. I've never seen him like this. If he were anyone else, I'd touch his arm, or say his name, or . . . just simply *acknowledge* the strain I can feel in the air. But as Rhen said, Grey never yields. Not to his brother, not to the magesmith who once cursed him, not to the threat of war. Not even to pain. He once hiked five miles through the woods when he had an arrow wound through his leg and a dozen lash marks across his back. I was all but crying from the agony of it, but Grey never broke.

While I stand there deliberating, he lets out that breath slowly. His hands lower, and his eyes are clear, his breathing steady. In control again, which should be reassuring, but I just lived through the last thirty seconds, so it's not.

He rubs a hand over the back of his neck and looks away. "We lost the baby."

It's my turn to stop breathing. Four simple words spoken so plainly shouldn't have the impact of a thousand arrows. I thought all this emotion was about something happening to Sinna.

I don't have the right words. I don't even know if the right words *exist*. But I can't stand here in the face of so much pain and do nothing. I step forward and wrap my arms around him.

He's startled for a moment, which isn't surprising, as Grey isn't usually one for affection, and our relationship has been tense for weeks. But then he hugs me back, and he doesn't let go.

"I'm sorry," I say quietly.

He says nothing, but I can feel the weight of his sorrow. If he's crying, he's doing it silently, but he also hasn't pulled away. I wait, and I breathe, and I wonder why fate is so cruel as to bring two men to tears in my presence today.

After a moment or an eternity, Grey pulls back and straightens. His eyes gleam in the firelight. He looks as raw as Lia Mara. I wonder how long ago it happened. He looks like he hasn't slept in days.

"Dice and whiskey?" I say. It's a common expression among the soldiers when someone has suffered a loss. Usually it's followed by a lot more drinking than gaming.

Grey shakes his head. His throat jerks as he swallows.

"Cards?"

He hesitates. "Yes."

We sit. I deal.

Grey picks up his cards, but he doesn't look at them. Instead, he slides them between his fingers and stares into the fire. "It was three days ago," he says, and his voice is as low as I've ever heard it. "Sinna had slipped away from the nanny. You know how she is. Loves to sneak, loves the chase."

I nod.

"But an hour went by," he continues. "Then two. Three. No one could find her. I tried magic, I tried ... everything. She wasn't in the palace. Lia Mara was ..." His voice catches. "She was distraught. The baby began to come. There was so much blood. Noah couldn't stop it. The midwife couldn't stop it. Sinna was missing, and Lia Mara was fighting them to go looking for her daughter, and I just—"

He stops speaking for a long moment, and then he shakes himself and looks at me. "I couldn't do anything. For either one." He rubs at his eyes again. "I tried to use magic on Lia Mara. To stop the labor—but it was too far. Too early. Maybe I made it worse." He grimaces. "I saved her, but the baby . . . the baby was already . . ."

I put a hand on his wrist. "You didn't make it worse."

But as I say the words, I don't know for sure. I remember Lia Mara sitting at breakfast. *You don't know what it would do to the baby.*

"I might have." His eyes meet mine, and I see the guilt and worry there.

"You *didn't*," I say again, and there's a part of me that's trying to convince myself. Grey only ever wants to use his magic for good, but there are times when emotion gets the best of him and his power can flare without focus. It happened when I was fifteen and we were chained to the wall of Rhen's castle. It happened during the Uprising, when hundreds of people surged into the palace.

I don't move my hand. "Where did you find Sinna?"

"In the forest," he says. "Beyond the guard barracks. Well out of the range of my magic. She made it into the mountains. I still don't know how, whether someone lured her or she made it on her own. We found her asleep under a tree. Lia Mara is terrified to allow her out of sight. She doesn't even trust the guards. I'm shocked she fell asleep."

I study him. "When is the last time *you* slept?"

"I catch an hour here and there." His jaw tightens. "No one knows about the baby yet, Tycho. No one but Noah and the midwife. There was so much panic about Sinna, and with as sick as the queen has been . . . we don't want to spread further rumors yet."

I nod. "No one will hear from me."

His mouth twists. "She's been so ill for so long. Noah says it may have happened anyway, that there's no way to know. But I can't help but think that I—" He breaks off and takes a long breath and rubs at his eyes again.

I think of everything going on in Briarlock, but right now, none of it matters. Right now, he's not a king, and she's not a queen. He's a grieving father and she's a heartbroken mother.

"*You* should sleep," I say to him. "You need it as badly as she does."

He gives a humorless laugh. "Well, right now, I don't trust the guards either."

"Sleep," I say quietly. "I'll sit sentry."

He goes still, studying me, and for a flicker of time, I see everything that's unspoken between us. He draws a long breath, and I can't tell if he's going to refuse or acquiesce, so I say, "Go. Rest with your family. I'll stand guard. Sinna won't get past me." I hold his gaze. "Neither will anyone else."

He hesitates, but then he stands, slipping his cards back onto the pile. He puts a hand on my shoulder and gives it a squeeze.

Then he's through the door, and I keep my word.

CHAPTER 33

CALLYN

I'm up before the sun, packing a basket with sugar-glazed muffins, apple tarts, and meat pies for Jax. I don't think my cheeks have cooled since last night. The smell of the sugar and cinnamon in the bakery nearly makes me swoon.

I need to get a hold of myself.

But every time I think about the feel of Alek's hands on my waist or his mouth against mine, my entire body seems to go weak.

If I follow you out to the barn, we won't be sparring with pitchforks.

I brace my back against the wall beside the ovens and inhale deeply.

All I smell is sugar and cinnamon. I need to get outside.

The cool morning air is sharp against my cheeks, and it helps. I stroll down the dimly lit lane, expecting to hear clanging steel at any moment, but when I reach the workshop, the forge is cold and dark, the tools still hung in their places. I rap lightly at the door to the house, but there's no answer, and when I ease the door open and call out his name, my voice only echoes.

I frown and exit the house, pulling the door closed behind me.

I take my basket with me, because I don't want rodents to get into the food if no one is here. Worry forms a pit in my belly. I should've come last night to see if he was back.

As I walk back down the lane, I become aware of an unusual sound out in the woods. The sun hasn't risen far enough for me to see much in the shadows, but the sound isn't an animal. It's not loud enough for an ax either. It's like . . . like a branch breaking? Not quite repetitive.

Thwick. Thwick. A long pause. *Thwick. Thwick.*

A hunter? Or maybe a fur trader? I grab hold of my skirts and stride through the underbrush. We don't often have hunters near the bakery, and when we do, I send them on their way. The last thing I need is Nora catching a wayward arrow.

I spot the man between the trees long before I get to him. He's deeper into the woods than I expected, a good hundred yards, but the shape of a bow is unmistakable. He draws back the string with practiced efficiency, and a second later, I hear the arrow strike a tree somewhere in the distance. He's barely more than a shadow in the early light, but I'm not being very quiet, and he turns, lowering the bow to his side.

"Callyn," he says in surprise.

I stop short. "Jax?"

"What are you doing?" we both say at the same time.

I answer first. "I . . . I was bringing you food." I pause, striding forward again to face him. "I heard about your father."

Jax's eyebrows go up, but his eyes skip away and his mouth forms a line. "Thank you."

I glance down at the bow in his hands. There's a leather bracer buckled around his left forearm and a quiver of arrows over his shoulder, and his crutches are leaning against a nearby tree.

"Your turn," I prompt.

He glances at the bow as if he forgot it was there, and then the corner of his mouth quirks up. "Do you remember Lord Tycho?"

"Of course."

His eyes lock on mine. "Right. Of course." He pauses, and that tiny smile vanishes. "He taught me to shoot. I've been practicing."

I look past him to discover targets set out in the distance, small panels of wood that have been nailed into tree trunks, with several suspended rings hanging here and there. The ropes look weather-worn, and several of the rings are spotted with rust.

I knew Jax and I had drifted apart, but with as busy as the bakery has been, I hadn't really noticed how much time had passed. Seeing this seems to drive it home. "You've been doing this for a while," I murmur.

"Not really," he says casually, and I somehow forgot that low rasp in his voice when he's uncertain. "I've only been out for a quarter hour."

"No—I meant—" I shake my head. "Never mind. Are you all right?"

He nods, then shrugs, but his shoulders are tight. "They're going to hold Da for a fortnight."

I can't tell how he feels about that. Things feel so awkward between us, and they've never been awkward. "Well—I said I'd make sure you had enough to eat—"

"I can hunt for my own food now." A dark light sparks in his eyes. "But I'll pay you for anything I take."

"No! Jax, you don't—I'm not—" I make a frustrated sound. "Forget it. I'll leave the basket at the forge. When you need more, you know where to find me."

I turn and head back out of the woods, my feet loud through the dense underbrush. I don't know how he makes it through here on his crutches, because there's hardly a path, but maybe he's been getting a lot of practice at it.

"Callyn!" he calls, but I don't stop.

After a moment, he swears, and I hear his crutches striking the ground. "Would you *stop*?" he snaps. "Clouds above, you know I can't chase you."

That makes me stop and turn, just as the sun breaks fully across the horizon, flooding the woods with buttery light. He's actually pretty good at chasing me, because he's nearly right on top of me when I turn. I'm not sure what about Jax looks different, but there's . . . *something.* Some element of determination or confidence that never seemed to be lacking, but seems to radiate from him now.

He stops in front of me, and his hazel eyes are shadowed but earnest. "Cal. Whatever I've done . . . whatever happened between us . . . I'm sorry."

I frown. He thinks *he* did something? He thinks I'm mad at him? "Jax—"

"I know you were anxious about the Truthbringers. But you were right. I asked for too much silver—and they found someone else to hold their messages. I was so relieved when you seemed to be getting more business—"

"Jax."

"—even though we're still scraping by for enough to pay the rest of what we owe." He runs a hand across the back of his neck. "I know I've let you down, and I'm sorry. I don't know how I'm going to keep up with the work when Da is locked up—"

"*Jax.*"

He breaks off. "What?"

My chest is tight and I can't fully understand why. But I remember the panic in my gut yesterday, when the magistrate went galloping down the lane. I know I've missed my best friend. I stride forward and throw my arms around his neck.

"I've missed you," I murmur.

He keeps hold of one crutch, but hugs me with his opposite arm. "I've missed you, too. I've had no company but Da, and you know how that goes." His tone turns dark, and I remember how the magistrate was dragging his father yesterday. I wonder what happened between them.

I draw back to look at him. "But you just said you've been spending time with Lord Tycho."

"Oh! No. Just a time or two."

I tug at the quiver strap across his chest. "This seems like more than a time or two."

"I've been practicing on my own." A bit of pink finds his cheeks, and he glances away. "He's very busy."

I study him. He studies me back.

I hate that we're uncomfortable with each other. I *hate* it.

I think of Lord Alek, how things are so different from the first night he came into the bakery. How I was ready to draw a knife on him that evening—and I was ready to tug him up the stairs to my room last night.

My own cheeks are probably turning pink.

"Well," I say.

"Well."

I don't know how we've gotten to this point, but I don't want to stay here.

"Do you want to come to the bakery for a bit?" I say in a rush. His eyebrows go up, and he hesitates, but I keep going. "Nora is still sleeping, but we could have breakfast. I mean—unless you don't have time. I know you're . . ." I glance past him, at the archery course he's obviously set up. It's a bit shocking, to think that he's been doing something like this and I had no idea. "Ah . . . busy."

For an instant he says nothing, but then he smiles. "I can spare some time."

I brew tea and set the muffins out on my work table. Jax takes the stool where he always sits, placing his crutches against the wall where they always lean, only this time he leaves his bow and quiver there, too.

I shove the muffins in his direction, and he unbuckles the leather bracer before taking one.

While I pour the tea, I nod at . . . everything. "Tell me how that all happened."

He tucks a loose lock of hair behind his ear and makes a face. "I'm . . . not sure, really. I told you about the day Lord Tycho brought Mercy up the lane for new shoes. Da was being . . . well, himself." Jax frowns. "Tycho said he needed someone to accompany him to town to see about some repairs. I thought he was going to drag me out to the woods and leave me for dead."

I remember him telling me. He said they talked. He said Alek showed up and fought with Tycho. Archery never made it into the conversation. "But he taught you to shoot?"

Jax smiles. "Well, not right away. I think . . . I think he's lonely. A bit."

I'm staring at him. I don't think I've seen Jax blush like this since we used to whisper over Mother's racy novels.

You fancy him, I said to Jax weeks ago. He didn't deny it. He's not denying it now.

He shrugs and takes a sip of his tea. "I've been practicing on my own. With Da's old bow. I didn't see Tycho for weeks. Months, really. I didn't think I'd ever see him again." That blush deepens on his cheeks. "Ah . . . until yesterday. Da was drunk and he came after me. Tycho stopped him. He took me into town and healed the worst of it. He was here with another man from the palace—Lord Jacob. They were looking for Alek. Honestly, Cal, I'm glad of how things turned out. You were right. It was too dangerous. I was taking too much of a risk. Maybe with Da locked up, I can scrape together enough coins to pay for next month. Your business has clearly been doing well with all the travelers, so—" He must notice my expression, because he breaks off. "What? What's wrong?"

There's too much. I don't know what to say.

Nora chooses this moment to skip down the stairs. "Jax!" she cries.

He smiles. "Nora!" he teases. "Those hens still pecking your fingers off?"

"Every *day*," she says dramatically. She sweeps into the room, her skirts spinning. "I need Cally-cal to marry a lord from the Crystal City so we can hire someone to—"

"Nora!" I snap.

"Oh, she's marrying you off?" Jax says to me, smiling. "Do you have a line of suitors?"

My face feels frozen. They're teasing, but it's all too close to home.

"*I* told her to marry Lord Tycho," Nora continues. "He was so handsome," she sighs. "But he hasn't been here in quite some time—"

"Nora," I say quickly. "Muddy May needs milking."

"I just put on my new skirt!" she says. "I don't want to get straw everywhere." She spins again, and I realize she *is* wearing a new skirt. It's a deep maroon, with green ivy stitched along the hem. I wonder if Lord Alek or Lady Karyl brought it to her, and I'm deathly afraid she'll volunteer this information next.

"Fine," I say. "I'll do it. Here. Have a muffin."

She scoops one off the table and shoves half into her face.

Jax leans in to murmur, "What were you going to say? Are you short on silver, Cal? I can see what's left of the stash I have buried."

"We're not short on silver," Nora says brightly around a mouthful of muffin. "Lord Alek has been sending customers our way for *weeks*. Sometimes we run out of food and we have to turn them away."

Jax goes very still. His eyes lock on mine.

"Jax," I whisper.

"I thought he was scary," Nora prattles on, "but he's truly very kind. He brought me new boots last week."

"Oh yeah?" Jax says tightly. His eyes don't leave mine. "What else has he done?"

"He fixed the barn," she says. "And the loose hinges on the door. Just there." Her voice turns devious, and she cuts a glance at me. "And last night, I caught Cal *kissing*—"

"NORA."

Jax is already off the stool, stooping to fetch the quiver and bow. His eyes are hard and ice cold.

"Wait," I say. "Jax. Wait."

He rounds on me. "All this time, and I thought you were mad at me for ruining it. I didn't realize you'd taken my place."

"No!" I cry. "That's not it at all! He was going—he was going to hurt you—"

"Yet you were kissing him. Sounds like a great deal of concern went through your thoughts."

"You don't know anything about it!" I snap, but he's already at the door, and he throws it wide.

"I *do*," he says viciously. "I do know something about it. Because I was *doing* it, and I saw how he treated me, and I saw what he did to Lord Tycho. So whatever he's told you, whatever he's promised, it's a lie, Callyn. I may have been using them for silver, but now they're using *you*." He gives me a pointed up-and-down glance. "For more than just passing notes, I'm assuming."

I draw a sharp breath. "Don't you dare."

"You're risking your neck," he says. "At least I had nothing to lose." He glances at Nora. "I don't care how much silver he's paying you. He's conspiring against the Crown. He's committing treason. And now *you're* the one helping him. What will happen to your sister when you're caught?"

"What?" Nora whispers.

"What if the king is using *magic* against the queen?" I snap. "You know what he did to my father. How is it treason if Alek is being loyal to the queen?"

Jax swears. "He got to you. Now you're on their side. I should have figured."

"You were also committing treason! And now you're lusting after the King's Courier!"

He flushes, but his eyes are full of nothing but anger. "You're right. So turn me in. We can hang beside each other, just like you wanted." Then he slams the door.

I throw a muffin at it.

It's not satisfying.

Nora is staring at me with wide eyes. "Is he right? Are you committing treason?" she whispers.

"No," I say sharply. "Of course not."

For half a second, I expect her to start pelting me with questions, and I'm going to be tempted to throw myself into the ovens. I press my hand over the pendant that hangs over my heart and draw a slow breath.

Instead, my sister strides across the floor to wrap me up in a hug. "It'll be all right," she says, and it's only then that I realize I'm crying. "It'll be all right, Cally-cal."

"I know," I whisper, hugging her back.

But I really have no idea whether it will or not.

CHAPTER 34

TYCHO

When I'm wary and uncertain, I often seek out the infirmary. It's usually where I find Noah. Grey may have taught me how to defend myself—how to *save* myself—but when I was younger and terrified of what fate might have in store, Noah always gave me a safe space to heal. He's always steadfast and unflinching, no matter what he sees—or what I tell him.

Today, of course, he has patients, so I have to wait. I don't mind, though. The infirmary is warm and tranquil, and Salam has trailed me down here to sprawl in the late afternoon sunlight that beams down through the windows. After traveling all day yesterday and sitting sentry all night, I slept most of today away, and I'm still not quite awake. I send for tea and entertain myself by teasing the cat with a piece of straw, smiling when he leaps to bat at my knuckles with barely sheathed claws.

Eventually, though, I'm alone with Noah, and he begins unpacking a crate full of supplies.

"I heard about Jax," he says without preamble. "I figured you'd find your way down here eventually."

"Hmm," I say noncommittally. Jake must have told him about what he discovered in the workshop. "I haven't told Grey about all that yet."

"'All that'?" he echoes.

I glance at him. "The sketches and seals."

"Oh." Noah is quiet for a moment. "Why not?"

"Last night wasn't—it wasn't the right time." I shrug, then run a hand over the back of my neck, remembering the weight in the room when Grey admitted what had happened, confessing his fears. "Well. You know."

Noah nods solemnly. "I know."

"And then this morning," I continue, "Grey gave me leave and said he was due to meet with Lia Mara's advisers. That didn't feel like the right time either." At daybreak, he was cool and distant, as stoic and reserved as I've ever seen him.

Or maybe I was just looking for a reason to postpone a conversation about how I might have been sharing breath with a man conspiring against the Crown.

Noah says nothing, but he glances over. He pulls a large fold of muslin from the box and uses a knife to tear it into more manageably sized strips. And he waits.

I don't know what to say. I know I'm supposed to be thinking about my duties here, about my responsibility to both Syhl Shallow and Emberfall. I carry a lot of secrets and truths, and what I learned last night is one of the deepest, darkest secrets I've ever been given. I have no idea how Grey and Lia Mara will reveal this loss to the people. Word of the queen's pregnancy has already begun spreading among the citizens of Syhl Shallow. Jake and I even caught wind of it in a few of the taverns on Emberfall's side of the border. Could the Truthbringers have been involved in whatever happened to little Sinna? There have never been threats against the princess. The queen's children, especially daughters, are always held in high regard in Syhl Shallow, and that's been consistent the whole time I've been here.

And why would Jax have seals bearing the Truthbringer sigil? What are he and Callyn involved in? Does Alek have anything to do with it? Years ago, his sister was a traitor to the Crown, but Alek has always staunchly denied any involvement. He might hate me, and he might hate Emberfall, but that doesn't mean he's plotting against his queen.

The worst part about all this deliberation is that thoughts of Jax keep pushing everything else aside. I'm imagining the silken feel of his hair between my fingers. Or his hands, a little rough and a little uncertain. Or his eyes, cool and focused when he drew back the string on my bow.

I'm remembering the tearstains on his cheeks after his father nearly killed him. I'm thinking of his hand holding mine as he showed me how to feed steel to the forge. I'm thinking of him brandishing a red-hot iron in front of Lord Alek.

I'm thinking of the taste of his mouth.

"Tycho."

I blink and look up. "What?"

Noah keeps tearing muslin. "When I said *I heard about Jax*," he says gently, "I wasn't talking about plots against the king and queen."

I make an aggrieved sound and flop back on the cot where I'm sitting.

Noah laughs. "You're not the first kid to fall for someone acting a little shady."

My insides clench. I keep my eyes on the ceiling. "I let myself get distracted. I should have stayed focused on my duties, Noah."

"I don't think that's how life works. Like you can just stay *focused* and nothing will ever go astray." He pauses. "People will surprise you, Tycho. For bad, for good, in so many ways you'll never expect."

I turn that around in my head for a bit. "I don't know," I finally say. "Grey is never distracted. Jake isn't. Lia Mara. Nolla Verin. *You*."

He chuckles softly. "Tycho, I'm *here*. If you don't think being yanked out of Washington, DC, was a distraction—"

I scoff. "That's not the same."

"Fine. I can tell you I was plenty focused when I was a doctor. *So* focused. I graduated at the top of my class at Georgetown—that's a really fancy, expensive school for medicine. Then I landed at Hopkins for my residency—one of the best places you can get into. I had my whole future lined up. But I forgot my wallet one day, and there was this . . . this . . ." Noah looks up at the ceiling, searching for words. "I'm trying to think of what you'd call it here. Like . . . a scruffy young outlaw, I guess. He was in line behind me. He paid for my coffee. He was probably a heartbeat away from prison—or, hell, a grave. He had *trouble* written all over him." Noah rolls his eyes. "Even once I got to know him, he'd never tell me what he was doing, but I could tell it was bad. He'd show up with bruises. Once he got a cut over his eye and I had to drag him to get stitches. Sometimes he'd have blood in the creases of his knuckles, and I'd have to pretend not to notice. I probably should have steered clear—stayed *focused*—" He gives me a look and rips clean through another piece of muslin. "But on that first day, there was something . . . something *gentle* about the way he offered me two bucks. He looked like someone you wouldn't want to meet in a dark alley, but as soon as he spoke, I was no good."

I study him. "Who was he?" I say. "What happened to him?"

Noah startles, then bursts out laughing. "I'm talking about Jake."

I sit straight up. "Wait. Jake was a *scruffy young outlaw*?"

"The scruffiest."

"What was he doing?"

"He was shaking people down for money. Threatening them if they couldn't pay what they owed."

"Huh." I try to reconcile that with the man who sat next to me on a horse and lectured me about my duties to the Crown.

A servant appears in the doorway. "My lords." She bobs a curtsy. "His Majesty requests your presence in the library, Lord Tycho."

"Of course," I say, though the request sends a tiny spike of dread right into my heart. I wish I could shake the worry that I've been carrying around for *weeks*. "Right away."

"Tycho." Noah's voice catches me before I'm through the door, and I pause, looking back.

"Jake wasn't doing good things," he says. "But he didn't think he had any other choice. He was trying to protect his family."

I nod. "I know. Jake is a good man."

"He was a good man *then*, too." He pauses. "You're not distracted. You're not reckless. If your heart tells you someone deserves your attention, listen to it."

The library is on the far side of the palace, with thousands of books, dozens of tables and armchairs, and countless shadowed corners where anyone could sit and get lost in a story. Huge floor-to-ceiling windows look out over the Crystal City, allowing the sun to flood the space with warmth in the afternoon. I don't think Grey has ever summoned me *here*, and I'm surprised at the location he's chosen—until I reach the library and find him sitting at a table with a sheaf of papers, while Sinna sits at a distance with a middle-aged woman I've never met before. Sinna is playing with her dolls in front of the windows.

When she spots me, she sprints across the velvet carpeting. "Tycho!"

I reach out to catch her, to throw her in the air.

Grey looks up. "*Sinna*," he says sharply, and she skids to a stop.

"Forgive me," she says primly. She offers me a crooked curtsy, then whispers, "Da has been cross all afternoon."

I want to frown, but I school my features to stay neutral, then bow in return. "No apologies are necessary, Your Highness," I say, then wink, and she giggles.

The older woman has caught up to Sinna. She looks more regal than the usual nannies who chase the princess around the palace, which makes me wonder if they've hired a governess instead. This woman has gray hair in braids that are coiled on top of her head, and one eye is blue while the other is brown. She curtsies to Grey and then to me. "Forgive *me*, Your Majesty. My lord." She takes little Sinna by the hand and leads her back to the sunlit spot by the windows.

I brace myself and approach the table, but Grey gestures to a chair. "Tycho. Sit."

I sit. He looks better rested than he did last night, but there's still a tension around his eyes that's never been there before. I wonder if it's about Sinna and the baby—but the king wouldn't have called me here to talk about that. Maybe Jake finally told him what we found at the forge. About what happened with Jax.

Despite everything Noah said, Grey is the king, and he deserves the truth. I can own up to my mistakes. Warmth crawls up my neck, and I inhale to do exactly that.

But Grey says, "My brother tells me we're at odds." He shoves a leather-bound folio in my direction.

I freeze, then clamp my mouth shut. So much has happened over the last week that I almost forgot about my conversation with Prince Rhen. I let out a long breath. "I did not say we're *at odds*—"

He taps the letter. "See what he wrote."

I hesitate, then look down at the first few lines of Rhen's perfectly even script.

Dear Brother,

I have many thoughts on the Royal Challenge and your impending return to Ironrose, but I would be remiss if I did not open my letter by insisting that you resolve this discord with Tycho.

I snap my eyes up. "Grey. I didn't tell him to write this."

"I rather doubt you could tell Rhen to do anything he didn't want to do himself." His eyes flash. "Keep going."

I bite my lip and look back at the letter.

> You and I have had our disagreements, including that one time we assembled armies to settle our grievances, but I have seen Tycho's loyalty to you since the very moment you were both dragged into the courtyard at Ironrose. You yourself went seeking your freedom before claiming your throne, and I encourage you to recognize that while Tycho may wear no crown, he may well seek the same escape.

I wince. I don't want to read the rest of this letter. I can just imagine what it says. "I'm not trying to escape," I say quietly.

Grey's eyes are unyielding. "Is there conflict we must resolve?"

I think of everything I've done wrong: Nakiis. Alek. Jax. Magic. Briarlock.

I think of all the measures Grey took to mitigate risk: Keeping me here. Sending Jake with me to Ironrose.

The worst part is that he was *right*. I shouldn't have freed Nakiis. I shouldn't have threatened Alek.

I . . . shouldn't have lingered with Jax.

"No," I say. My insides feel tight and uncertain, and I can't tell if my deep-seated worry is about arguing with Grey or about denying everything I've felt up till this moment. "There isn't." I pause. "Grey. I'm sorry."

He sighs, then runs a hand over the back of his head, casting a gaze at the window, where Sinna is now lining up her dolls to peer out through the glass. His gaze softens when he looks at his daughter, and it reminds me of the heady emotion from last night. Sinna is talking to her dolls, but her voice is so soft that I can't quite make out everything she's saying.

"We have to watch the skies," she's murmuring. "You can all look."

"Lia Mara wants to make a statement about the baby before rumors can begin to spread," Grey says, dragging my attention back to him. "I expect she'll want to do it first thing in the morning, if not this very evening." He pauses. "But Jake tells me there were some complications in Briarlock again. He seemed surprised you hadn't spoken a word of it."

I freeze.

"Is this more of the conflict we're not having?" Grey says.

I frown. "Last night didn't seem the best time—"

"I'm not just talking about last night." He taps a hand on the letter from Rhen. "You haven't been forthright with me for *weeks*."

I bristle. "I've never lied to you."

"Deceit isn't always about lying." His eyes are intent and focused.

Deceit. My emotions hit me so fast that I can't seem to sort through them quickly enough to respond. I'm frozen in place, simultaneously hurt and ashamed, belligerent and repentant.

"Tycho." He smacks the table. "*Talk.*"

I jump, and from the corner of my eye, I see the governess flinch. At the window, Sinna whirls. She clutches the dolls to her chest.

Not all of this is about me. I know that. The king is buried in his own emotion, and I wasn't even here for the last few days—days that must have been filled with heady fear and worry.

But my jaw is tight. Maybe we *are* at odds—and a lot of that is from his side.

I've never faced Grey like this. Every muscle in my body is tense, and I'm very aware that anything I say, anything I *do*, is going to be witnessed by little Sinna.

A page appears near the archway. "Your Majesty," she says. "Lord Alek of the Third House has arrived for an audience with the queen.

He says he has an urgent matter for discussion. Her Majesty requests your presence."

"Right away," he says, and the page curtsies before slipping away. But Grey's eyes haven't left mine. "Is Alek bringing us any surprises?" he says.

"No—I—" I swear and break off. Of *course* Alek would arrive at exactly this moment. "Grey, I don't know what he's doing. But I'm not keeping any secrets. I've never been disloyal." The words almost hurt to say.

"Good." He rises from the table. "Come along. Let's see."

CHAPTER 35

TYCHO

I'm not one for murderous thoughts, but for Alek, I'm making an exception. I'm wishing I hadn't left my bow with Jax, because I long to nock an arrow on the string and let it fly. I imagine Alek flailing on the floor of the throne room, writhing as he tries to pull a shaft free of his chest. His blue eyes would be clouded with pain and anger, and he'd be trying to swear at me, but the arrow would've punctured his lung.

I bet you'd accept a bit of magic now, wouldn't you, I'd say.

Much like Grey's barely restrained temper wasn't all about *me*, mine isn't all about Alek.

But some of it is.

I should probably join Jake by the side of the dais, but I'm still smarting from Grey's comments, and I don't need to be chastised again. Instead, I linger by the wall a bit apart from everyone. Alek stands in the middle of the throne room, dressed for travel, armed for battle. His expression is troubled and wary, but he bows respectfully when the queen gestures for him to come forward. "Your Majesty," he says. "I hoped to speak with you alone."

Lia Mara is resplendent on her throne, wearing glistening red robes with a black satin belt, her hair long and shining over her shoulder. There's no hint of distress or dismay about her expression, but she takes Grey's hand and holds it when he joins her on the dais. His thumb strokes over her knuckles slowly, and just that tiny movement steals some of my agitated worry. Their pain is invisible, but it seems to radiate throughout this entire room.

"We issued a summons weeks ago," Lia Mara says evenly. "If you wished to speak with me alone, Lord Alek, you've had ample opportunity. Now you will address my court and explain yourself."

"I sent word—"

"You attacked the King's Courier. You assaulted a member of this court."

"I defended myself, Your Majesty." His voice is just as even as hers is. "As is my right. If the king has seen fit to grant *magic* to those in his circle, you should be aware when those powers are abused."

I was defending myself, too. I want to speak so badly that my fingertips are digging into my palms.

"Tycho doesn't abuse his power," says Grey.

"How do you know?" says Alek. "Have you asked him?"

I have to bite the inside of my cheek to keep myself from speaking.

"Do not question me," Grey says coolly. "You were summoned here to answer for what *you* did."

"I *have* answered for what I did," Alek says. "Tycho should be forced to answer for *his* actions." He pauses, gazing around the room dramatically. "Did I injure him so badly that he cannot speak for himself?" His eyes land on me, and they're ice cold.

I'm sure mine match.

"No," Alek continues frostily. "He's right there. He bears the magic to heal himself, so these claims of *assault* seem rather frivolous to me." He pauses, his eyes finding mine again. "Would you like for me to do it again, and we can all have a demonstration?"

I have never wished for a sword and dagger as much as I do this very moment. "Go ahead and try," I say darkly. "We shall see how it ends."

He draws blades. "Gladly."

"*Hold.*" Lia Mara's voice is clear and sharp over the sudden murmur that echoes through the throne room. "I will not abide bloodshed in my court."

Alek's gaze hasn't left mine. My heart is pounding in my chest, and my hand clenches near the hilt of a sword that's not there.

Danger sparks in his eyes as he says, "The old queen would not have minded a bit of sport."

"I am not my mother," Lia Mara snaps, "and you would do well to remember that, Lord Alek. Now put up your weapons."

He slides his sword and dagger into their sheaths as quickly and smoothly as he drew them, then bows again with perfect gallantry. "As you say, Your Majesty."

The court falls silent again—or maybe the rush of my pulse is blocking any sound. I force myself to look away from Alek, to see how this interaction is being received. As always, there are many people here who don't trust the king, just like Alek. There are many people who love the queen—just not the man at her side. It wasn't different four years ago, when we first came to Syhl Shallow. But in the months since the Uprising, this feeling has grown darker, more insidious. A dagger in a shadowed corner instead of open rebellion.

Alek has taken a step forward, and his tone is repentant now. "Had I known you bore such doubts about my response, Your Majesty, I would have returned to court at once. I assure you, I meant the King's Courier no harm. I knew he had magic, and I assumed we were simply . . . having a disagreement."

"That involved bloodshed," she says flatly.

"I contend that he threatened me with magic first," says Alek.

He's not lying. Grey looks at me, and his gaze could cut steel.

I have nothing to say.

The queen is still looking at Alek. "Tycho is not one to pick a fight," she says, and the king leans in to murmur something to her.

"Perhaps not one to pick a fight," says Alek. "But I would ask that you inquire about his dealings in the small town of Briarlock. He has been seen many times with the young blacksmith who held a message for me." Alek's gaze shifts to Grey. "I believe your man-at-arms discovered some effects that indicate a link to the Truthbringers in the blacksmith's workshop, did he not? I have heard that the boy is hungry for silver, and your so-called courier enjoys a good bit of freedom." He looks at some of the other House ladies and lords who are gathered in the throne room. "Rumors have been flying in the city that Princess Sinna was at risk. Missing for *hours*, in fact. I believe we all deserve to know whether you've brought someone into your confidence who seeks to work *against* our queen—"

"Enough," says Grey, and his voice is low and vicious. "Tycho is not working against the queen."

A low murmur has filled the throne room again, but Alek looks at me. "Were you in Briarlock yesterday?"

"You know I was there," I say tightly. "Inquiring as to *your* whereabouts."

"Were you?" he says, putting a finger to his lips. "I saw Lord Jacob, but not you. He was well informed of my reasons for being there." He pauses. "Where was the young blacksmith, then?"

I swallow tightly. Every eye in the room is on me—including Grey and Lia Mara.

"Answer," says Grey, and there's absolutely no give in his voice.

"He had nothing to do with this!" I say. "He was injured, and I—"

"Used the king's magic to heal him?" says Alek. "A young man who'd displayed evidence of working with the Truthbringers? Who else have you been working with, Tycho?"

I inhale to snap at him, but the room explodes with noise and commotion, including nobles who are suddenly demanding a formal inquiry. Many others are yelling for the queen to separate herself from the king.

Jake appears beside me. "Not another word," he says.

"He's *lying*," I seethe.

"They don't think he is," Jake says under his breath. "If he's trying to be misleading, it's working."

The queen is on her feet. "I will have silence," she declares. "And I will have order, and I will have—"

She makes a tiny sound, very much like a gasp, and it's such a small noise that I almost don't register that I've heard it. But her hand goes to her abdomen, and she gasps again. Almost as quickly, she's straightening, her free hand clutching at Grey's hand. Her face has gone pale, but she's clearing her throat.

"I will have silence," she declares.

But the room is already silent. I'm not the only one to have noticed.

Everyone has gone still. Almost every eye has fallen to that hand that rests above her stomach.

Grey leans close to her and says something, his voice very low. Her jaw is tight, and she draws a slow breath before straightening.

Some of the contempt has slipped out of Alek's expression, and his gaze shifts from the queen to the king. Instead of disdain, his eyes flicker with outright hostility when it comes to Grey. The court might not know what's happened yet, but Alek is savvy enough with court politics to know *something* is amiss. It's bad enough that there are already rumors about Sinna's disappearance.

"I will meet with my advisers to discuss what has been said this evening," Lia Mara says, and her voice is strong and clear.

"Perhaps the King's Courier should be stripped of his magic until these questions have suitable answers."

I go still. This suggestion comes from a woman of the court, Lady Delmetia Calo. She's the head of the Fifth House, which isn't known for being closely allied with Alek. I've never had an issue with her—and to my knowledge, she's never been outright opposed to Grey either.

For her to suggest this means the distrust of magic may run even deeper than I thought.

"Take them off," Jake whispers. "Do it now, before anyone orders it. Do it before it looks like you have a problem with it."

I *do* have a problem with it.

All eyes are on me again, so I tug at the steel rings, pulling them free of my fingers. I've worn them for so long that they scrape past my knuckles. The whole time, I'm waiting for the king or queen to tell me to stop, to speak in my defense, to tell the court that Alek's accusations are baseless lies.

But they don't.

This is worse than humiliating. I'd almost rather the guards cut my fingers off and take them by force. My jaw is so tight I don't think I'll be able to speak, but I step onto the dais and bow to them both, then hold out a hand with the rings.

"I will answer any questions you have," I force out. I don't know what else to say.

I would never betray you.

That's what I want to say. But I shouldn't have to. They should know it.

Grey takes the rings from my palm. "Return to your quarters. We will send for you."

"Yes, Your Majesty."

I bow again, then stride out of the room.

I expect someone to follow, but no one does.

It's bizarre to think that last night, I was sitting sentry so the king and queen could get a night of sleep without worrying for the princess, and now I'm sitting alone in my room, wondering if I'm going to lose my position at court.

I don't know what Jax is doing. I don't know what Alek is doing.

I do know I'm not working with the Truthbringers.

But I remember how Lady Delmetia Calo said I should relinquish any access to magic. The way the court erupted in shouting. Maybe Alek has sowed enough doubt in me, in magic, in the king, that truth won't matter. Just perception.

I flop back on my bed, staring at the ceiling. I'm not a prisoner, but I feel like one. I wonder how long I'll be forced to wait.

Salam helpfully pads across my bed, lies down on my chest, and begins to purr.

I sigh and absently go to twist the rings around my fingers, but they're not there. My hands feel weird without them. My *thoughts* feel weird without them. It's not a feeling of vulnerability, not entirely, but . . . maybe a little.

My door clicks softly, and I startle. Salam scrabbles off the bed to dash out of sight.

Little Sinna slips through the gap, letting the door fall closed behind her.

I sit up straight. "Sinna!"

She puts a finger to her lips. "Shh. I'm hiding."

The last thing I need right now is the princess sneaking away from her governess and hiding *in my chambers*. I stand and put out a hand. "You need to go back. Come. I'll take you."

"No!" she whispers, then dashes to the opposite side of the room, climbing into the window seat. "I need to look."

"Look for what?" I stride across the floor. "If you go missing again, your new governess will be dismissed—"

"I can't see the woods like you can, Tycho." She presses her tiny hands against the glass. "He said I have to be patient, but he would come back."

My heart seems to stop beating for a bare second, then kicks hard against my ribs. "Who?" I demand. "Who said he would come back?"

"Shh," she whispers. "He said Da would not like it."

I'm staring at her. "Sinna. Who?"

"He doesn't have a name, but he could *fly*, Tycho! He gave me a leaf made of ice, too. It was so *cold*—"

"*Silver hell.*" I run a hand over the back of my neck and swear under my breath.

She looks at me crossly. "Mama says those words are only for the battlefield."

I drop to a crouch in front of her. "Sinna—how did he fly?"

Her face screws up. "With *wings*, silly." She kneels up on the window seat and presses a finger to my lips. "But we can't tell Da."

I make a choking sound. Of course they wouldn't find tracks around little Sinna. Nakiis wouldn't have to leave tracks when he could fly out of sight.

I don't know why he'd come after the princess, but I do know how he feels about Grey—about any magesmith, really.

They've been suspecting Truthbringers or some kind of plots against the throne, but whoever lured Sinna into the woods was some-one I let out of a cage.

I scoop Sinna into my arms. "I need to bring you back. You can't be here right now, Sinna."

She howls and wiggles and tries to climb over my shoulder. I ignore her thrashing and head for my door. When I throw it open, there are already guards in the hallway, and I hear voices down at the other end calling Sinna's name.

"I have her," I call. "Sinna snuck into my room."

"Let me down!" She kicks her feet. "Tycho, you let me down!"

Lia Mara appears before me, and she takes her flailing daughter into her own arms. "I have had enough of your sneaking—"

"I want to look at the woods!" she says.

"*Sinna.*" Grey's voice is sharp, like the crack of a whip, and the toddler jumps.

So does Lia Mara. "Grey," she begins softly.

"She cannot keep doing this," he says, and his expression is like thunder.

"She's fine," I say. "She wanted to look out the window at the woods—"

"No!" Sinna shrieks. "Don't tell him, Tycho!"

There's an audible gasp among the guards. Every head in the hallway turns to look at me, and I nearly flinch.

Grey takes a step toward me, and he looks like he could burn me to ash without thinking twice. "You had *better* tell me."

"*Of course I'm going to tell you,*" I snap.

There's no gasp this time, just the brittle tension of a dozen held breaths.

I force my hands to unclench and fall back a step. "Your Majesty."

He points at my door. "Inside. Now."

I expect him to slam the door once we're inside my room, but he doesn't. He eases it closed, then leans against it, arms folded.

"Talk," he says.

I swallow. I've never been on this side of his anger. I told Jax that

I would take a knee and swear fealty again if Grey demanded it—and I meant it when I said it. I would do it right now.

But for the first time, after what transpired in the throne room, I find myself wondering where Grey would stand if I needed *his* help.

His eyes are dark and unyielding, and I'm worried I've already learned the answer.

"She snuck in here," I say quietly. "She said she wanted to look out the window. Just like she was doing in the library earlier."

"That's not a secret," he says. "What else?"

"She said she's looking for *him*," I say. "I don't know who *him* is." I hesitate. "But I'm worried it might be Nakiis."

His eyes don't thaw one bit. "Why?"

"He told her not to tell you that he was here. She said he had wings. She said he made her a leaf out of ice. You remember how Iisak used to—"

"I remember."

I take a breath. "She said she doesn't know his name, but he told her not to tell you about him." I pause. "She said he would be coming back."

He studies me for the longest time, and I refuse to wither under his gaze. The silence is unbearable, though. When he says nothing, I start talking.

"He didn't hurt her, Grey—and he could have. You saw my armor. You know what they're capable of. She's so tiny that he probably could have carried her out of here—"

"Tycho." His voice isn't sharp anymore, and he runs a hand across the lower half of his face. Underneath all his anger and worry and doubt, there still flows a current of pain.

I hear what he's *not* saying, too. Nakiis might not have hurt her—but that doesn't mean he wouldn't have. Or that he wouldn't have used her against Grey.

"He let her go," I say softly. "He left her unharmed."

"He said he would return."

"I know."

"There is already such distrust for magic, and now—"

"I *know*."

"And now I am to warn my guards and soldiers that a magical threat may come from the *sky*."

"He's *one* scraver—"

"You hope." He gives me a look.

I bite my tongue.

He's silent again. So quiet that wind rattles my windowpanes, and I nearly jump.

"Jake told me of what happened in Briarlock," he finally says. "About Jax."

I flush and look away, fidgeting. "Grey . . ."

"Even when I felt an attraction for Lia Mara, I knew my duty to Emberfall. And later, to Syhl Shallow."

I frown. "I know."

"I know you're not working with the Truthbringers, Tycho."

I look up in surprise.

His gaze hasn't softened. "But it doesn't matter what I know." He pauses. "At court, your loyalty is in question. The company you keep is in question. Your *actions* are in question. You may hate Lord Alek, but you heard the reaction to his accusations." His eyes seem to darken. "Your position won't get better once I warn the soldiers about Nakiis. To say nothing of Lia Mara."

"Forgive me," I say. "I would never—"

"I don't want apologies," he says.

I freeze. "As you say."

"I want you to return to Ironrose," he says.

My eyebrows go up, but I know enough to keep my mouth shut now.

"The first event of the Royal Challenge is nearly upon us," he says. "You would be expected to travel ahead, so you may as well go now." He pauses. "I will follow shortly. Lia Mara will remain here with Sinna. We have a new governess from a highly respected House, and she has impeccable references. I will ensure she does not leave Sinna's side."

My chest is still tight. This should feel like a relief—but it doesn't.

It feels like I'm being sent away.

"I'm not worried about one random blacksmith," Grey continues. "And all messages point to a threat against me alone. I will worry less if the queen is not with me during my travels." He pauses. "But you are to ride straight through to Emberfall without deviating from your path. Am I clear?"

I nod once. "Yes," I say hollowly.

"Good." He claps me on the shoulder. "If you pack now you can leave by full dark."

I blink. "You wish me to leave *tonight*—" I catch a glimpse of the fire in his eyes and I break off.

If I leave tonight, I will need to ride hard to make it across the border to my first safe house before midnight, when they lock up.

I highly suspect Grey knows this.

I nod again. "Yes. Of course. Your Majesty."

Half an hour later, I have a full pack strapped behind Mercy's saddle, and I've replaced the bow I left with Jax. I can't shake the feeling that I'm forgetting something important, but I ignore any lingering worries. I've hardly been given time to say goodbye to anyone, but I'll need to ride fast to make it across the border, so I don't want to linger. There's a tension among the workers in the stable, and a few sideways glances cast my way. I wonder what gossip has already sparked in the air around the palace.

There's a part of me that's relieved to go.

Mercy is eager, leaping into a canter once we're free of the palace gates. I rarely leave at night, and her ears are pricked as we cover ground swiftly. Maybe she can sense my mood, because she doesn't tug at the reins or distract me. She's steadfast as ever.

I wish I had a distraction. My thoughts are swirling with the events of the last twenty-four hours, of everything that's happened in the palace.

But at the forefront is Jax, the warmth in his eyes, the strength in his hands, the wild tangle of hair he keeps knotted at the back of his neck.

He can't be a traitor. He can't be plotting against the king. He can't.

An hour passes, then two. We're nearing the turnoff for Briarlock. Again, Mercy must sense my thoughts, because her pace slows.

Jax. *Jax, Jax, Jax.*

I'm in so much trouble already. I need to make the safe house by midnight.

But I need to know for sure.

I sit down in the saddle and Mercy responds immediately, dropping to a slow lope when we reach the guidepost. The night is pitch-black, and I shiver under my light cloak.

For the first time, I consider that I might have been followed. Maybe by Alek—or maybe guards, sent by Grey's order.

I hate this. I draw Mercy to a halt.

If Alek *has* followed me, I won't hold back. I'm not worried about political appearances now. He may have gotten the best of me once, but he won't again. I'll burn *him* right to ash.

But I wait and hear nothing. Eventually, Mercy paws at the ground, eager to move.

I slip the rein and we ride on. We're close now. I'll get some answers, for good or for bad.

But it's not until I ride toward the bakery that I flex my fingers on the reins and realize what I'm missing.

Grey still has my rings.

CHAPTER 36

JAX

I don't know what wakes me.

The house feels absolutely silent, but I'm suddenly alert, my eyes on the pitch-dark ceiling overhead. I'm used to my father stumbling home from the tavern at all hours of the night, but he's never quiet about it—and he's locked up with the magistrate anyway. I can't imagine they'd turn him loose in the middle of the night.

My ears pick up a soft whisper of sound somewhere nearby, and every muscle in my body goes completely still.

Another sound, though this one is familiar: the tiny creak of the door that leads into the forge workshop.

I sit straight up in bed. The blankets pool around me, and the cold night air bites at the bare skin of my chest. My heart is pounding.

I think of Callyn—but she wouldn't be sneaking into my house in the middle of the night. Especially not now.

Lord Alek.

The instant his name appears in my thoughts, I can't shake it. Even if it's not him, anyone slipping into my house at this hour is a threat.

I still have that dagger hidden under my mattress, but I don't know how to use it.

My hand has already closed on the bow alongside my bed anyway.

By the time I hear the creaky spot in the floorboards of the main room, I have an arrow nocked on the string.

When a cloaked figure appears in my doorway, I catch the glint of light on weapons.

I don't think. I shoot.

The man is quicker than lightning, ducking sideways and deflecting the arrow with his bracer. He's got a blade in his hand before I can nock another arrow, but I try anyway.

He's too quick, and he grabs hold of the bow before I can shoot again. I don't try to hold on to it. I dive out of his reach, thrusting my hand under the edge of my bedding, hoping I find the dagger.

Just as my hand closes around the leather-wrapped hilt, I'm slammed onto the gritty floorboards and pinned there. One of his hands grips my wrist with the dagger, the other is attached to the sword against my throat.

I'm breathing hard, my heart pounding with fear and fury—but I'm terrified to move, because that cold steel promises pain if I do.

But then he's leaning close, the hood of his cloak hanging a bit askew. I recognize the strong slope of his jaw, the gold in his hair.

"Tycho?" I whisper.

"I came to ask if you were truly my enemy," he says. "Am I getting my answer?"

"Your—*what*?" Maybe I'm still sleeping. Maybe this is a dream.

"Jake showed me what he found in your workshop. Are you working with the Truthbringers? Are you plotting against the king?"

"What?" My eyebrows knit together. "I don't know what you're *talking* about." I hiss a breath as the sword bites into the skin at my neck.

Tycho swears and draws back—but he doesn't let go of my wrist that holds the dagger. "Drop the weapon, and I'll let you go."

"Clouds above, why—"

His grip tightens until it turns painful.

"Fine!" I snap. The dagger clatters to the floor.

He keeps his word and rolls off me, but he takes the dagger, slipping it under his belt. His sword stays in his hand.

I stare up at him, and I shift to sit against the bed. My heart is still skipping along, unsure whether it's time to settle. I don't understand how he can be so dangerous and so alluring all at the same time. I'm still shirtless, and there's a part of me that feels the need to run, but there's another part that wants to swing a fist, just so he'd have a reason to throw me to the ground again.

I have to scrub my hands over my face.

"Why were you shooting at me?" he demands.

I jerk my hands down in disbelief. "Why were you breaking into my house?"

"I knocked," he says. "No one answered."

I wonder if that's what woke me up. "So you broke in?" I give him an irritated once-over. "I believe you said you didn't *like* common soldier-ing, my lord."

His gaze seems to darken, but he sheathes the sword, then extends a hand to help me up.

I smack his hand away, then get my foot underneath me on my own. "What would've happened if I didn't wake up?" I touch a finger to my neck, and it comes away wet. I wince at the spark of pain. "Would you have cut my throat in my sleep?"

He reaches out a hand as if to touch my throat, and he sighs. "No. Jax—"

I plant my hands on his armor and shove him square in the chest. "Keep your magic."

His eyes light with surprise, but he shoves me right back.

I don't have the leverage to stay upright. I sit down hard on the bed.

I can't tell if I'm overjoyed that he's not treating me like a "crippled blacksmith"—or if I'm furious. Probably both. I get back on my foot and shove him harder, throwing some real strength into it, and I'm gratified to hear him grunt and take a step back.

Something about this is terrifying—but also exhilarating, especially when he steps forward and knocks me back down.

"You want to fight?" he says. "I can do this all night."

I'm flushed and angry and stirred up and a whole cadre of emotions I can barely identify. I force myself to standing again. "Promise?"

"Try me."

My heart skips. It's definitely not fear.

A spark lights in his eye, and I wonder if he feels exactly the same way.

But then my thoughts settle on the first thing he said, when he pinned me to the floor. It steals some of my intensity. "Why..." My voice is husky, and I have to clear my throat. "Why did you ask if I'm your enemy?"

He blinks, then frowns and draws back. "Lord Jacob found seals in your workshop. Sketches. They bore the mark of the Truthbringers." He pauses. "My intent was to *ask* you about them, but then you started shooting at me—"

"Because you *broke in*—"

"I know." He pauses. "But that doesn't change what he found."

I take a breath and look away.

Tycho catches my chin and drags my gaze back. "And I would like the truth."

If he were rough, I'd shove him away again. But his fingers are gentle against my jaw, and his eyes are intent on mine.

After a moment, I touch my fingers to his and nod. "Come. Sit. I'll fetch a lantern." I hold his eye. "Would you care for tea, my lord? Perhaps one cup before you drag me off to the stone prison?"

I'm partially teasing, partially not, but the edge of his lip quirks up. "Sure."

I light a fire in the stove and fill the kettle, then join Tycho at the small table in the corner. I've only ever sat here with my father or Callyn, and I'm acutely aware of the chairs held together with rusted nails, or the cups with chips in the porcelain. I found a linen tunic in the corner of my bedroom, then loosely tied my hair into a knot, small tasks that took me less than thirty seconds, and gave me absolutely no time to stall before confessing my sins to him.

I wish I could dim the light from the stove and the lantern, because the flickering warms his features and spins gold in his hair, reminding me of the first night we met. I want to reverse time by a matter of minutes, when my pulse was pounding and he said *Try me.*

I'm such a fool. If I could reverse time, I'd go back to the moment Lady Karyl first appeared in the workshop.

I'm doubly a fool. If I could reverse time, I should go all the way back to the moment that wagon crushed my foot.

Or possibly the moment the very action of my birth killed my mother.

"Jax," says Tycho quietly. "You know my secrets."

Not all of them. I think of the scars on his back. "You should know . . ." My voice catches. "You should know that I wanted to tell you on that first day. The day you came to Callyn's bakery. You—you were so kind. And clearly someone of importance." I hesitate. "My father had been spending our tax money on ale, but I never knew until the tax collector showed up. Suddenly . . . the forge was at risk. Callyn was in the same situation. Her father had given all their money to the

Truthbringers, but she didn't know it until later, after the Uprising. So when a woman named Lady Karyl offered me good silver to hold a message . . ." I glance at him to see if the name sparks recognition, but it doesn't. I run a hand over the back of my neck, which is suddenly damp. "I suspected it was for the Truthbringers, too. But . . . you must understand. It was so much silver. I'm not—well, I'm not suited for any other work." My voice shakes, and I have to clear my throat again. "Lord Alek was—he was terrible. But he said he was loyal to the queen. You know what the rumors about magic are like, the stories we hear of the king. I didn't have any reason to not believe him. He paid what I asked for, so I held his messages. We were able to make our first tax payment. It was easy, and we're a long way from the Crystal City, and Cal and I figured there was little harm.

"But then . . . then you healed my hand. It scared Cal—and it scared me too. But even after I yelled at you, you still came back. The day you taught me how to shoot." I draw a breath. "The way you spoke of the king . . . I've never met anyone close to him. And you were so loyal, and so kind, and I began to think that for someone like *you* to call him a friend . . . well, the rumors might be wrong."

Lord Tycho is quiet, listening, his expression unchanged. My eyes meet his briefly, and I have to look away.

"When Alek showed up that night, I thought he was going to kill you. I realized then that I was on the wrong side of this. But he took his message and left." I pause. "I haven't seen him since. I thought maybe he'd found someone else, because it's been *months*. I spoke true about that. But this morning . . ." I hesitate. This part isn't my secret.

"Tell me."

His voice is even, and not cold, but tonight is the first time that I've seen the true *force* behind all the weapons and armor. It's like seeing a friendly dog snap at a threat and learning that the fangs aren't just for show. I have to take another breath before I can speak again. "This morning, I discovered he's been sending his messages through Cal. He's been sending business her way, buying her attention with his favor, and I had no idea. But she thinks I'm the fool, because I was trying to trick him out of extra silver." I have to look away when I say this. "But it wasn't for me. I'm just trying to save the forge. I was trying to help her save the bakery. The lords seem to have endless silver, and we scrape for every coin." I swallow hard, remembering how generous he was. "It wasn't greed or trickery. I swear—"

My eyes fall on his fingers and I break off.

His rings are gone. All of them.

My eyes flash to his. "What happened to your rings?"

"I had to return them to the king." Before I can reason that out, he says, "This doesn't explain the seals, Jax."

I glance at his hand again. "When I shot at you, I could have killed you."

"I deserve a *little* more credit than that."

I reach for his wrist, and there's a tiny slice along his bracer, where he deflected the arrow. A tiny stripe of blood clings to his arm, where the arrow must have skidded off.

"No rings," I say. "No healing."

"No healing," he agrees.

I trace a finger over the injury, but the kettle whistles, and I jump. I grab hold of the counter to pull myself out of the chair, then pour water into the cups, followed by a scoop of tea leaves into each.

"I don't have honey," I say.

"I prefer it without."

He speaks from right behind me, and I turn in surprise.

He takes the cups from my hands and sets them on the table, but now he's blocking my path.

"The *truth*," he says evenly.

"I made the seals," I say. "I made the sketches."

His eyes go a bit steely, so I rush on. "Alek was very forceful. I thought he'd kill me if I read one of his letters. But it was so much money, and such a risk. I wanted to know what he was saying. So Callyn and I devised a plan to open the letters and reseal them in exactly the same way."

"And what did you discover?"

"Nothing," I admit. "Alek fought with you before I was able to re-create the right stamp. We were never able to open them." I pause. "I spoke the truth when you asked me before. And I'm speaking it now. If I could go back to that first night and tell you right then, I would. I've wanted to tell you a thousand times since."

He frowns. I can't decide if he's disappointed there's not more information to be had—or if he's relieved.

"Do you believe me?" I say.

He nods, then sighs. "I know what it's like to be desperate." He frowns. "So does the king, for what it's worth. I don't know of a Lady Karyl, and I know most people among the Royal Houses."

"I remember thinking it was a fake name when she said it to me," I say. "But Lord Alek's was real."

He thinks about that for a moment. "Maybe it had to be, because I recognized him when he came into the bakery." He pauses. "Callyn didn't tell you that she was working with him?"

I shake my head. "I knew she was getting a lot more business, but she never mentioned him." I pause. "But she thinks I'm the fool for trusting *you*."

His eyes meet mine. "Because of the magic."

It's not a question, but I nod.

His gaze centers on my neck, and he makes a *tsk* sound. His thumb brushes against the wound.

"Forgive me," he says. "I shouldn't have been so rough."

"It's just a scratch." His fingers are still there, tracing along my hairline, and my pulse jumps. "And I *was* trying to kill you."

"You're a good shot," he says. "The army would be lucky to have you."

I roll my eyes. "You stopped me with your *arm*."

"Just barely. There's a reason I tackled you to the floor."

I flush, because that's a memory I'll replay later. "Well," I begin, but I choke on my breath. Because he's shifted forward, and his free hand is at my waist, his thumb pressing into the muscle. I all but melt when the warmth of his breath eases along my jaw.

Then he tugs the pin free of my hair, and when his teeth graze my neck, I have to grab hold of his shoulder because my knee wants to go weak.

"Yes?" he whispers.

I nod quickly. My fingers are hooked on a strap of his armor. It seems unfair that he can shift his grip and find skin in seconds, but he's all trussed up in leather and steel. I think of his secrets that I *do* know, and I wonder if that's intentional.

I stroke my free hand up the column of his neck, and when his mouth goes still for the barest second, I know it is.

He could likely kill me in fifteen different ways without thinking about it, but *this* kind of closeness gives him pause.

I remember the day he fought with Alek, how the other man pinned him down by the throat. Tycho retaliated with magic, but now I understand there was more to the fight than what it looked like.

He said the king took his rings. I wonder what happened.

He's tense under my touch now, so I draw back. "Your tea will go cold."

"Ah, yes. The tea." But he doesn't let me go right away, and when he does, his hands are reluctant.

I all but fall back into my chair myself, and even though we're close to the stove, I shiver anyway and take a sip.

Tycho unclasps his cloak and sweeps it around my shoulders. I'm so stunned that I don't know how to react, and I find myself staring at him.

He drops into his chair. The lantern light glints off his eyes, casting shadows along the muscle of his arms revealed by his armor. "You seemed cold."

I wasn't shivering because I was cold, but there is absolutely no way I'm admitting that *now*. "I continue to doubt your claims of *little courtship*," I tease.

He smiles. "I spoke true."

I keep my hands wrapped around my cup, because otherwise I'm going to make a fool of myself. But then I consider the hour and frown. "Lord Tycho—"

"Tycho."

"I'm not saying it for your benefit. I'm saying it for mine."

His eyebrows go up.

I shrug and refuse to elaborate. "Why *are* you here at such a late hour?"

The smile slips off his face. "I have been ordered to return to Emberfall."

"In the middle of the night?"

He nods, then takes a sip of his own tea. "I should have crossed over the border by now. My safe house will be locked up until morning."

I stare at him for a long moment. "So . . . what will you do?"

"I can ride through the night. Mercy won't lead me wrong." He pauses. "I won't sleep on the road. I have messages from the king, and now that I have no rings, I have to be vigilant."

He'll leave again. I don't expect it to hit me like an arrow, but it does.

But I study him across the table. He doesn't look like he's in any hurry to move.

"You could sleep here," I offer. "Leave at daybreak."

For an eternal moment, his eyes hold mine, the brown of the irises glittering gold in the candlelight. There are a thousand reasons he could refuse. *Should* refuse, most likely.

Before he can, I rush on. "Surely that would be safer than traveling alone in the darkness. If nothing else, I wouldn't have to worry about you galloping headlong into a tree."

"You'd worry?"

Warmth crawls up my cheeks. "I'm sure you'd cross my mind at least once."

He smiles. "Then I'd best do as you say."

CHAPTER 37

CALLYN

So turn me in. We can hang beside each other, just like you wanted.

I've been hearing Jax's voice in my thoughts all day.

All night, too. Nora is snoring across the hall, but I've been staring at the ceiling. I remember my conversation with Jax when I was begging him to re-create the seals.

If we're committing treason, I said, *we should know.*

Now I'm the one holding messages, and I'm the one who doesn't know. Alek showed me one innocent letter, but none of the others. The magistrate dragged Ellis out of here, but I'm still not sure what they caught him doing.

I'm so tired. My parents worked hard, and our lives weren't necessarily *easy,* but . . . their relationship seemed like it was. Our *family* seemed like it was.

None of this is easy. None of this is fair.

In the midnight silence, the bakery doorbell chimes.

I sit straight up in bed. It wasn't a full chime, as if the vibration started and was immediately stopped by a hand on the steel. Such a short burst of sound that I could almost pretend it was my imagination.

But it wasn't.

I slip out of bed carefully, my bare feet padding across the floor. I can see Nora in her bed from here, an arm flopped over the side, her mouth open and her hair splayed across her pillow. Sound asleep.

I hold my breath, my ears straining.

Another sound, down in the bakery.

Goose bumps spring up on my arms, and I shiver. All my good knives are in the bakery, but Mother's weapons are here, wrapped up and tucked beneath the bed. I tiptoe back to the bed and slide my hand around until I find a hilt. I expect a dagger, but I get a sword.

It pulls free with barely a whisper of sound. My heartbeat grows loud, but I stand straight, feeling the weight of it.

Too late, I sense movement behind me, and I try to whirl. An arm catches me around my neck, the hand slapping over my mouth. Another hand grabs my wrist, fingers clenching tight. I can tell from the size that it's a man—and from the weight at my back, he's armed a lot better than I am.

I squeal and struggle, trying to wrench free.

"Shh," he whispers against my neck. The hood of a cloak brushes my cheek. "Don't wake Nora."

I freeze. *Lord Alek.*

His grip on my wrist gentles the slightest bit. "Can I let you go?"

I nod fiercely.

His arm slips loose, and I spin free of his hold, lifting the sword in front of me. All the heat from our kiss is missing now that he so clearly broke into my house. "What are you doing?"

He doesn't even do me the grace of lifting his hands in surrender. "Do you know how to use that?"

"I know it'll do a lot more damage than a pitchfork."

He reaches out a hand to touch a finger to the blade, tipping it sideways half an inch. "Army issue. Your mother's?"

I nod. "You didn't answer my question."

"I won't be interrogated at sword point, Callyn."

There's a dangerous tone to his voice tonight, and it sends a chill through my veins.

"Put it away," he adds. "We're not at odds."

No. We weren't. But I can't ignore Jax's warnings ringing through my thoughts. The way he said Alek was using me.

What will happen to your sister when you're caught?

I've been frozen in place too long. Alek's eyes are barely a gleaming shadow under the hood of his cloak.

"Or are we?" he says.

I lift the sword another inch. "Tell me what you're doing here."

He sighs. "Fine."

Then his sword spins free of its sheath, and he swings before I'm ready. I haven't used a sword in years, not since my mother took me into the yard to spar with her. Alek knocks the sword out of my hand, and it goes clattering across the floor. I suck in a breath and look to the doorway, but it's all the moment of distraction he needs. Suddenly Alek's sword point is at the hollow of my throat. I can feel the kiss of the cold steel.

I lift my hands and take a step back. He pursues me until I hit the wall. My pulse is still thundering.

"A sword isn't a weapon of warning," he says. He steps closer, changing the angle of the blade so it remains at my neck. "If you aren't willing to use it, you may as well put it down."

I keep my breathing very shallow. The edge is right there. I flick my eyes at the doorway. No Nora. *Good.*

"And you're willing to use it?" I whisper.

"Always." He's moved very close, until I can feel the warmth of his body. The blade is a narrow barrier between us.

"Is this going to be our standard greeting?" he says. "Should I always arrive armed?"

"Don't you anyway?"

He smiles and his eyes gleam. "A day ago, you were going to drag me into the barn. What changed?"

"You broke into my house."

"I didn't want to wake you. But Lord Tycho was ordered to return to Emberfall, and instead he has come to Briarlock. He's lost the king's favor. I thought he might come here for answers."

"So you're making sure I don't say the wrong thing."

His eyes don't leave mine, and that sword doesn't leave my throat. "I'm making sure you're not in harm's way."

My heart is pounding so hard that it might wake Nora. I don't know who to trust or what to believe.

"Desperate people do desperate things," he says.

"Are you talking about him or you?"

He startles, then smiles, but it's a little vicious. "Likely all of us." The cool steel of his blade touches my throat.

Then he leans in and brushes his lips against mine.

I plant my hands on his chest and draw up a knee to hit him right in the crotch.

He's a good enough fighter that he drops back, avoiding my hit, but it gets that sword off my neck. I duck and spin away from him, swiping Mother's sword off the floor in one movement.

This time his smile is real. "As I said."

"Are you just using me?"

"Look at the state of your bakery. It seems we're using each other."

I flush. "That's not what I mean and you know it."

"What is it you want, Callyn? An oath of devotion? A profession of love? A declaration of innocence? What would you trust, if not all my actions up to this point?"

"I'd settle for you putting away your sword."

The weapon slides right back into its sheath. "Done. Now you."

That felt too easy.

He takes a step toward me, and I raise my sword a few inches.

He lifts his hands, but he doesn't stop. He touches a fingertip to the blade again, pushing it to the side lightly before stopping right in front of me.

"I think the problem is that you don't want to admit what *you* want," he says softly.

"That's not true." I swallow. "I want to be true to my parents. I want to protect Nora." I take a breath. "I want to be a good friend to Jax."

"None of that is about *you*." He steps closer. "If you want me to leave, I'll leave. I can watch your house just as easily from the outside as the inside."

"Just like that?"

"Just like that." His blue eyes are shadowed and cool. "When have I ever forced anything on you, Callyn?" He reaches out and strokes a thumb across my cheekbone. "The choice is always yours."

When has the choice ever been mine? My choices have always been shaped by the decisions of others.

Until now, I suppose.

I shiver, then change the grip on the sword until the blade points down. I hold it out to him. "You don't have to leave." I pause. "I shouldn't have pointed this at you."

"On the contrary. I'm rather fond of your greetings." He takes the sword and tosses it on the bed behind him. That hand that stroked my cheek buries itself in my hair, and I half expect him to pull me into a kiss.

He doesn't. He pulls me close, his hands strong yet gentle, his free arm going around my back. He leans down to place a kiss under my ear. "What do you want?"

I don't know. I want to stop feeling like I can't trust anyone.

I hesitate, tense for a moment, worried he'll turn it into more. Jax's words about Alek using me are still loud in my thoughts.

But Alek simply adjusts his arms until he's doing nothing more than holding me. I hear the breath ease out of his chest. My head relaxes against his shoulder.

What would you trust, if not all my actions up to this point?

He's right. I'm the one who always greets him with a weapon, with a sharp word, with wary distrust.

He's the one who shows up with silver, repairing the barn, bringing gifts for Nora, sending nobles to the bakery so we have enough money.

He's the one who shows up to *protect* me, expressing his worry instead of making demands.

With a start, I realize he's been protecting me since the first day I saw him, on the steps of the palace. On the day my father died.

Within the circle of his arms, my body has begun to relax against him, but he holds up my weight effortlessly. He's stroking the hair down my back, and I don't ever want it to stop. I take a deep breath for what feels like the first time in months. Years. Ever.

My face is pressed to his shoulder, and I inhale the warm scent of his skin. I can't remember the last time anyone *held* me, but it's very nice. My sleeping shift is thin, and I can feel every buckle, every weapon, every ridge in the leather strapped to his body. I'm keenly aware of his size, the strength in his arms. When his hand drifts to the small of my back for the dozenth time, it ignites a small flame in my abdomen, and I suck in a tiny breath.

He notices immediately. I'm not sure how I can tell, but there's a sudden alertness to his body. A quickening of his pulse. This time, when he strokes a hand down my back, his hand slips lower, pulling a true gasp from my mouth.

He hesitates. Waiting. Assessing, his breath warm against my temple.

I tighten my grip on his neck, my palms suddenly damp. He takes that for an answer. Without warning, he dips a bit, his hand hiking the length of my shift, his hand sweeping the length of my calf, followed by a brief stroke over my knee, and then a slow agonizing trail up the line of my thigh.

His mouth hovers over mine now, his eyes glittering in the darkness, his fingers so light they're barely touching me. "Yes?" he whispers.

I can't think. I can't wonder. I can't breathe. I'm nodding vigorously, but he captures my mouth with his own, and suddenly, I'm drowning. Everything is too warm, too intense. A fire, waiting to burn. Then his fingers find me, and the only thing holding me upright is my grip on his shoulders. Somehow, at some point, he's unlaced the front of my shift, because his mouth closes on my breast, and between that and his talented fingers, I cry out.

"Shh," he says, laughing under his breath. "If you wake your sister, we'll have no shortage of questions."

"Right," I gasp. "Right. Yes." I still can't think. I'm not even sure which way is up. His hand has slipped to the safer territory of my hip, and I'm pulling him closer, as if every inch of my skin is longing for him.

"Does your door lock?" he murmurs into my ear.

I nod without thinking. Suddenly, he's gone, and I'm left shivering in the dark.

A scrape of wood precedes a click of metal, and then he's back, tugging at the shift until I raise my arms.

But then I remember myself—almost too late.

I'm choking on my breath as I say, "Wait. Wait. Nora."

His voice is rough and low in my ear. "The door is locked."

"I know—I know—still—"

"As you say." He tugs me, still dressed, toward the bed, where he sits on the edge, then pulls me to straddle his knees. My shift hikes up again, but now I'm more aware, more vulnerable. There's a knife hilt under my left thigh, cold against my skin. The air finds every exposed bit of skin, and I flush, self-conscious. I want to tug at the fabric, to cover myself.

But Alek's hands are soft on my face, and he's kissing me, gentle and sure. He tastes like cinnamon and sugar and—

I jerk back. "You ate some of my apple tarts," I whisper fiercely.

"Well, if you're going to leave them on a platter, you certainly can't blame an enterprising visitor."

"An enterprising *thief*—"

The words die on my tongue as his mouth finds my breast again. I hiss a breath just as his fingers slip between my legs. His arm snakes behind my back, pulling me tight against him. My world centers down to this moment. His lips, his teeth, his fingers, the press of his body. The warmth, the intensity, the yielding in my body when my head falls against his neck, my forehead damp, my breathing quick and full of whimpers until I settle with a sigh.

I wait for him to pull away, to disentangle.

He doesn't. He holds me as closely as he did when he touched my sword to the side.

He brushes a kiss against my hair. "I'm no thief, lovely."

I kiss his throat, feeling his pulse, tasting his skin.

"No," I whisper. "You're surely not."

CHAPTER 38

TYCHO

When Jax invited me to stay, my thoughts were wrapped up in pro-longing my eventual departure, because as usual, our time together feels too short, and my list of responsibilities seems never-ending. But when I go out to tend to Mercy, the cool night air bites at my skin, chiding me to be on my way. I have duties. If the king knew I stopped here—if *anyone* knew I stopped here—there'd be trouble.

But as I strip Mercy of her gear, I see my bare fingers, the skin a bit more pale where the rings used to sit. There's *already* trouble.

I think of the look in Grey's eyes when he was demanding to know why Sinna was in my room.

The way he took his magic back without speaking a word in my defense.

The way he hit the table. *Tycho. Talk.*

If he doesn't trust me, what am I risking, really? He didn't send me to Emberfall out of necessity. He sent me back to Ironrose Castle to get me out of the *way.* The thought is a tiny spear of bitterness that lodges somewhere near my heart. I tether Mercy and find her a bucket of water, with a promise of a large measure of grain for the morning, then go back into the house.

Jax is still curled in the chair with a mug, my cloak hanging askew, his hair a tumble of loose dark waves hanging over his shoulder.

It's a *sight*, and I almost stumble to a stop.

He offered to let me sleep here, and I'm no fool. I know what it *means*. But my heart is tripping along, and needles of tension find my spine. I don't know if I want it to mean that. I don't know if I can handle it meaning that.

I can't quite believe he started shooting at me. I wish he'd do it again. I know what to do with violence. It's intimacy that feels frightening.

He surveys me for a long moment, his eyes glinting in the light from the lantern, and I wonder if he can sense every doubt I'm not voicing. A shadow crosses his face, and he stands, setting the mugs aside and reaching for his crutches.

"I can take Da's bed if you like," he says softly, easily. "You can have mine."

I falter. I can't tell if I'm disappointed—or relieved. "I don't want to chase you out of your own bed."

"Well, I have no idea about the state of my father's bedding," he says. "But I promise I'm giving you the better option."

When I fail to move, he studies me, his eyes searching mine.

"Is that what you want?" I finally say.

"No," he says. "But I'm not taking anything you don't want to give."

The words hit me harder than I'm ready for. Not just in a romantic way. In *any* way. No one's ever said anything like that to me. Not even Grey. It's not just the words, it's the heavy truth behind it. I have to close my eyes and take a breath.

"Should I get the bow and shoot at you again?" His voice is low and teasing.

"That would likely be easier." My eyes flick open, and my chest is tight with emotion. "What do *you* want, Jax?"

His eyes search mine again. "Do you need me to choose, Lord Tycho?"

Maybe I do. "I'm very good at following orders." I mean for it to be honest, but it sounds a little coy, and I can feel warmth crawl up my cheeks.

"In that case, come keep me company. An armed man broke in earlier."

That makes me smile. "If I lie beside you, I rather doubt I'll be able to sleep at all."

"Good," he says decisively. He steps forward and taps me right in the center of my breastplate. "You'll be well suited to guard against intruders."

I catch his hand and hold it there, then lean in. "I wouldn't let anyone put a hand on you."

His breath catches, and now it's his turn to blush. "Go on then," he says, and his voice is rough. "I can't drag you."

I let go, then take hold of the lantern and obey.

In his bedroom, Jax unbuckles the cloak and hangs it neatly over the back of a chair. I don't pay this much mind, but then he jerks his linen shirt over his head. The golden light from the lantern traces the cords of muscle across his shoulders and down his arms. My brain entirely stops thinking. I'm frozen in the doorway. By some miracle I don't drop the lantern.

I have absolutely no idea what I'll do with myself if he drops the trousers, but he flops onto the bed and pulls a blanket over himself.

"Oh, stop with that look," he says. "I'm sure you've seen hundreds of soldiers undress."

"Hundreds of soldiers aren't you." I ease the lantern onto the side table, then reach for my sword belt.

"True enough." He gestures at my armor. "Surely all that is going to take a bit longer."

I smile. "Less time than you'd think."

I can—and have—removed armor in the dead of night in a snowstorm, so my fingers are swift and methodical, slipping buckles free. I lay the sword alongside the bed, within easy reach, along with two throwing knives and my dagger on the ledge above the pillows. My breastplate, bracers, and greaves are piled nearby, but I keep the folded length of leather containing royal messages and tuck it beneath the edge of the mattress.

Jax watches me the whole time, which is both unnerving and flattering, but his eyebrows go up when he sees me tuck the length of leather away.

"Messages from the king and queen," I say. "Meant for Prince Rhen in Emberfall. I keep them with me always."

"What happens when you're not sharing a bed with a wayward blacksmith?"

"If I have to share a room with a stranger, or if I have to make camp on the road, I sleep in my armor."

"Really?"

I nod and unlace my boots, then kick them free. When I straighten, my hands land on the hem of my shirt, and I freeze.

He's right—I have seen hundreds of soldiers disrobe. And I've never hesitated to yank a shirt over my head before. My scars aren't a secret.

But this isn't the training barracks. This is Jax. And we're alone.

"I've seen your scars," he says softly.

My gaze snaps to his. His eyes are pools of darkness in the shadows.

He shrugs a little. "After you healed the damage my father caused. You removed your armor. I caught a glimpse." He leans across the bed to douse the wick of the lantern, and the room plunges into moonlit darkness. "Do as you like, my lord."

He eases back to the far side of the bed, then draws up the blankets.

I'm still frozen in place.

He puts an arm across his eyes. "I'm rather tired anyway," he says, and yawns. "That brigand who broke in earlier woke me from a sound sleep."

I smile, but it still takes me a full minute to force my limbs to move.

I'm not taking anything you don't want to give.

I want to wrap those words up in my thoughts and hold on to them forever. It's such a gentle statement. Such a *patient* statement. He spoke of my kindness, of my generosity. But it's him. He's the kind one. The generous one.

I take a deep breath and pull the shirt over my head. The bed shifts under my weight, but Jax is immobile. His breathing is soft and even, his arm still thrown across his eyes.

There's at least three feet of space between us, but I keep my voice very low. "I know you're not asleep."

He doesn't move. "I was plotting how to get your weapons."

I grin. "Want to try?"

He bursts out laughing, and his arm slides off his eyes to land in the spill of hair above his head. "You really would fight all night."

"I would." I pause. "I wasn't sure," I say, "that you saw them."

"Scars are nothing to be ashamed of," he says. "I'm missing an entire foot and somehow the King's Courier is in my bed."

"The King's Courier considers it an honor."

He blushes deeply, but his eyes hold mine. "Was it done to you by those men who were after your father?"

"No," I say. "It was done by Prince Rhen."

He rolls up on one arm to look down at me. "In Emberfall?"

I nod. "When I was fifteen."

"I hate him," he says immediately.

I laugh softly. "Jax."

"I do. Take me with you. I'll tell him to his face."

He probably would. I can just imagine Rhen's reaction.

I also can't stop the thrill of intrigue that races through my thoughts when he says *take me with you.*

"It was a long time ago," I begin.

"Not too long. You can't be much older than I am."

"I'll be twenty by midsummer."

"As I said."

"Prince Rhen was trying to protect his kingdom," I say. "He bears his own scars. I've made my peace with it."

"Truly? Then let me see."

Well, he's got me there.

Jax stares down at me. "You were *fifteen.* Barely more than a boy. I'm sure you were a huge threat to the kingdom of Emberfall."

"King Grey was the rightful heir," I say. "He would not reveal himself."

"And what does that have to do with you?"

"I alone knew his secret." I pause. Much like what happened with the soldiers when I was young, I don't often discuss this—with anyone. "The . . . the whipping . . . it was done to us both."

These words fall into the darkness like a stone into a pond.

"But the king has magic," Jax says. "He couldn't protect you?"

"He didn't know how to use it then." I pause. "He bears the same scars." I take a long breath, run a hand down my face, and roll onto my stomach before I can lose my nerve. "You can see."

Now it's his turn to freeze.

He's absolutely silent, but I can see the moment his gaze shifts from mine to my back. My head rests on my forearms, and I watch the tiny movement of his eyes as he traces the lines.

When he reaches out a hand, I tense, but I force myself to remain still.

His hand stops before reaching me, though. "Can I touch you?"

The question takes me by surprise. It's four simple words, almost ridiculous words, considering we're lying beside each other. But maybe that's what allows me to nod. It's the patience. The waiting. A request instead of a demand.

He doesn't touch the scars, which is what I expected. His hand drifts along my shoulder, down across my biceps, following my forearm until he reaches my face and lets his fingers run through my hair before he does it again. And again.

By the fourth time, the tension has eased out of my body, and my eyes flicker closed. I want to stay awake, to keep talking, to listen to the easy rumble of his voice. There's still a tremor of worry in the back of my thoughts, that this will lead to more before I'm ready for it, but his hand never strays from the chaste path along my arm. My thoughts begin to drift and loosen.

When the stroking stops, I wonder if he's begun to fall asleep, too, but the bed shifts, just the slightest bit, and my eyes barely open to find the tiniest smile on his face, his arm reaching over my head.

Jax barely has a hand on the blade before I pin him to the bed, trapping his wrist.

He gasps in surprise, but then he laughs, full out.

"You're dangerous," I say ruefully.

"I was curious about how serious you were."

"Well, now I'm very serious about not sleeping."

He frowns. "You're not really, are you?"

"No." I wince. "Maybe? Not because of you," I add. "But Alek.

Anyone." I flex my fingers. "It's very different to be on the road without my rings."

"You mean, you're just like the rest of us?"

That gives me pause, and it reminds me of the day I healed his hand. "Yes," I admit.

He glances at his hand with the knife, which is still trapped against the mattress. "You clearly don't need them."

I wonder if that's true. Maybe I've grown too reliant on magic, and I've forgotten how to rely on *myself*.

"Maybe not." I hesitate and think of the moment Alek thrust that dagger under my ribs—or the battle with Nakiis in the arena. I frown. "But . . . sometimes I take risks I otherwise wouldn't."

"Sometimes risks remind us of what we have to lose." He flexes his wrists under my grip. "More of your soldier training?"

I nod.

"Show me how to get free."

I smile and squeeze his left wrist. "Slide this one straight overhead. It'll break my balance. If you do it fast, you can push off with your foot and flip me—"

He flips me onto my back so quickly that it takes me by surprise. He really is stronger than he knows. I think it takes *him* by surprise, because he's wide-eyed and staring down at me.

"I told you the army could use you," I say. "Now you're in a position to punch me in the face or cut my throat."

He smiles and lets go of my wrist to set the knife back on the ledge, but then he leans down close, his hands braced beside my shoulders, his hair tickling my skin. But there's a part of this that's making my heart skip in a way that's wary and uncertain. I wish I had my armor back.

Maybe he can tell. "Can I kiss you instead?" he says, and his voice is quiet.

Every time he asks, it's like a bit of the unease in my chest melts away, dissolving into nothing. I wonder if he knows.

I look into his earnest eyes and nod. "Yes."

When he closes the distance, his mouth is gentle and soft, and he bites at my lip in a way that steals my thoughts and lights a fire in my belly. My breathing goes rough and ragged at once, and he draws back to study me.

He's straddling my waist, and my hands fall on his knees. His pants are loose, but revealing shadows are everywhere. If he were to shift his weight by a few inches, my lustful thoughts would be no secret either.

I slide my hands up his thighs, and he sucks in a quick breath—then traps my hands under his own. I go still, but he smiles, then lifts my hands to press them into the mattress, threading our fingers together. It leaves him all but hovering above me.

"Forgive me," I whisper.

"You've done nothing wrong," he says, and there's a smile in his voice, but a note of seriousness as well. "But too many people have taken too much from you. I don't want to be one more."

My chest constricts in a way that's both painful and exquisite. "Jax," I whisper.

He kisses me again, and this time he's more sure, his fingers tightening on mine, his knees tight against my rib cage. He finally does shift, and our chests meet. Our hips meet. I gasp into his mouth. That fire in my belly turns to liquid honey that spreads through my veins. I'm desperate, wanting, making small sounds low in my throat. When I get a hand free, I grab his waistband to pull him tighter against me, and I'm gratified to draw a gasp from him as well.

But then he smacks my hand away and grins. He touches his nose to mine and whispers against my mouth. "No."

"As you say."

I expect him to pull away, but he grinds against me harder, burying his face in my neck. As his teeth graze my skin, his hand finds my waist, his fingers five points of heat. His hand slips under the edge of my trousers, finding the bare edge of my hip.

I can't breathe. I'm all but panting underneath him, my hands wanting skin but clutching the night air. I get a fistful of his hair, and he growls against me. That almost does me in.

"Jax," I'm gasping. "Jax."

His response is slow, languorous, murmured against my throat. "Yes?"

"I—I—"

His hand goes still. "Stop?"

I shake my head fiercely. "No—no—I—"

"Then hush. And take for once."

I want to protest, but his teeth find my bare chest, and I forget everything I wanted to say. His tongue brushes my nipple, drawing it into his mouth, and I forget my own *name*.

Then his hand slips the rest of the way under my clothes, his gentle fingers closing around me, and I shudder. I hear him whisper, but the words don't find my ears. My body knows, though, and I'm nodding without thinking, my fingers sliding through his hair. Every breath feels like fire, and my back is arching against the mattress under his touch.

Jax kisses his way down my chest, tugging at the waist of my trousers. I'm aware of the cool night air, of the way our legs have tangled together, of the sudden warmth of his mouth. I'm aware of his eyes, still dark and intent on mine. I'm aware of his patience. Of his gentle kindness.

And later, when I tug him back up my body, whispering my devotion, my gratitude, my reverence, he presses his lips to mine, and I kiss him deeply. I have a momentary worry that he's going to pull away, that he's going to leave. But Jax tucks his face into my neck, his breath sweet and warm against my skin, his palm a spot of heat against the center of my chest.

This is a different kind of magic, one that no one can take away from me.

CHAPTER 39

CALLYN

I don't mean to doze off, but Alek's arms are so warm, and I can't remember the last time I felt so safe, so secure. But time passes, and somehow I'm under my quilt, my hand reaching out in the darkness, finding nothing more than an empty bed beside me.

For a quick moment, I wonder if I dreamed everything. My eyes blink sleepily, and I see that the door is no longer closed and locked, the very edge of Nora's bed visible across the hall. Candlelight flickers off my walls, so I roll over.

Alek is sitting in my chair beside Mother's old writing desk. The chair is angled so he can see out the window, but his eyes are on one of her books.

Definitely not a dream.

"You didn't strike me as a reader," I say softly.

He turns a page without looking up. "Whyever not?"

"You seem like the kind of person who would be *having* adventures," I say. "Not the kind of person who has to read about them."

"Surely I can do both." His blue eyes flick up and find mine. "As can you."

Said like someone with no shortage of silver—and no younger siblings to consider. "You don't want to sleep?"

He glances out the window for a bare second. "No," he says. "I told you why I came here."

I'm making sure you're not in harm's way.

Again, this feels too easy. Too comfortable. My thoughts conjure the memory of his hands against my skin, and I shiver. I think of all the things he's said to me in the weeks we've known each other, and I can't reconcile it with the way he treated Jax.

He looks back at the book. "Perhaps I'm reading about all the other things we could do together." He flicks another page.

Clouds above. I know what kind of book he's reading *now*. I pull the blankets over my head.

He laughs, the sound warm and low in the confines of my room. I don't hear him move, but a moment later, the blankets pull free, and he flops down on the bed beside me. He's removed some of his armor, but he's still fully dressed, sheathed blades everywhere.

"My mother had quite a collection of books as well." He pauses. "Some like these, but also history, artistry, military strategy—everything you can imagine. I had tutors since I was very young."

Of course he did.

Then his voice takes on a heavier note. "I used to read them when she was away. And then . . . after."

The weight in his voice tugs at my heart. "Me too," I say softly. "Jax and I would sit and read for hours. I always liked the stories of romance, but he was partial to the ones about magic."

"Ah." He reaches over and tickles my nose with a worn piece of paper. "What is this?"

I frown, reaching for it. I have to squint in the dim light, but as soon as I recognize it, I flop back on my pillows.

"It's the note from the tax collector," I say. "From the midwinter levies." I want to crumple it up. I should have crumpled it up weeks ago. So much stress and worry and harm over one little note.

"That's quite a sum."

I roll onto my back to stare at the ceiling. "I'm sure it's nothing to you."

Alek touches a finger to my chin and turns my gaze to meet his. "It's not nothing to *you*."

I don't know what to do when he's like this.

"Yes, well." I bite at my lip and wonder if I'm revealing a secret. "Jax owed twice as much."

"Truly?"

I can't read anything from his voice. We could be discussing the weather.

"Yes. Truly." I tug the blankets back up. "Why do you think he started carrying messages at all?"

"I have no idea." He pauses. "So now he's conning silver out of the King's Courier?"

"I don't think he's conning anything. Jax isn't like that. He was very regretful that he lost your trust." I pause. "Especially since you brought your business to me."

Alek is studying me now. "I didn't trust him the first time I saw him speaking with Tycho. He couldn't expect to play both sides. I told you before, if he doesn't like dangerous games, he shouldn't play." He tickles my nose with the note again.

I grab it and crumple it in my palm. "He didn't bring him here." I pause. "I didn't bring *you* here."

"Would you like me to leave?"

"No. I just . . ." My voice trails off. I stare at the ceiling.

He touches my chin and brings my gaze to meet his. Those blue eyes are so intent on mine. "Tell me your thoughts, Callyn."

"These notes you're passing," I say quietly. "They're not *really* about fabric shipments."

"Some of them are," he says.

"But not all."

He traces a finger down my nose. "Not all." His finger drifts along my cheek, to my jaw, and then down my neck, sweeping along my collarbone until I shiver and catch his hand.

"Are you trying to distract me?" I say.

"Are you distracted?"

"No." But yes. I am. He's shifted closer, and he's warm against me. His hand is like a lit coal under my own, burning against my skin. When he slides his hand under the fabric of my shift again, I inhale sharply.

But then his fingers close around my mother's pendant. "Where did you get this necklace you wear?"

"It was my mother's." There's a part of me that's tense about him touching it, as if he'll yank it off my neck just because he can. "It was given to us with her things. After . . . after."

As always, he doesn't take anything. He just eases it back against my skin, the warm, familiar weight settling into place.

Then he says, "It's Iishellasan steel."

I freeze. "What?"

He nods. "From the ice forests. It can bind—"

"Magic," I whisper.

His eyebrows go up. "You know." A dark look flickers in his eyes. "Ah, yes. The king's pet used his rings to heal the blacksmith. So you've seen what it can do."

I touch the pendant the way I've done a thousand times. I suddenly expect it to feel cold, but it's warm as ever under my fingertips. "My mother . . . my *mother* had a *magic* pendant?" I say.

Alek shrugs a little, as if this conversation is somewhat dull, as if he hasn't completely knocked my world off its axis. "Likely not. Iishellasan steel can be bound to *repel* magic just as easily. The Truthbringers have found many such artifacts of old. There are swords and daggers and even arrows that can bring harm to a magesmith—but there are a few, like this, that can bring protection to the wearer." He taps the necklace. "I'm glad you wear it. You're lucky she left a bit of protection for you."

I close my fingers around the warm steel. My throat is tight with so much emotion I'm not sure what to do with it. If my father had been wearing this necklace, would he still be here today?

Or did it keep me and Nora safe when we were mere feet away from the magic that burst through the Crystal Palace?

Oh, Mother. There are so many things I wish I could go back and ask her.

Alek traces a finger along my hairline, and I blink up at him. "You said the Truthbringers have a lot of this steel?"

"More than a bit. Less than *a lot.*" He pauses. "The Truthbringers are loyal to Syhl Shallow. We would never seek to harm the queen."

I stare at him, the candlelight flickering over his features. I can't decide if he looks passionately earnest or terrifyingly sinister. Somehow, as usual, it's both.

"You want to kill the king," I whisper.

"I'm not the only one. You were there on the day of the Uprising. Many of those people had no desire for violence—but they all died anyway. There are rumors that he can't control his magic. That he's injured the queen somehow, but they're hiding it." He pauses, his eyes searching mine again. "What would *you* do, if the king were to show up on your doorstep?"

"Faint from shock."

"Callyn."

"I would! What would you do?"

"The king *has* shown up on my doorstep."

Of course. He's probably had all manner of royalty on his doorstep. I almost laugh—but something about his expression stops me, and I study him carefully. "And what did you do?"

"It was years ago. He'd just returned from claiming his throne in Emberfall." Alek hesitates. "He and the queen arrived with news that my sister was a traitor. That she'd been killed during a skirmish with soldiers from Emberfall. That she had worked against the throne. They wondered if I was doing the same. If I was disloyal."

I roll up on one arm to face him. "And were you?"

"No. I'm not disloyal now."

I feel like we're finally speaking truths. There's a part of me that wants to back away from this conversation. So much that we've said would already be considered treasonous. But ever since Jax took that handful of coins from Lady Karyl, I've been desperately wondering what was in these notes. What they're planning. What I've become a part of.

"Would the queen think the same?" I say carefully.

"My sister was an adviser to the queen. She was never disloyal." He pauses. "But . . . she was never loyal to our new king. Our mother was a tactician in the army. A strategist. Her death . . . it hit us hard."

"I know." My voice is soft yet full. My mother's death hit me equally hard.

He lifts my fingers to lay a kiss across my knuckles. "I know you know."

"So you're hoping to avenge your mother and your sister?"

"I am hoping to restore Syhl Shallow to what it once was. When the magesmiths first crossed the Frozen River, the queen refused to allow them to settle here. When they settled in Emberfall, you've heard the stories of what happened. Their former king tried to kill them all. Only a few survived—and look at the trouble they caused. Look at the deaths, the destruction. There's a reason they were not allowed to settle here, and now one is married to our *queen*?"

He's right. I've read the histories a dozen times.

"Are you the leader?" I say.

His eyes flash to mine. "Me? The leader of the Truthbringers? No."

"You're so . . . assured. I assumed."

"I was only seventeen when my sister was killed. My family has the old texts. Several of the old artifacts. I was recruited early. Because of my access to the royal family, I have some power. Some sway. But like you, I am but a soldier for the cause."

"And your messages are about killing the king?"

"No. Nothing so overt. We learned from the first attempt that the king cannot be overtaken by sheer numbers. So we have discovered . . . other methods."

Other methods. So there must be a limit to his willingness to share information. He strokes a finger across my cheek. "Have I shared enough to earn your trust yet?"

"Maybe."

He grins. "That's an honest answer if I've ever heard one." He leans down to brush his lips over mine. His fingers drift across my breast, pulling a gasp from my throat before I'm ready.

But then he stops there, and speaks low. "I'll earn your trust one day, lovely. For now, you need your sleep." He pulls his hand free and kisses me on the forehead.

I don't know if I should be disappointed or relieved.

My body is *definitely* disappointed.

My head is, too, when he slips out of the bed to take a seat by the window again. My entire body seems to be humming.

He picks up a book. "Sleep. I'll keep watch."

"I'm not scared of Lord Tycho."

"I'm not scared of him either." He pauses. "But he's lost the king's trust. As I said, something has happened with the queen. The rumors at court are . . . exceptional. I don't know what to believe, but I don't know what Tycho will do now that he's been stripped of his magic and sent away."

I study him. "So you think he's working against the king, too?"

Alek snorts disdainfully. "No. I think Tycho would cut his own throat if the king asked him to." He hesitates. "He knows I've painted a target on his back—but it's not as if he didn't give me the opportunity. He's not happy about it. Even a lapdog knows how to bite."

I remember the first day I met them both, how the tension in the bakery shot to a point of discomfort. "Why do you hate him so much?"

"At first, it wasn't personal." He shrugs. "I hated everyone the king brought with him. They represented a country that stole too much from ours. But after he and the king killed my sister, Tycho took an active role in trying to make sure I had no place at court. As if *he* had a right to be there. I had to fight my way back in."

I consider that for a while. I remember thinking about the nobility, how their problems seemed petty and far distant from Briarlock. But I hear the current of pain riding below Alek's glib words, and I realize that we're all affected by grief and loss, even if we're from wildly different stations in life.

"I'm sorry, Alek," I say.

He gives me half a smile. "You don't have to be sorry. You've done nothing wrong. You're helping me put things to rights for our queen." He glances at the window again, then lifts his book meaningfully. "Now sleep."

My thoughts are swirling. I don't think I'll ever sleep again.

But he's so quiet, and it's so late, and I'm so tired. I do.

When I wake, the room is cold and full of sunlight, and he's gone.

Beside me on the bed are two pieces of paper.

The first is a folded note, sealed with a broad circle of green-and-black wax, the silver stars in the seal familiar.

The second is the crumpled slip of parchment that has the tax collector's handwriting on one side.

Alek has written a note on the other.

> *Callyn,*
>
> *Lady Karyl will arrive for this letter in a matter of days. Take care. This message isn't for your eyes, but it's not about fabric orders at all.*
>
> *Hopefully this tiny admission is enough to buy a bit of your trust.*
>
> *Yours,*
>
> *Alek*

My heart is pounding.

Yours. It's meaningless. Meaningful. I can't tell. Like we've moved away from the business of passing messages, and now my heart is on the line. Much like when he calls me "lovely," it lights me with joy and inserts a spike of worry in my chest.

Something has happened with the queen.

I am but a soldier for the cause.

As I think back over all our words, I realize that he answered many questions—which is why I didn't notice how he so skillfully dodged others.

You're helping me put things to rights.

I think about everything he didn't say, and I realize I don't know if that's true at all.

I remember discussing the queen with Tycho and Nora, how my sister was spinning in circles and imagining the baby as if she'd be welcoming her own little sister. Alek said the queen was very sick and the king wasn't using his magic to heal her. We hear so many stories here, though. I'm not sure what to believe—or *who*. I know my father believed everything said about the king. It's part of why he participated in the Uprising—and part of why I agreed to work with Alek. I often think my mother would be doing the same.

But I touch my fingers to this pendant. Would she be part of the Uprising? My mother was loyal to the queen. I know that much for sure. She took great pride in her role as an officer in the army.

Alek, too, keeps declaring his loyalty to Syhl Shallow, to the queen.

But our queen married a magesmith—which the Truthbringers *hate.*

Where does that put their loyalty? Can you respect someone and still deride their choices? If they want to kill the king, *is* that loyalty? Or is that treason?

Mother told Father he should have enlisted, but he didn't. She didn't force him to do it. She didn't take his choice. Just like he didn't want her to go off to war—but he didn't stop her.

Is it any different from Alek repairing my barn when I told him not to? He thinks he's doing the right thing, and from the outside, it *looks* like a benevolent action . . . but is it?

I don't want to think about this too hard. I'm too involved, and the answer feels like it will hurt. But I'm realizing what's at the heart of my distrust of Alek.

Taking a choice away from someone else isn't devotion, and it isn't loyalty.

He talked about Jax playing dangerous games, but Alek is playing the most dangerous one of all. A game of make-believe with lethal stakes: disguising *control* as faithful devotion.

Disguising assassination as an act of *protection*.

I just wanted to save the bakery. I just wanted to protect my sister.

It was just supposed to be a few letters.

"Cally-cal?"

I look over. Nora stands in my doorway.

"Good morning," I say. "I'm going to need you to milk Muddy May. I have something I need to do."

CHAPTER 40

JAX

Tycho was wrong. He's been sleeping soundly for hours, his chest rising and falling with each breath. I feel rather certain I could grab hold of those knives and he'd have no idea.

Or maybe not. He surprised me before.

I don't try. He has many days of travel ahead of him. He should rest.

I, on the other hand, have been awake all night. I've all but convinced myself that the instant I fall asleep, I'll awaken to an empty room full of sunlight. Every time I begin to drift off, my thoughts remind me that he's here, that he's real, that I can inhale his scent and taste his skin and feel the beat of his heart.

It's early, but not *too* early. The room is dark and cool, but I can see the bare start of light through my shutters. Any other morning, I'd be clanging away beside the forge already, getting a head start on the day's projects.

Right now, there's no way I'm moving.

Once day breaks, he'll be gone. He'll wake, buckle his armor in place, and ride off on his horse. This may as well have been a dream.

My gaze falls on his fingers, loosely curled against the blanket. I wonder what happened with the king. Tycho is always close-lipped when it comes to royalty, by virtue of his position, I'm sure. Last night was no different.

But he's always spoken of the king with such devotion. I saw the shadows in his eyes when he confirmed his rings were gone.

Something happened. Especially since he's returning to Ember-fall so quickly. I truly didn't expect to see him for another week, at *least.*

Tycho inhales deeply, and his eyes blink open.

For an instant, I'm frozen in place. My chest tightens before I'm ready for the emotion.

But his eyes find mine, and he presses his palm to my cheek. "Jax," he says, and his voice is soft and low. There's a tiny edge to his pronunciation of my name, as if his accent is stronger when he first wakes, which makes me smile. But then he says something I can't understand at *all*, and I turn my head to kiss the inside of his wrist.

"Unless you need me to shoe a horse," I say, "I can't speak much Emberish."

He startles, then smiles. His voice is rough and worn from sleep, and he rubs at his eyes. "Forgive me," he says in Syssalah.

I was right: his accent *is* stronger. It's silly, but it feels like a secret only I know, and it makes me shiver. "Tell me what you said."

"I said . . ." He blushes. "Well."

I shift closer, lifting up on my elbows to look down at him. "Tell me!"

"I said you're incredibly demanding in the morning." His hand finds my cheek again, his thumb tracing over my lip.

I lean closer. "Would you rather tell me what you said last night?"

His hand goes still. "What did I say last night?"

"I have no idea. An accounting of every weapon you carry? A list of all the royal secrets you know? I can say with certainty that shoeing horses never came up." I trail a finger down his chest and whisper, "You may recall I was rather busy."

He hisses a breath and catches my hand. His eyes are full of light, and I expect another playful response, but he kisses my fingers and speaks low. "I said you're magnificent. Exquisite. Flawless. I thanked fate for leading me to your door."

"Oh," I say, and my voice catches. I've spent so many years hearing that I'm good for nothing more than misfortune, so my heart thumps hard in my chest. "Is that all?"

"Ah . . . let me think." He gazes at the ceiling. "I said you're unexpectedly *talented*—"

I give him a shove. "You're a scoundrel."

"With archery!"

That makes me laugh. I forgot how good it feels to laugh with someone, to share a *moment* with someone. My chest tightens again, and this time, my eyes feel damp. It's not just about leaving, it's about everything that's happened over the last few months. I've been so alone—and I'm about to be again.

On that note, I need to get out of this bed before thoughts of his departure become truly brutal. I kiss his cheek and begin to extricate myself. "I'll see to our breakfast, my lord."

He catches me before I can get far. His hands are always so gentle that I forget how strong he is.

"Tycho," he whispers. "Just Tycho."

"Just Tycho," I say dutifully.

His thumbs brush at the skin of my arms, and his voice is husky and low. "Stay."

You stay.

But I can't say it. It would hurt him; I know it would. It's hurting me to think it.

"I'm not risking the queen's anger for delaying her courier," I say.

He frowns, thunderclouds rolling into his eyes. I don't know what he's going to say, but I try to shift free, and he lets me go. Out near the forge, I hear a light repetitive banging, and I force a smile.

"I think your horse is hungry, too," I say, reaching for my shirt and my crutches. "I'll see to Mercy first."

The workshop is cool in the shadows, but Mercy pricks her ears and whickers to me when I come through the door. Tycho tethered her at the post under the overhang, and I'm not surprised to see he left her with a bucket of water. She paws at the bucket, splashing water everywhere.

"You're making a mess," I say lightly. I pull a measure of grain from the barrel we keep for ornery horses or needful travelers, then replace the water bucket. Mercy thrusts her face into the food, then presses her nose against my chest, trailing wet bits of grain down my shirtfront. I rub her neck anyway, peering at her feet, looking to see if the nails seem secure, if the shoes seem worn.

The instant I realize I'm trying to think of a reason to further delay him, I tell myself to knock it off. I turn back for the house.

But then I feel . . . something. A quick chill that seems to come from nowhere. The hair on the back of my neck stands up.

I turn and look out at the yard in the early morning silence. Shadows hang between the trees, and the grass glistens where dew clings to the blades, but nothing moves. I can't hear anything over the sound of Mercy rooting for her grain, but I frown and wait.

Nothing.

I sigh and light the forge so it can begin warming for all the work I have waiting.

Once I return to the house, I can sense movement in the bedroom. Tycho must be dressing. Arming. Whatever.

I sigh again.

The cabinets yield biscuits and hard cheese, along with some dried beef. I'm almost hesitant to load them on a platter, because I remember the food we shared in the boarding house, and this seems like a paltry substitute.

There's still water in the kettle, so I light the stove. When I turn away, he's right there behind me, and I draw a sharp breath. "Clouds above, you move like an assassin—"

"Get used to it." And then his lips are on mine, and it's a good thing he's *not* an assassin, because I can't breathe, I can't think. One of my crutches hits the floor, but Tycho has a grip on my waist, his hands strong and secure against me. He's buckled into all of his gear, and again I find leather and steel and weapons in every place my hands seek skin and warmth. But none of that matters because I'm drowning in the taste of his mouth.

This will make it harder, more painful, but right this moment, I don't care.

Especially when his teeth graze my neck and his hands slip under my shirt to find my waist. Heat has already pooled in my belly, and I'm clinging to his armor.

"Can you stand?" he whispers, and it nearly takes me a full minute to realize he's asked a question.

"Yeah." I swallow hard, my head nodding almost without me being aware of it. My heart is racing along in my chest, but I unwind my fingers from the buckles at his shoulder.

"Good," he says, and then he drops to one knee.

I lose any sense of myself. I should stop him, but his fingers are so warm, and his mouth is so wicked. My fingers twist in his hair, but I have to grab hold of the table. There's a good chance my knee will give out, but I'm more worried my heart will take flight. Tycho's hands are firm against my waist, holding me upright, holding me close. My vision fills with stars, and when I cry out, my hands grip tight to his shoulders. He supports my weight like it's nothing.

He eventually straightens, tugging my clothes back into order as he rises. His hands don't let go of me, and I realize I dropped the other crutch at some point. My breathing is still shuddering, loud in the space between us. His brown eyes are so intent on mine, seeking, searching. *Seeing.* No one has ever looked at me like that. No one has ever made me *feel* like that. Like I'm a reward, not a hindrance.

I blink, and my eyes blur. My chest is tight again.

"Are you all right?" he says softly.

I nod, slowly.

He leans in to kiss me. Lightly, tentatively.

I don't kiss him back. Instead, I wrap my arms around his neck and hold him tight.

I expect him to sigh, to pull away, to tell me that this was meant to be his *goodbye.* That he has obligations and he's already delayed them long enough.

But he doesn't. His arms are tight at my back, and he holds me for the longest time. He holds me for so long that I rest my cheek against his shoulder and think it would be acceptable for time to stop right this instant, for my world to shrink down to nothing more than this.

Eventually, he speaks, and his voice is very low, very soft, just for me. "I will do my very best to return before your father is released, but it may not be possible."

I frown and sniff and begin to pull away, but his arms tighten. "Just listen," he says, and I go still against him.

"I will leave you with silver," he continues. "If I have not returned by the time he is released, it should be enough to pay for passage to Iron-rose Castle—"

I snap my head up. "What?"

He grimaces. "Things are rather tense with the king right now, or I'd hire a carriage this very instant. But I don't want to leave you with no escape—"

"I can't—I can't just come to Ironrose Castle—"

"Sure you could."

"I don't even speak the language!"

"Syssalah is much more prevalent in the castle than it ever was before. Prince Rhen himself has gotten rather good. You wouldn't be at a disadvantage." His eyes spark with mischief. "I wouldn't lead off with how much you *hate* him, however."

I can't stop staring at him. I can't believe we're even discussing this.

The smile slips off his face. "If you'd like," he says finally. "You don't have to."

"No! I just—I've never even left Briarlock."

His eyebrows go up. "Really! Then I must return to make the journey with you. The mountains are rather spectacular from the other side. And the first events of the Royal Challenge will be quite entertaining."

My heart is pounding so hard I don't think it will ever stop.

"Promise you'll take the silver. Promise you'll leave if he returns." He strokes a lock of hair back from my face. "I'll worry for you while I'm gone."

I swallow. "You'll worry?"

The corner of his mouth quirks up. "I'm sure you'll cross my mind at least once."

I blush. "I promise."

He ducks to fetch my crutches, then kisses me. "If I could stay for another day, I would." Out in the workshop, Mercy knocks at her bucket again, followed by a muffled whicker.

I smile, though it feels a bit watery. "Your horse is ready to leave."

"Mercy is always impatient." He takes a step back, and traces a finger down the length of my chin. "Be well, Jax."

I take a deep breath and close my eyes. I don't want to watch him leave. "Be well, Tycho."

His boots barely make a sound on the wooden floor, but I know the sound of the creaking hinges, and my eyes snap open. But the kettle whistles, and I turn to take it off the heat. By the time I make it to the door with one crutch and a cup of tea, he's gone.

I sigh and return to the forge, stoking the coals. Tycho has left a small bag of silver on top of my tongs, and I feel the weight of it, then sigh and shove it into my pocket. At least I don't have to worry about my father stealing it.

Passage to Ironrose Castle.

I can't even imagine.

It's still early, so I feed an ingot of iron to the forge and wait for it to heat. I've been shooting in the mornings, but right now that would make me think too much of the man who just left, so I might as well work.

A foot scrapes on the path, and I look up in surprise.

Callyn.

My heart almost stops in my chest. I remember the last thing I said to her—but I also remember the last things she said to me. Is she coming to have it out with me again? To tell me how amazing the treacherous Lord Alek is?

My face must wear a warning because she stops a short distance away. It feels like a mile.

"Did Lord Tycho visit you last night?" she finally says.

"Yes." I turn the iron in the forge. "Did Lord Alek visit *you*?"

I'm being sarcastic, but she nods. "Yes. He did."

I snap my eyes to hers. "He did?"

"He was worried Tycho was here to cause trouble."

I hate the spike of worry that's going to be lodged in my heart until I see him again. "Lord Alek should be more worried about *himself.*"

"Maybe he's not, but I am."

I frown, trying to make sense of that.

She takes advantage of my silence to stride across the distance between us. "Look," she says in a rush, "I don't know if Alek is using *me* or if Tycho is using *you*—"

"He's not using me, Cal."

"—but we're both wrapped up in *whatever* is going on, and I don't think we should be on opposite sides. Alek isn't telling me anything. Is Tycho telling *you* anything?"

"He's not *using* me, Callyn!" I jerk the iron out of the fire and smack it against the anvil.

"That's not what I asked you."

I lift the hammer—then freeze. No, he's not really telling me anything at all.

"He's the King's Courier," I say. "He's bound to secrecy, I'm sure."

"Maybe so." She pulls a folded slip of parchment out of her skirts. "But we're not."

It's a message, held together with the same green-and-black seal I've seen half a dozen times already.

I don't reach for it. "I don't want any part of that anymore."

"Oh! So high and mighty now!" She kicks dirt at me. "You're the one who started this, Lord Jax."

I cannot believe she just did that. I scoop up a handful of dirt and fling it at her like we're six years old and arguing over the last sweetcake. "To save the forge! To save your bakery! I didn't shove him under your skirts."

She flushes.

Oh. I was teasing. I didn't realize she'd actually done that.

I grimace. "Sorry, Cal. I didn't know."

"Forget it." She turns away.

UGH.

"Stop," I say. "Just . . . what do you want me to do with that? Do you need me to hold it?"

She stops, but for a moment, I don't think she's going to face me. Finally, an eternity later, she turns around. "No."

"Then what?"

"Do you still think you can re-create the seal?"

"I don't know. Maybe."

She lifts the note. "I think it's time we figure out what's really going on."

CHAPTER 41

TYCHO

Preparations for the first competition have been well underway, and the transformation of the fields surrounding Ironrose Castle is impressive. Markers and targets have been set out for archery, both for long range and accuracy. Small sand arenas sit ready for close combat, either sword fights or hand-to-hand. Longer tracks have been arranged for mounted or foot races. Flagpoles stand at each end, banners with both the green and black of Syhl Shallow and the gold and red of Emberfall snapping in the wind.

Along the far side of the competition fields, nearly a hundred tents have been built, and even though the matches aren't due to start for at least another ten days, many are already occupied. Pennants and banners in an array of colors already hang from the tent eaves, blues and yellows and greens representing cities and towns and families. Anyone with status has been invited to stay in the castle, but I learn from the Royal Guard that the array of tents is already proving to be a site of revelry and music late into the night.

The prince and princess are away when I arrive, which is both a relief and a disappointment. I've been jittery since I left the forge, as if Grey might have sent scouts to make sure I got where I was supposed to be. He didn't—at least, not as far as I can tell. But I'm *sure* he and the queen made mention of the goings-on at court in their letters. If I'm going to hear an earful from Rhen, too, I'd rather get it over with.

I try to make the best of my evening alone, turning Mercy loose in a pasture for a few hours of liberty, then sinking into a hot bath for myself. There's no formal dinner since the prince and princess aren't in residence, but the castle kitchens always lay out a late meal after sundown, which I prefer anyway. A few stars have begun to twinkle in the twilit darkness outside the windows, and I can hear faint music coming from the distant competition yard. I smile and fill a cloth napkin with slices of bread and cheese and salted meats, then turn for the door to go explore. If I've been granted a short reprieve from anyone's disappointment, I may as well enjoy it.

But I walk through the door and find myself face-to-face with Alek.

I'm so shocked by his presence that I nearly drop my food. He looks like he's only just arrived, still trussed up in armor and weapons, his red hair a bit windblown, his face unshaven. His own guards are at his back—and though castle guards are on duty down the corridor, right now I'm alone.

My heart pounds, my thoughts replaying that moment in Jax's workshop when I faced Alek months ago. My free hand is automatically reaching for a sword that's not there. I'm not even wearing a dagger. I've never had need for weapons in the halls of Ironrose.

That will change if Alek is here.

He must see the quick burst of alarm in my expression, because his smile is predatory. "Tycho. I'm glad to see you arrived in a timely manner. I know the king had concerns."

Concerns. The word is barbed, every point aimed at me. I had no idea Alek was attending the competition. I suppose I shouldn't be surprised.

I grit my teeth and tighten my grip on the food. "If you'll excuse me."

He moves to block my path. "Something happened to the queen before you left the palace. What was it?"

I think of the queen's sorrow, the king's tense worry, both of which are wrapped up in a tragedy that might have been caused by an action I took. I won't give Alek *any* of that.

"You'll have to address your questions to the queen." I glare at him, thinking of how much doubt he cast on me in the throne room. "You remember how to do that, I'm sure. Now move."

He doesn't. "You're hiding something," he says, his voice low. "The *king* is hiding something."

"Hiding something from a man rumored to work with the Truth-bringers?" I say. "What a surprise."

"Are you referring to yourself? I believe those rumors now point at *you*."

I want to throw a punch. My hand has already formed a fist.

Alek leans in and says, his voice low, "I know where you went, and I know what you did."

My chest constricts, and I suck in a breath—but I hold my temper and try to shove past him.

I should know better. Alek isn't one to let a physical altercation pass him by. He grabs hold of my arm, and I whirl, letting my fist fly. Maybe he didn't expect me to retaliate so quickly, because I get him in the jaw an instant before he ducks to drive an arm into my abdomen. I regroup to hit him again, ready to seize one of his blades, but an arm grabs me from behind.

I struggle, thinking it's his guards, but Alek has been grabbed as well. It's Emberfall's Royal Guard. Commander Zo is standing between us, Princess Harper at her side.

To my surprise, they let me go, but they keep hold of Alek.

"You will *unhand me*," he snaps in Emberish. "Do you know who I am?"

"I know you assaulted a member of this court," Harper snaps back. "Do you know who *I* am?"

Alek inhales like he's going to spew venom. He probably *does* know who Harper is, but he bears nothing but disdain for Emberfall.

Prince Rhen speaks from the end of the hallway. "Watch your words, Lord Alek. *I* know who you are. I will remind you that you are in the heart of Emberfall, not your home country." His tone could slice through steel. "My brother may need to pander to you, but I do not."

Alek grits his teeth—but we're surrounded by guards now. He looks at Harper. "Forgive me, my lady," he says, and if I didn't hate him so much, I'd be impressed at how quickly he can strip any disrespect from his tone. One of Rhen's guards still has his arm pinned, but you'd never know it. "It's been a long ride. I shouldn't have let Tycho provoke me. I let my temper get the best of me."

These words slice into *me*, and my gut tightens. Just like in Syhl Shallow, he'll be forgiven. Another arrow of doubt will pierce my reputation.

But Harper says, "If Tycho provoked you, he probably had a good reason." She looks at the guard pinning his arm. "Let him go."

The guard does. Alek tugs his armor straight.

Prince Rhen has crossed the short distance to stand at her side. "If your travels have been so wearying, I suggest you spend the remainder of your evening in your quarters. I'd be happy to have the Royal Guard escort you."

A threat hides in his words, and a shred of Alek's arrogance lights up his eyes, but it doesn't make it into his voice. "Of course, Your

Highness," he says craftily. "I trust your servants can deliver a full meal for me and my guards?"

I'm hoping Rhen will tell him to eat the food I've dropped on the floor, but the prince simply says, "Certainly," and his voice is just as smooth as Alek's was.

Alek bows to them both, then turns away. Rhen looks at Zo and speaks quietly. "Make sure he doesn't find any further provocation."

She smiles. "Yes, my lord."

Once they're gone, the tension in the hallway evaporates, leaving me with more shame and embarrassment than any latent anger.

I know where you went, and I know what you did.

I have no idea if he spoke true. But even if he's doing nothing more than fishing for information, my reaction likely said enough. I'm sure he'll deliver that news to Grey in as compromising a way as he possibly can. He'll probably wait to announce it in front of a crowd.

Rhen looks at me and lifts an eyebrow. "Politically tricky, you say?"

That almost makes me smile. I'm grateful for their intercession—but mostly regretful that it happened at all, especially in front of them. "Forgive me. He took me by surprise."

"You'll tell me if he harasses you again," says Rhen.

The words light me with a little glow. I'd begun to forget what it felt like for someone to speak out on my behalf. But I grimace. "Please don't take action at your expense."

"At my *expense*? I am the brother to the king. Acting regent in Grey's stead. If Lord Alek chooses to attack a member of this court, then the expense will be his own."

I'm staring at him, half in shock, half in wonder.

Harper smiles, then laughs a little wickedly. "Grey might be good with a sword, and he might have the magic, but when it comes to words and strategy, no one beats Rhen." She rises on her tiptoes to kiss him on the cheek.

He smiles, then traces a finger under her chin. "Certainly not that one. He's playing a game I perfected *ages* ago."

My cheeks warm at their casual affection. I take a step back, intending to excuse myself, to leave them to their own meal, their privacy, their time together.

But Harper hooks an arm through mine and kisses *me* on the cheek as well. "Come on, Tycho. I wanted to get back in time to hear the music. Some of Zo's old musician friends have taken up a tent. We can fill a basket and make a picnic. Walk with us?"

That little glow that lit in my chest builds more fully. I haven't fractured *all* my relationships. "Yes, my lady. As you say."

The night air is cool, and widely spaced torches light the paths between the tents. A large open area sits at the center, and a bonfire burns, sparks flaring into the night. The area isn't crowded, but enough people have gathered to listen to the music that I'm glad I fetched some light weaponry before leaving the castle. The Royal Guard will follow wherever we go, but if I'm walking with the prince and princess, I don't want to be another liability.

Drums and stringed instruments create a percussive rhythm I can feel through every fiber of my body. I'm not the only one—many people are already dancing, creating long, lively shadows. We find seats on logs that have been arranged around the fire, and I could almost forget the mess I left in Syhl Shallow. But firelight flickers along dozens of unfamiliar faces, and a tiny part of my brain warily seeks the shadows for Alek.

The fire warms my skin as I watch the dancers, though, and a bigger part of my brain wishes I could seek the shadows for Jax. I can close my eyes and hear his voice, a little rough, but never uncertain.

Do you need me to choose, Lord Tycho?

A cool wind slides through the camp, causing the bonfire to flicker and throw sparks. Some of the dancers yip and laugh as they scatter away from the burning embers. The musicians play on.

The morning I left, he held on to me so tightly.

I should have hired him a carriage right there on the spot.

"What are you smiling about?" Princess Harper bumps me with her shoulder.

"Ah . . . nothing." I flush and take a sugared pastry from the basket. I'm glad for the cloaking darkness. I wish I knew what Grey had said in his letters. Both she and Rhen are being so kind that guilt keeps pricking at my thoughts.

"Hmm," she says knowingly, and I smile.

She shifts closer to me, slipping a slice of apple onto a piece of flatbread smeared with goat cheese. "I'll let you keep your secrets."

Secrets. The word is a barb, but I know it's not intended, so I nod. "Much appreciated."

"Will you tell me their name, at least?"

I look at her in surprise, and she shrugs.

"I've been smitten before," she says, as if that explains everything. "I know the signs."

For a moment, I can't say his name. Right this instant, it *feels* like a secret, shared only between us. If I speak his name, I make it more. I make it bigger. I make it real.

"Jax," I say, and it's like the wind pulls the name from my lips. Like he'll hear me say it on the other side of the mountain.

The sentimentality of that makes me blush again, and I try to scowl it away.

I fail. The music plays on.

"Good name," Harper says.

"Yes," I agree.

I say nothing else. She doesn't pry. The wind settles, and the dancers move closer to the flames. Prince Rhen has moved away to speak with a man across the clearing, his guards shifting almost invisibly to track his movements.

Harper takes another slice of apple from the basket. "Rhen said you offered to spar with him the last time you were here. That was very kind."

"I didn't mean it as a kindness."

"I know you didn't. I think that's why it meant so much."

I glance over.

She shrugs a little. "He hasn't picked up a sword since he lost his eye. But . . . well, since you and Jake left, I've caught him in the court-yard a few times. Going through the footwork. Early in the morning. You know."

I study her. She takes another apple slice, pressing it into the cheese.

"I don't think he'd ask you," she says carefully, her voice very low. "But if you offered again, I don't think he'd turn it down."

I nod. "I will."

Then Rhen is back, and we sit and listen to the music for a while. Harper's lady-in-waiting, a kind woman named Freya, joins us, her daughters twirling to the music. Her son, a boy who must be eight or nine by now, is lingering close to some of the fighters, probably hoping to be drawn into their midst. Soon, Harper and Freya are spinning with the girls, leaving me on the log with Rhen.

I've been waiting for him to confront me about whatever Grey's letters said, but the prince hasn't said a word. Tension has been building in my gut as guilt and worry grow to fill the space. The music and light-hearted atmosphere should be soothing, but it's not.

Especially when Rhen says, "Do you care to walk?"

It's not an order, but it might as well be, so I rise from the log. "As you like."

He heads away from the bonfire until we've walked beyond the light, and the shadows grow long between us. I wait for him to talk, but he says nothing, and the music fades as we meander among the rows of carefully built tents.

Finally, I can't take his silence any longer. "Forgive me," I say. "But aren't you going to say anything about Grey's report?"

He glances at me. "I was waiting for you to tell me. He simply wrote 'Tycho will tell you all you need to know.'"

Grey could have fired an arrow over the mountains to strike the ground at my feet and I'd be less shocked. I turn these words over and over in my head, and that pool of anxious tension moves north to grip my chest.

He didn't write *anything*.

No wonder Rhen and Harper have been so casually amiable. No wonder they defended me from Lord Alek.

I think of the way I carefully wrapped up any papers to keep them safe—and there was nothing truly confidential to protect. "So he didn't trust me to deliver the message securely."

Rhen peers at me in the darkness. "Or he trusted that you'd do exactly as he said."

That tightness in my chest doesn't ease. I'm glad we've moved away from the flickering torches, because I have no idea what expression is on my face. I feel like I'm breathing through quicksand. "I don't think so."

"Prove him wrong then."

Rhen says these words so simply that I blink and look at him. "What?"

He lifts one shoulder in a shrug. "If you think he wrote *nothing* because you'd betray him somehow, prove him wrong. Tell me all I should know."

Is this a test? This feels like a test.

I inhale to answer—but there's *so* much. Too much.

Rhen catches my arm lightly and stops walking. "At the very least, tell me *something*." He pauses. "Grey's message did not give me the impression that there was trouble. Is there?"

I feel like I'm about to ruin the last scraps of any trust I have with the royal family.

But because I *am* loyal, and I *am* trustworthy, I square my shoulders and tell him everything.

CHAPTER 42

TYCHO

If Grey is a man of action, then Rhen is a man of deliberation. I know they were trapped in Ironrose Castle together, cursed to repeat an endless autumn for what must have felt like *centuries*, though time in Emberfall didn't move much. Maybe that time is part of what made Grey so resolute and decisive. If so, it had the opposite effect on Rhen. He's patient while I talk, rarely interrupting. I tell him everything I can think of, from sitting sentry after learning about Lia Mara losing the baby to Grey's worry of the news reaching the court.

He exhales heavily when I get to that part. "A terrible secret to have to keep." He glances over. "How were they when you left?"

"Not good."

He nods solemnly.

I backtrack, telling him about Jax's father and everything that happened between us afterward—including Jake's findings in the workshop, and how it implicated Jax and Callyn, and then how it complicated the conversations between me and Grey. I tell him about the tourney and Nakiis and what little Sinna said about the woods. I tell him about Alek confronting me before Lia Mara's court on the night that I left.

And finally, I tell him about the lateness of my departure, how I deviated from my journey to demand answers from Jax.

"And were you satisfied with his answers?" Rhen says.

We've wandered far from the bonfire by now. The night air is cool and quiet, heavy with darkness, only punctuated by the occasional sound of the guards' boots when we find gravel.

"Yes," I say. "But maybe it's naïve to trust him."

"He could have killed you while you slept and no one would've been the wiser. Not for *weeks*. I didn't expect you to return so quickly."

I wince. "I know."

"You misunderstand. My point is that your instincts seem sound."

"I don't know about that."

"We can only play the cards that fate deals."

"Well, I keep playing them badly." I pause. "I don't know if Alek is plotting against Grey—or if he's innocent and he truly does think magic is a risk to Syhl Shallow. I don't know if I inadvertently led Nakiis to the Crystal Palace—and then put Princess Sinna in danger." My breath catches, and I fight to steady it. "I don't know if it's my fault that she went . . . that she went *missing*, which then caused the queen to lose—"

Rhen catches my arm. "No. Do *not* do that."

His grip is tight, his voice sharp. A command. It's steadying. Stabilizing.

I swallow past a knot in my throat. "Yes, Your Highness."

He lets go and keeps walking. "There's little use dwelling in self-doubt. Grey used to tell me that all the time."

I think of the moment when the king's breath hitched when he told me about their loss, and I wonder if he still believes that.

"I'll talk to Alek," Rhen says. "Perhaps I can get *someone* from Syhl Shallow to play cards instead of dice."

I snort. "You think he's going to admit to treason?"

"No, but I can convincingly share a distaste for magic and see what he says."

"I look forward to hearing how *that* goes."

Rhen laughs, but not like anything is funny. "Ah, Tycho." He claps me on the shoulder. "I expect you to *join* us."

The following day is warm, the sky overcast. Rain drizzled from the sky all morning, but I ignored it in favor of walking the tracks between the tournament fields, watching competitors practice their skills. Many are amateurs, hoping to get lucky, entering for the right to say they were here. But there are a few clear outliers, men and women with obvious talent and focus. Some competitors from Syhl Shallow have made the journey, and I greet them in Syssalah, remarking on their weapons, wishing them luck, because I know they've breeched a narrow chasm of discomfort in competing *here*.

I wander because I want time to pass slowly, but fate insists on shoving shadows along the ground at a rapid clip. Before I'm ready, it's well past midday, and I am due to meet with Rhen and Alek.

The library at Ironrose is vastly different from the one in the Crystal Palace. The windows here are narrow, the space lit by numerous lanterns and one large chandelier that hangs over the center of the space. Books are everywhere, shelves reaching for the ceiling.

Alek reaches the library entrance at the same time I do. He's dressed in finery, his clothes made from expensive cloth and lined in black leather, revealing only a few details in green. The colors make it very clear where his loyalties lie.

I didn't give my clothing much thought, so I'm a bit more casual in breeches and boots and a belted jerkin. Though I learned my lesson yesterday, and I'm fully armed.

So is he.

For a solid minute, I think about drawing blades. We could settle . . . *whatever this is* right here. He's been eager for it for years, and I wouldn't mind a rematch after what happened in Jax's forge.

But Alek keeps his hands away from his weapons and gives me a clear up-and-down. "Tycho," he says. "You couldn't be troubled to dress appropriately to meet with the brother to the king?"

"I don't usually dress up for a game of cards."

"Ah." He *tsks*. "Your poor upbringing revealing itself again."

"Go to hell, Alek."

He smiles. Rhen appears. We move to a table near the windows.

I try to keep a scowl off my face while they exchange bluntly barbed pleasantries. They may love the verbal parry, but I hate it. I don't want to be here, and I'm sure it's obvious. My attention drifts, and my gaze falls on the window, watching clouds roll through the sky.

Despite all my guilt and uncertainty, I can't stop myself from thinking of Jax. Will he use the silver to hire a carriage? Will he come here?

I'm sure you'd cross my mind at least once.

It's been a lot more than once.

Alek cuffs me lightly on the arm. "You should pay attention to the rules of the game."

I glare at him darkly. "You should take your cards and shove them—"

"Be civil," Rhen says equably as he begins to deal.

I have no idea what we're playing. I *should* have paid attention. But I gather up my cards and glare at Alek across the table. "Forgive me, my lord," I say, without a lick of contrition.

"Forgiven," he says grandly, as if he's the benevolent sort, and I'm the intolerant one.

I turn my glare on my cards. There are six in my hand. Rhen lays out three on the table before us, the setup for Mules and Mares, a common betting game in Emberfall, so at least I'm familiar. Soldiers and guards just call it Mule. It's uncomplicated, but has a tendency to be a *long* game, with many chances for betting and deliberation per round, making it good for long nights and late watches.

They don't play cards much in Syhl Shallow, so I wonder if Alek has ever played at all. It's an interesting game choice, but I look at my cards. I have two threes—the *mules*—but I find no queens—the *mares*—in my hand or on the board, so I toss a copper down to bet.

Alek's eyes flick between his hand and the cards on the table. I can see him trying to recount the rules, the elements of strategy, but he's surely too arrogant to ask for clarification. After a moment, Alek tosses his own coin onto the table, and the round proceeds. Rhen deals more cards, adding to the initial three on the table. We bet again. No one speaks.

After what he said yesterday, I expected Rhen to launch an interrogation. It's what Grey would have done. It's what *I* want to do. But Rhen is even tempered and cordial, to such an extent that I begin to wonder if he's on my side, or if he's handed Alek another opportunity to dig at me.

For the final round, a queen turns up on the board. I have two threes in my hand, but Rhen declines to bet, leaving it to me and Alek. I bet, and he calls, so we have to show our cards.

He also has two threes, along with a queen of his own. I say nothing, just frown and shove my coins his way, acknowledging the win.

"I *like* this game," he says, and there's a taunting note in his voice.

I inhale to fire back, but Rhen says, "I do too. Your dice games are quick, but there's so little time for thought and reflection." He shuffles the cards and deals another round.

We play in silence again, round after round after round, until servants bring a pot of tea and a carafe of wine, along with small platters of biscuits, sliced cheese, honey, and spiced nuts. The room has grown warm as the sun changed angles, and Rhen's jacket now hangs over the back of his chair. My own sleeves are pushed back. Only Alek is still as buttoned up as he was when we entered this room. We've all gathered a small pile of coppers and silver.

The game and the quiet have given me time to think, and most of my indignant fury has bled away, leaving me with nothing but questions. After a while, I can no longer take Rhen's silence.

I look at Alek. "You followed me when I left the Crystal City."

"I did." He doesn't look away from his cards, and after a moment of deliberation, he puts a copper on the table.

"It's the only way you could have gotten here as quickly," I say.

"I didn't deny it."

Rhen says nothing. He tosses a coin on the table and deals more cards.

I don't even look at them. "Why?"

"Because the day I hired that greedy blacksmith, he demanded twice as much silver as was offered. Again and again. And then I found him whispering with the King's Courier, after I and others had paid for his confidence." His gaze flicks up from his cards. "You remember, I'm sure. You set me on fire, then went crying back to the king about *my* transgressions."

"That's not what happened."

He raises his eyebrows. "It's your bet."

I make an aggravated sound, then glance at my cards. I have three queens in my hand, and there's a three on the board already. I toss a silver onto the table.

In that short span of time, his words rattle around in my thoughts. *You set me on fire, then went crying back to the king.*

For the first time, I wonder if that's what he believes. That *I* attacked him, when he was the one pinning me to a work table.

It makes me think of Callyn flinching away from me after she learned I had magic.

For one tiny fraction of a second, it rattles my foundation. But I know what he did. I remember how he acted.

"Why do you need to pay for his *confidence* if you're not doing anything wrong?" I demand. "There are courier channels all over both countries."

He surveys his cards, then lazily tosses his own silver onto the table. "If they're so secure, why do you have a job at all?"

I inhale sharply, but Rhen says, "I believe we can all agree that there are some messages that should not be delivered with the same degree of urgency and surety as a plowman reporting how much he needs a second set of oxen."

I clamp my mouth shut.

"So you believe Tycho may not be trustworthy?" Rhen says.

"I think it is a telling measure of judgment and character that a high-ranking nobleman would be dallying with a poor laborer who's shown a willingness to . . ." His eyes flash with rancor. "Shall we say . . . to do just about *anything* for a few extra pieces of silver?"

I nearly come out of my chair.

"Tycho," says Rhen, and his voice is quiet. Not a rebuke or an order.

I stay in my seat, but I'm gripping my cards so hard that they're beginning to fold.

Alek hasn't moved. Rhen hasn't moved. I feel hot and cold all over, like I can't say or do the right thing. My cheeks are surely burning.

I hate this. I hate him.

"I'm not the only one *dallying* with a laborer," I snap.

"You're the only one casting a shadow on the integrity of the entire royal family."

"Only because of your lies."

"When have I lied?" he says. "You bring the king's doubt upon yourself."

"Who are you working with, Alek?" My breathing feels tight and shallow. He's too clever. I know Rhen brought him here in hopes of uncovering something, but Alek always knows how to twist things so the outcome is exactly what he expects.

His expression doesn't flicker. "I have customers and vendors all over Syhl Shallow. You know this."

"That's not what I mean and you know it. Who's Lady Karyl?"

He looks up. "I have no idea. Is that someone of importance?"

I want to punch him. "That's who left you a message with Jax!"

He sighs as if bored of my interrogation. "I cannot keep track of the name of every servant sent to leave me a message, Tycho. At this point, I wouldn't even know which message this might apply to."

"So if it is not a matter of trust," says Rhen, bringing the conversation back to the matter at hand, "do you question Tycho's loyalty?"

Alek slides his cards together, then surveys the board. He must be satisfied by what he finds there, because he lays a coin down, then looks at me. "In fact, no. I don't question your loyalty at all."

That shocks me still.

"If anything, Tycho's loyalty is rather . . . impressive," Alek continues, and his voice is just as even as Rhen's. "I personally would find it rather challenging to devote myself to a king who once fled his duty, hid his identity, lied about his abilities, and then allowed me to be chained to a wall and flogged."

There's blood on my tongue. I've bitten the inside of my cheek. I don't think I'm breathing.

Alek glances at Rhen. "To say nothing of carrying that devotion so far as to sit here politely playing cards with the man responsible."

I expect that to make Rhen flinch, because I feel the impact of those words like a sledgehammer. But he doesn't. He doesn't look away from

Alek. "A man in power has to think about more than just the life of one person—or two, as it was. I had a country to protect. A choice to make. So I made it."

"I don't fault you for it," says Alek.

"I honestly don't care if you do or not." Rhen sets down a coin. "Tycho, the bet is yours."

I have no idea how they're continuing to play cards right now. I don't even look at the cards in play; I just add another coin to the pile. I feel like I'm simultaneously being strangled and set on fire.

Alek does this every single time. It's diabolical. Masterful, the way he makes me reconsider every decision I've ever made.

But then I realize what Rhen just said.

I honestly don't care if you do or not.

It wraps up with the words he said to me last night.

There's little use dwelling in self-doubt.

I look at Rhen. My chest feels hollow, but my voice is steady when I say, "You may not care for my opinion either, but I also don't fault you for it."

"On the contrary," he says. "Your opinion means quite a bit. Alek, where do your loyalties lie?"

"With Syhl Shallow," Alek says. There's no tension in his voice, but I can see that his eyes are no longer studying the cards, and are instead studying Rhen. "As I hope you would expect."

"Of course." Rhen pauses. "So I would assume you are loyal to your queen?"

"As you are loyal to your king, Your Highness." Alek shrugs. "The problem arises when one's subjects begin to question the king and queen's loyalty to each other."

"Is it a matter of *questioning* their loyalty," says Rhen, "or judging it?"

Alek says nothing. He senses a trap.

"Your queen has chosen to marry the king of Emberfall," Rhen continues. He looks at his cards, surveys the arrangement on the table, and lays down a coin. "So you can see where *her* loyalty lies. And surely you would have no question about mine."

"You're loyal to Emberfall."

"Yes. And to Grey. And to those who are loyal to him." He pauses. "I understand my brother made a choice when you and Tycho had this . . ." He glances at me. "*Altercation* in Briarlock."

"Are you questioning his choice?" says Alek.

Rhen smiles dangerously. "Never." He pauses. "I can say without hesitation that I would have made a different one." He shuffles. Deals. Shrugs. "I would have questioned you both and acted accordingly." When he looks at Alek, his gaze is piercing. "Had you failed to appear, I would have considered that an admission of guilt."

"How lucky I am that you were not making the decision, then."

"Indeed you are. The bet is to you, Tycho."

I toss a coin on the table without any care for the cards in my hand. I've watched a thousand sword fights, but none have come close to the level of tension in this room.

There's something fascinating about that. I've spent years with Grey on the training fields, but this is a different skill altogether. I was ready to draw a weapon a moment ago. But with Alek, I need to be smarter. To figure out a way to rely on more than just my talents with a blade.

"You bear a distrust for magic," Rhen is saying to Alek.

"You do too, I'm told." He glances at Rhen's hands. "You do not wear the rings your brother has shared with an honored few."

"I have no need for magic," Rhen says. "But I do not begrudge my brother his talents."

"I do," Alek says. "I've seen the damage magic has caused to the people of Syhl Shallow. *You've* seen the damage magic has caused to Emberfall. Grey has been king for four years, but where is magic's benefit to either country? Our former queen was formidable. No one would dare attack her court. And now we have a queen who's been attacked more than once. She refuses to allow her guards and soldiers to act, under the guise of wanting *peace*. Instead of peace, we had protestors slaughtered in the castle hallways."

Alek leans in against the table. "And now, his magic seems to be putting our queen at risk. Her lingering illness is no secret to those at court. The princess's disappearance has not been explained. If the king cannot be trusted to use his magic to protect the royal family, why should anyone else trust him?"

Rhen's eyes flick to me, but I say nothing. The king and queen were planning to make an announcement, but I don't know if they actually did. I may have lost my position at court, but I still know how to keep secrets.

I glare at Alek. "You keep implying everyone else is unworthy of trust, but it's you. You're the liar. You're the one sowing discord."

"Again," he says. "When have I lied?"

"Tycho is suspicious of your motives," Rhen says. "That makes *me* suspicious of your motives. What are you really doing in Briarlock?"

Alek shrugs lazily. "Nothing."

I grit my teeth. "If your intention is to harm the king—"

His eyes flash to mine. "How could *anyone* harm the king," he says, his tone low and mocking, "if he has such powerful *magic*?"

Something about those words lodges in my thoughts. I'm not sure what, and I turn them around in my head.

"If you are found to be plotting against the king," says Rhen, his voice just as low, "it will not go well for you."

Alek bets. "Are you attempting to threaten me?"

"Threaten you!" Rhen laughs. "No. I am attempting to *warn* you."

I'm frozen in place, but I'm hardly listening now.

How could anyone harm the king?

I know how. I flex my fingers. Just like my rings gave me magic,

Iishellasan steel can be charged to repel magic. I've seen a dagger that could cause injuries Grey was unable to heal.

I remember a line from one of the first letters we found.

Gather your best silver.

We thought they were gathering funds. Planning another large attack on the palace.

But everything else was in code. *Mama fed the goats, . . . Papa . . .* Why not *silver*, too?

My heart is pounding again. Have they been gathering Iishellasan steel? Has Alek found weapons that would block Grey from using his magic? The thought is chilling.

Alek lays down his cards. One mare and three mules. "With all due respect, Your Highness," he says, his voice even, "I don't need your warnings." He reaches to gather the coins on the table.

"My win," I say, and he looks up in surprise.

I lay down three queens, which beats his hand.

He scowls and shoves the coins in my direction.

I stack the silver slowly, tallying my win. "*With all due respect,*" I say, mocking his arrogant tone, "I'm beginning to think you should take all the warnings you get."

CHAPTER 43

JAX

Fine metalworking generally isn't among my top skills. Farmers don't ask for detailed designs along the blade of a sickle. Even the weapons we create are crafted to be practical, not beautiful. No one needs elegant etchings on a dagger for it to draw blood.

As before, re-creating this seal perfectly is something that requires a lot of practice.

There's a part of me that just wants to rip the message open. Surely that's what the recipient would do. They wouldn't examine the seal too closely.

But if they're plotting against the king . . . then maybe they would.

And the wax! Callyn walked into town to the stationers for a few cubes of colored wax, and she's been trying to re-create the perfect swirls of green and black and silver. But no matter what she combines, the colors mix into sludge that doesn't look similar at *all*.

All the while, time ticks away. Without my father here to handle some of the business, I work late into the night trying to keep up with everyone who needs something from the forge. I listen to travelers' chatter whenever I can. The king will be traveling to Emberfall in a matter of days. The queen is ill and will remain behind with the young princess. The Royal Houses are openly distrustful of magic. The king and queen are at odds. There are whispers of a scandal involving the King's Courier.

I swallow hard when I hear these words, but I keep my head down and work.

A scandal.

I wish he'd told me what was going on.

I'm sure you'd cross my mind at least once.

Only every waking moment. I think of that bag of silver he left. I imagine myself hiring a carriage to Ironrose Castle. Arriving with soot on my knuckles and a nail pinning my hair in a knot, bearing a potential letter of treason.

And what would happen to Callyn and little Nora? Could I take them with me? Is this enough silver to bring them along?

If we *all* left, would the Truthbringers come after us? Callyn said that Alek had people watching her. Surely they were watching me too. Are they still? Was it a threat—or was it true? Are they people in Briarlock, or people from the Crystal City?

There are too many questions.

Callyn comes down the lane every morning now, bringing me eggs and meat pies and a good dose of contrition that we both seem to feel. The air between us is still raw, but it helps to have a common goal.

I want to ask how she could trust a man like Alek—but she must not. Not fully. Not if she brought me this letter. Not if we're doing this.

She probably wants to know how I could trust a man like Tycho, someone whose entire life requires secrecy, someone whose only opportunities to see me are when he happens to be crossing the mountain border on someone else's command.

By the end of the fifth day, I have a workable replication of the seal itself. I use Callyn's sludge-wax to practice, and the pattern of stars is identical, at least to my eye. When she arrives on the sixth morning, I show her my results.

She says nothing, just chews on the edge of her lip.

"I don't think I can get any closer," I say. "I had to build new tools to create the narrow lines and stars in the upper half. It's so tiny that it kept getting too hot. I don't have a small firebox like the fine forges have."

She still says nothing.

"*What?*" I demand. "Do you not want to open it now?"

"No," she says. She pulls the folded parchment from a pocket in her skirts. "I already did."

The archery competition is on the second day.
Father will be on the fields to observe.
Use your best arrows, and do not miss your target.

"I can't believe I've been burning my fingers for days over *this*. It's not exactly an assassination plan." The message surely isn't meaningless—why would it be worth so much?—but it definitely doesn't say anything we could run to the palace about. We couldn't even take this to the magistrate.

I fold the parchment back together. There's a dark spot where the wax sat. A clenching in my chest when I consider that we might be killed by Lord Alek or his people for daring to do this.

"What made you open it?" I say quietly.

"I kept trying to re-create the wax mixture, and it wasn't working. I thought perhaps I could melt a bit of this one. I held it over a steaming pot, and it softened right up." She pauses. "It might not be a plan, but it's definitely a time, right? An opportunity?"

"Would *Father* be the king?"

"Maybe." She bites at her lip, studying the letter. "Alek told me of a special steel from Iishellasa that can affect magic. Like the rings Lord Tycho wears."

The ones he doesn't wear anymore.

"He said the steel can work *against* magic, too," she says. She tugs at the pendant under the neckline of her blouson, pulling it free. "He said this was made of the same steel."

I reach out, running my fingers over the metal. It's darker than the rings Tycho wears. "Like some kind of ward against it?"

She nods. "Maybe." Her voice drops, and she closes her fingers around the pendant. "I've been wondering if perhaps it kept me and Nora safe during the attack on the palace."

My eyes flick up to meet hers. "Do you really think that?"

"Maybe." She reaches out to tap the letter. "*Use your best arrows.* I think they have weapons that will hurt the king."

My chest clenches.

"They passed Briarlock a day ago," Callyn continues. "Did you hear?"

"Who?"

"The king and everyone who'd travel with him."

"No. I didn't hear." I don't know what to do. I don't know who I can take this to.

Tycho.

But that's just as dangerous as it would've been when I wanted to take it to him *sealed*. I don't even know if I'd be able to make it in *time*.

Cal sighs, then digs a hand into her pocket. "I brought the original wax. If you've made a seal, at least we can put it back together."

"Yeah." I stand, take the ball of swirled wax, and move to melt it over the heat of the forge.

But then I stop and unfold the paper against the table. I take a piece of wrapped kohl and rewrite the words on a new slip of parchment.

"What are you doing?" demands Cal.

"I want to make sure I have the exact words." I hold the wax over the fire, and it begins to melt.

Almost immediately, the colors begin to blend.

"Too much!" Cal says. She pulls the spoon from my hand, then hastily pours it onto the juncture of parchment. It's a wider splotch of wax than before, and only half bears the swirls of color, but I press the seal into it carefully.

Then we're done. It's resealed.

"Does it look close?" she whispers.

Yes. No. Maybe. "I don't know how closely the nobility examines sealed letters," I say.

She blows lightly on the wax to cool it, then nods at my scrawling. "What are you going to do with *that*?"

I hold my breath for a moment. I remember when we first started doing this. We were only planning to pay our taxes. We had no love or hate for the royal family—just a need for silver.

But I'm not naïve enough that I don't think this is a message plotting to kill the king. It's a time. A moment of opportunity. This has gone far beyond a few messages that will never affect us.

There's so much at risk. I have no proof.

But I have a bag of silver next to my bed. A hidden dagger. A good bow and a quiver of arrows.

What are you afraid of?

I look at Cal. "I'm going to take it to Tycho."

I fill a sack with a few supplies, but I keep it light, because it's a long way into town to hire passage. I don't have a dagger belt, so I bury the weapon at the bottom of my bag. The archery bracer buckles onto my forearm like an old friend. The satchel and quiver crisscross my chest securely, followed by the bow across my back.

I remember Tycho buckling into his armor. The way he taught me to break his hold.

I told you the army could use you.

Warmth crawls up my cheeks even though I'm alone. This is a bit of gear. A shred of confidence. I'm no soldier. It shouldn't matter.

But . . . it does.

I tuck the silver into my bag with the note, then take hold of my crutches to head into the main room of the house. I'll need to leave a note beside the forge, though Callyn said she'd try to look out for any customers while I'm gone. I'll wrap up the meat pies she brought so I can take them with—

My father is sitting at the table.

I choke on my breath and stumble to a stop. I'm so shocked that I nearly drop the crutches.

I can't breathe. I can't think.

"What are you doing here?" I scrape out.

"I told the magistrate that my boy was a cripple and he'd starve without me here." He takes one of the meat pies Callyn brought, holds it up to his face, and inhales deeply. "I suppose I was wrong."

My heart is pounding so hard that it hurts. "They—they just let you go?"

"Aren't you glad to see me?"

He's sober—which is a relief.

His tone is low and dangerous, which is not.

He rises from the table, and I shove myself back a step involuntarily.

He smiles. "What are you up to, Jax?"

"I'm not up to anything," I growl.

"You look like you're going somewhere."

I inhale to lie—but it'll be obvious. I am clearly prepared to leave the workshop. "I was heading to town." I grit my teeth. "I'll be back soon."

"What do you need in town?"

"Food."

I say it quickly. Too quickly, because his eyes narrow. "There's food here." He takes a bite of the meat pie.

For an instant, the air hangs with tension between us. I can't run. He knows I can't run.

But now I've been quiet for too long. It's too late to lie.

When he makes a move, I'm ready for it. The bow comes over my head, my fingers finding the string with practiced ease. I have an arrow nocked.

He tackles me just as I release the string. A sound bursts from his throat, surprise mixed with pain.

Then we hit the floor. He's heavy, and he lands on top of me. The wind rushes out of my lungs.

He punches me right in the face. It's so quick and unexpected that my head snaps to the side.

Maybe next time we should work on how to block a punch instead of shooting arrows. Ah, yes. Next time, Lord Tycho. Next time.

There's blood on my tongue. My arms are up, but he doesn't hit me again.

Instead, he's tugging at my satchel.

It takes too long for the implications of that to catch up with me. "No," I cry. "No."

He finds the bag of silver, and his eyes go so wide they look like they're going to fall out of his head. "Oh, Jax. What are you doing?"

"Nothing."

He grabs hold of the straps across my chest and lifts me slightly to slam me back against the floorboards. *"What are you doing?"*

I'm bleeding. Aching. Failing.

He finds the note next and swears. "What's this?" He leans down close, until I can smell his breath. It's bad enough that I miss the ale. "What kind of misfortune are you bringing to me this time?"

My own breathing is hitching. I don't feel strong anymore. I was stupid to think I could be anything more than what I was.

"Nothing," I whisper.

"You're damned right it's nothing." He smacks me on the side of the head and gets up. He's got the dagger now, too. I didn't even see him unearth that from the bag. For an instant, I think this is it. He'll cut my throat or stab me in the chest, and I'll die right here on the floor.

"Get up," he snaps. "I've been gone for days. There's work to do."

CHAPTER 44

CALLYN

Jax is going to take the contents of the letter to Tycho.

I can't decide if this is brilliant or if it's the dumbest idea he's ever had.

I haven't seen any of Alek's guards in the woods, but he's told me before that he has people watching me. The message is tucked securely in my skirt pocket, fully sealed and ready for Lady Karyl. After I returned from the forge, I sent Nora out to fetch the eggs from the hens. When she crossed the barnyard, I watched the woods. A cold wind swept through the space, but I didn't hear anyone. I didn't see anyone.

Regardless of how I feel about magic, I don't want to be a part of an assassination. If I've learned anything from interacting with Alek and Tycho, it's that there are a lot of secrets being kept, and I don't know the truth at all.

I am but a soldier for the cause.

Surely a soldier would have to believe in the cause.

I don't know if I believe in this one.

I'm spreading flour across my pastry table to make tarts for the afternoon when I realize Nora has been gone for a while. I expect irritation to wash over me, but instead, a prick of fear needles me between my shoulder blades.

I dust flour from my hands and head for the door.

Nora is standing in the barnyard, a basket of eggs hung over one arm. Her eyes are wide, her breathing quick.

She's facing Lady Karyl, who's backed by ten soldiers.

Behind the soldiers is a wagon with two horses, the contents covered by a long stretch of canvas that's been tied down. I think it's there to cover supplies, but a small hint of motion at the back tells me there's someone under the canvas.

That needle of fear in my spine turns into a dagger.

"Nora," I say, keeping my voice even. "Don't trouble Lady Karyl if she's here on official business. Go back in the bakery."

"She's no trouble," Lady Karyl says. "I understand Lord Alek left you with a message for me?"

Her voice is simple and calm, completely at odds with the ball of tension in my chest. I have to force my legs to move, and I stride forward, pulling the message from my skirts.

She examines it carefully, and I'd swear my heart stops beating when her eyes fall on the seal.

I expect her to put it in her purse, as she's done with others, but she hands it back to me. "Burn it."

I almost choke on my breath. "Wh-what?"

"Our plans have changed. Burn it." She pulls a silver from her purse. "You have my gratitude."

I'm all but shaking. I can't demand an explanation without admitting that I've read it.

Have I been tricked? Has Alek? Is there a plot against the king or not?

"Callyn?" Lady Karyl is peering at me. "Are you well?"

"Yes," I say. I have to clear my throat. "I—sorry. Yes, my lady. I'll burn it."

"We'll be needing your barn for the next few weeks as well," she continues. "Surely you won't mind offering shelter to my guards and soldiers for a few days after Alek so graciously repaired your outbuildings?"

I glance behind her at the soldiers again. Ten doesn't seem like a very big number, but it sure is a lot of swords and daggers. That cover on the wagon shifts again.

I look back at Lady Karyl. "I don't want any trouble here."

"Then you'll agree."

I inhale. A soldier puts a hand on the hilt of his sword.

Nora pulls close to me. "Cally-cal," she whispers.

I nod at Lady Karyl. "Yes, my lady. What we have is yours."

CHAPTER 45

TYCHO

After our card game, I expressed my concerns to Prince Rhen, that Alek might have weapons that could harm the king. The prince agreed to have the man's chambers searched.

That search turned up nothing.

I'm not surprised. Alek wouldn't make it that easy.

But it leaves me ungrounded, because Alek has done such a good job of turning any suspicion *away* from himself. I have no proof. I'm not even sure I have Grey's trust any longer.

Grey isn't one to stand on ceremony, so there isn't much fanfare when he arrives, but his presence in the castle is impossible to ignore. Even if I can't go directly to the king, Rhen takes my concerns seriously, and I see that he's assigned additional security to any spaces Grey might linger. Lord Alek is never left to linger alone. Syhl Shallow guards suddenly line the hallways along with the Royal Guard of Emberfall. The languages of both countries can be heard in the Great Hall, on the training fields, in the arena.

If the queen were here, I know she'd be admiring the occasional sense of unity, of collaboration and trust.

She wouldn't be ignoring the undercurrent of tension. The words muttered in Syssalah or Emberish when backs are turned. The exchanged glances between guards, underscored with distrust.

I doubt the king is ignoring it, though I have no idea. He's been here for days, and I've been keeping my distance. The competition has started, so he's always surrounded, always busy, always with both Rhen and Jacob and a dozen guards at his side.

The tension, the *waiting*, is terrible. I keep watching, expecting a trap to be sprung, for Alek to make his move.

But he doesn't. He's cordial. Polite. The perfect courtly gentleman, enjoying a bit of sport on the field.

By the fourth day, nothing has happened, and I begin to doubt *myself.* I'm sure Grey knows the source of my concerns by now, and the daily lack of any true danger must seem like one more failure on my part. The competition fields have turned to foot races, which I don't care to watch. Instead, I head for the stables, which are mostly deserted, to fetch Mercy.

To my surprise, I find Prince Rhen there as well, feeding his horse a caramel. He's still dressed in palace finery, which he's worn to the competition every day. Palace guards from both countries are on duty in the aisle. I'm so startled that I stop short in the doorway, my eyes seeking Grey.

Rhen notices my expression, because he gives me a knowing look. "Don't worry. The king is expected to watch the competitors, so you've got a few hours of safety left."

I inhale to protest, but he's too savvy—and I'm not one to lie. "Am I so obvious?"

"Yes." He holds out a handful of candies. "Here. For your mare."

Before I've even taken them, Mercy has her head stretched out of her stall, reaching for the sugar, as if she can inhale them from ten feet away. I feed them to her, then tether her to fetch her saddle.

"Were you going somewhere?" says Rhen.

I nod, then shrug. I'm not sure how to admit that I couldn't keep waiting for . . . nothing to happen. I wonder if he's feeling the same. A flicker of guilt pulls at me. "Nowhere of consequence. You?"

"A destination may be more prudent." He pulls open the tack closet beside his horse's stall. Much like Grey, when it comes to horses, Rhen isn't one to pass on the care of his mount to another. "Either way, I'll join you if you don't mind the company."

I hesitate, trying to figure out his tone.

I must wait too long, because he stops with a saddle hung over one arm. "That's not an order. If you prefer the solitude, simply say so."

I *do* prefer the solitude—but I've discovered over the last few weeks that I don't mind Rhen's company either.

Then I notice something else: he's armed. A sword hangs at one hip, and a dagger is belted to the other. Maybe it's for appearance's sake, since he's been at the king's side all week.

But . . . maybe it's not.

"I welcome the company," I say.

"Good." He slips the saddle onto the back of his buckskin. "Do you know the forests north of the castle? There's an old clearing a few miles beyond the creek. Nearly half an acre of fresh clover. A good spot to let the horses graze."

"I know it." Barely. I've seen it once or twice. I think.

Rhen smiles, then buckles the girth into place. He looks to his guards. "You will remain behind. Tycho will be adequate defense."

I stop with my hand on Mercy's bridle. "Your Highness, are you certain that is a wise—"

"I'm certain you're about to be left behind." He slips a bridle on his own horse's head, then leads the animal out of the stall. Without hesitation he swings aboard.

Then he's *gone*.

I lose a moment to shock. Another to the buckles on her bridle. She's already tugging at the reins.

But I smile for what feels like the first time in *days*. "Come on, Mercy. We've got a race to win."

The only time I've ever ridden with Rhen, it's been sedate journeys to distant towns, surrounded by guards or advisers. Everything I know of him is careful planning and thoughtful deliberation. I didn't expect him to take off like an arrow shot from a well-strung bow.

He keeps a lead as we fly past the competition fields and dive into the shadowed woods north of the palace. I expect Rhen to stick to the broad, winding road through the woods, but his horse slips between branches to skip curves, leaping over fallen trees without hesitation, trusting that the ground won't fall away on the other side. My heart is pounding in time with Mercy's hooves against the turf.

I should be responsible here, should call for a slower pace, because if the king's brother goes flying headlong into a tree, I'm pretty sure there'd be no forgiveness.

But the wind is in my hair, and the thrill of competition is in my blood, so I slip Mercy another inch of rein. "Come on, sweet girl."

She flicks an ear in my direction and redoubles her speed.

It's not enough to make up for Rhen's head start. When we burst into the clearing, he's at least three horse-lengths ahead of me. Both horses are breathing hard when we draw to a stop, but they're fit and we haven't gone far. Mercy is prancing in place, pawing at the ground in protest, wanting to run again.

Rhen is red-cheeked and windblown. His hair has fallen across the leather mask that covers his missing eye. "I haven't done that in *years*."

I smile. "Well, you couldn't prove it by me."

"You didn't *let* me win, did you?"

That makes me laugh. "No. Mercy might feel better if I say that I did."

He says nothing to that. He looks out at the stretch of sunlight-dappled grass, then swings down from the saddle and pulls the bridle free, giving his horse the freedom to graze. After a moment, I do the same with Mercy.

"You used to race with Grey?" I guess.

"I did. He could almost always best me in the arena, but I rarely find a horse that can beat Ironwill." Rhen pulls another caramel from a pocket, slipping it to the buckskin.

I consider the sword at his side. The race. The lack of guards. The fact that we're miles away from the competition fields and the watchful eyes of his brother.

"Did you drag me out here to practice swordplay?" I say.

He glances over. "No. I dragged you out here so you could freely ask about your king."

I feel *that* like a fist to the gut. "Oh."

We stand there in silence for the longest moment. I don't know what to say.

Eventually, I put my hand on the hilt of my sword. "Perhaps we could do both."

He studies me for a long moment. Then he takes hold of his own weapon. "Fine."

I'm prepared for him to begin slowly, to ease into swordplay like a beginner, with straightforward thrusts and parries. Luckily, I have years of warnings from Grey about underestimating an opponent, so when Rhen comes at me like he means to wage war, I deflect and spin and disarm him in less than ten seconds. His sword lands in the grass, and he swears.

"I didn't let you win that time either," I say.

Rhen gives me a rueful glance. "Noted."

He attacks again. I disarm him again.

He swears again.

"We could begin more slowly," I say.

"Don't make me stab you."

"Haven't you been trying?"

He looks startled, and I worry that I've poked at his pride too hard. But he laughs under his breath and claims his blade. We begin again. And again. And again. It's not just that he's out of practice, though that's part of it. Some is his vision—but there's nothing he can do about that. It's his disappointment in himself. His impotent rage. He's tireless, though, and he attacks with such surety.

I disarm him every time.

Eventually, sweat threads his hair. He abandoned his jacket long ago, and a few stripes of blood decorate his sleeves when neither of us could deflect quickly enough. I want to suggest returning to the armory for training blades, but I think he really would kill me.

But as time passes . . . he begins to compensate. His stance changes as he tries different angles. He's begun to learn my movements. The arrogant frustration has slipped away, revealing a cool focus.

Before I'm ready, he blocks, swings, gets inside my guard, and ends with his sword against my throat.

We're both breathing hard. I lift my hands. "I yield."

He sheathes the blade, then runs a hand across his face. He has to lift the hem of his shirt to wipe away the sweat. When he speaks, his voice is quiet. "Thank you, Tycho." He hesitates, then glances at me. "There haven't been this many people at Ironrose in ages. After everything we've learned about the Truthbringers, I've worried that my closeness to Grey would make me . . ."

His voice trails off. I frown. "Would make you what?"

"A liability. I can't fight like I once did."

Maybe he really did want to get away from the castle as badly as I did. "You will," I say. "With practice. Again?"

"I'd rather finish while I don't feel like a *complete* failure. I'm going to be sore for days as it is." He swipes at his face again, then drops to sit in the grass. He peers up at me. "Why didn't you enter the competition? You're very good."

I shrug and drop to sit in the grass beside him. "I had a good teacher."

"You didn't answer my question," says Rhen.

I shake my head. It was bad enough sparring with Jacob a few weeks ago. Fighting in a competition in front of the king would be ten times worse. "It felt inappropriate."

"You didn't ask anything about Grey."

I'm not sure I want any answers. "That feels inappropriate, too."

"You know I took your warnings seriously. For what it's worth, Grey did as well. But I've spent long hours watching the competition in Alek's presence. He speaks highly of the queen, and his worries about magic seem genuine. He's either very clever or very innocent."

I frown and wait for him to say more, but he doesn't.

A cool wind sweeps between the trees, bringing a light drizzle of rain. In our time out here, poor weather has moved in again.

Rhen looks up at the sky. "We should return. My guards will come looking."

"As you say." I sigh and uncurl from the ground, then whistle for Mercy. I wait for him to have the bridle over Ironwill's head before I say, "Your Highness?"

He looks up.

I leap into my saddle. "I'll race you back."

We fly through the woods again, cold rain stinging my eyes. This all feels a bit reckless, but the footing is sure, and I can hear his horse not too far behind me. I'd almost forgotten what it felt like to enjoy something simple. My heart feels lighter than it has in *weeks*.

Then we burst out of the woods and slam right into a group of men and women on horseback—guards from Emberfall and Syhl Shallow.

"Whoa!" I sit down hard in the saddle, and Mercy responds immediately, skidding in the wet grass, fighting my grip on the reins. The rain is pouring down, soaking us all. The guards shout in surprise, scattering a bit so we don't collide with anyone.

And of course that leaves Mercy to skid right into the king's horse, who prances and kicks out, leaving his rider looking aggrieved.

What's worse is that Alek rides just behind him, astride his own mount. "Have some control of your horse," he says to me.

If I have to apologize to him, I'm going to do it with a sword. I keep my eyes on the king. "Forgive me," I say. "Your Majesty."

Rhen skids to a stop beside me. "You interrupted our race," he says.

The rain pours down. The king glares at both of us. "I came looking for you both."

"If you'd waited five more minutes, we could be having this conversation in the warmth of the stables. Join us for a sprint?"

"No." Grey's tone is as cold as the rain.

"Very well. Tycho?" The prince clucks to his horse and turns away.

My heart is beating in my throat. I absolutely do not have the mettle to race away from the king. I can feel Alek's eyes on me.

Grey catches Rhen's rein and sighs. "I'll ride back with you, Rhen. Just not at a full gallop."

"Of course. As my king commands." Rhen's voice isn't flippant, but almost.

Something about his tone makes me take notice. Maybe I *should* have asked questions. The tension here isn't all between me and Grey. I wonder if Rhen taking my side in regard to Alek has painted *him* in a bad light, too.

But they begin walking, so I turn to follow. Grey says, "No. Ride alongside."

I do as he says, though I feel like I've swallowed a handful of ash. Alek catches my eye, and I see something like triumph in his gaze. Rain sneaks under my jacket to make me shiver, reminding me of miserable assignments when I was a soldier. My fingers tighten on the slick reins.

Grey is never one to mince words, and he doesn't now. "Alek has mentioned that you did not cross the border into Emberfall as I ordered."

Silver hell. I've been so focused on threats against the king that I completely forgot about Alek's threats against *me*. I steel my spine and answer. "You said you were not concerned about one random blacksmith. But I was."

"You could not have shared your concerns with me?"

"I wasn't hiding anything," I say tightly. "You ordered me to leave, so I did."

"I ordered you to cross the border and reach the safe house before midnight."

I hate this. I don't want to be at odds with him. I don't want to feel like every choice I make is a poor one.

"And even if you thought you knew *best*," Grey continues, "you didn't think to tell me about this . . . *investigation* on the day I arrived?"

My eyes are fixed on Mercy's mane, my jaw tight. "Jax didn't know anything," I say, keeping my voice low. "He wasn't working with the Truthbringers."

"Just like Nakiis would never cause trouble?" he says.

I wish he would pull his sword and end this right here. All the peace and joy from the race with Rhen, from the swordplay, is now shriveled in my gut.

Prince Rhen speaks into my silence. "We all make choices that seem right in the moment," he says, "that turn out poorly later. I believe you've made a few such choices yourself, Your Majesty."

"Enough." The king's glare is so lethal it's a miracle it doesn't knock Rhen off his horse.

That isn't better. "I won't disobey orders again," I say. "I swear it."

"Will this oath be similar to the one you already swore?" says Alek.

I glare at him. I wish I had the talent to strike a blow with words, the way Prince Rhen can. "You may be able to convince everyone else of your innocence, but I know you're turning everyone against *me* to keep the suspicion off yourself."

"What suspicion?" Alek says. "You've made countless accusations, Tycho, but it seems *you* are the one trying to point the blame at *me*. Don't think I didn't know who suggested that Prince Rhen's guards search my things."

I bite the inside of my cheek to keep from snapping at him, and look at the king in the rain. I say the only thing I can think of. "I'm sorry I failed you. If you don't need me here, I'll return to the Crystal Palace and await further orders."

I don't know what I'm hoping for him to say, but he nods. "Fine."

That wasn't it.

I'm going to make the ride at night again. The rain continues to poor down, but I've got an oilcloth cloak over my armor, and I haven't been scared of thunder since I was a child. Mercy's tack is still slick from when I went galloping with Prince Rhen, but I don't care. My chest is tight and my heart is heavy and I just want to be . . . gone.

A boot scrapes on the stable aisle, and I turn, expecting Rhen again. He won't convince me to stay. He won't convince me that I haven't lost whatever trust I might have had.

Instead, I find the king.

I'm shocked into stillness, but I recover quickly. I frown and grit my teeth so I don't swear at him. I'm sure he can read every expression on my face anyway.

I can't read *anything* on his.

Mercy butts at me with her head, and I'm glad for an excuse to catch her bridle and fiddle with a buckle unnecessarily. To my surprise, Grey joins me at her side, unnecessarily adjusting a buckle himself. His eyes meet mine, and he stops, so I do too.

I feel like I've failed him in so many ways that there aren't enough words to make up for it. But I feel like he's failed me too.

Maybe that's unfair. I don't know what he's waiting for me to say.

I don't find out, because a guard from Syhl Shallow steps into the aisle. "Your Majesty," she says breathlessly. "A runner from the sentry station at Willminton has arrived with urgent news of the queen."

The king turns, our conflict forgotten. "What news?"

"I haven't heard the report. I was sent to—"

"Grey." Rhen bursts through the doors, a roll of damp parchment in his hand. "Lia Mara and Sinna have been taken." He holds out a palm, and a ring set with three diamonds glints in the light. "Her ring was sent as proof."

For half a second, Grey is frozen in place, stricken. He takes the ring, running his thumb over the stones. When he speaks, his voice is thin. "The scraver?"

"No. The Truthbringers."

Grey strides forward to take the parchment before Rhen can even hold it out. "How?" he says, his words clipped. "Where?" He doesn't even wait for an answer. He looks to a guard. "Saddle my horse."

"It will take four days to ride to the Crystal City," Rhen says. "We should arrange a team—"

"It won't take *me* four days."

I can hear the panic in his voice, though. Even with magic, it will take time. Even if they used runners from every sentry station instead of one single courier, there's no way to send a message in less than two.

"They aren't demanding a ransom," Rhen says. "I know this is a shock, but you must—"

"I didn't ask for your counsel, Rhen."

"I'm giving it to you anyway. This message took days to arrive. An hour to formulate a plan won't—"

"I'm not giving them one extra *second*." Grey turns to me, and his eyes are like fire. He hits me in the chest with the parchment, and I'm so startled that I fall back a step.

"Jax doesn't know anything," he says flatly, mimicking what I said to him hours ago. "Jax isn't working with the Truthbringers."

I frown, grabbing the parchment. "He's—he's—"

"Read it." A guard leads his horse out of a stall, and Grey takes the reins, turning away without hesitation.

I stare down at the damp parchment, the words scrawled hastily.

> We have the queen and your daughter.
> They will be treated well if you return to Briarlock to face judgment.
> Our loyalty is to our queen.
> Syhl Shallow will rise.

Jax wouldn't be involved in this. He couldn't be. Could Callyn? But wouldn't that point the blame right back at Jax?

And . . . Alek? Despite everything, Alek has always seemed loyal to Lia Mara. As much as I hate him, I can't see him being involved in a plot to kidnap the queen. And he's been *here*. Not there.

I keep thinking of that moment during the card game, when he asked how someone could harm the king. Rhen said he's either very innocent or very clever.

Maybe there's more going on here than we realize. Maybe he's *both*.

"Send whatever team you like," Grey is saying to Rhen, and his voice is vicious. "Whoever took them will be dead by the time you get there."

Without another word, the king swings aboard his horse, tearing out of the stable with as much speed as Rhen used earlier.

I don't have time to think. Grey might hate me. He might see me as a disappointment. He might kill me for coming after him—or he'll just use magic to accelerate his pace to where I can't keep up.

But Jax didn't do this. I *know* he didn't. Maybe I've made mistakes, but on this point, I'm sure. Whatever's waiting for the king in Briarlock is bigger than Jax and Callyn.

I remember the Uprising, how so many people died in the attack. How Grey's magic tore through the Crystal Palace and killed anyone in its path. I remember walking the halls with the queen, looking for survivors.

I don't want to consider what will happen when he gets to Briarlock.

And just as I have the thought, I realize why we didn't find Iishellasan steel among Alek's things. I realize why he's been spending so much time in Briarlock.

Of course it's not here. It's *there*.

I yank the tie on Mercy's tether and look at Rhen. "It's a trap. I need to go after him."

I don't hear his answer. I don't even know if he'll figure it out. But I've already swung into the saddle, and Mercy flattens into a gallop before my feet find the stirrups.

CHAPTER 46

TYCHO

Grey sets a brutal pace. Wind and rain whip at my face, stinging my eyes, sending my cloak streaming out behind me until it makes no difference. Mercy feels the urgency, because she puts her head down and throws her head into the run. Grey doesn't have a long lead, but it's far enough that I'm not sure he knows I've followed. Just when I'm beginning to worry that Mercy won't be able to keep up, Grey's horse slows to a canter, and I'm able to draw alongside.

I don't know if he thinks I'm trying to *help* him or trying to *stop* him—and honestly, I'm not entirely sure myself. But I don't get a chance to say a word. He only keeps a tight grip on the rein long enough to say, "Don't fall behind," and then his horse digs its hooves into the mud and springs ahead.

And then . . . I feel his magic. Or maybe I simply sense the change in Mercy. Her breathing is no longer labored. Her stride feels effortless, despite the cold rain and the mud underfoot. The sky is pitch-black, the rain pouring down, but she feels like we could gallop for hours.

And we do.

I lose track of time. The rain eventually stops, but the wind from Mercy's speed keeps me shivering under my cloak. Whatever magic Grey is using to keep the horses from tiring doesn't extend to us—or at least to *me*. I alternate holding the reins in one hand so I can hold the other under the warm saddle blanket while she runs. My joints begin to ache, and by the time the sun creeps over the horizon, a dull knife of hunger has begun to twist in my gut. In a way, I'm glad for the soreness and irritation, because it pulls my thoughts away from everyone who might be in danger. Jax, accused of something I'm sure he hasn't done. Callyn and Nora, wrapped up in something bigger than they realize. The queen and little Sinna, at the mercy of . . . *who*? Who else is Alek working with?

I don't know. But I can't stop thinking of the tears on the queen's cheeks on the night I learned they'd lost the baby. Little Sinna's voice. *He said I have to be patient, but he would come back.*

Nakiis? I can't quite make that work out in my head. Alek hates magic. He wouldn't be working with a scraver. The queen and the princess would have been surrounded by a full contingent of palace guards, anyway. No one could simply walk into the palace and kidnap the queen. Few people could have gotten close.

My thoughts spin and spin . . . and go nowhere. Mercy gallops on. I knot the reins and hook my fingers in her mane in an effort to stop them from cramping.

If Grey feels the effects, he's ignoring it.

I try to do the same.

Once the sun rises, I begin to recognize landmarks. Without having to stop, we've covered almost two days' worth of travel in what I estimate to be twelve hours. If we continue at this pace, we'll tear into Briarlock in the middle of the night.

Exhausted. Starving. And alone.

I need to think about this like a soldier. I was never a tactician, but close proximity to the king allowed me access to a lot of senior officers, so I know how to plot an assault. We have no idea who we'll be facing—and it'll be *days* before anyone from Ironrose can reach the small village. We have no idea who else read that letter either. The courier channels aren't the most secure. Would word have reached the Crystal Palace? Will there be soldiers to meet us? Now that Emberfall and Syhl Shallow are at peace, the guard stations at the two mountain passes are only minimally staffed, mostly with longbowmen and messengers—few true combat warriors.

When the Truthbringers attacked the palace, there were hundreds of them, and all at once. They swarmed into the castle and nearly overtook the guards and soldiers. We weren't prepared.

We're not prepared now. Are there hundreds waiting to ambush the king in Briarlock? Hundreds of people with weapons made from Iishellasan steel? We need a plan.

I don't know who I'm fooling. We need an *army*.

Don't fall behind.

I'm trying. My mouth is bone-dry, and my bladder has been begging me to stop for what feels like hours. The sun has dried my cloak and warmed my skin, but now I'm sweating beneath my armor. I keep thinking of how Rhen said Grey would never yield, and he spoke of that like a failing.

Right now, it feels like a massive victory, because I'm not sure how much longer I'll be able to keep this pace before my body gives up.

We've reached the open fields far northwest of Ironrose Castle, and the mountains are clearly visible in the distance. The terrain here is uneven and rocky, terrible for galloping, but Grey's magic must be flattening the ground or supporting the horses, because Mercy's steady hoofbeats never vary. Dusk is hours away, and I want to beg for a break, but I know he'll leave me behind. I can sense it.

I have to keep up. I'll tie myself to the saddle if I have to.

Out of nowhere, Mercy's gait falters. She stumbles hard on one rock, then another. It's so unexpected after miles and miles of a fluid pace that I nearly drop over her shoulder. Ahead of me, the king's horse stumbles, too, throwing its head down, pulling the reins free. We're heading toward rockier turf. I expect Grey to swear or reach for his rein or try to maintain control—but he does nothing.

Then I realize he's *falling*.

I put a heel against Mercy's side, heedless of the rocks. Her hooves slip and stumble, but she responds, lurching alongside the king's horse. I grab hold of his armor, fighting to reach for his reins. Grey's body is limp. Lifeless.

The horses stagger again and I lose Mercy's reins. "Whoa!" I cry. I can't control them both. His horse feels Grey slipping and shies away.

I don't think. I use my grip on his armor to haul him over Mercy's withers—just as his horse puts a foot down wrong, stumbles hard, and falls, its momentum sending the animal tumbling onto the jagged rocks.

"Whoa," I say again. Mercy slows, but her sides are heaving, her neck slick with sweat. Grey is still motionless, half his body barely over Mercy's neck, but I can't reach the reins. She prances, agitated, stumbling on the terrain. Grey's horse thrashes at the rocks, one leg tangled in its tack as it tries to get to its feet. There's blood on the rocks. A horrific, panicked keening sound peals from its throat.

Too much has happened all at once. We're out in the open, close to the Syhl Shallow border. If people are waiting to kill the king, now is the time to do it.

Then I see the source of the blood. The horse's left hind leg is broken, blood and bone glistening through a torn patch of dark fur.

My chest goes tight, and I leap down from the saddle. "Grey," I gasp. I pull him down from Mercy's back. "Grey—you have to—you have to—"

He all but sags in my grip, sliding to the ground. His head nearly slams into a rock.

All the while, his horse is screaming. Fighting. Blood is all over the rocks now. The fractured leg flails awkwardly.

I reach out a hand automatically before remembering—*again*—that I don't have my healing rings.

"Grey," I say, and my voice is rough and ragged. "Grey, please." I tug at his armor, searching his pouches, hoping, *praying* that he may have my rings in his possession.

He doesn't.

I choke on my breath just as his horse manages to get to its feet.

That's *worse*. The animal is clearly in shock, half the tack broken from its struggling against the rocks. And that leg, the hoof hanging, barely attached by sinew and muscle. It takes a step and falls again, then redoubles its fighting. Mercy shies away.

"Steady," I say, and my voice breaks.

I can't do this. I can't.

I didn't want to become a soldier, but I did. I didn't want to be vicious, but I was. I didn't want to kill anyone, but I *did*.

And now, I don't want to kill a horse. An innocent horse. A *good* horse. A brave animal that ran far harder and longer than any good steed should.

But I can't let it bleed to death. I can't let it suffer. I can see the panic and terror in its eyes.

"Grey," I say. I look at his pale skin, damp with sweat, red where his armor rubbed his neck and elbows raw. His breathing is slow and uneven. He doesn't move. I beg anyway. "Please. *Please*."

It seems selfish to beg for a horse. The queen is in danger. The princess. Their lives are at risk.

But this animal knows none of that. This animal only knows pain and suffering and wants it to *end*.

So I draw my sword and end it.

The silence is sudden and profound. I stand for the longest time, watching the blood soak into the earth. Eventually, Mercy noses at my hand, and I draw a shuddering breath.

"Mercy," I whisper. The sun beats down. We're miles away from anything, and the king is unconscious at my feet.

And, I now notice, Mercy has a bowed tendon on her left front leg. She wasn't just stumbling. She was *limping*.

Silver hell.

At least she can walk. I don't have to . . . to do what I did. I don't know if I'd have the strength to do that to Mercy.

But she can't bear the weight of a rider. Not even an unconscious one.

I scrub my hands over my face, then assess my surroundings. I don't know *exactly* where we are, because I don't ride across these rocks when I head for Syhl Shallow. But I know the mountains, and by my estimation, we're a few hours south of the closest mountain pass. We can't stay here. The dead horse will draw predators. We're too exposed.

I take two minutes to attend to human needs and try to think of a plan.

I don't come up with a good one.

Finally, I drop to a knee and take hold of the king's arm, pulling his weight over my shoulders. He's taller than I am, but this is a common soldier drill. I can carry him for a while. The woods are only a few miles off. We'll find shelter, I'll wrap Mercy's leg, and Grey can wake up. And then . . .

I have no idea. I take hold of Mercy's reins, sigh, and start walking.

By the time we reach the tree line, darkness has begun to creep toward the mountains. I have flint, so I'll be able to start a fire, but we're still nowhere near a stream, and I need to rest. I can't leave the king, but at some point I'm going to have to. I can't carry him all the way to Syhl Shallow—especially not if I'm starving and thirsty and exhausted.

I strip Mercy of her gear and start a fire. Grey hasn't made a sound, not even when I pulled his weapons and armor free. He lies in the dirt beside the growing flames, and I have no idea what to do.

I think of Jax, his kind, wary eyes, the rough edge of his voice. He can't be a part of this. He can't. There's a part of me that feels like I'm trying to convince *myself.* Maybe Grey's right, and I am a fool.

Maybe I should have followed orders.

The fire is warm, but I shiver anyway. I need to find water.

Every muscle in my body begs me to wait, to rest, to sit here for just one more minute. Against my will, my eyes flicker closed.

When I open them again, the sky is a true black overhead, only a few stars twinkling between the tree branches. The fire has dwindled.

And there, leaning over me, his clawed fingers making five points of pain against my throat, is the scraver Nakiis.

CHAPTER 47

CALLYN

The soldiers don't allow me or Nora into the barn. I worry about the hens, about Muddy May, but the soldiers bring me buckets of eggs and milk every morning, so at least the animals seem to be tended. I worry about Jax, about Alek, about all the choices I've made over the last few months and whether they've been the *right* ones.

The day after Jax was to leave, I heard clanging up at the forge, and I don't know what it means—and I'm too nervous to go check. There are too many soldiers here. Too many guards. It's . . . weird. Nora peers out the windows every night.

"What do they want?" she'll whisper. "Did Lord Alek send them?"

"I don't think so," I say, remembering the way Lady Karyl told me to burn his message.

I didn't. It's under my mattress near all of Mother's old gear. I've read it a dozen times, but I don't understand why she'd tell me to burn it without reading it. *Our plans have changed. Burn it.* Is Lady Karyl tricking me? Or was Alek tricking me?

On the seventh night, Nora is lightly snoring beside me when I hear a sound down in the bakery. I freeze in place, thinking of Alek. The worst part is that I can't decide if I'd be relieved by his presence right now, or alarmed.

I slip out of bed in my sleeping shift and move to the top of the stairs.

Down below, a shadow slides along the far wall, and my heart clenches. But then I hear a tiny voice whisper, "More sweetcakes!"

I frown, hesitating, then ease down a few steps as silently as I dare.

There in the middle of the bakery, carefully licking frosting off her fingers, is a little girl no more than three or four years old. Her clothes are filthy and ragged, her curly hair a wild mane of tangles that reach her waist.

No Alek. No soldiers. No Lady Karyl.

Oh good. Now I have more questions.

I ease down a few more steps, and she spots me. Her eyes grow wide and she gasps, her expression trapped in that moment between fear and curiosity. I know it well from Nora.

I may not know how to stop an assassination, but I know how to be a big sister. I don't want her to be afraid of me, so I smile. "Where did *you* come from?" I whisper, peeking around like we're co-conspirators.

"I'm sneaking," she says.

"I see that." I hesitate. "Can I have a sweetcake, too?"

She studies me for a moment, then must decide I'm acceptable, because she smiles back and nods.

I come down into the bakery and take one off the platter. The fire in the hearth has gone to embers, but up close, I can see that the girl's hair is as red as Alek's. "I'm Callyn," I say. "What's your name?"

"I'm pleased to make your acquaintance, Lady Callyn," she says prettily, then curtsies as perfectly as a noble from one of the Royal Houses, completely at odds with the stained and wrinkled skirts she's wearing—or the fact that we're standing in the middle of my little bakery, and I'm no lady. I smile, bemused, until she adds in her tiny voice, "My name is Sinna Cataleha, but that takes too long, so everyone calls me Sinna."

My heart stops before she gets to the end of that sentence. I'm frozen in place. That bite of sweetcake turns to stone in my mouth.

I have to force myself to speak. "Sinna?" I say, and my voice is strangled. "Sinna, like the princess?"

She nods emphatically and takes another sweetcake. "Mama says we're playing a game with Da, but I don't like it very much."

I don't know what to do. Why would the princess be inside my bakery in the middle of the night? Where did she come from? We're *four hours* from the Crystal Palace!

While I'm standing there deliberating, I hear a shout from outside— followed by a woman yelling. The voice is raw and strangled—and *loud*. "Where is she? What did you do to her?"

Soldiers are shouting now, too. They're going to wake Nora.

Sinna's face turns white, and she drops the sweetcake. Her voice is a whispered rush. "Mama is cross."

Mama. The queen.

I'm sure *my* face is white.

I don't know what's happening, but I do know I don't want to be a part of it.

The woman outside is still shouting, her tone turning panicked. "I have done as you asked! You will *give me back my daughter!*" she screams in rage. "You will *let me go!*"

Sinna's lower lip begins to tremble.

I scoop her into my arms. "Let's go make sure your Mama is all right."

I expect her to struggle, but she wraps her arms around my neck, tangling her sticky fingers in my hair. I burst through the door and a dozen crossbows are suddenly pointed in my direction.

A dozen more are pointed at the woman standing in the barn doorway. Her skirts are as rumpled and filthy as Sinna's, but there's no mistaking the power in her stance, the assuredness of her expression, as if being queen was a quality that could fill the very air around her.

"Don't shoot!" I cry. "The princess snuck into the bakery."

"Oh, Sinna," the queen says, her voice half relieved, half a sob.

One of the guards approaches me. "I'll take her."

Sinna cringes away from him, clutching my neck and squealing.

"Don't you *touch* her," the queen says, and there's a vicious note in her voice that makes me shiver—and makes the guard hesitate.

I glance from the guard to the queen. "She's not hurt," I call to her. "She just ate some sweetcakes. I didn't—I didn't know who she was."

The queen stares back at me, and it feels like she's studying every fiber of my being, judging me by measure.

I remember standing with Jax in the bakery, when we discussed the first note. How the palace and the royal family felt so far off.

It's just one note, I remember thinking.

As I stare across the yard at the queen, as I feel her daughter's shaking breath in my ear, I realize it's about more than one note.

I don't know what Alek did, or where the king is, or what Jax was able to do.

But I know what I've done. And I don't know if I can undo it.

"I can bring her to you," I call.

The guard looks to someone else: a superior officer. The woman nods.

I don't waste time. As I stride across the distance between us, I feel as though a thousand eyes are on me.

"Mama is mad," Sinna whispers in my ear.

"She's not mad at you," I whisper back.

When I reach the queen, I discover details I couldn't see from the bakery door. Her cheek and jaw are shadowed with dark bruises, and a split on her lip has scabbed over. Long red hair is roped into a braid, but tendrils have escaped to frame her face. Blood speckles her clothes, including one long streak on her sleeve. Her eyes are like steel.

"Mama," Sinna says lightly, without letting go of my neck, "this is Lady Callyn. She gave me sweetcakes."

There are so many guards surrounding us. I'm afraid to let go of the little girl—and also afraid to keep standing here. But the queen's eyes are on mine, and she's in worse shape than I am. If she can stand here stoically, so can I.

"Are you unwell?" I say quickly. "Are you—"

"I am being held against my will."

"I didn't know you were here," I say. "I didn't—I didn't know—"

"You must know something," the queen says, her voice dangerously quiet, "or they would not have brought us here."

Heat rushes to my cheeks. "I had no idea," I whisper, and my voice breaks. "I only held messages for Lord Alek and Lady Karyl. He never— *they* never—I thought—"

I don't know how to finish that sentence. I'm not sure how to tell the injured woman in front of me that I thought they might be plotting against her husband, the king.

I don't know how to tell her that I might have been helping them.

"I didn't know what I thought," I finish.

She says nothing to that. "Sinna," she says softly, then raises her arms.

The little girl goes to her mother, clinging to her neck the way she did to mine.

"The woman you know as 'Lady Karyl' is a traitor," the queen says firmly. Loudly. "Lord Alek may be as well."

One of the guards snorts. "The king is the traitor. Get back in the barn."

She glares at him. "*You* are the traitors."

He lifts his crossbow. "I don't have to kill you to make you regret that—"

"No." My heart is pounding, but I step in front of him. "I don't know what's going on here, but please. Just stop." I don't know what kind of person would point a crossbow at a mother holding her child, much less the queen.

"You don't need to risk yourself," the queen says. "They won't dare to put an arrow through me. The king's magic will find and destroy anyone who tries." She pauses. "They know what happened the first time they attacked the castle. They are clearly eager to meet the same fate."

My mouth goes dry. I don't know what's right anymore. I don't know what's wrong.

"Mama," says Sinna. "I don't like this game anymore. When will it be over?"

The guard hasn't lowered his crossbow. "Go back in the barn," he bites out.

What the queen said clearly unnerved him.

"I will go," she says to him. "But you will not touch my child."

I turn before she can leave. My eyes search her bruised face. "Are you hurt?" I say. "Do you need supplies?"

She studies me for a long moment, then says loudly, "You will come with me. I will give you a list of what we need."

She doesn't even look at the guard for approval; she simply turns and steps into the barn as if it's as regal a building as the Crystal Palace.

If I look at him, I'm going to falter, so I scurry after her, hoping I'm not going to get an arrow in my back for my trouble—and hoping Nora won't wake up and come looking for me.

The queen walks to the far corner of the barn, where I store hay and straw for the animals. A lantern is hung from one of the posts, and a few random quilts are laid out over the ground and the hay bales.

I can't help but stare. "Is this where you've been sleeping?"

"It's not the worst place I've ever slept." She lays her child on one of the quilts, then tucks the blanket up and around her. "You're wasting time. They won't allow you to stay here with me for long. Who are you? Why are they holding me here?"

"Your Majesty, I'm—I'm no one. I'm just a baker."

"There must be a reason they chose this place. Lady Karyl is a governess from the Crystal City. Her real name is Lady Clarinas Rial—or maybe Lady Karyl is her real name, and she presented us with a false one." The queen sighs. "She has no relation to Alek. She should have no business here. You said Lady Clarinas—I mean, Lady Karyl has been sending messages through you?"

"Yes—but they're always sealed. I don't know what they say." I hesitate. "Did they hurt you?" I cast a glance at her midsection. Her clothes are too rumpled and stained for me to tell anything, but I remember all the gossip about the queen's pregnancy. "Is the baby . . ." I let my voice trail off.

"There is no baby anymore," she says, and even though her voice doesn't waver, the words are hollow.

I gasp. "They—they beat you so badly—"

"I will not speak of this with my captors, Callyn. And certainly not in front of my daughter."

I freeze. Sinna is watching us both with wide eyes. "I'm not your captor," I whisper. "I swear. I didn't know they were doing . . . this. We thought—" I break off, glancing at the tiny princess again.

"You thought what?" says the queen.

"We thought the target was the king. His magic."

"The king is my husband. The father of my child. An attack on him is an attack on me. If you think otherwise, you are fooling yourself."

"I know. I know that now."

"Did they force you to carry these messages?"

I swallow. "No."

"They paid you?" Her eyebrows go up.

"Yes," I admit softly.

"And you knew they were associated with the Truthbringers?"

"Yes, Your Majesty." Now it's my voice that sounds hollow.

She studies me for a long moment, thinking. "A *baker*. You're the baker Tycho met, aren't you? Does that mean we're in Briarlock?"

"Lord Tycho mentioned me?"

Something in her gaze sharpens—or maybe it shatters. Her eyes gleam in the dim lantern light. "Is Tycho a part of this, Callyn?" she whispers.

"I don't know. I don't think so." I pause. "It's Jax who's seen him more than I have. He's the blacksmith."

She doesn't look reassured. "Jacob said that the blacksmith was found with marks of the Truthbringers, too."

I bite at my lip. "We wanted to break the seal. We wanted to see what kind of messages we were carrying."

"And what did you discover? What are they planning?"

"I don't know! Truly. We were only able to open one letter, and it looked like a plot to kill the king—"

Sinna gasps and sits up. "Da!"

"Hush," says the queen, and her voice is soothing, no hint of tension. "This is all part of our game, remember? We need to solve the puzzle."

Sinna lies back down, but she doesn't look convinced.

"The message from Alek said *Father will be on the fields to observe*," I say to the queen. "*Use your best arrows, and do not miss your target.*"

She goes very still. "*Father* has been a reference to the king."

"But Lady Karyl didn't take the message," I say. "She told me to burn it. So I don't know if the plot was real—or if she was trying to mislead someone else." *Like Alek*, I think. I pause, trying to work that out in my head, but it's too complicated. "That's the day she arrived with the guards." I think of the covered wagon, which was clearly hiding the queen and her daughter. "The day you arrived here."

"They're holding us here for a reason." She presses a hand to her abdomen like it pains her. "It doesn't matter. Grey is days away in Emberfall. They must know that. *Everyone* knows that."

She's right. Even I know it. And if Jax is able to get to Emberfall to share the message with Tycho, it'll take days—maybe weeks!—before he'll be able to return to Briarlock. And even then, there'd be no reason for the king and his entourage to stop here. They'd head straight for the Crystal Palace.

I think of the clanging I've heard at the forge. I don't know if Jax went at all.

The queen is stroking her fingers over Sinna's hair now, and the little girl's eyes drift closed. I watch the motion for a moment, then remember something Alek said about the king's magic only being extended to a select few.

"Do you not have rings like Tycho's?" I say in surprise.

She looks at me ruefully. "I did. But they were smart. They attacked Sinna first. I was forced to remove them."

"Won't people in the palace know you're missing?" I say quietly.

She sniffs, then swipes at her face. "Most everyone of importance went to Emberfall with Grey. Lady Clarinas thought a series of spring visits to my Royal Houses would be an enjoyable way to pass the time. That it would give Sinna a bit of fresh air since the baby—" Her voice breaks, and she drops to sit on the hay bale. "I was so foolish."

The guard opens the door. "That's enough time," he barks.

I shift to leave—but hesitate. "I'm going to figure out a way to help you," I say. "You weren't foolish. I was."

She looks up at me. "I always wish for the best for my people, Callyn. I always *expect* the best. I know it is seen as a weakness. I have heard the gossip. The rumors that I am not as strong as my mother. That my husband has somehow tricked me or is using his magic against me." Her voice turns to steel, and she glances at the guard in the doorway. "But expecting more from my people is not a weakness. It is hope. It is patience. It is grace. But those virtues don't mean the absence of viciousness. The true weakness is to think a queen is powerless."

"Just wait," calls the guard. "We'll see who's powerless."

"Yes. You will see. Because when you fail—and you *will* fail—you will learn that I am stronger than my mother. You will learn that the king's magic reaches farther than you even imagine." Her eyes flash with danger. "And you will learn that instead of standing here pointing a weapon at my child, you and the rest of the traitors should have been finding a place to hide."

CHAPTER 48

TYCHO

The scraver's eyes catch a gleam of light from the dwindling fire. It feels like he's got one knee on my chest, the other pinning my right arm. His claws are like five daggers against the skin of my throat. I have no magic, so he could kill me with a twist of his wrist. My throat is parched, my lips chapped from hours of riding in the wind.

I wonder if he's been waiting for an opportunity to kill the king.

I wonder if the king is already dead.

"Nakiis," I breathe, and my voice is rough and worn. My throat stings. His claws have broken the skin.

"I trust you've been well?" he says mockingly.

"I've been better." I slide my left hand through the dirt carefully, seeking my dagger.

Nakiis hisses, his claws tightening. More blood flows, and I freeze.

"I can see in the dark, you foolish magesmith," he says.

"I'm not a magesmith." I grit my teeth and try to strain away from him, but his grip is strong. My mouth feels like I swallowed fire. "Perhaps—perhaps you could let me go if you want to talk."

"I should kill you both right now," he growls. His claws tighten, and I close my eyes. I try to swallow but his grip is too tight. I can't fight. I can't breathe. In a moment, that'll be permanent.

We're in the middle of nowhere. Whoever Rhen sends might never find our bodies. All my loyalty and duty and honor would be nothing. The only memory anyone would have would be my failure to protect the king when his family was in danger.

But the pressure on my neck eases. Wings flutter, and the weight disappears from my chest. I cough, choking on air, rubbing at my blood-slick neck. It takes me half a minute to sit up. Nakiis is a short distance away, his eyes glittering at me from twenty feet up in a tree.

I ignore him and crawl quickly to Grey. He's still breathing, but it's shallow, and a bit ragged like my own. He doesn't appear to have moved from where I laid him when we stopped here. His lips are as chapped as mine feel. The sweat has dried in his hair, and he seems more pale, though it's hard to tell in the dark.

"I filled your water skins," the scraver says.

The words hit me slowly, as if my brain can't process what he's saying—and then all at once. My eyes search the ground and locate the water skins near the dwindling fire, and I all but dive onto them, tugging the laces free as quickly as I can. I pour the liquid straight into my mouth without pausing to wonder about whether it's safe. I want to ask why or how he did this, but I don't even care. The water is cold and sharp and nothing has ever tasted better.

Once I've drunk so much that I'm worried I'm going to spit it all right back up, I pour some into my hand and touch it to Grey's lips, as if a taste of water might bring him around.

It doesn't. The water trails over his lips to disappear into the shadows.

I'd give anything for my magic-bearing rings. For Noah, who'd surely know what to do. I try to remember everything he's ever taught me, but my lessons in the infirmary were always few and far between. I press my fingers to the king's neck, finding his pulse, which beats steady against my fingers.

Still, he doesn't wake.

Mercy must smell the water, because she nickers low in her throat, pawing at the ground where she's tethered. I don't have a bucket, but I cup my hands and offer it to her sip by sip.

Throughout all of this, Nakiis stays high overhead, clinging to the branch where he's taken roost. While Mercy slurps water from my hands, I look up at him. The scraver's skin is so dark that he's almost invisible amid the leaves.

"Thank you," I say. It feels odd to thank him when he was seconds away from tearing out my throat, but I don't know what else to say. I don't want to provoke him when I don't know why he's here.

He peers down at me, and an icy wind whips through the trees. "The creek isn't far. A mile on foot perhaps."

"I thought it was farther." I try to realign my sense of where we are, then look back up at him. It's interesting that he just had his claws around my neck, but now he's way up in a tree. I try to puzzle that out, and I can't quite comprehend what I come up with: he's wary. Maybe even afraid.

I should kill you both right now.

But he didn't.

While I'm thinking this through, Nakiis disappears from the branch with a flutter of wings and a rush of cold air.

I frown, then sigh. I don't understand—and it probably doesn't matter. I rekindle the fire, building it until the flames reach for the sky, then try pouring another handful of water over Grey's lips.

Nothing.

I offer more water to Mercy, then crouch to look at her leg. The tendon is hot and swollen, the hoof partially lifted off the ground. She noses at my neck gently, blowing warm breaths into my hair as if to say *fix it, please.*

"I'm sorry, sweet girl," I murmur to her, and she presses her face to my chest.

Everything is terrible.

I return to sit beside Grey, dropping next to the fire. I pull a whetstone from my pack, then draw my dagger. It doesn't need sharpening, but I need something to do or I'm going to bash my head into a rock. I'll have to hunt soon, but I don't want to leave him, especially with Nakiis lurking somewhere in the darkness.

"Anytime you'd like to wake up," I say, "I wouldn't mind the company."

Nothing.

"I can't carry you to Syhl Shallow," I say, passing the blade over the stone. "Though I must say I'm grateful for all the drills that allowed me to get you this far."

Nothing. It doesn't matter. I'm used to talking to Mercy. I can outline our next movements to an unconscious king.

The blade scrapes over the stone in rhythmic fashion. "I suppose I can carry you to the nearest major road. Rhen will send a team through as quickly as possible. I estimate it will take them at least three days to get this far—and we've already used up one. I don't have a map, but I believe we're about twenty miles west of the King's Highway. If I start walking at daybreak, I should be able to beat them there."

Twenty miles, carrying a man on my shoulders. A daunting task on my best day. I'm so exhausted right now that it feels impossible.

A screech splits the night, and then a dead wild goose lands in the dirt right in front of me. I jump and nearly put the blade right through my hand.

I look up as Nakiis settles back onto the branch. He stares down at me wordlessly, and for a moment, I don't move.

"Again," I say finally, "thank you."

He says nothing. I suppose I'm the only one making conversation, then. I start plucking feathers, then quickly and efficiently slice the meat from the bone before laying it on rocks in the fire to cook.

He brought me water and food—but he also lured Sinna away from the palace. I'm not sure how to proceed.

I slice the heart free and hold it out to him. Those gleaming eyes look back at me, but he doesn't leave the branch.

"Iisak always asked for the heart," I say. "It's yours if you want it."

He still doesn't move.

I think of what he's said before, how he doesn't want to be *bound*. I've never lived my life as someone who keeps track of implied debts for things that should be considered a simple kindness. But maybe Nakiis does. Maybe he's had to.

"Offered without expectation," I say. "As thanks for your generosity." After the longest moment, I add, "Otherwise, I'm going to throw it into the fire."

His wings beat at the air as he leaps off the branch. He barely lands before swiping the flesh from my palm, then darts to the opposite side of the fire.

It's so hard not to think of his father, of the similarities and differences between them. There's a part of me that pulses with longing, with *loss*, because it's been so long, and so much about this moment reminds me of *before*.

But Iisak wouldn't have kidnapped a child. Iisak wouldn't have had his claws wrapped around my throat.

I swipe my bloody hands in the dirt to dry them, then brush them off on my trousers. "What are you doing here?" I say.

I don't expect him to answer, but he does. "You were pouring magic into the air for *hours*," he says. "I could feel it from miles away."

"I wasn't." I cast a glance at the king. "He was."

"You allowed him to burn through his power, then."

"He burned through his magic?" I stare across the flickering fire. "Is that why he can't wake up?"

Nakiis tears a bit of flesh from the heart with his fangs, and I'm both glad that it's dark and glad that I *do* remember his father, because I don't flinch from the sight. The look he gives me is shrewd. "I tasted your blood in Gaulter," he says. "You cannot hide your magic from me, boy."

I hold up my naked hand. "That was his magic, too. I had rings of Iishellasan steel. They're gone."

His eyes widen, but he tears another piece of the heart and studies me. I turn the meat on the rocks. I'm so hungry that I'm tempted to eat the poultry as raw as he does.

"You wore magic-bound steel against your skin?" he says.

The way he says that is interesting, and I frown. "Yes."

"For how long?"

"For . . . years."

He mutters something that sounds like a swear, then flicks disdainful eyes at Grey. An ice-cold wind swirls through the clearing to make me shiver. "As I said," he growls. "Foolish magesmith."

"Why? Why does it matter how long I wore them?"

He studies me again. "Why should I help you?"

"I don't know. Why are you?"

He says nothing.

"You could have killed us both and had *two* hearts," I add.

He curls his lip, baring his fangs. He licks a drop of blood off a claw. "As if I have any taste for a magesmith's heart."

I think of little Sinna being at his mercy, and I have to suppress a shudder. But she wasn't afraid. She seemed eager to see him again. I can't seem to make that match up in my head either. Then again, I was barely more than a boy and I was never afraid of Iisak, no matter what terrible things I saw him do.

One of the tiniest pieces of meat is beginning to brown on the rocks, so I pull it free, shoving it into my mouth, heedless of the pain when it burns my tongue. I'm too hungry to care. I wash it down with another pull from the water skin, then grab another that's still a bit raw.

Nakiis watches this, his eyes glittering in the firelight. Eventually, he finishes the heart, but he doesn't return to his spot in the tree. He doesn't attack me either.

By the time I move to shove a third piece of meat in my mouth, I have the patience to let it cool first. He stares at me across the flames, and I can't read anything from his expression.

I hold his gaze. "Why did you kidnap the princess?"

"Kidnap!" he growls. His wings flare, and the bare edge of his fangs flash in the light. "The king surrounds his child with humans who mean her harm, and you accuse *me* of kidnapping?"

"You lured her away from the palace."

"I lured her away from potential captors."

I turn that thought around in my head. "Who?"

"I keep my distance from the palace. I do not know the names of everyone at court."

"How did you know she was in danger, then?"

"I can hear much, from the air. So many whispers. So many secrets."

That's right. I forgot about that. The scravers have magic of their own, but it comes from the wind and sky. Iisak used to be able to hear at a good distance—and he could keep himself from being heard as well.

Nakiis adds, "There are many who conspire against your king."

"In the palace?"

He nods, and a chill wraps itself around my spine. One of the only reasons Grey felt safe leaving Lia Mara and Sinna was because they'd be surrounded by guards.

"*Many* in the palace conspire against him," he says. "Are you among them?"

"No!"

His fangs glisten in the light again. "Because you have magic in your blood, yet you spare *none* to save him."

"*I am not a magesmith!*" I snap.

He tackles me into the dirt with enough force to drive me back a few feet. Rocks and underbrush dig into my neck. I grunt and swear and try to get my hand on a weapon, but he's quick. Those talons sink right into my forearms, only an instant before his fangs find the space between my throat and my armor. The pain is so quick and sudden that I can't think of anything else—except for the fact that Iisak once did exactly this to Grey, to prove to him that he could use magic.

Only Grey truly *is* a magesmith.

I am not.

I can't catch my breath. I might be whimpering. I might be *crying.* I'm straining against him, but my arms are on fire. My throat is on fire. My vision begins to darken.

His teeth let go of my skin, and I realize the last sight before I die is going to be my blood on his jaw.

"It's in your blood," he growls at me.

"If I were a magesmith, you'd be dead by now," I growl back.

His fingers tighten on my arms. I swear I feel his talons touch bone. "Prove it," he says.

"I can't—I don't—" There's too much pain. I can't *think.* "I don't have my—"

"Stop talking and use your magic!"

"I don't have magic!"

He leans down close, until his black eyes fill my vision, and his forehead nearly brushes mine. "If you are unwilling to try," he says softly, "then you deserve to die."

I taste blood on my tongue, and it reminds me of the night Alek stabbed me in the side. I think of Jax leaning over me in the flickering shadows of his workshop, his hair unbound and panic in his eyes.

I think of his hands on a bow, the day I taught him to shoot.

What are you afraid of?

I think of my rings, taken. Gone. But I remember the feel of them. I remember reaching for the magic.

Like a pair of boots that don't fit quite right, I remember saying. Because it's not my magic. It's Grey's. It was in the rings.

It's in your blood.

Is it? I imagine the rings on my hands, the magic at my fingertips. I try to remember what it felt like. Where it came from.

But my thoughts begin to drift and loosen, and I realize I've lost a lot of blood. Something soft brushes against my cheek, then my jaw, and then my hair. A warm burst of air fills my ear, and then a low nicker.

Mercy.

And then, I feel a spark. A tug. The tiniest flare of magic in my veins.

And then another. And *another*. The magic, slow at first, causing more pain as it tries to find the injuries. Then stronger, more sure. I can flex my fingers.

A moment later, I can sit up.

I stare down at my forearms. Blood is everywhere, but they're unmarred. Whole. I slap a hand to my neck and feel no pain.

Silver hell.

Mercy is nosing at me again, her tether broken and dragging in the dirt. I lift a hand to stroke her muzzle, then stare across the fire at Nakiis, who's keeping his distance again.

"Your horse was very worried," he says.

"Yeah," I say. I hold up my hand again, as if I have to convince myself that it really happened. "Me too."

CHAPTER 49

TYCHO

Despite the evidence right in front of me, I can't quite believe what just happened. My dagger is in the dirt, and I want to slice open my palm to see if I can heal it again.

Then Mercy noses at my hair again, and I realize I don't need to.

I kneel beside her injured leg, then run a palm down the swollen tendon. At first, nothing happens, but I remember Grey's early lessons with Iisak—and later, Grey's lessons with *me*, how magic can't be rushed, can't be forced. Slowly, I feel the magic in my fingertips, the sparks that felt so familiar when I had my rings, yet somehow feels foreign and new now. Mercy flinches when the magic begins to work, but I murmur to her and she settles.

In less than a minute, the swelling is gone. When I let go of her leg, she bears weight fully, then noses at my shoulder as if to thank me.

I let out a long breath, then look back across the fire. Nakiis hasn't moved.

"How?" I say to him. "I'm not a magesmith. Truly."

His eyes flick disdainfully to the king. "Did he give you the rings?"

"Yes."

"Then he knew. He knew what it would do to you."

I frown. "I don't think so." I pause. "The king wasn't raised as a magesmith. There's no magic here. There are a few books in the palace, but magesmiths were driven out of Syhl Shallow long ago. The scravers are on the other side of the Frozen River."

"I know where the scravers are."

I suppose he does. "Well, he's been on his own since your father died. It took a long time to bind magic into the rings as it was."

A cold wind blows through the clearing, making the fire flicker and sparks fly. "So your king kept my father as a *resource*."

"No," I say evenly. "I've told you before. Iisak was a *friend*." He stares back at me impassively, and I add, "If the king needed a scraver on a chain, I could have left you in that cage in Gaulter, ridden back to the Crystal Palace, and told him where you were. Then he could have come to fetch you himself."

The scraver still says nothing, so I make a disgusted sound and return Mercy to the tree where I kept her tethered. I'm thinking like a soldier again, making plans. If we have a sound horse, at least one of us can ride ahead to meet whoever Rhen sent.

If I can get the king to wake up.

I kneel by his side. His breathing is still shallow. I don't even know where the injury is. His head? His heart? I put a hand to his forehead and try to summon the magic again.

"If you send magic through your body," Nakiis says, "a small bit will always linger. But if you bind it with Iishellasan steel, the magic will be more potent." He pauses. "This is elementary magic. When the mage-smiths lived in Iishellasa, their children used magic-charged steel to practice before coming into their power fully. But rarely a human." His eyes shine in the darkness. "For obvious reasons."

I wonder what this means to the others who have rings. Jake and Noah. Lia Mara. Harper.

I put the thought aside. None of it matters now. The queen and the princess are at risk. If they are being held prisoner in Briarlock, then Jax, too, is likely at risk. A time will come when I need to make decisions on how to proceed.

I would have followed orders, Tycho.

As usual, there's no one with me to give them.

And despite the magic at my fingertips, Grey has not woken. I press my palm to his chest instead. "Come on," I whisper. "Wake up."

"You cannot heal him," Nakiis says. "He is not truly injured. As I said, he burned out his spark."

Wind whips across my cheeks again, and I shiver.

"There's so much magic in the air," the scraver says. He stretches like a cat, his wings flaring. "Can you not feel it?"

"How do I get it back to him?" I demand. "Why hasn't this happened before?"

"Magic calls to magic," he says easily. "It may eventually find its way back to his blood."

I want to punch the ground. "How long?"

"Days? Weeks? It's possible he may not survive it. I have never seen a magesmith so effectively ground himself. What possessed him?"

His wife. His daughter. *Days. Weeks.* Lia Mara and Sinna don't have that kind of time. The note demanded the king's presence, not mine. Even if I have magic, I'm still one person—and I have no idea what kind of weapons the Truthbringers will have amassed. I have no idea what kind of force we'll encounter.

Again, I need a plan. I don't have one.

Or . . . maybe I do. I look at Nakiis again. "The magic is in the *air*," I say. "You could help him."

Without hesitation, he says, "I could."

"So do it!" I exclaim. "Tell me what to do! Do you need to touch him? Do you need—"

"I need some assurance."

"Anything," I say immediately. "Tell me what you want me to swear. He won't harm you. He won't imprison you. He won't—"

"You cannot make a vow for him," Nakiis says, and ice coats the rocks at his feet. "I want a vow from *you*."

My gaze narrows. "What kind of vow?"

"There will come a time that I will need a magesmith to fight at *my* side. To obey *my* will. When I call, you will answer."

"Who are you fighting—"

"That is my offer," he says. His eyes gleam in the darkness. "Accept or not."

It's too open-ended. There are too many unknowns.

Just like everything else right now.

"For one day," I say. "I'll fight at your side for one day."

"A year."

"Never."

He regards me coolly. I regard him right back.

"Six months," he says.

He has something at stake here. I'm not sure what it is, but he needs something, too, if he's willing to negotiate.

"Two days," I say. "And I'll fight in your defense when you ask, but I'm not a mercenary. I won't kill for you."

"A month. And I can help you get to Syhl Shallow much faster than horseback."

My eyebrows go up. "How?"

"Make the deal and see."

I chew on my lip for a moment. "A week."

"Done." Wind, cold and sudden, blasts through the tiny clearing, bringing rocks and dirt to sting my eyes and spook my horse. I can feel the magic now, burning at my skin, tugging at my armor, simultaneously so cold and so hot that I can't tell if my blood is freezing in my veins or boiling under my skin. I have to close my eyes from the force of it. My eyes are full of white light anyway, like a thousand suns all at once. The sound of the wind becomes so loud that I can't hear anything else, but somehow, underneath the force of it all, I hear Nakiis's voice, softer than before.

"I've brought the magic to you," he says. "Now give it to him."

For an instant, I don't know how. The magic is everywhere, a million stars filling me up and tearing me apart, wonderful and terrible all at once. It's addictive, this power. Unstoppable. A terrifying part of me wants to hang on to it, to keep this magic to myself. But my hand is still on Grey's chest, and that one tiny point of contact is a reminder of every moment we've endured together, from the very first instant I discovered his magic.

I swore my life to him once. I told Jax I would do it again, without hesitation.

I would do it now.

The wind builds, roaring so loudly that I think my ears will burst, until I lose all track of up or down. With a final wrenching pull, the magic blazes through my hands. I hear Grey gasp, a terrible breath that sounds like the end of a life—or the beginning of one. For one moment, I see his eyes. I hear his voice.

"Tycho."

And then I lose all sense of myself and know nothing more.

I awaken to the king crouching over me, his worried eyes staring down into mine. The sky above is still thick with stars, but a faint pink haze has appeared on the horizon. When I blink up at him, Grey lets out a breath and sits back, running a hand over his face.

I expect to feel sore and achy, but I don't. "What happened?" I say, and my voice is rough, like I've slept longer than I intended. I shove myself to sitting.

"I was hoping you would be able to tell me." He pauses. "You were out for a long time." Another pause, this one heavier. "I couldn't wake you."

I put a hand to my head. I feel disoriented and dazed. *He burned out his spark.* Did I do the same? "I don't know."

My eyes search the ground, the trees, the sky. Mercy is tethered not far off. But with a start, I realize there's no trace of the fire I set last night. These aren't the same trees.

I snap my gaze back to the mountains. We're on the Syhl Shallow side.

I can help you get to Syhl Shallow.

"Where is Nakiis?" I say.

Grey frowns. "The scraver?"

There's a note in his voice that I don't fully understand, as if he could wrap up worry and anger and fear and surprise all in one word.

"Yes." I hesitate. "He's not our enemy. He helped me. He helped *you.*" I look around again. "He got us into Syhl Shallow." I have more questions than I started with. I don't know how he did it. The king's magic has never allowed him to travel a far distance in the blink of an eye.

But then I realize what Grey said. *You were out for a long time.*

I blink at him. "I'm surprised you didn't take Mercy to go after Lia Mara and Sinna."

He stares back at me. His eyes are so dark and shadowed. "You thought I would leave you unconscious and alone in the middle of the woods?"

Yes, I think. But I don't have the courage to say it.

I don't think I need to. Grey runs a hand over his jaw again. As usual, I can't read much from his expression, but after a while, he rises to standing. In control, no doubt or hesitation.

"Can you walk?" he says.

I have to think about it for a second. "Yes."

"If we're inside the border, I don't want to waste time. You can explain what happened while we walk."

Good. We'll stick to the matter at hand. No need to venture into the conflict between *us*.

But I think I liked it better when he was unconscious.

"Yes, Your Majesty." I don't say it flippantly, but he gives me a look anyway. I ignore it and head for Mercy's side. I partly expect him to call after me, but instead, he begins buckling his armor into place.

There's a part of me that feels like the last few hours were a dream. Like maybe Nakiis wasn't here at all, and Grey just happened to wake before me.

But . . . we're in Syhl Shallow. I couldn't dream that.

I drop to a crouch and run a hand along the back of Mercy's foreleg anyway. No swelling, no injury.

I stand, then draw my dagger and press it against my fingertip until blood wells.

I hold my breath and search for the magic.

The wound closes. Effortless, as if I never lost my rings at all.

It wasn't a dream.

From behind me, the king says, "Maybe you should start with that."

I explain about Alek's comment during the card game, how I think the Truthbringers have been securing Iishellasan steel that may be used against him, and that's why I followed. I tell him how Nakiis proved to me that wearing the rings for so long would allow the magic to seep into my blood until I would no longer need the rings at all.

"Iisak used to tell me that any tools fashioned from that steel would be closely guarded," Grey says. "I thought he meant because of how much power it would grant the bearer. But maybe it was more."

"You're not upset."

He frowns. "No. Relieved, actually, to think Lia Mara might have some protection if they're holding her. I'm sure they would have taken her rings first."

"Lia Mara is no fool," I say. "How would they get close enough to take her?"

He's quiet for a long moment. "Sinna."

I swallow. "Nakiis said there were many traitors at the palace. That he was trying to lure Sinna away from danger."

"And you believed him?"

Grey doesn't sound skeptical. He sounds like he wants a genuine answer. So I nod. "If he truly held a grudge against you, he could have killed us both right then and there. He'd have no reason to lie."

"Does he know who's holding them in Briarlock? Does he know what weapons they have?"

My chest constricts. I should have asked—but I didn't. "I don't know." I pause. "We should wait for Rhen's forces."

"They have my wife and daughter. I'm not waiting." He looks at me. "If Nakiis is so innocent, why did he leave?"

"I don't know that either." I glance at him. "He's very wary of your power."

Our power.

The instant I have the thought, a jolt goes through me. From the instant I met Grey, the magic has always been his. Any bit of power that I could use came from *him*, was granted by him.

Now . . . it's not. I flex my fingers by my side, feeling stars in my blood, ready and waiting.

Magic of my *own.*

I expect him to come up with a plan, now that he knows what we might be facing, but the king says nothing more. There's a part of me that wants to leap aboard Mercy and finish racing toward danger—but a bigger part of me knows it would be the worst kind of reckless.

And if anyone goes racing off on my horse, it's going to be him. My heart beats hard with every step, waiting for him to make the demand, because this time I'd have no way to stop him—or help him.

But he doesn't. "Why did Nakiis help us, if he was so wary?" he says.

"I bartered for his help."

He's quiet for a moment. "Why?"

"*Why?*" I round on him so quickly that Mercy throws her head up and snorts. "You ask *why*? Because you were *unconscious*! And Mercy was lame! The queen and your daughter are in danger! Do I need more reasons? My only other option was to carry you twenty miles while leading an injured horse. Forgive me if you feel that would've been more prudent, but you went tearing out of Ironrose without a plan, so—"

"Enough."

I clamp my mouth shut. My fingers are tight on Mercy's reins, my shoulders tense as we walk.

"What did you barter?" he asks.

The words stop on my tongue. I can't say it. My vow to the scraver could ultimately mean nothing, or it could mean everything. I don't even know when or how Nakiis will claim his time. Or who his enemy will be.

It could be Grey.

The thought hits me with a start, and a tiny lance of fear pierces my heart.

I set my jaw. "I would rather not say, Your Majesty."

"Tycho, if you call me that again, I am going to punch you in the face."

"Good." I let go of Mercy's reins and shove him square in the chest. "Do it."

He falls back a step. "Don't do this."

I shouldn't. I *know* I shouldn't. It's not the time or the place, and we have bigger issues. But I'm exhausted and discouraged and my emotions won't settle.

I go to shove him again, and he deflects, catching my arm. I expect him to attack, but he doesn't. He grabs hold of the breastplate of my armor and holds me back.

"Stop," he says, his voice low.

"I know you *want* to hit me," I growl. "Just do it."

"I don't, actually." He lets me go. "But you clearly want to hit *me*. So go ahead."

I'm swinging a fist before he's done speaking. I truly don't think he expected me to do it, because he takes the hit fully. He stumbles back and ends up in the dirt.

He swears and spits blood at the ground, then looks at me, rubbing his jaw. "Silver hell. You really meant that."

"I did."

"Do you feel better?"

"No." I feel *worse*. I turn away and take hold of Mercy's reins. "I shouldn't have delayed us." I don't wait for him. I start walking.

He falls into step with me very quickly, but I don't look at him. We walk in silence again. The tension between us is unchanged.

Grey does not yield, Rhen said.

Obviously.

"What did you barter?" Grey says after a while, as if the last ten minutes never happened.

Fine. I can play this game. "I'd rather not say, Your Majesty."

"Tycho."

"I'm very good at keeping secrets. Perhaps you remember."

"I never forgot."

If he said it arrogantly, I'd punch him again. But I can't read his voice, and despite myself, I glance over. He doesn't look angry. Or defensive. He looks . . . remorseful.

I don't want remorse. I want . . . something else.

"I'm surprised that you followed me," he says. "If you're this angry at me."

"You needed to know what you were heading into," I say tightly. "And I didn't want you to kill Jax. I don't care what you think of me, but he's not behind this."

"So you didn't seek to help me. You sought to *stop* me."

There's no judgment in his tone, but I bristle anyway. "Can it not be *both*?" I demand.

He says nothing. It's a good thing, because I'm not done.

"I love them, too," I snap. "You rode heedless out of Ironrose. You have *no idea* who took Lia Mara. There could be hundreds of them. I may not be an officer anymore, but I still know you don't send one man off to battle without a plan. You may just see me as a messenger now, but I'm not a liability or a hindrance. I'm not a *child*. Stop speaking to me as if I am."

"I don't just see you as a messenger, Tycho."

I don't want to be having this conversation. And honestly, we're walking right into a trap. We'll probably both end up dead and none of this will matter. "There are already rumors of rebellion and violence against you after what happened in the Uprising," I say. "It's one thing to protect the royal family from a palace invasion. If you level a town, there will be no quelling the rumors. No matter what they've done to the queen."

"If they've hurt them . . ." He breaks off, and there's no disguising the promise of violence in his voice. "I once had a conversation with Iisak about what he was willing to risk to find Nakiis," Grey says. "I didn't fully understand then." He pauses. "I do now."

I stop on the trail and look at him. "Iisak died."

"He died trying to save his son."

"No. He didn't. He died because he crashed through a window to attack an enchantress. He died because he was blind with anger or fury or vengeance. He died because he didn't take a moment to figure out what was happening *in that room*, Grey." I glare at him. "Just like you did, when you got on your horse without waiting."

I've never spoken to him like this. He stares back at me in the shadowed darkness.

I make an aggravated sound, then turn to start walking again. But I stop short.

We've reached a crossroads. The road that leads to Briarlock. I let out a long breath.

I can almost *see* a dark light spark in Grey's eyes. I grab hold of his arm before he can leap aboard my horse and martyr himself or stab Jax or set all of Briarlock on fire—or all three.

"I know my way through the woods," I say. "Let's get off the road. We can approach from the rear, where we won't be spotted. They won't be expecting you this quickly—and likely not alone. We don't have much darkness left, but we'll have the high ground, and we can assess the size of their force, if they have one."

He glances at my hand on his arm, then back at my face. If he's surprised now, it doesn't show.

"Well advised," says the king. "We'll do as you say."

CHAPTER 50

JAX

The bruise Da left on my jaw hasn't faded. The ache in my gut promises to linger a bit longer, too. I think there's a chance he bruised a rib.

None of that matters, because the resentment in my heart doesn't fade at *all*.

"I've cleaned up your mess," he said to me on the second day.

I didn't answer him. I just gritted my teeth and kept working.

He smacked me on the back of the head. "You should be grateful. I've figured out what you were doing. Who you were helping. I turned it around for us, boy. You're lucky you didn't get us both thrown in the stone prison."

"So lucky," I muttered.

My weapons are gone. I'm not sure what he did with the dagger, but Da broke Tycho's bow into pieces and fed them to the forge while I watched. Then the arrows, one by one. He may as well have been feeding *me* to the fire.

He's threatened to. More than once. "You try anything, and you'll wish it was just your hand in the forge."

I have no weapons. No silver.

No options.

I've thought about escaping. Sometimes late at night I imagine it. Easing through the house, making my way through the woods in the darkness. But I'm not fast, and I'm not silent. If he caught me . . . I don't like to think about the repercussions.

Every time he and I are in the forge together, I think about clocking him in the face with one of my tools. I just haven't yet found the courage to do it.

What are you afraid of?

Right now, a whole lot.

So every day, I keep my head down and work. I don't know why I thought for even a second that I could escape my misfortune. If the Truthbringers really did intend to kill the king, I have no way to warn anyone. I have no proof. And if they succeed . . . well, I was a part of that. In a small way.

If they don't, it'll still be weeks before Tycho will pass through Briarlock again.

This morning, I'm in the workshop before sunrise while Da boils some eggs. I spare a moment to hope that he'll choke. The sky glows pink over the mountains, but it's still dark down here, so I light a lantern before I set a spark to the forge. A cool breeze winds around me, tugging a tendril of hair free, and I blow on my palms to warm them. But a sudden stillness seems to overtake the morning. A hesitation. A *waiting*. The hairs on the back of my neck stand up.

I grab my crutches and rise, peering out into the shadows, then turn to look back at the door to the house. I can hear Da banging around in there, so it's not him.

When I turn back around, there are two men striding through the shadows beyond the forge, and I jump. No one ever shows up at this hour—at least not for any good reason. My heart is pounding, and I glance back at the door, wondering if I should call for Da. I inhale sharply.

Before I can say a word, a hand slaps over my mouth. Familiar brown eyes fill my vision. "Jax," Tycho whispers. "Be at ease. It's just me."

Despite his words, my heart won't settle. He wouldn't appear at this hour if all was well. He wouldn't be whispering. I glance from him to the other man in the shadows. I can't make out his features in the dim light, but it doesn't look like Lord Jacob. He's taller than I am, with black armor buckled to his frame. His eyes catch a gleam of light from the lantern.

So do his weapons.

I think of the letter that Callyn and I intercepted, and I swallow. My fingers tighten on my crutches.

"Look at me," says Tycho, and his voice is just as quiet, potent with urgency. "*Jax*. Look at me."

I bring my gaze to his. A loud cough sounds from inside the house, and my father swears.

The man at Tycho's back draws a sword. "Tycho. He's not alone."

Tycho's eyes haven't left mine. "Who else is here?"

"Just my father. The magistrate released him." I glance between him and the other man. "Who—what—what are you doing here?"

"There are soldiers in the woods surrounding Callyn's bakery," Tycho says.

My eyes flick to the road, but I can't see anything but darkness and trees. "Soldiers? The Queen's Army? Or from Emberfall?"

"The Queen's Army." The other man steps forward. His eyes are so dark they're almost black, and there's absolutely no give to his expression. "At least three dozen. Maybe more. Is that where they're holding the queen?"

I frown. "I don't know anything about the queen." *I only know about a possible plot to kill the king.* I hesitate. I'm unsure how forthright to be.

Inside the house, the floor creaks. My father is moving around again. I can't decide if it would be a good thing or a bad thing for him to walk outside right this instant.

"Talk," says the man, and nothing about his voice is calming. "If you've done nothing wrong, you have nothing to fear."

He's more intimidating than Tycho and Alek combined. I can all but taste my heartbeat.

I must hesitate too long, because he steps closer. "Answer me. Where is the queen? Are you working with the Truthbringers?"

"I don't know anything about the queen." I stumble back with my crutches because he won't stop advancing.

"Do you know why I was summoned to Briarlock?"

"I don't even know who *you* are." I back into the work table, and a crutch rattles to the ground. He looks like he's a breath away from putting that sword right through my belly, but Tycho grabs his arm.

"Grey. *Grey.* He spoke true. I told you. He doesn't know."

I stare into the dark eyes of the man nearly pinning me against the table. "Clouds above," I breathe. "You're the king."

"I am," he says. "So talk. You know *something.*"

"I—I don't know anything about the queen," I say, and my mouth is dry. I don't know if I'm supposed to kneel or to bow or to start begging forgiveness for everything I've done wrong. "Callyn opened Lord Alek's last letter. It didn't say anything about the queen. It said something about the archery competition on the second day. That *Father* would be on the field. It wasn't a threat, but . . . almost."

The king's expression is so unyielding. "Nothing about the queen? Nothing about Sinna?"

And then I hear it in his voice. The fear undercutting everything else.

I shake my head quickly and look at Tycho. "I was going to try to get to Emberfall. To warn you somehow. But my father came home. He took the silver."

Tycho and the king exchange a glance.

"I watched the archery competition," the king says. "Alek was at my side the whole time." He pauses. "And this doesn't explain the soldiers down the lane. Nor the message I was given."

Tycho frowns. "Where is the letter now? Who claimed it?"

I inhale to answer, but the door at my back clicks.

Tycho's eyes go wide. "Grey!" He lifts an arm and shoves the king to the side.

I hear the *snap* of a crossbow, but I don't register the sound until a bolt appears in the king's shoulder.

Then my father's voice. "Good job, Jax. You've finally done something right."

CHAPTER 51

TYCHO

The king is struck before I can fully block him. He takes the first shot in the shoulder, but it's better than his neck.

I lift an arm to block a second shot with my bracer, and the arrow slices right across my bicep.

The sudden pain nearly brings me to my knees. I've been shot before, but not like this. The arrow burns where it breaks the skin, stealing my breath. Jax's father already has another bolt loaded.

The next one hits Grey in the leg, and he goes down.

"Da!" shouts Jax. "Da, stop!"

I go for my throwing knives, but the fingers on my injured arm are slow and clumsy. Silver hell.

"The arrows," Grey gasps. His knee hits the dirt. "You were right. They're Iishellasan steel."

I don't have an arrow embedded in my arm, but blood flows freely down my sleeve. Stars flare in my blood, but I can't heal it at all.

Jax's father hasn't fired again, but he's got another bolt loaded and aimed right at us both. I'm panting, but I slip a throwing knife into my left hand. My aim won't be anywhere near as good, especially with him behind the table, but I wait for a clean shot.

"They weren't attacking me!" Jax cries, as if his father could possibly be seen as *defending* him.

"I know that," Ellis says. "We've been waiting for him to show up. Now go down the lane to tell the guards at Callyn's that we've got the king, too."

Too. My heart clenches.

I wonder if that means Callyn is part of this.

Ellis stays behind the work table. I'm sure Grey's got a weapon in hand, but there are two steel arrows driven through his skin. He's breathing harder than I am.

"Can you use magic?" I whisper to Grey in Emberish.

Grey's eyes are dark with fury. When he speaks, his voice is strained. "If I could use magic, this man would be dead already." He looks at me. "You need to find the queen."

"I'm not leaving you."

"I can see what you're planning," Ellis says. "But I have no problem killing you both. They knew you'd come here! They knew!" He's all but crowing with glee. "They'll probably give me a *reward*. Boy! I told you to go down to Callyn's!"

"I'm not helping you do this," Jax snaps.

Ellis turns his glare on his son, his eyes red with rage. "*I told you to—*"

I see my chance. Those knives spin free of my hand before he can shoot. It's a bad angle, so the first one misses, but the second one skips right across the man's shoulder. He cries out, then aims to shoot *me*. I fight to get a third knife.

Jax tackles him. He doesn't have the strength to bring his father to the ground, but they grapple for the weapon, and the shot fires wildly. The lantern shatters and the workshop goes dark. Jax cries out, and my head whips around.

"Tycho!" Grey says. He's got blades in his hands now, too. "You need to find Lia Mara," he says. His breathing is quick and ragged. "You don't know what other weapons he has." He winces. "Go now, while you can."

I don't want to leave him. I don't want to leave Jax.

Ellis has another bolt loaded. I hear the click of a crossbow, and time seems to stop right in that moment. There are too many people at risk.

"I'll do my best to keep him alive," says the king. "*Tycho.* If they've taken the royal family, they've taken Syhl Shallow."

He's right.

I run.

CHAPTER 52

CALLYN

I'm woken by shouting.

No, cheering. The soldiers in the barnyard are cheering. Excited whoops and victorious hollers that are definitely going to wake Nora.

I try to make sense of the noise to figure out why they're so happy. I move to the window to look down. Several lanterns have been lit, and the soldiers are excitedly milling about.

"Callyn."

Nora stands in the doorway of my bedroom, her face tight and worried. She knows who's in our barn—and she knows that cheering from the queen's captors is likely not good news.

"Go get dressed," I say to her quickly, then move to do the same for myself. I press a hand to my mother's pendant. I don't know what's going on, but after what happened with the princess, I don't want to deal with it in a sleeping shift.

Minutes later, we're down in the bakery. Nora draws close and clutches at my fingers as we hide just inside the door to peek out.

The soldiers are still cheering. There are dozens of them now. Maybe over a hundred.

Where did they all come from? Were they sleeping in the woods?

"What are they saying?" Nora whispers. "They keep chanting. *We caught . . .*"

"The king," I say breathlessly. "They caught the king."

And the queen is held prisoner in my barn.

Alek asked me where my loyalties lie. He said he was loyal to the queen—but now she's been imprisoned by the very people who were supposedly protecting her.

I want to honor my mother's memory, but I can't imagine she'd be doing *this*.

My father did.

The memory burns. If this was his plan when they raided the palace the first time . . . then he was wrong.

The guards and soldiers are everywhere now, but they've been allowing me to bring food to the queen since I first learned of her presence. I don't see why that would change if they've caught their quarry.

"Help me pack a few bags with food," I say to Nora. "We need to make them heavy so I have a reason for you to be with me." I think quickly. The soldiers were checking the bags of food at first, but either they grew bored with it or they stopped worrying about me planning anything. They're so busy celebrating now that they surely won't bother this time. "Fetch Mother's daggers from under the bed. Pile the loaves from yesterday on top of them."

Her eyes go even wider. "Why?"

"Hurry." I glance out the window of the door again. "I don't want to leave you here."

"Why not?"

"Because we're going to try to save the queen."

CHAPTER 53

JAX

I'm surprised Da didn't shoot *me* with the crossbow. After he punched me, he reloaded the weapon and pointed it at me for a solid minute. I was so sure he was going to pull the trigger that I laid on the dirty floor of the dim workshop and peered across the piles of iron and half-finished projects to meet the pain-stricken eyes of the king.

"Forgive me," I said to him. "I didn't know—"

"Don't ask him for forgiveness," my father snapped. "Go in the house, if you can manage that much. Find the shackles under my bed."

I didn't move.

"Do it," said the king, and his voice was strained. "Don't give him cause to shoot me again."

So now he's chained to the forge, which is hot enough that sweat threads his hair. The arrows are still embedded in his skin, and he's all but panting from the strain of it. The first rays of sunlight have broken over the mountain, and I can see that blood has soaked into his shirt and the leather of his armor. His weapons lie in a pile on the other side of the workshop, well out of reach, courtesy of my father. Swords and daggers and a bow like Tycho's.

Da left five minutes ago. Presumably to tell whoever he's working with, because I heard a cheer go up down the lane, near the bakery.

No matter what I think of my father, he's no fool. He snapped my crutches before he left. "Guard him," he said.

That's a joke. I've offered the king water, which he refused. He doesn't trust me. I can see it in his eyes.

I don't blame him.

Tycho is gone, too. I was surprised how many soldiers seemed to be down the lane. I'm not sure what that means.

I do know Tycho can't hold them all off. Not without his rings. Maybe not even *with* them.

And then there's the matter of my friend. Have the Truthbringers done something to Callyn?

Or did she know all along?

The king shifts his weight and winces. I rise to my knees and move to approach him, but his eyes flash to mine, and I freeze.

Most of Syhl Shallow is afraid of this man, and I've heard all the rumors of what he's capable of. I know there are many people who'd be relieved to see him chained to a forge, powerless. Many of them are apparently down the lane. But all I keep hearing in my head is Tycho saying, *He is* good *and he is* just *and he will do everything in his power to protect Syhl Shallow* and *Emberfall*. I keep hearing the king's unyielding voice demanding answers—followed by the emotion in his tone when he asked about the queen and the princess. His wife and daughter.

King Grey might have terrifying magic, but he's not the sum of all the stories that Callyn and I have heard.

He might be in pain, but his eyes are picking me apart. I wonder what he sees.

"Tycho swore to me that you were not plotting against the throne," he finally says.

"I wasn't," I say. "It was just supposed to be messages. We're so far from the Crystal City." I have to fight not to look away. "We were so desperate."

"You had to know your father was a part of this."

"I didn't. Truly." I frown, though, remembering Lady Karyl. On the very first day, she was looking for Da, but I didn't think he could be working with the Truthbringers. Not after what happened to Callyn's father.

But maybe he and I were on opposite sides of the same coin: desperate for silver and not caring how we got it.

You should be grateful. I've figured out what you were doing. Who you were helping. I turned it around for us, boy.

Even when he captured King Grey, it had nothing to do with resentment for magic or protecting Syhl Shallow.

It had to do with money.

I should kill you both, he said. *They'll probably give me a reward.*

"I should have known," I say bitterly. The king winces and shifts his weight again, and I glance at his injuries. "Would it help if I pulled the arrows?"

He studies me for a long moment. "I don't know." He swallows, and even that looks painful. "I don't know what power is bound into them. It might make it worse if I can't heal." He flexes his wrists, then winces. "Can you unchain me?"

"Da took the keys." I hesitate. "The links are too thick to cut. I could try to melt the chain using the forge, but it wouldn't be quick."

"Do it."

"It'll hurt. And if he catches me—"

"Then do it now, before he returns." His voice doesn't rise, but there's a command in his tone that makes me jump and scurry for my tools.

The leg of the forge isn't close to the opening to the firebox, and the chain isn't very long. The king has to lever himself backward a few inches, and I tug the chain until his shoulders are twisted to a near inhuman angle. He sounds like he's breathing through his teeth.

"I'm sorry," I say. "I'm sorry—"

"This isn't making it faster, Jax."

"Yes—yes, Your Majesty." I manage to get the very edge of the chain over the lip of the forge. "It's not long enough."

He tries to rise onto one knee, but his leg won't support him. Not with an arrow through his thigh. I wrench his arm back another inch, and he makes a sound—then quickly follows it with, "Don't stop."

I get a link into the fire, wedged there with my tongs so it'll get hot enough. I'm so close to the heat that sweat slicks my forearms already, but I don't dare let go. The pain is almost unbearable, and a gasp escapes my lips.

Then the king says, "When these soldiers come, who will you stand with?" He pauses. "Who will you fight for?"

I don't know what to say. I never thought it would *come* to this.

But of course it *did*. I made a choice then. And I have a choice to make now. No one has ever asked me a question like that. Fear sits like a ball of lead in my stomach—but so does determination.

For the first time, I think I understand the note in Tycho's voice when he said, *The actual soldiering, not so much.*

I do know one thing for sure. "I don't stand with the Truthbringers," I say. "I stand with Tycho. If he would fight for you, so will I."

"Tycho risked his position at court for you," the king says. "He risked his *life* for you."

I inwardly flinch, then blink sweat out of my eyes. "I know." I draw a shaky breath and watch blisters erupt on my fingers where they grip the chain. "I know."

"Make it worth it."

I nod. The chain begins to glow red.

"Almost," I say. "Just another minute."

"Do you have any soldier training?" the king says, sounding like he's speaking through clenched teeth. "Can you fight, if it comes to that?"

I'd laugh if it weren't all so serious. "No. None." I hesitate. "Well . . ."

"Tell me."

The chain turns yellow. I reach for my pincers. "I can shoot. Tycho taught me." The chain gives, and the king's arms pull free so quickly that he almost falls over.

My heart is pounding. If my father catches us, he might leave the king alive, but he'll kill me.

I realize the sound of the cheering is growing louder.

"They're coming back," I say.

"Weapons, Jax." He's breathing heavily again, but his voice is strong. "Now."

I have to crawl for them, and I start with the biggest blades. He quickly separates a dagger belt from the weapon, double wraps it around the thigh with the deeper arrow wound, and buckles it tight.

Without warning—without even a moment of hesitation—he jerks the arrow free and swears.

Blood flows down his leg. I stare. "You need—"

"I need more weapons. Throwing blades next."

Again, I scurry. I carry as many as I can at a time, pinning them to my chest with one hand and crawling with the other.

"Can you heal it?" I say to him on my third pass.

"Not yet." He looks like his skin has paled a shade. "The bow and arrows next."

I tug the full quiver over my shoulder, then crawl with the bow in hand. When I hold it out for the king, he shakes his head.

"That," he says, "is for you."

CHAPTER 54

CALLYN

I was right. We're able to get into the barn without much resistance. The soldiers are used to me bringing food now, so they let us pass. Nora huddles near my side.

The queen is sitting in the corner with her daughter, and she looks up in surprise when we approach with a lantern. Sinna is in her arms.

"What's happening?" the queen asks quietly.

"I'm not entirely sure," I say carefully.

"They say they've caught the king," she whispers.

"I know." I swallow. "I don't know how. I don't know what it means."

A shadow slides along the wall of the barn. A male voice says, "It means Grey is trapped."

The queen gasps, but Sinna struggles free of her arms to run across the straw. "Tycho!"

He catches her in his arms and swings her into the air, but the movement is sedate, and his expression is serious. "The king is injured," he says quickly. "I don't know what they've shot him with, but they seem to have a supply of Iishellasan artifacts. He can't use

his magic. There are at least four dozen soldiers on the road. I recognize many from the palace guard. They could have more." He
draws close, his eyes narrowing when they fall on the queen, taking
in the blood on her clothes and the bruising to her face. "Your
Majesty. Forgive me. He ordered me to find you. I could not keep
him—"

She strides forward and throws her arms around his neck so forcefully that he takes a step back.

"I'm so glad you're here," she says, and her voice almost breaks. "We
have to save him, Tycho."

"We will," he says, but even he doesn't sound entirely sure.

She draws back to look at him. "How did you get in without being
seen?"

"I broke the lock on the back door. Everyone is in the barnyard
celebrating his capture," he says. "It's barely sunrise. I look like any
other soldier in the shadows." He glances up and around at my barn.
"I thought I might need to sneak into the bakery, which would've been
a bit harder, but I remembered all the repairs I'd seen to your barn."
His voice turns rueful. "I thought perhaps Alek had set this up."

Sure enough, he did.

I flush. I was so foolish.

The queen wastes no time on my remorse. "We will sort out the key
players once we are all safe in the palace. Tycho, how many soldiers do
you have with you? Can we be sure of their loyalty? If we take a stand
against these Truthbringers, will we—" She catches a glimpse of his
expression in the flickering lantern light. "What?"

"No soldiers," he says. "You have me."

The words fall into the silence and hang there.

The queen reaches out to squeeze his hand. "There are few people
I would rather have at my side."

He smiles, though it's a bit wistful, full of words unsaid. "Well, I'd feel better if we had a full battalion. I feel certain Rhen has sent soldiers to follow, but they could not travel as fast."

"A full battalion!" says Nora, and I can't tell if she's fascinated or afraid. "Will there be a war right here in Briarlock?"

"A war!" says the princess, and her tiny voice is the same. She clutches tightly to Lord Tycho's neck.

"Maybe," says the queen. "How soon do you expect them?" she says hopefully.

"Not for another two days," says Tycho. "At least."

She stares at him. He stares back.

"As I said," he says quietly. "You have me."

"So it is up to us," she says decisively.

"Yes. If we move quickly, before the sun is fully up, I believe we can escape into the woods without being spotted."

The queen looks at me. "Callyn, you swore to me that you wanted to help. If I am to rescue my husband, I will need you to look after little Sinna."

There are so many shocks in that sentence, I don't know where to start. But her eyes are so intent on mine that I can't do anything but nod. "Yes, Your Majesty."

"I'll help," says Nora.

Dutifully, the princess holds out her tiny arms to me, and I take her from Lord Tycho. She winds her fingers in my hair exactly the way Nora used to do.

"We should keep them with us," says Tycho. "I don't think it's safe to leave them here."

"Oh, I intend to," says the queen. Another cheer goes up outside, and she frowns. Her voice grows very soft. "They want to kill him, don't they, Tycho?"

He nods. "Let's get to a safe place, and let's make a plan. Once they realize you're gone, they have enough people to search these woods."

"As you say," says the queen. She takes hold of Lord Tycho's hand and gives him a rueful glance. "Right now I am very sorry we made you give up your rings."

"Oh. Right." He picks up a piece of straw and holds it up. In an instant, a flame crawls to life. Nora claps. I stare. The queen gasps.

"Your Majesty," says Tycho. "The king is no longer the only one with magic."

CHAPTER 55

JAX

Soldiers are coming down the lane. We can hear them chanting, clear as a bell.

Kill the king! Kill the king!

My heart slams hard against my rib cage, and I hear every breath that rattles into my lungs. The king has managed to get to his feet, but he seems less steady than I am, and that's saying something. He's pulled the final arrow from his shoulder, but his magic is still slow to work, and blood soaks the side of his armor. His arm hangs limply. I've got an arrow nocked and waiting, and the king's bracer on my forearm. He's been giving me a litany of instructions.

If they're wearing armor, the throat is the most vulnerable, but it's a narrow target.

Better to aim for their legs. If they can't walk, they can't advance.

Or the face. No one can fight with an arrow in their eye.

Don't wait to see if your arrow strikes true. Either it does or it doesn't. Find your next shot.

Don't forget to breathe! Take time to aim. Don't waste your arrows.

I've never even hit a moving target. I don't know if now is the time to tell him that. Probably not.

"I'm not a soldier," I say to him, as if there's any chance he wasn't sure.

"No one really is until they have to be."

He says this like it's nothing, but the words lodge in my heart and stick there. In a way, this reminds me of shooting with Tycho that first day in the snow. This could be a lesson. Nothing at stake except a little bit of tree bark.

Then the king shifts his weight, and his breath hitches the slightest bit, the only sign he's still in pain.

There's a lot at stake.

I swallow as the sun fully climbs above the mountains, giving us a clear view of the path.

"Any magic yet?" I say. His wounds seem to have stopped seeping blood, but I can't tell if that's a good sign or a bad one.

"Some. Nowhere near enough." He looks to the sky, then glances at me. "But I've beaten bad odds before."

There are dozens of soldiers coming. I only have twenty arrows in this quiver. Even if every single one shoots true, that won't stop them all.

"This bad?" I say.

"Fate has already drawn a path beyond this moment, Jax. Let's follow it through."

I've never believed in fate, but his voice is so sure that I nod. "Yes, Your Majesty."

The soldiers come into view. There are so many. They seem to blur together, and I realize it's sweat dripping into my eyes. For an instant, I can't breathe. I can't think. My fingers shake, and I tighten them on the arrow.

"Hold," the king says, as he pulls his sword. "Wait for my order."

I nod. My hand is slick on the bow.

"Breathe," he says, and I exhale slowly.

The soldiers must realize the king is no longer bound, because a shout goes up, interrupting their eager chanting. I see bows and crossbows lift. Some are pointed at the king—but others are pointed at me.

My father is among them. I see the shock register in his eyes as he sees the bow in my hands—but he lifts his own weapon. I can't tell if he's aiming at me or at the king, but it doesn't matter. There are so many of them, and all at once.

"Now," says the king, and I loose the arrow, just like I've practiced.

CHAPTER 56

CALLYN

From the woods, I see Jax's father fall, but it's so quick that he disappears under the other soldiers as they swarm forward to attack. Other soldiers begin to fall as well, as Jax's arrows take them down. There's a man at his side who must be the king. But there are so many soldiers that move to surround the forge, and Jax vanishes from view. The queen and Lord Tycho have edged forward in the woods to attempt to use magic somehow.

Jax. Against my will, tears blur my vision, and I'm glad I have a toddler clinging to me or I'd join the fray myself. He's not a soldier. He's not a fighter. He has one bow and a wounded man at his side.

I keep hearing his voice, that first day he took the coins. *You're my best friend.*

I said I was willing to hang beside him. I should be beside him now.

"Cally-cal," whispers Nora in the early morning shadows. "Will Jax be all right?"

I have to swallow past a hard lump in my throat. "I don't know." My voice is a worried rasp, but I clear my throat, because Nora looks to be on the verge of tears. "Here, Your Highness," I say to little Sinna. "Would you like to sit with Nora? She loves sweetcakes almost as much as you do."

I don't even wait for either of them to answer, I just ease the young princess into Nora's arms. She immediately strokes a finger along Nora's braid. "Mama plaits her hair like this, too." Her face contorts like she's trying to figure something out. "Are you a queen or a princess?"

Nora's mouth drops open, and I say, "She's a princess."

A smile flickers through Nora's tears. "Princess Nora. That's me. Shall I plait your hair, too?"

While they chatter, I ease forward a few feet. The soldiers seem to have slowed unnaturally, but I don't know if that's the king's magic, or if Tycho and the queen have done something. Many soldiers have fallen, arrows jutting from their bodies.

Many others haven't.

The press of bodies part, just for a second, and I see Jax, the bow in his hands.

Then the soldiers shift again, and he's gone.

A burst of flame erupts in the underbrush in front of Tycho and the queen, and I gasp. The fire spreads quickly, crawling forward along the ground, seeking the slow-moving soldiers. The women and men scream as they see it coming, and they try to change course to run. Some succeed, scattering into the woods.

Others catch fire. The screaming is terrible.

I realize this is how my father died. The magic in the palace during the first attack.

The realization is staggering. The same magic that killed my mother.

Fire is suddenly everywhere: in the leaves, in the trees, burning everything it touches. The soldiers have realized where the magic is coming from, and they're no longer attacking the forge. Armor-clad women and men who've evaded the magic are surging up the hill toward *us*. Lord Tycho already has a sword drawn. I shift to return to Nora and Sinna when I see a man sprinting through the woods, his crossbow pointed right at the queen's back.

I don't think. I dive for her, tackling her to the ground. We roll, finding fire and rocks. Above me, Tycho drives his sword right into the man's throat. Blood is suddenly everywhere. The queen is tugging at my arm.

Then I hear Nora scream. The world shrinks down to the sound of my sister's panic.

I look, and it's as if the magic is still making everything slow, but I know it's exactly the opposite: everything is happening too quickly. A soldier backhands Nora across the face, knocking her to the ground. He snatches a screaming Sinna up into his arms.

"No!" screams Nora. My brave, fearless sister.

She launches herself off the ground to attack him.

He drives his sword right through her body.

My world stops spinning entirely. I can't breathe. I can't think. I'm going to shatter into a million pieces. There's so much blood in the air. On her dress. In her braids. She's coughing. Choking. Dying.

The soldier is yelling. "I have the princess!" He's got an arm around her waist, trapping her against his chest. The other hand holds a blade against her throat. He glares at the queen. "Stop the magic, or she will die."

CHAPTER 57

TYCHO

I'm frozen in place. Too much has happened.

Little Nora lies in the leaves, motionless. Sinna is clutched in the arms of a soldier. A tiny stream of blood runs down her neck, and she squeals. My chest clenches. There are blades in my hands, but his dagger is too close to her throat. A dozen arrows and crossbows are pointed at us.

On the ground, Lia Mara is gasping. "Please," she says. "Please."

"No more magic," the soldier says. I recognize him. Ander, from one of the regiments stationed at the palace. I've recognized a *lot* of them.

Many in the palace conspire against the king.

Yes, Nakiis, I see that now.

"Drop your weapons," Ander says.

"Mama," whimpers Sinna.

"Let the princess go," I say.

He must squeeze Sinna, because she squeals. More blood drips down her neck.

"Tycho," gasps Lia Mara. "Tycho, do as he says."

I don't want to. *If they've taken the royal family, they've taken Syhl Shallow.*

If the king had his full power right now, all of these women and men would be eviscerated where they stand. I'm not as fast as Grey when it comes to magic, but I feel the stars in my blood, waiting for a command.

Ander narrows his eyes. "Now, Tycho."

"I've fought at your side," I say to him. "You've fought at the *king's* side."

"He turned his magic against our people," he says. "There's a reason Emberfall's king slaughtered them all."

Sinna whimpers.

"Sinna hasn't done anything wrong," I say. Somewhere behind me, I hear Callyn speaking tearfully to Nora. "You've already killed one child. The Truthbringers always claim to want the best for the queen. Her daughter—"

"Our queen married a magesmith," says Ander.

"Da," Sinna screams. Another stream of blood appears beside the first. "Da, help me."

"He's coming," Lia Mara gasps. "Sinna, he's coming."

But he's not coming. He's not here.

These were impossible odds before we even got here. I knew. The king knew.

I think of the power Nakiis helped me pull out of the air. I think of the magic the rings allowed me to do.

I feel those stars spin in my blood, ready for action. I'm not practiced with large-scale magic. I'm not practiced with much more than healing.

But maybe that's all I need.

"Put her down," I say to him. "This is between you and the king. He came, just as you asked. Let Sinna and the queen go."

"We're not letting anyone go," he says. "We're ending the line of magic right here." He jerks Sinna's head back, and she cries out.

I drop my weapons and leap for him, magic flaring in my hands.

I don't know if I'm going to be quick enough. Strong enough. Skilled enough. But I grab hold of his wrist just before he can use that blade. I send my magic right into his skin. Taking apart instead of putting together. The bones of his wrist begin to snap, just as a crossbow fires. Ander shouts, and I try to grab hold of Sinna. Instead, I feel the bite of the arrow. My magic dies. Sinna screams.

Again, I'm going to fail.

But then an inhuman screech splits the air.

Followed by a dozen others.

CHAPTER 58

JAX

At first I don't know where the screams are coming from. My heart has been pounding so loud for so long that I almost can't recognize anything else. I only have one arrow left, and the king has gone to his knees with yet another arrow in his leg. We can barely see past the press of soldiers. But for a moment, I catch a glimpse of a man on the hill with a little girl with red hair clutched against the front of his body. I see Tycho tackle him before taking an arrow himself.

Then a dark winged creature soars out of the sky to rip the toddler right out of the soldier's arms.

"Nakiis," says the king, and he doesn't sound panicked. He sounds relieved.

The answer comes on a blast of cold wind. "Your daughter is safe, magesmith."

Suddenly, the man is wide open, his arms bleeding from whatever the winged creature did to him. He's still got a dagger in one hand, and I watch him turn on Tycho. He's wearing a breastplate, and he's at least seventy-five yards away, but I can see every inch of exposed skin.

I have one arrow left.

I know soldiers who can't hit a target at that distance.

I'm shooting before I even mean to. The arrow goes right through his neck.

"Nice shot," says the king.

I don't have time to enjoy the praise. Whatever magic held the others seems to have snapped loose, because Grey and I are suddenly facing ten more swords. But more screams fill the air: impossibly beautiful and terrifying winged creatures with fangs and talons come out of the sky from every direction.

They slice into the remaining soldiers viciously, severing limbs without hesitation, until none are left standing.

I can't breathe for an entirely new reason. I think of all the stories I used to read with Callyn, and it's like seeing them come to life. I don't know if I should be terrified or grateful. I'm a little bit of both.

But the first, the one the king called Nakiis, lands in front of us with the little girl. The other scravers cling to the trees surrounding the clearing. I can't stop staring.

The little girl reaches for her father tearfully. "Da. I don't like this game."

The king struggles to get to his feet, but his leg won't hold him.

"I don't either," he says.

I put out a hand, and he blinks at me in surprise—then takes it. The little girl grabs him tight around the waist, and he winces, but he doesn't pull away.

He looks at the winged creature. "The queen?" he says quietly.

"And . . . Tycho?" I say hopefully.

"Both are being attended to." Nakiis sighs, but he's looking at the steel bolt protruding from the king's thigh. "*Why* do you fools keep leaving charmed steel against your skin? Your magic will never recover." Without warning, he reaches out, grabs the steel, and yanks it free.

The king swears and cries out, but he grips the table and stays on his feet.

I stare out at the fallen bodies surrounding the forge. Blood is everywhere. I don't see my father. I don't see Callyn. My breathing is shaking in my chest.

Then the princess draws back to look at the king. "Da. If you're done, we have to see to Princess Nora."

CHAPTER 59

CALLYN

Nora isn't dead. That should be a relief, but it's not.

Blood is trailing out of her mouth while she chokes. Her eyes were desperate for a while, but now the life in them is beginning to fade. I'm holding her hand, kneeling in the leaves. I'm terrified. I'm pleading. Stars keep flaring in my eyes, and I must be lightheaded from the shock.

"Please," I'm crying. "Please."

The queen has her hands on Nora's chest. "I'm trying," she whispers. "I'm trying. I'm not like Grey."

One of the winged creatures who attacked the soldiers lands in the leaves beside us, and I shriek, covering my sister. "No!"

"Be at ease," the creature says, and her voice is softer than I expect, behind the fierceness of her countenance. The first one had gray skin and dark wings, with a length of black hair, but this one has purple markings on her skin and the underside of her wings, with a long purple streak through her hair. The air around us turns ice cold, and she reaches a hand toward Nora.

"Please," I whimper. "Please don't hurt her."

"Children are sacred. We do not harm them." She lays a hand over the queen's. "Pull the magic from the air." Ice forms on the leaves around us, and I shiver. My tears freeze on my cheeks. Nora's blood crystallizes along her jaw.

Magic. Every beat of my heart wants to rebel against it. I've spent my entire life fearing it.

But I can't. Not when it's Nora.

"There," the creature says, satisfied. "You feel the magic more clearly now, Your Majesty."

Those stars are still flaring in my vision, and I'm worried I'm going to pass out. As I watch, the wound on Nora's chest begins to close, and I gasp.

From behind us, a man says, "You don't need me at all."

The queen lets out a sound that's almost a sob. "Oh, Grey. I've never needed anyone more."

Grey. The king.

I'd take a moment to examine that, but Nora coughs, and I blink away the stars to look down at my sister.

She's peering up at me. "Cally-cal? I'm so cold. Can we go home yet?"

CHAPTER 60

TYCHO

There's an arrow through my shoulder, but I've managed to get to my knees. I feel like I'm going to be sick in the leaves. The queen is alive, off to my left, helping little Nora, whose injuries are more pressing. I think I've heard the king's voice, so I know he's still alive.

We're surrounded by bodies. I haven't seen Jax.

I put my good hand against the leaves, then move to shove myself to my feet.

Before I can, one of the scravers stops in front of me. I barely have time to recognize Nakiis before he wrenches the arrow right out of my shoulder.

It's so unexpected and so painful that I go to my knees again. This time I *do* vomit in the leaves.

Stars flare in my blood, but they're slower than before, sluggish to heal the injury from the Iishellasan steel. I'm coughing and trying to stop when a cold wind sweeps through the clearing, Nakiis lending his magic to mine. The scraver says, "Come now. Even your king did not do that when I pulled his arrow."

"Oh, that makes me feel better," I say huskily. "Thank you." The air is ice cold and full of the scravers' magic, and I inhale deeply. I can barely think past everything that's happened, but I need to find Jax.

A gauntleted hand appears in my line of vision. "That doesn't mean I didn't want to," says Grey.

I hesitate, then take his hand to pull myself to my feet. "Grey. Grey, I need to find—"

But then I stop short, because Jax is right there beside him. There are blisters on his hands and blood on his cheeks and his silky hair is a tangled mess, but that's all I notice before I ignore the pain in my shoulder to throw my arms around his neck.

"You're alive," I say, and I feel a bit breathless. "You're alive."

"I'm alive," he says, and his voice wavers as if he's surprised to hear it, too.

I only hold him for a moment before I pull back to examine him more closely. "Where are you hurt? Tell me."

"I'm not." He shakes his head fiercely as if he has to convince himself. "I'm not hurt."

"No one got close," says the king. He nods down at Ander's body, which I now see has an arrow protruding from his neck. "He even took out that one, Tycho."

My eyes widen, and I wrap my arms around Jax's neck again. "I *knew* you were a good shot."

He laughs breathlessly against my shoulder, but there's no humor to it. "I'm sure it'll do me a lot of good when I'm locked up for treason."

I go still. Despite everything, I forgot Jax's role here. He and Callyn might have helped, but they're not innocent.

I look up and find Grey's eyes. As usual, I can read nothing in his expression.

But after everything, he can't be lenient. Not now. Not about this.

I swallow and wonder if I'm going to end up in a cell right beside Jax, because there's no way I'm going to let Grey lock him up.

But after a moment, the king reaches out and claps Jax on the shoulder. "You risked your life to protect the king," he says. "Surely that's worth discussing a pardon, don't you think?"

As injuries are assessed and words of gratitude are shared, the scravers begin to withdraw. Wings beat hard against the air, and they leap into the trees. Nakiis is among them.

"Wait!" I call to him. "Where are you going?"

"I'll find you when I need you," he calls back. "Remember our bargain, young magesmith."

Jax is by my side, and he looks over. "'Young magesmith'?" he echoes.

"That's going to take a bit of explaining."

The king's eyes are on me, and I know his focus is on the other half of that statement. *Remember our bargain.*

I wait for him to ask me again.

He doesn't.

"We'll have to secure this lane," he says. "And wait for Rhen's forces to get here. There's no telling what's waiting for us at the palace. They surely had a plan beyond this."

The queen rises from where she was kneeling with Nora, and she looks at the sky, at the retreating scravers. "I will take the girls to the bakery," she says. "Callyn says we can see the road from there. We'd have plenty of warning." Without waiting for an answer, she moves away to do exactly that.

I look around the stretch of forest, at the aftermath of the battle. We'll have much to do before Rhen's forces get here. I shake out my aching shoulder and sigh.

"I'll help you back to the forge," I say to Jax, and he nods.

"Tycho," says the king, and I stop. His gaze is intense, unyielding. "Whatever it is," he says, "does it put you in danger?"

I'm not sure how to answer that—because I truly have no idea. So I give him an unyielding look right back. "No more than what I do for you."

CHAPTER 61

JAX

I've heard a lot of stories about war. After the strife with Emberfall, I remember soldiers coming through Briarlock with tales of what happened on the battlefields. I know about what happened to Callyn's father, and there's no shortage of travelers willing to talk about the Uprising.

I've never really thought about the aftermath.

The lane between the bakery and the forge is littered with bodies. Many more have fallen in the woods. Dozens are badly burned, and the sickly sweet smell fills the air. There are worse smells, too. I've heard that nothing about death is dignified, and I'm seeing the proof.

I'm glad that Callyn and the queen took the younger girls to the bakery, that they'll be watching for travelers and stopping them before they can come down the lane and find . . . this. But it left me in the woods with Tycho and the king, and there's clearly a tension between them that the battle didn't erase.

After Tycho offered me his arm, he glanced back at the king and said, "I'll be back in a minute to strip and drag."

I didn't want to be a burden when there are so many more important things to worry about, but I didn't want to trip and fall face-first into a corpse either, so I took his arm, and now we're making our way back down the hill.

I don't want to search the bodies for my father, but I can't help it. My eyes skip over armored men and women, but I don't see him. My heart keeps beating at a rapid clip. Maybe he escaped. I can't decide which option I should hope for.

"Are you all right?" Tycho says quietly.

I try taking a deep breath and regret it immediately. I focus on not breathing through my nose. "I don't know yet." I think of how closely he's guarded royal secrets, and I wonder how much I can pry. "Are you?"

He gives me half a smile. "*I* don't know yet."

At the forge, Tycho finds my crutches, which are in pieces, and he sighs. "I'm sorry."

As if this is the worst thing to happen today. I shake my head. "I have tools. Just leave them."

Tycho nods. His demeanor is cool and detached, the only sign that everything that happened here affected him, too. "This will take us a while," he says. "But I'll be back when I can."

"What does that mean?" I say to him. "'Strip and drag'?"

"We'll pull the weapons and armor," he says. "Anything worth salvaging. And we'll identify who we can." He hesitates. "Then we'll drag the bodies into the clearing at the end of the lane to burn them."

I stare at him as if I don't comprehend.

But I do.

The actual soldiering, not so much.

I want to pull him into the house and lock the door, as if I could somehow trap all this horror out here and that would erase the bleak look from his expression.

But he wouldn't want that. Of all I've learned about Tycho, he's not one to sidestep duty and obligation.

I've been quiet too long, and Tycho speaks as if I need a better explanation. "It's late spring. Dead bodies get a lot worse before they get any better. Prince Rhen's soldiers won't be here for days."

"No. Yeah." I have to shake myself, because I don't want to think about that too closely. "Go. I'm fine."

He squeezes my hand, then moves away.

There's a part of me that wants to go into the house and pretend none of this is happening—but a bigger part doesn't want to feel like a coward. I need my crutches, so I set to repairing them while Tycho and the king go about their task.

It's slow work, with what must be hundreds—*thousands?*—of buckles. Quiet work, too, because they say little aside from the occasional comment that they call to each other in Emberish. The king is favoring the leg that took an arrow, and when I look more closely, I notice that Tycho is favoring his injured shoulder. But they begin to make a pile of weapons and armor—keeping the Iishellasan steel separate, from what I can see—and they carry on.

I wonder what all the gossip-hungry travelers would make of this version of King Grey and Lord Tycho: injured men who should be taking respite in the palace, but are instead kneeling beside fallen soldiers to do what needs to be done.

Lord Alek might be a skilled fighter, and he might claim he's loyal to the queen, but I could never, for one minute, imagine him doing *this*.

I swing my hammer to bolt my crutches back together, then slip them under my arms to support my weight.

Then, before I can think too closely about what I'm doing, I step out of the workshop to help.

I underestimated. There seem to be *millions* of buckles. I remember Tycho disarming in the lantern light, his fingers quick and deft. I'm slower, lacking practice. When I first began, I expected Tycho and the king to exchange a glance and send me back to the forge, to leave this work to the real warriors. Instead, they acknowledged my presence in the lane and switched to Syssalah for their sparse conversation, admitting me into their company. The sun beats down as the day goes on, and I see exactly what Tycho meant about dead bodies getting a lot worse before they get better.

When I struggle with unfamiliar equipment, they call instructions. *Unbuckle those greaves from the bottom. It'll loosen the other straps.* Or, *There's a hidden hook under that pauldron so you don't need to unbuckle it.*

Sometime around midday, I've grown a bit numb to what we're doing, and I drop to a knee beside a man's facedown body, then absently grab hold of his shoulder to lay him out on his back.

He's not dead. He growls with rage and swings a hand with a dagger. "Magic sympathizer!"

I cry out in surprise and fall back, but I'm not quick enough. His dagger slices a gash right across my ribs. I gasp and try to scramble backward, but he's coming after me.

Before he gets far, a knife hilt appears in his neck. Then another. Pain and shock flare in his eyes, but then nothing else. He collapses back to the ground. Truly dead this time.

My heart is hammering against my rib cage. I can hear my breathing rattle in my chest.

Tycho is at my side almost instantly. I don't know if he threw those blades or if the king did, but I press a hand to my waist and I'm stunned at how much blood I find on my fingers.

"Was it just a regular dagger?" Tycho is saying. "Jax. Jax, let me see." He drops to a knee beside me. Before I'm ready, his fingers press into the wound, and I flinch—but then it's healed.

"Are you all right?" he says.

I nod, then run a wrist across my damp forehead. My heart is still pounding. "He just took me by surprise."

I expect him to tell me to stop, that helping might be too dangerous, but the king calls, "Fit him with a breastplate, Tycho. There may be others."

Tycho finds me a breastplate—and a pair of steel-lined leather bracers, too. As he helps me lace and buckle the armor onto my body, I try not to think too hard about the fact that the last person to wear these died in them.

Tycho surprises me when he adds a dagger belt with a weapon strung along the length.

"I'd rather you have one if you need it." He tugs at the strap, pulling it tight, then stands back to look at me. "You make a good soldier."

That sparks a light in my heart, and I have to look away before my throat tightens. I shake off the emotion, hook my crutches under my arms, and move to the next body.

I have to do a double take, because it's my father.

He's clearly dead. He wore no armor, and there's an arrow through his chest. I remember the moment I saw him lift that crossbow.

Tycho goes still beside me, then puts a hand on my shoulder. His voice is very soft. "Jax."

I try to breathe past my shock. I wait for remorse to hit me just as hard, but it doesn't.

Resolve does.

My father made his choice, and so did I.

What are you afraid of, Jax?

Not my father. Not anymore.

I reach down and jerk the arrow free, then plant my crutches in the ground to move on to the next.

CHAPTER 62

CALLYN

There's a queen in my bedroom, and a king down the lane, but somehow Nora is snoring away, little Sinna asleep at her side. Honestly, I'm glad they're asleep. The men have been searching bodies and stockpiling weapons all day, but now they've moved on to dragging corpses farther down the lane. My little sister doesn't need to see that. The princess definitely doesn't.

I'm down in the bakery, wiping counters that don't need to be wiped and setting dough to rise for bread I'm going to feed to the royal family. I feel like I'll never sleep again. Maybe I'll be hung for treason tomorrow, and I really *won't* ever sleep again.

I heard what the king said to Jax, but he didn't say it to me.

And Jax wasn't the one who invited Lord Alek right into her bedroom.

I swallow and glance at the front window. Those scravers left hours ago, but I won't be able to erase what I saw them do. I won't be able to forget how the queen used magic to save my sister.

Or maybe . . .

I stop my thoughts in their tracks. I hold a hand to Mother's pendant, feeling its warmth press into my skin.

Alek said it was charmed *against* magic. But I remember having my hands on Nora's chest, how she was able to breathe while we waited for help. I remember the stars in my vision before the queen even touched her, how those stars seemed to multiply when the scravers arrived. I remember how Tycho explained to the queen that their rings allowed magic to seep into their blood.

I thought I was lightheaded from the panic and worry, but maybe it was something else.

I pause in my scrubbing and reach for one of my knives. Before I can think about it too closely, I touch the blade to a fingertip, and a drop of blood almost immediately wells up.

I close my eyes, thinking of those sparks and stars, imagining them. My finger is stinging something fierce, and I feel foolish.

I sigh and open my eyes, then use my rag to swipe away the drop of blood.

No injury remains. I stare at my finger, breathless.

Magic.

No. It's not possible.

I grab a new rag and start swiping the counters twice as fiercely. I need to worry about my sister. No matter what they do to me, there must be a way for me to protect Nora. Maybe Jax will look out for her. My shoulder aches from scrubbing so hard, but I move on to the bench in front of the window. I beat the dust out of the cushions, then set them aside to scrub the wood.

"Callyn?"

My breath catches, and I straighten. The queen has come down the stairs. She's changed out of her stained attire into one of my loose linen dresses. Her bruised face is freshly scrubbed, her hair neatly braided in a plait that hangs down over one shoulder.

I curtsy hastily. "Your Majesty."

She inhales to say whatever she came down to say, but I'm deathly afraid she's going to take me away from my sister or chain me up in the barn, so I start babbling. "Are you hungry? I can make you anything you like. Would you care for a meat pie? Or an apple tart?" I sound addled, but I can't seem to stop. "I believe Nora and Sinna finished the sweetcakes—"

"Callyn. Please—"

I recognize my error and flush. "Oh! Excuse me. Ah . . . I mean, Her Highness, *Princess* Sinna—"

"*Please,*" the queen says. "Stop."

I stop.

But I *can't* stop. I feel my face crumple, and I press my fingers to my eyes. I choke on my voice as I say, "Please don't hurt my sister. Please—please, Your Majesty. She didn't know. She wasn't a part of this. Please—please—Nora is so kind, so good, so innocent—"

"Callyn," she murmurs.

And then, to my absolute shock, the queen's arms come around my shoulders, and she's holding me. She's so warm and reassuring, and I'm clutching at her in response, soaking my tears into her shoulder before I realize what I'm doing.

But she's stroking my hair down my back the way I do for Nora when she's had a nightmare. She's holding me up when I feel like curling into a ball.

"Your sister," she says quietly, with a bit of humor in her tone, "got my daughter to fall asleep in mere *minutes,* which means I owe her a great debt, and I may in fact hire her to be a royal bedtime adviser."

It's so startling and unexpected that I giggle through my tears.

"She read Sinna a story," the queen continues. "She's quite animated when she does the voices."

I draw back and swipe at my eyes. "She loves the voices."

The queen brushes the tear-damp hair back from my face. "She said you always do them when you read to her, so she wanted to do the same for little Sinna."

I swallow a hard lump in my throat. "I do. Mother used to do it for me, and when she died—" My voice breaks, and I touch a hand to my pendant again.

Oh, Mother. I don't know what to do with this.

The queen wraps me up in her arms again, and I almost can't believe it's happening.

"Forgive me," I say tearfully. "I shouldn't cry." On the *queen* of all people.

"Oh no," she says. "You should cry all you want. Big sisters rarely get the chance."

Eventually, I stop and draw back. I have to swipe at my eyes, and I'm surprised to find that hers are red-rimmed, too.

"We have much to discuss," she says to me. "Perhaps we should have a cup of tea?"

Yes. Good. Something to do. I nod quickly and dry my hands on my skirts, then move to set the kettle on the stove.

The queen sits on one of the stools beside my pastry table, the spot that Jax usually claims, and it's bizarre to have her here in my bakery. But also . . . not.

She glances at the window, at the dimming sky. "The king does not think it would be prudent to return to the Crystal Palace until Prince Rhen's forces arrive. We don't know how many more members of the army and the Queen's Guard may be disloyal. For all we know, they may have taken the palace. So for a few days, we will be staying here."

My eyebrows go up. "There are far finer places in town, I promise you—"

"And far too many people," she says. "Far too much risk. Grey will assess how many rebels may have escaped, but it is easier to keep a

remote bakery secure than a boarding house in the middle of town."
She pauses, and a note of uncertainty enters her voice. "Especially as
we have no idea how deeply this insurrection runs."

An insurrection I was a part of. I swallow, twisting my fingers
together.

Again, I think of little Nora.

I remember telling Alek that I'd hang beside Jax.

The queen notices my fretting, and she puts out a hand on the table
between us. "I'm not going to harm your sister," she says. "Nor you. But
I am going to need you to tell me everything that has happened here in
Briarlock. With Lord Alek and with Lady Karyl." She pauses. "And with
your friend Jax."

I swallow and nod. "Yes, Your Majesty." My voice is rough. "I'll tell
you anything you want to know."

But I rub my healed fingertip against my thumb. The tiny injury has
disappeared so completely that I might have imagined it. I probably
did imagine it.

I do tell the queen everything she asks.

But for now, I leave that part out.

CHAPTER 63

TYCHO

It's been two days, and Prince Rhen and his forces have yet to arrive.

By now, there's little left of the battle in the woods. To avoid suspicion, we've begun allowing people down the lane for business at the bakery or the forge. Callyn warns the queen that she's had much business from nobles due to Lord Alek, so Lia Mara stays out of sight, listening to what's said. I sit sentry during the day, waiting in the woods, walking a perimeter with Mercy as I watch to see who comes and goes. Grey relieves me at night.

This battle might be over, but there's a tense aura of a bigger one coming, and all of us feel it. When I change shifts with Grey and walk down to the bakery for dinner, even little Sinna asks me when the war will begin.

The second night, Grey doesn't appear until midnight. Once he takes watch, I return to the forge, where I learn from Jax that once the sun went down, the king sat in the workshop for hours, asking questions.

"Interrogating you?" I ask.

"At first," he says, "I was worried that's what it was. He's very forthright."

I laugh without any humor.

Jax hesitates, and his tone turns slow, thoughtful. "He was just . . . asking. Asking about the people we see, the rumors we hear. He had many questions about Lord Alek and his notes. About Lady Karyl and her guards."

"Hmm." I still can't make all those puzzle pieces fit together. If Lord Alek left a message about an attack on Grey, it never came to pass.

And we haven't seen Lady Karyl. She wasn't among the dead.

Besides which, *no* message has ever mentioned an assault on the queen.

I'm too tired to figure this out tonight. I run a hand through my hair, then rub at my eyes.

"You need to sleep," says Jax. "Have you eaten? I saved you some boiled eggs. And there's bread from this morning. Go disarm. I'll bring you some."

I'm struck by the calmness in his tone, as if this tiny house is a brief respite from all the tension that swirls in the lane.

Or maybe it's just a respite from the tension between me and Grey.

But no, it's not just that. It's a quiet stillness I usually find when I seek out the infirmary with Noah.

Minutes later, I've removed my boots and armor and washed my face. Jax appears in the doorway, a crutch under one arm, and a plate in his opposite hand. He sets the plate on the table by the bed and shifts to leave.

"Where are you going?" I say in surprise.

He gives me a rueful look. "Da's room. The king was very clear that he expects you on duty at sunrise."

I'm sure he was. I give Jax a sidelong glance. "We're a long way from sunrise."

He laughs under his breath. "You *are* a scoundrel." But he doesn't come closer, and I know he's worried about whatever Grey said.

I sit on the edge of the bed and draw my legs up to sit cross-legged. "At least keep me company while I eat. I've had no one but Mercy all day."

He considers for a moment, but the king must not have been *too* scary, because Jax eventually acquiesces, dropping his crutch to the floor to sit cross-legged beside me. It puts our shoulders close, our knees brushing. Despite my reason for asking him to stay, I say nothing, so Jax is quiet, too, and I relax into the silence.

Eventually, the food is gone and the lantern has gone a bit dim, but neither of us moves. His hand is resting on his thigh, and I reach out to thread my fingers through his, slowly, gently, until our palms are almost pressed together, and the warmth of his touch seems to wash over me.

"Prince Rhen should arrive tomorrow," I say quietly.

He nods drowsily. "The king said the same."

"I do not know what action they will take." I hesitate. "It's likely I will be given new orders."

Jax snaps his head up to look at me.

"My position at court was precarious," I say. "It still might be. And if there's insurrection in the Queen's Army, Grey may want me to return to the ranks as a soldier."

I hate the way the idea of *new orders* fills me with dread. It's clearly doing the same to Jax.

I should be eager. There once was a time when I would have been.

But I'm not. I squeeze his hand. "It won't be weeks or months or never, Jax. I promise you."

Once again, we are back where we started.

I expect him to protest, but he draws a long sigh. "I know who you are, my lord."

I frown, but he shifts closer, then rests his head on my shoulder. It's the most endearing thing anyone has ever done, and for a moment, I'm not sure how to react.

Then he lifts our joined hands to press a kiss to my knuckles. "You're right," he finally says.

"I'm right?"

He turns his head to brush his lips against my neck. Then his teeth find the skin just below my ear, and I gasp. "You're right," he says again. "We are a long way from sunrise."

I grin. "*Now* who's the scoundrel—"

But his hand lands on my thigh, and I discover there are better things to do than talk.

I sleep fitfully and wake early. Duty and obligation have been drilled into me for too long to be cavalier about an order from the king. My goal is to dress in silence, but Jax's eyes blink open before I've even slipped out of bed.

"Sleep," I say to him. "I'll be quick."

He shakes his head and rubs at his eyes. "I'll make tea."

But then we hear voices outside, speaking low. The clear sounds of horses.

Jax's eyes snap to mine.

I reach for my breastplate with renewed speed. "Rhen's soldiers must be here."

He watches me work the buckles. There's a bleak look in his eyes that mirrors the moment I told him I'd be given new orders. "Should I wait inside?" he says. "Or should I join you?"

My fingers go still. Then I smile and reach for the armor he wore on the day he helped us search the bodies. I toss it onto the bed beside him. "Join me, Jax."

Prince Rhen brought hundreds of soldiers, dressed and ready for battle, with claims that a full regiment stands ready just over the border in Emberfall.

He also brings news that Lord Alek is being held under heavy guard, awaiting the king and queen's interrogation.

I wish he were being held in the dungeon, but I keep those thoughts to myself and revel in the *imagining* of it.

After two days of quietly standing guard over the lane, my hours are suddenly full of obligation. I'm sent with Lord Jacob to find the magistrate, who has no knowledge of what transpired with the queen. Later, we're sent back to the Crystal Palace with a handful of guards, to assess whether the capital city has been taken.

Once there, we discover that there's little panic. Jake and I seek out Nolla Verin, the queen's sister.

She's surprised to see us. "I sent word to Emberfall days ago," she says. "Lia Mara was to be visiting her Royal Houses with Sinna, but she should have returned before now. I have been quietly making inquiries—"

"She's in Briarlock," I tell her. "Near the border. She said that if you were alive and unharmed, you should return with us."

Her eyes flare at the words *alive* and *unharmed*. "I will assemble a team of guards at once."

I shake my head, thinking of Ander and all the others who betrayed their queen. "You should come alone, and quietly."

We make it back to Briarlock by early evening, where I find that the king has put Jax to work. The blacksmith has sweat threaded through his hair and soot on his fingers, and he barely glances up from the horse he's shoeing when I arrive.

"Well met," he says, and there's more than a little sarcasm in his tone.

It makes me smile. "I see you've been busy, too?"

"Apparently when an army assembles hastily, there's little attention given to the hooves of its horses." His hands are full of tools and glowing iron, so he blows a lock of hair out of his eyes.

I reach out and tuck it behind his ear, and that earns me a grateful smile.

"Tycho." The king's voice speaks from behind me, and I turn to find him standing with Queen Lia Mara, Prince Rhen, and a half dozen advisers.

I don't know how I know that orders are coming, but I do.

There are so many things going on that are more important than *me*, but I can't stop the clenching tightness in my chest. I think of the moment I punched him in the woods, declaring so vehemently that I wasn't a child.

As before, if I mean it, I have to *prove* it.

I stand at attention. "Yes, Your Majesty. How may I serve?"

CHAPTER 64

JAX

Again, midnight arrives and Tycho hasn't returned to the forge. It's so late that I've begun to wonder whether he'll return at all, or if the king has already sent him on a mission, and I won't receive word for weeks or months.

It won't be weeks or months or never, Jax. I promise you.

But he can't promise that when he doesn't know what his future holds. I've known all along that his life was at the mercy of the king. Now more than ever.

But just as I begin to drift to sleep, I hear the squeak in the floor, and I sit up sharply in bed.

"Don't shoot," he calls ironically from the main room. "It's just me." He appears in the shadowed doorway. His face is in darkness, his weapons catching glints of light from somewhere. "I didn't mean to wake you."

"I'm getting used to it."

He smiles, but something about it seems a bit reluctant. "May I sit?"

I can already hear it in his voice. "You're leaving."

He doesn't beat around the bush. "I am. At daybreak."

My throat tightens almost at once. I try to breathe past it, but my voice is still husky when I say, "You can sit."

When he does, I waste no time. I wrap my arms around his neck, heedless of the armor that he hasn't removed. This reminds me of the first night he slept here, when his leather and weapons seemed to protect him from emotional wounds as strongly as physical ones. "Tell me."

"The royal family will return to the palace almost immediately," he says. "It seems that the assault on the queen is not well known, and they do not want to allow much more time to pass, because rumor will spread quickly. Queen Lia Mara needs to be on the throne before people begin to speculate. But they will be joined by a contingent of Emberfall's forces, along with half of Emberfall's Royal Guard. Everyone in the Queen's Guard will need to be interrogated. The Truthbringers have begun to form factions in Emberfall, but the level of insurrection in Syhl Shallow runs deep."

"So you're staying here," I say. This doesn't sound *too* bad. It's only a few hours away. "In the Crystal Palace."

"No," he says. "I've been asked to take residence at Ironrose Castle for the time being."

I freeze. "Why?" I say. "For how long?"

"For weeks." His body is so still against mine. "Likely months. Before the first events of the Royal Challenge, Lord Alek spread rumors of me being involved with the Truthbringers, and those have not dissipated. There were accusations that I was using magic for personal gain. The king and queen cannot afford any impressions of weakness or subversion. Not right now."

"So the king is sending you away?" There's heat in my voice. "After all you've done?"

He nods. "I made a bargain with the scraver Nakiis to save Grey's life, and there is no way to know when he'll demand my services. You saw Callyn's reaction when the scravers swooped down from the trees to save us in battle. Can you imagine if they appeared in the midst of the Crystal City? It's a variable the king doesn't want right now. I may not like it, but I understand it."

I remember the king's words when he was broken and bleeding on the floor of my workshop. *Tycho risked his position at court for you. He risked his* life *for you. Make it worth it.*

I did. And Tycho may have survived—but he's being punished anyway.

I frown against his shoulder. "I'm sorry for what I put you through. I wish I could go back to that first day and undo it."

"Jax. Jax, no." He pulls back to look at me, then brushes a thumb against my cheek. "I don't regret one minute of it." He pauses, and his voice turns careful. "I've also brought you an offer, from Prince Rhen."

I straighten. I've caught glimpses of the blond prince, either with the king or between soldiers. Every time I see him, I think of the scars on Tycho's back and I want to throw a hot bar of iron right at the man.

Tycho sees my expression and chuckles. "Perhaps I should keep it to myself. There's a part of me that does not want you to feel . . . obligated."

"I am not obligated to him," I say darkly.

"No . . . I meant obligated to me. Because I know there will be challenges."

I stare at him. "I don't understand."

"The prince intends to offer you a job, as a resident blacksmith for the Royal Guard. You would not be alone. He has a crew of metalworkers to supply the castle. But I know you have your forge here, and your life is here, and your—"

I throw my arms around his neck again. "Yes. *Yes.* Why didn't you lead with that? *Yes.*"

He's laughing softly against my shoulder. "You can't throw the prince in the forge, though."

"He could always trip."

"Jax."

"Shh. Allow me to imagine it a bit longer."

"I will still have duties and obligations," he warns. "I will still have my position as King's Courier."

"Would I leave with you at daybreak?" I can't disguise the eagerness in my voice. "Or would I have to wait?"

"You could leave with me. There will be many soldiers traveling by wagon."

That same eagerness is echoed in his own voice, and I kiss his cheek. "Help me pack."

He laughs. "All right."

I'm shoving clothes into a linen bag when I have another thought. I feel like a terrible friend that it took me so long.

"Tycho?" I say. "What about Callyn?"

CHAPTER 65

CALLYN

The queen is preparing to leave.

She hasn't said as much to me, but it's obvious that the soldiers who arrived are making preparations to depart. Wagons are being packed. Horses are being freshly shod. The king and queen have been meeting with advisers and generals all day, while I've been in the bakery trying to keep Nora and Sinna out of everyone's hair. The princess is addicted to sweetcakes just like my sister, but she's fascinated by Muddy May and all the milk she produces, so I've sent them out to the barn a dozen times just to keep them from eating their weight in frosting.

When night falls and the preparations don't cease, I realize that they intend to leave *soon*. I sit up in the bakery, waiting on the queen, feeling foolish. She's surrounded by guards and soldiers now. I don't need to have a role of playing lookout.

But the events of the past few days have been too tumultuous, and I've grown fond of the queen and her kind firmness. I think of my mother, and her devotion to soldiering, how I've always worried I was making the wrong choice in staying here to run the bakery. But I've begun to realize that strength comes in many forms. I remember how Lord Alek kept questioning the queen's actions, saying he was protecting her.

But he wasn't. He was simply taking away her choices.

As if my thoughts summoned her, the queen eases through the doorway, reaching up to quiet the bell before it can ring fully.

She seems surprised to find me waiting up. "Callyn. I thought you'd be asleep."

"The girls are," I say. "But I wanted to make sure you—" I stop myself. I was about to say, *you were all right*, but of course that's ridiculous. "That you had everything you needed," I finish.

"Not quite," she says.

"Tea?" I say. "Or I could make you—"

"No. I wanted to talk to you." She gestures to the pastry table. "Could we sit?"

I nod. We do.

"We will be returning to the Crystal Palace in the morning," she says.

I nod. "I've been watching the preparations all day." I pause, then feel warmth crawling up my cheeks. "I believe Nora will be heartbroken to lose her new shadow."

The queen smiles. "Well, after what happened with Lady Karyl and the Queen's Guard, the king and I are wary of leaving Sinna in anyone's care in the palace. Right now, we don't know who to trust." She hesitates. "So I would like to humbly request that you and Nora accompany us to the palace, in an official position as the princess's ladies-in-waiting, but unofficially to be my eyes and ears around little Sinna, because I cannot—"

"Your Majesty," I gasp.

She smiles. "Is that a yes or a no?"

"It's—it's—" I'm staring at her. "I—yes? I think?" I flush and touch a hand to Mother's pendant, thinking of the magic I don't want to acknowledge. "But I—you—you should not. I made so many mistakes. I should be hung for my crimes—"

"Lord Alek and Lady Karyl didn't just deceive *you*," she says. "If everything proves to be true, there are *many* who've deceived the royal family." Heat fills her voice. "You acted to protect me. To protect my daughter. You risked your life, Callyn. I could not ask for anyone better to stand as my daughter's guardian when I cannot."

My thoughts are spinning. Nora will be beside herself.

The queen's hand reaches out to cover mine. "You and your sister could be in danger. This is not a decision to be taken lightly. Nolla Verin has stated that she would begin instructing you in self-defense, and we will be bringing a large contingent of Royal Guards with us from Emberfall. We were nearly overcome once, Callyn. This is not a position without risk."

I swallow and nod.

"But," she continues, "I have also considered that you may be at risk remaining here. The Truthbringers are rumored to be quite vicious when it comes to those who turn against them."

Those words are chilling, and I shiver. "Yes, Your Majesty."

"All the same," she says, "I would not make the choice for you. This is not an order or a demand. I have taken care of the tax debt your father left. If you do not want this, I would ensure you are given everything you need to protect the bakery."

I keep thinking about the choices my mother would have made. Maybe it's time to start thinking for myself.

I take a deep breath and straighten my shoulders. "We'll do it."

The sky is pink, the woods lined with purple, but I walk down the lane to Jax's house at dawn. The forge is silent and cold, and I expect to find him still asleep, but instead, I step into the workshop just as he comes through the door on his crutches.

"Cal." He stops short. So do I.

He's wearing sparse armor, which is a surprise, his hair tied back tightly. He's wearing a thick boot on his foot, complete with leather greaves, and it all serves to make him look a bit taller, a bit more intimidating.

He sees me looking and blushes. "Tycho is worried we may encounter ambushes on the road."

My eyes go wide. "On the road?" I say. "You're leaving?"

He hesitates, then nods. "I was actually coming to see *you*." He pauses, and a bit of wry humor slips into his voice. "Thank you for saving me the walk."

I have so many things to say, but so much has changed in the last few months that I can't think of a single word until I stride forward and give him a hug.

He catches me solidly, and it's so odd to hug him in armor.

I have to draw back and stare at him again. I remember seeing him during the battle, the clear focus in his eyes when he was drawing back the string of his bow. "You were so brave, Jax."

"So were you."

I study the lines of his face, the light in his hazel-green eyes. "I'm leaving, too."

He nods. "Tycho told me what the queen was going to offer." He pauses. "I knew you'd accept."

I shove him in the arm. "Oh, you did not!"

He grins. "I knew Nora would kill you if you didn't."

"Well, that's true enough." I can't help it. I reach forward and hug him again. "I don't know when I'll see you again."

"The king said something, in the midst of battle," Jax says quietly.

"He said that fate has already drawn a path past this moment. That we should follow it through." He pauses. "Let's follow it through, Callyn."

I nod and kiss him on the cheek. "Let's follow it through."

The door at his back opens, and Lord Tycho steps out. He sees me and smiles, then offers a bow. "Lady Callyn. I am honored to meet the newest lady of the court."

I was going to give him a shove just like I did to Jax, but those words draw me up short. *The newest lady of the court.* I press my hands to my cheeks.

His smile widens. "Don't get too excited. Sinna is an escape artist. You'll be covered in dust and cobwebs by the end of the first day."

I smile, hesitate, and decide to throw caution to the wind. I stride forward to give him a hug as well.

If he's surprised, he doesn't show it. "Tell Lady Nora that the palace kitchens always have sweetcakes in the morning."

"I will." I kiss him on the cheek. "You take care of my best friend."

"I swear to it, my lady."

That makes me blush again. Tycho begins to pull away, but I hold tight, then meet his eyes. "I'd ask for one favor," I say to him.

"Anything," he says.

"If you're going to Emberfall, punch Alek right in the face for me."

His smile turns a bit wicked. "That won't require a favor at all. It will be my absolute pleasure."

CHAPTER 66

TYCHO

I've spent so long traveling by myself that I forgot how different it is to make the trek to Emberfall with a unit of men and women. With loaded wagons, the going is slower, and there are too many of us for an inn, so we have to make camp at night. I hear the muttered comments about what happened in Briarlock, and I wonder how far gossip will stretch this time. Tensions were already high between both countries, and knowing their king is in Crystal City, the target of an attack, is not endearing anyone in this group to the people of Syhl Shallow.

Jax is a bit shy with the soldiers, and I'm not sure how much of that is an unfamiliarity with the language and how much is the newness of finding himself in an unexpected role. After everything that happened in Briarlock, I was concerned that the soldiers might be a bit hostile to him. But I needn't have worried: they've heard about how he fought at Grey's side, and they've already started exaggerating his role in protecting the king.

"I heard he got a man in the neck from a hundred yards," one of the guards murmurs to another when they're unaware I'm listening.

I smile and don't bother to correct them.

There's never any shortage of work, but once dusk falls and bedrolls have been laid out, I dig a deck of cards out of my pack and try to coax Jax into a game with the guards and soldiers.

At first he's reluctant, uncertain, but a soldier named Malin pulls a bottle of amber liquid from somewhere and holds it out. "Come," he says in heavily accented Syssalah. "Drink. Lose silver."

Jax huffs a surprised laugh, but he joins the game. Later, we lie in the darkness and stare at the stars, and he begs me to teach him words in Emberish, so I do, anything I can think of. *Sky* and *camp* and *night* and a dozen others, until Malin throws something at us and says, "How about *sleep*?"

Rhen travels with us, but he doesn't linger with the soldiers. He keeps his own tent, and we meet in the morning while the others break camp. He outlines his plans to provide support to the king from here, to root out any insurrection on this side of the border. There's no worry in his voice when he speaks to his guards, but I hear it when he speaks to *me*, of the challenges we will surely face in the months to come.

"Tycho," he says, and his voice is very quiet. "For the time being, it would be best if you kept your magic a secret."

I hesitate, surprised at the pulse of rebellion that flickers in my heart, but I nod. "As you say."

"You haven't mentioned it among the soldiers?" he presses. "Not even in jest?"

I shake my head. "Jax knows. The royal family knows. Anyone else who witnessed it died in the attack."

"Do you trust Jax to keep your confidence?"

"I do."

"Good." He pauses, studying me. "Grey said you would not tell him what you bargained with the scraver."

I startle, then flush. I didn't realize that conversation would've gone beyond the king, but of course I should have. "I made that bargain to save his life."

"He said as much." Prince Rhen pauses. "And I believe I understand why you would not trust him enough to reveal whatever you yielded."

"No! It wasn't a matter of trust. It was—" I stop short, thinking of everything unsaid between me and the king over the last few months.

It *was* a matter of trust.

Rhen waits while I work this out in my head. I'm not sure what to say.

"I know you wouldn't offer anything to put him at risk," Rhen eventually says. "For what it's worth, Grey knows that, too. That's the only reason he's allowing you to keep this secret."

I bristle. *He's still sending me to Emberfall. He's getting me out of the way.*

I don't say it. I don't think I need to.

As if confirming my thoughts, Rhen gives a nod of finality. "You're dismissed. We have a long way to go today."

I turn to leave the tent, and for some reason, my insides feel jangled up and uncertain in a way that's becoming too common.

But then Rhen calls me back. "Tycho. Wait. I do have a question."

The soldiers outside are calling taunts at each other, striking tents and loading the wagons. I should be helping them, but I stop and turn. "Yes?"

"Do you trust me enough to tell *me*?"

It's an honest question, delivered with more gravity than it should need. Maybe that's why I take a moment to consider, instead of flippantly refusing, the way I did with Grey.

My vow to Nakiis has been rattling around in my head for days. I truly don't know what he'll ask for—or when. Maybe I am a fool, and I have no desire to have someone else confirm it.

But as I stare back at Prince Rhen, I think of our conversation on the day he steered me away from the courtyard. The day we shared secrets and vulnerabilities. Or the way he found me in the stables when I was avoiding the king, the way we raced through the woods on horseback. The way he challenged Lord Alek on my behalf.

Prince Rhen is the last man in the world I ever thought I'd look at as a friend, but just now, that jangled uncertainty in my chest seems to smooth over.

"Yes," I say suddenly, surprising even myself. "I do."

EPILOGUE

ALEK

I've watched nine sunsets from this room, and when the sun begins to disappear beyond the forests surrounding Ironrose Castle, I know it'll soon be time for me to watch my tenth.

I shouldn't be watching *any*. I shouldn't be locked in the castle. I should be at court in Syhl Shallow, watching the ladies of the court attend to a grieving queen.

An assassin was supposed to have killed the king in the middle of the archery fields.

An assassin who never showed.

Callyn. I have no way of knowing if she delivered my note to Lady Karyl.

I have no idea who attacked the queen. That was never part of the plan.

Betrayal could have come from both sides. It burns at my thoughts during my long hours in this room. The Truthbringers have always had one goal: protect the queen.

As the sun turns red along the horizon, a guard knocks at the door with my dinner. It's a bit theatrical, as the door is locked from the outside.

"Enter," I call, as if I have any say in the matter.

Today's guard is a man named Vale, a man well into his thirties with graying hair and armor that's straining, just a bit, to adequately cover his midsection. He's a seasoned guard who's served in the castle for three years.

He's also steadfastly loyal to the Truthbringers.

I know this because we placed him here.

Prince Rhen might be a cunning bastard, but even he has his limits.

"A runner arrived this afternoon," Vale says quietly. "The prince is returning with a small contingent of guards and soldiers. The rest are remaining in Syhl Shallow to determine how deep the insurrection runs."

I swear. "What of the royal family?"

"They survived." He pauses. "From what I hear, it was close. The King's Courier is returning with the prince."

That makes me smile. His relationship with the king is still fractured, then. "Any casualties?"

"Unknown. I'll do my best to find out."

A guard calls from the hallway. "Vale! What's taking so long?"

"Punch me," I say in a whispered rush. "Say I attacked you."

He swings a fist, and I have to force myself to take it. My head snaps to the side, and I taste blood. I allow myself to fall back, stumbling to a knee just as another guard appears in the doorway.

"He went for my dagger," Vale snaps.

I touch my fingers to my lip. "I was just trying to take the tray, you fool."

He stares at me as if he's waiting for me to provide his next line, and I all but roll my eyes.

"I'll have words with your prince when he returns," I declare. "You should all prepare to be dismissed."

"You're lucky you're getting a meal at all," says the other guard. "Come on," he says to Vale. "Just leave him."

They leave the room, and the click of the lock echoes.

The sky is fully red now.

My lip is still bleeding, and I sigh. I lift the cover from the tray of food.

Shellfish. I make a face and cover it back up.

If the prince is returning and the royal family is returning, they will have to let me go. There's nothing to signify my involvement with the Truthbringers. No proof. No matter what happened to the queen, I was here in Emberfall. No matter what happened to the king, it was done elsewhere.

Casualties? Unknown.

I think of Callyn: her cynical glances, her wicked smile, her challenging eyes. I remember stroking a finger across her cheek. Asking, *Have I shared enough to earn your trust?*

And then, like a fool, I gave her one small shred of truth.

If Lady Karyl deceived me, I shouldn't be surprised. I've never trusted her, and I was likely a fool to have allowed her as much unchecked freedom as she enjoyed.

But Callyn . . .

I sit in the chair beside the window and watch my tenth sunset, the red gleaming in the trees in a way that reminds me of the light on her hair.

I make a very dangerous enemy, Callyn.

If she betrayed me, she'll learn how very true that is.

ACKNOWLEDGMENTS

I somehow set a precedent of writing long acknowledgments, but listen: I'm on deadline, so I'm going to have to make this quick.

This is my fourteenth (!!!) published novel, so at this point, it should go without saying that I am incredibly grateful to my husband, Michael. I could not do this without him by my side. I am so thankful for every moment we have together, and look forward to every moment in the future. Thank you for being my best friend for all these years.

Mary Kate. MARY KATE! Mary Kate Castellani is my incredible editor at Bloomsbury, and I swear my books would only be half as good without her input. Mary Kate, I am so very lucky to work with you. You know why this paragraph is so short (I'm writing book #15 as fast as I can, I promise!!), but I want you to know how very much I love working with you. You're brilliant.

But also Suzie. SUZIE! Suzie Townsend is my incredible agent, and I would be running in circles without her guiding me down the right path. I just have no words. I am so incredibly lucky to have you and the team at New Leaf on my side. Thank you so much for everything.

The entire team at Bloomsbury continues to stun me with their eternal dedication to every book they work on, and I am so grateful for everything. Huge thanks to Claire Stetzer, Noella James, Erica Barmash, Faye Bi, Phoebe Dyer, Beth Eller, Valentina Rice, Ksenia Winnicki,

Diane Aronson, Jeanette Levy, Donna Mark, Adrienne Vaughan, Rebecca McNally, Ellen Holgate, Pari Thomson, Emily Marples, Jet Purdie, and every single person at Bloomsbury and Macmillan who has a hand in making my books a success. Special thanks to Lily Yengle, Tobias Madden, Mattea Barnes, and Meenakshi Singh for their incredible work on managing my Street Team.

Speaking of the Street Team, if you're a part of it, thank YOU. It means so much to me to know that there are *thousands* of you interested in my books, and I will never forget everything you've done to spread the word about my stories, whether you've been a part of it since *A Curse So Dark and Lonely*, or if you've more recently joined to learn more about the *Defy the Night* series, or if you're here to get secret insight into Tycho, Jax, and Callyn. Thank you all so very much.

Huge debts of gratitude go to my dear writing friends, Melody Wukitch, Dylan Roche, Gillian McDunn, Jodi Picoult, Jennifer Armentrout, Phil Stamper, Stephanie Garber, Isabel Ibañez, Ava Tusek, Bradley Spoon, and Amalie Howard, because I honestly don't know how I would get through the day without your support. I am so grateful to have you all in my life.

Several people read and offered insight into parts of this book while it was in progress, and I want to take a moment to specially thank Jodi Picoult, Mary Pearson, Reba Gordon, Ava Tusek, Jim Hilderbrandt, Kyle Fereira, and Dylan Roche.

Huge thanks to readers, bloggers, librarians, artists, and booksellers all over social media who take the time to post, review, tweet, share, and mention my books. I owe my career to people being so passionate about my characters that they can't help but talk about them. Thank you all.

And many thanks go to YOU! Yes, you. If you're holding this book in your hands, thank you. Thank you for being a part of my dream, and for loving Tycho so much that you wanted a book all about him and his adventures. As always, I am honored that you took the time to invite my characters into your heart.

Finally, tremendous love and thanks to the Kemmerer boys for following in Daddy's footsteps and supporting me every bit as much as he does. You surprise me every single day, and I am so very lucky to be your mom. Yes, I copied that paragraph from the last acknowledgments that I wrote, but alas, it's time to go pick you up from school. I still mean every word.